BUZZ

By Sharleen Davidson

Published 2008 by arima publishing

www.arimapublishing.com

ISBN 978-1-84549-257-1

© Sharleen Davidson 2008

Printed and bound in the United Kingdom

Typeset in Garamond 11/14

In this work of fiction, the characters, places and events are either the product of the author's imagination or they are used entirely fictitiously. Any resemblance to actual persons, living or dead, is purely coincidental.

Swirl is an imprint of arima publishing

arima publishing
ASK House, Northgate Avenue
Bury St Edmunds, Suffolk IP32 6BB
t: (+44) 01284 700321

www.arimapublishing.com

Anyone could write, but to write well was what Susan wanted. She had typed out these words on the first space of her screen, for that was all the encouragement she needed. The screen stared back at her, empty.

Susan knew she was dying, just like her father a few months ago, but she was not going out without a fight. Nor had he, right up to his dying day. He was a tower of strength to her, as was her husband Jamie whom she adored. He had encouraged her to occupy her mind and with a letter beside her typewriter giving her full permission from the Chief of Police of the City of Camgonga no less, that's what she had decided to do.

Beside her on the desk lay the files for 1951 with 'Top Secret' stamped in red across them. Some thirty years had passed and Susan was now just fifty years old but to look at her you would think she was sixty-five at least. Her hair was grey, what was left of it, and her eyes, once beautifully clear and piercing blue, were now watery and sullen, and her skin was pale and yellowing. She was not the only one like this. There were many others. It was as if a bomb had been dropped on them all, but this was not the case.

In Susan's hands lay the full story. It was up to her to co-ordinate them and put them all together, something she would have liked to have done years ago but was unable to do until now when circumstances had changed and the file had been released.

The room was warm; the sun was shining brightly outside the open window. Susan was in the town of Zimba, now just one of the twenty people left alive who had lived in the town before. The others were dead or dying. Susan flexed her bony fingers; the ring that Jamie had placed there years ago swung round freely. Opening the first report she started with the words "Here goes…'"

Susan's story starts on January 4th 1964 in Africa, where we join Frank Parker in one of the city's zoos. Frank is in his early forties, about six feet tall and dark. He has just received a letter that he has been waiting for, for some weeks. The letter is to say that he has been accepted as game warden of the safari park of Camgonga, consisting of some thousand square miles of rough natural territory, some of which are mountain ranges. The new job involves him in having complete control of the thinning out of the animals, seeing that no poachers do their dirty deeds and controlling the natives who live within his area. To assist him in his duties he is allowed to take with him JoJo, a native boy in his early twenties and now almost one of the family since he has been with Frank and Ann for the past few years. We join Frank who has just come home after a hard day's work. He is very pleased with his news "Ann," called Frank, running up the driveway "darling, its come. I've got the job".

Ann came out into the hall; in her hands were some dead flowers she had just picked out. "Have you darling, that's good," she replied none too pleased.

"Good. Is that all you can say?" said Frank coming through the door which was draped with beads.

"For the time being, yes," said Ann.

"Why, I thought you would be pleased" he answered coming over and giving her a kiss.

"Well I was," she hesitated "that was up until last night," replied Ann, putting the flower heads down.

"Why what's happened to make you change your mind suddenly?" asked Frank.

"Oh nothing," Ann said dropping her hands to her sides, "nothing really just me being stupid that's all. Probably the time of year now Christmas is over. Here, drop these in the bin."

To which Frank replied, "now don't tell me, you went to see that lady after all. I told you not to get involved now didn't I? Why do you persist in going against my advice and filling your head with all this super voodoo nonsense? How many times…?" he asked as he dropped the dead flowers in the bin.

"But Frank, it's just something I like to study, that's all. I am interested. Why can't you face it?" She returned to the kitchen and Frank followed her.

"So," said Frank "what next? Soon we will have the kids getting interested. Then what?"

"Well, Mark is studying the language and is bound to be curious now isn't he? What do you expect living out here all these years? We can't hide it from him or James come to that. If they understand it then they can face it can't they?" said Ann.

"All right. You win," said Frank. "Anyway what did she say? Well, never mind it's obvious that you believe her. I'd say you are hooked. I just don't understand why, that's all. You can tell me about it later. It's time to start packing. We have just three weeks and by the way we can take everything along," said Frank as he waved the letter in his hand. "Tell the k ids I'll be back in a minute."

"Where are you going? Your dinner's ready," said Ann. "Do you have to go right away?"

"Yes, to drop a letter to your brother Keith. I'll just be able to catch the post if I hurry," said Frank. He was lucky the van was still at the box.

STILL IN AFRICA

In a downtown coffee house in Zimba on January 11th Dale and Keith's land rover stood outside when a radio call came through. It was John trying to contact them, but they were too busy talking to hear him.

"Dale, Keith, for god's sake where are you?" asked John.

Dale and Keith who were partners were inside the coffee house.

"Hey," said Keith, sipping at his coffee. "Have you heard the good news yet?"

"No. What's that then?" asked Dale. "Don't tell me... you've found yourself another girlfriend."

"Nar, nothing like that," replied Keith, feeling in his pocket for his cigarettes. "Anyway what's that to you even if I had?" he asked Keith as he frowned at Dale who wondered what he meant.

"What's that then?" asked Dale looking at Keith's tanned face, then went on to say, "hey did you hear about the woman who got raped last night?"

"Yes I heard," said Keith "I'd like to get my hands on that bastard, son of a ..."

"That's a bit strong isn't it?" interrupted Dale "even for you."

"No it's my sister, she's..." said Keith, but he did not have time to finish before Dale asked "Having another baby is she? She's not complaining about being raped is she?"

"Why don't you shut up for a minute? That's what I don't like about you," said Keith.

"Oh, for god's sake be quiet and tell me your news, I'm only teasing you, you idiot," said Dale. "I just like to see you trying to explain yourself. You always have had problems in that direction, haven't you?" he laughed. "I like to see you get all riled up, it adds to the spice of life, makes it less boring, you know what I mean? Here, have one of mine," said Dale, taking out his cigarettes. Keith took one.

"Thanks," said Keith. "No, its my sister and her husband, they're coming to town along with their two kids, Mark and James. Remember I told you some weeks back Frank's taking over as game warden."

"Oh, you mean the game warden is your brother-in-law?" said Dale still smiling. "That's nice."

"Yes that's what I was trying to tell you, but you kept interrupting me," said Keith.

Dale took out his lighter and lit Keith's cigarette.

"Aw come on, you should know me by now, nice for you I mean," said Dale lighting his own cigarette.

"Yes," answered Keith.

Just at this point in the conversation the town's doctor came in and ordered a coffee.

"Hi," called out Dale, "Why not come and join us?"

"Yes sure thanks. How's Jenny?" Doc asked. Turning to Keith "and you?"

"Oh, I'm fine thanks and how's Mabel?" answered Keith.

"Jenny's ok," said Dale.

"Oh, Mabel's ok. Off out down to the store, it's Nickki's fifteenth birthday today and Maria is giving her her first lesson on how to run the store. School days are over and all that," said the Doc.

The woman who ran the coffee house came over with Doc's coffee.

"Coffee, Doc," she said. "Any more for you two?" she asked.

"No thanks," Dale and Keith replied "we have to go back on duty now thanks."

"Ok. by the way Doc," asked the woman "Is it true about that woman who was...?"

"Yes, I'm afraid so," said the Doc. "Poor woman was terribly beaten up."

The woman left them shaking her head as she went.

"What's this I hear about you going on holiday in a couple of months Dale?" said Doc.

Dale looked at Keith; he had not had the time to tell him.

"No sign of Jenny having that longed-for baby yet then?" asked Doc of Dale. "Still you can't hurry nature can you?"

Doc had dropped two clangers.

Keith's face went sad as if he was jealous.

"You never told me," he said to Dale.

"No, sorry I wanted to surprise you," said Dale and looking at Doc he continued "it's ok Doc, Keith introduced us."

Doc gave a half hearted smile.

"Anyway where are you going?" asked Keith "Now that I do know."

"Switzerland," answered Dale "it'll be a complete change from all this heat won't it?"

"Probably end up with a stinking cold," said Keith.

"Well, who's going to complain?" said Dale laughing.

So did Doc as he drank his coffee. "Oh now I understand the glum look on your face," Doc said to Keith.

With that, Keith and Dale got up and stubbed out their cigarettes and pushed the ashtray away as they knew that Doc didn't like smoking.

"Excuse us," they said. "Duty calls, you understand?"

"Smoke many more of those things and you will have a longer holiday than you think. Yes, sure I understand, you go ahead," said Doc.

Dale paid for the coffee.

"Doc," said Dale "You are fathering us again."

He and Keith laughed.

"All right," said Doc laughing to himself "Mabel's always telling me that."

"Bye Doc," they said waving.

"Bye boys," said the woman behind the counter.

They finally got the message from John who had been trying on and off for the past ten minutes to contact them and reported to the office only to be told that they would be on night duty for the next month. In the meantime Frank, Ann, JoJo and the children were on their way into town. When they arrived, Frank went to the store, Ann went to the police station to see her brother and the boys stayed with Frank to give him some help. Mark fancied Nickki and JoJo went along to get some drinks. He saw a lovely girl in the bar and she made eyes at him. After everything was done they left town and returned to the bungalow in the scrubland.

JANUARY 1951

In Zimba the Chief of Police came into the office followed by his daughter Susan. She had a radiant natural beauty inherited from her mother; piercing blue eyes, long blonde hair naturally wavy and features that made men's heads turn. Her soft curving figure was like a wine bottle purposely shaped to attract the potential market. In spite of this Susan lacked the vital panache. Although outwardly confident, inside she was very unsure of herself, but that was due to inexperience, because her father had brought her up since her mother had died. Her father sat down at his desk and motioned her to sit too. Susan helped herself to a chair from behind the door, which was now closed.

"Cigarette?" asked her father taking a packet from the top drawer of his desk.

"Yes thanks," said Susan taking one. She eyed her father and noticed a sort of deep sadness in his eyes, one which he thought he was hiding from her. "Do you think I will be all right for this job then?" she asked. "You haven't said much since I came back from the city, and by the way, Jamie sends his regards. He's hoping to get here and see us in a few weeks."

A knock at the door interrupted Susan's conversation. Though she was trying hard to please her father she seemed to sense that he was worried about something.

"Come in," her father called, then glancing at Susan "Excuse me."

"Sure," answered Susan. Her father leant across and lit her cigarette. "Thanks," she said.

The door opened and Keith walked in.

"Sir," said Keith.

"Yes, what is it?" asked the chief.

"This report sir, on the woman who was…?" Keith hesitated as he looked at Susan.

"It's ok. You know Susan don't you?" asked the chief.

"Sure, hi nice to see you back again," said Keith smiling at her. "The one who was raped sir," continued Keith, glancing at the chief to see if he would disapprove of him saying such a thing in front of Susan. Keith would not have like to offend her.

The chief took the report from Keith, opened it and placed it on his desk. "Susan's about to start work here with us," the chief said to Keith, "after finishing her course at the police school in the city, so I should hope by now that it doesn't come as a shock to her what you say," he finished looking across at her.

For the first time Susan was confronted with the reality of the job she was to undertake and didn't want her father to see she didn't feel confident about it.

"Of course not father," she answered but inside she shivered at the thought of what it must be like to be raped and changed the subject quickly hoping that it would not be noticed.

"How are things with you these days Keith? Heard from your sister lately?" she asked.

"Funny you should ask that," said Keith. He had noticed the quiver in her voice and had seen the look on her face when she caught sight of the photo of the badly beaten woman, as it slipped from the file he had handed to the chief, at which he was now looking. "She and the family arrived here this morning. Frank has got the job of the game warden," said Keith.

"Time for all that later," said Susan's father brusquely.

The chief collected all the papers and photos and placed them back in the file.

"Boy, he's tetchy today," thought Susan. She had her doubts as to whether she had done the right thing coming home and moving in with him again. She had been away six months and he had retreated into a shell, almost as if he had died. What could be the cause of his snappy behaviour? This was not what she had expected her homecoming to be at all.

"Keith," said the chief "take Susan down to the canteen and introduce her to the others and get her off to a good start in her new job. This job is only temporary, things won't be easy for you and I want you to be aware of this. We are very short staffed and you will be expected to do a hundred and one jobs, some you have been trained for and others you have not. Do you understand? Are you still willing?"

"Yes father," replied Susan although hurt at the way she had been treated.

"Here you are one of a team," her father told her. "Outside you are still my daughter."

"Yes sir," said Susan respectfully.

Although Susan did not like it she had enough sense to see that it had to be that way. She followed Keith out of the office, replacing the chair behind the door as she went. For the first time in her life Susan was working and just like everyone else she knew that it would not be easy but she would enjoy it.

DAVID

Meanwhile back in England during this period, David, a very adventurous boy of ten is busy in the garden of his home with his friend Allen. They are building a slide for David's pet otter. David lives with his mother in Charminster, a village near Dorchester in Dorset. This is near a river. That's how David came to have such a strange pet, along with two red setters and when the weather is good a tortoise as well. The otter was left to die when its mother and father were killed on a farm. David had hand reared it since it was a pup and now he was building it something to play on. It was a mischievous little bugger and often came into the house. David usually let it roam freely as did his mother, since it was not able to look after itself. Today David would finish the slide for his pet, and he was talking to Allen. David was very good at woodwork for a boy of his age.

"Allen," said David. "Pass me that other piece of wood please?"

David held onto one small panel. "And some more nails please," he said looking up. "Over there," he pointed to the ground.

"Like I said," said David. "Tarzan came up behind this bloke and smashed him on the head with a piece of tree, and he fell to the ground. Then this native shot at Tarzan and he hit his head about here." David pointed to his temple. "Tarzan fell down and rolled over the clifftop and landed on top of some trees, Cheeta ran as fast as he could to get help, screaming and screeching as he did so to the boy who lived in the trees with Tarzan in the hut they had made. The boy quickly rescued Tarzan," David continued.

David took the nails from Allen. "Thanks," he said.

"I've seen that film," said Allen. "That's where they capture the girl and take her to the native village along with that hunter. Up on that big mountain isn't it?"

"Yes, that's right," said David. "When did you see it then?" he asked. "I thought it was brilliant didn't you?"

"Yes," said Allen. "I also liked that serial about the five boys."

"Yes, great," said David. "Pass me that hammer will you?" He pointed to it on the ground.

David's mother came out of the house and hung up some washing. She smiled at the two boys.

"Hi mum," said David looking up.

"How are you two getting on?" she asked David. "Allen would you like to stay to dinner?"

"Yes please," answered Allen.

"Good," David's mother said. "It's sausages and mash."

"Smashing, my favourite," said David. "Look mum all I have to do now is fix this side bit then it's finished."

"That's good," said his mother.

"When I grow up," said David "I want to go on a safari to see all the things Tarzan saw; tigers, lions and snakes."

"Do you?" said Allen. "I saw a film once where Tarzan fought a great big spider the size of a man".

"I'm going to do a lot of travelling," said David.

"Oh yea," said Allen. "That costs a lot of money doesn't it?"

"Yes I know," said David "but I want to see France, Germany where Hitler used to live and I want to see the statue of Abraham Lincoln in the USA, but most of all I want to go to Africa."

"Why?" asked Allen giving him a queer look.

"I saw Tarzan kill a great big spider in one of his films. I want to see one of those," said David.

"Don't be silly," said David's mother, "they are not really that size. They have been magnified, trick photography that's all it is" and picking up her basket she went indoors.

"They are only the size of a man's hand," she finished as she disappeared.

"Yes I know that mum," said David "but I still want to go."

"Are you in the school play this year?" asked Allen.

"Yes, don't remind me," said David.

"Why?" asked Allen, handing David the hammer.

David gave the side panel a hit with his hand. "Ha, get in there you swine," he said.

"I'll give you both a call when dinner's ready," called David's mother from the house.

"Ok. mum," said David looking up.

"I don't know whose bright idea it was," he continued "but I got the tail end of the horse in the play. Probably Mr Stebbing's. I'm sure he has it in for me ever since I stuck chewing gum on his ruler."

"What, you didn't get the cane for it?" gasped Allen.

Both boys laughed.

David held onto a piece of the slide and held it with his knee, then lined up the nail ready to hit it.

"Blast, I can't do this without your help, can you hold it for me Allen?" said David.

"Sure," said Allen as he bent down and held on to the piece of wood. "Are you going to the pictures again this week?" asked Allen.

"No, I'm going to save up and see the new Flash Gordon film," said David. "Why don't you do the same?"

"Yes I might," said Allen. "Can I let go? My arms are aching?"

"In a minute," said David holding onto the nails and trying to hit one with the hammer. "There, that went in ok didn't it?"

"So, how much does it cost?" asked Allen getting up. "Ouch that's better," he continued stretching his back.

"Thanks," said David. "About five shillings I think. Right, now the next nail."

David lined up the nail and had the hammer ready to hit it when his mother appeared.

"David, Allen," she called. "Dinner is ready."

David hit out at the nail and let out a cry. "Ouch that hurt," he yelled as he jumped around the garden waving his hand.

The two dogs came up and joined in running about to see what was wrong. Blood poured from David's thumb, but a nail had also gone into his foot.

"What's the matter?" called out David's mother, as she came running out of the house, and down the steps. Allen tore over to David's side. David had gone very pale. He looked at Allen and he seemed very far away. The pain was terrible, then he passed out.

David awoke and found he was in the ambulance on his way to hospital. His mother didn't have a car and had phoned them to take him there. Leaning over him was one of the ambulancemen.

"How do you feel son?" he asked David.

David's mother sat at the other side of the stretcher.

"Are you all right darling?" she asked David.

"My finger hurts," said David.

The ambulanceman looked at his mother.

"Is it only your finger that hurts son?" he asked.

"Yes why?" asked David. What's happened?"

"The nail went into your foot, that's what happened," said the man.

"No wonder you passed out. It must have hurt you a lot," said his mother.

"No, I can't feel anything," said David. He looked down at his foot and saw the nail sticking out. He shuddered. "Why can't I feel it mum?" he asked.

"I don't know," replied his mother.

"It's because you are in shock," said the man. "It often happens like that but don't worry we will soon have it out and you won't even feel a thing. Mind you I expect you will have a couple of days off school".

When they got to the hospital David was wheeled into the outpatients and a nurse was looking at his wound. "What have you been doing to yourself?" asked the nurse.

"Building a slide for my otter," said David.

The nurse looked puzzled and David's mother explained what happened.

"Oh I see," she said looking at the nail sticking out of his foot. "There's not much blood." She then checked David's thumb and cleaned it.

"We will have you sorted out young man," she said looking at his mother. "Is he always so pale?" she asked, and checked his eyes. "You seem to be a little anaemic," she said. "Does he eat properly?"

"He picks more than he eats," replied David's mother.

"Sleeps a lot?" asked the nurse.

"Yes," said his mother.

She washed and bandaged his thumb and froze his foot. "Just in case it hurts," she said to David, and then she removed the nail. "I'll be back in a moment."

She left David and his mother and went to the sister's office. She knocked on the door.

"Come in," called the sister. "What can I do for you?"

"Excuse me sister, I've a young boy in outpatients who has a nail in his foot," said the nurse.

"What's the problem then?" asked the sister.

"Oh, no problem really, it's just that there was no bleeding when I took out the nail," said the nurse.

"I suggest that you send some samples of his blood to the lab., He sounds as if he might be anaemic," replied the sister.

"Yes sister that's what I thought," said the nurse,

"Better see that he gets a tetanus jab too," she said, going back to her paper work.

The nurse returned to David and his mother.

"Is there anything wrong?" asked David's mother.

"No, just routine," replied the nurse. "We shall have to give David a tetanus jab so that any infection he may have picked up will be stopped, but I also want a blood sample to be sent to the lab., Is that all right with you?"

"Yes sure," answered David's mother. Deep down she had a strange feeling as David's father had died of such an infection some two years previously, but she did not want David to see she was scared. Samples were taken from David's arm, but he never flinched.

"There you are David," said the nurse. "You can go home now. Everything's done."

"Thanks," said David, with a smile on his face, relieved that he was now free to go back to Charminster.

TWO WEEKS LATER IN ENGLAND

David's mother had received a letter from the hospital in Dorchester to take David back there.. Since he had hurt his foot David had been listless and very sick at times. His mother had put this down to shock.

She had called to him several times to get up.

"David, David, are you up yet?" she called yet again.

She waited for his answer but there was no reply. All she heard was a moan from his room, so she went opened the bedroom door and found David still fast asleep.

"David, wake up sleepy head, it's time for you to get up. We have to go to the hospital. I've had a letter. They want you to go and have some more tests," said his mother.

"Go away," said David. "I'm still asleep. I don't want to get up yet."

"Come on, get up, you would sleep all day if it wasn't for me,"she said pulling off his bedclothes and continuing "Come on, our appointment is for eleven." She slapped his bottom gently.

"Ouch that hurt," said David opening his eyes "Do I have to mum?"

"Yes come on. What do you fancy for breakfast?" she asked.

"Nothing," said David rubbing his eyes.

"Nothing, why's that?" asked his mother. She bent forward and kissed his forehead.

"I didn't keep last night's tea down," said David. "And I had to get up in the night again."

"Oh dear, why didn't you come and tell me?" said his mother. "You are a funny boy aren't you?"

"I'm a man now mum," said David. "And a man doesn't make a fuss, does he?"

"No guess you are right there," said his mother.

She remembered how strong he was when his father had died and what a comfort he was to her when she was sad.

David sat up and looked around his room. On nearly all the walls there were posters of lions and things from Africa. On the corner was a larger stuffed elephant.

"Mum, if I was in Africa what would I have for breakfast?" he asked.

"Oh I don't know really," she said. "Maybe waffles or crisp bread followed by a strong cup of black coffee Why do you ask?" she asked. "You are always on about Africa," she said. "I don't know why you talk about it so much." She brushed his hair to one side and said, "It's not like in the pictures and books you know, most of the people are starving."

"Yes I know mum. I do read the books at school about it, but for some reason I feel I must go mum," said David thoughtfully. "If we start saving now do you think that by the time I leave school we will have enough to go?"

He was very excited when he said this and looked at his mother's face for an answer.

"Well, we shall have to see about that," she said. "But first young man, you must get up or we shall be late for our appointment, and don't forget to wash you face."

"Yes, ok mum," said David starting to get dressed.

Soon David was washed and dressed and he came downstairs and sat at the table. His mother was in the kitchen and came in and put a glass of milk in front of him.

"There you are," she said. "We can't have you going on an empty stomach."

"Yes mum," said David drinking it. She went off to the kitchen to finish the dishes. Then she got David's coat just as she heard the bus coming up the street. They caught it to town and David continued the conversation about Africa.

"Mum," he said. "Do you reckon that if I put all my pocket money in the building society that by the time I left school I might have enough saved up to go?"

I'm sorry darling," said his mother. "It will take a lot more than that to go there but I will see what I can do, maybe if I took out an endowment policy that would amount a bit more. Anyway we shall have to wait and see. Come on, this is where we get off," she said. David got up and they left the bus. "Tell you what," said his mother. "As soon as we get out of the hospital we will go to the office and ask some questions about it."

"Oh yes mum will you?" said David, very excited at the thought that perhaps his dream might come true.

MEANWHILE IN A CONVENT NOT FAR AWAY

In a convent near Dorchester a sister was attending another sick and elderly sister who was dying; she was very old and her time had nearly come. For many years she had been the Reverend Mother of the convent but this position had been taken over by a younger person. Now the old nun had pneumonia and was very ill and also she knew she was dying. Attending her was a young sister of about twenty-five. The chapel bell rings and the young sister leaves the patient's side and goes to a corner to say her prayers. She crosses herself and prays.

"Dear Lord in heaven, please help and guide me, and guide Sister Dominique to your side, make her end peaceful, she has been good to us all and needs your help," prayed the young nun.

"Sister Theresa," said the old nun. "Come here," she beckoned feebly.

"I'm sorry," said Sister Theresa. "I did not mean to waken you."

"You did not waken me," said the old nun. "When you have spent your life in convent then it's the bells that call you to prayer that you hear."

"What is wrong?" asked the sister. "Do you wish to have a drink?"

"No my dear, nothing like that, but I would like you to listen to me for a moment. For many months now I have been watching you and I have come to the conclusion that you are not happy. I have waited for you to ask my advice but you have not found the courage to do this, so now it's time for me to speak before it's too late."

"Oh have you Reverend Mother?" said the other sister, turning away so the other could not see her tears.

"Yes you know my dear that you don't have to stay if you don't want to, if the lifestyle is not to your liking", said the old nun. "Why then do you torture yourself and make yourself unhappy?" She put out her hand and gently squeezed the younger sister's hand. "There is a world outside you know my dear," she said.

"Yes I know, but I have chosen to be here," said the younger sister. "Why do you choose to speak to me now?"

"I can see this is not the life for you," said the old nun. "I have asked the Reverend Mother to release you. Now don't get upset. This doesn't mean you have failed in any way, but it can't go on. You have learnt to be a nurse and if you join the outside world you can become whatever you want to be."

"But Reverend Mother, I have been to confession and learnt humility and said my prayers so why do I have to leave?" she whispered. "I am sorry I have tried to be a good nun and I know if you let me stay I can be a good nun, please, I promise," said Sister Theresa.

"No my child, don't lie to yourself. Join up with the sisters on the outside and become a really good nurse, there is no shame, you have done well and you can do better,"

Later as Sister Theresa went down the corridor she was stopped by one of the other sisters and told to report to the Reverend Mother's office; so she went. "Come in," said a voice.

Sister Theresa entered and found Reverend Mother at her desk. She looked up from her papers.

"Oh come and sit down," she said. "I have some bad news for you, I'm afraid. Sister Dominic's condition is worse and she will have to go to hospital after all and I wish you to go along with her".

"Yes Reverend Mother," said Sister Theresa. She looked at Reverend Mother's face.

"She is dying, so you must stay as long as necessary. She has also asked that you be released from the convent; I have never questioned what she has said before so I will not do so now. She is a very wise lady and in this case I feel she is right. I, too have seen that you have not been very happy, thanks be to god you have been given the power to help others and one day you will make a really good nurse. God bless you, my child you were not meant to be locked away in here with us, but before you go you must sign this form in triplicate. Just a formality really," said the Reverend Mother.

She got out some papers from her desk and laid them on the table in front of Sister Theresa, then she walked over to the window calling to Sister Theresa to come and say prayers for the last time as a nun. Sister Theresa got up and they went to the corner of the room and knelt together and prayed; Sister Theresa got up and went to the desk and signed the papers. She left the office and heaved a sigh of relief, while inside the office Reverend Mother gathered up the papers and turned to say more prayers.

MEANWHILE

David and his mother had arrived at the hospital waiting room. David looked all around the room at the pictures on the walls while his mother studied the letter a bit more closely and wondered why they needed him there at all. Things kept creeping into her head, questions that she could not answer. Why was David sick? These thoughts kept haunting her mind.

David sat looking at the rows of chairs that lined the room when a boy came in and sat down next to him. He had his arm in a sling. David smiled at him. The doors were pushed open and the sick nun was wheeled in accompanied by Sister Theresa, and the nurse also came into the waiting room.

"Come into room five we have been expecting you," the nurse said to the nun. "The doctor will be along soon."

"Thank you," said the nun. "Is it possible I can go with her?"

"Not right away," replied the nurse. "But if you sit there for a moment you can then go up to the ward with her as soon as the doctor has seen her."

"Right thank you," said Sister Theresa and she sat next to the two boys.

"Does it hurt much?" asked David to the boy who sat next to him.

"No not now, but it did when I first did it," said the boy. "I fell down from a tree," he said. "And my dad came out and picked me up but that was three weeks ago, and today I am going to have the plaster off and a smaller one put on. I don't mind it doesn't hurt at all when they do that." He looked at David. "What did you do then?"

"Oh not much, I got a nail stuck in my foot a couple of weeks ago, that's all," said David.

"Richard Hale" called the nurse. "You can go in now."

"Bye," said David.

"Bye," said the boy. "See you around maybe.."

David then turned to the nun, who was waiting to go and see her friend.

"Hello," said David.

"Hello," answered the nun.

"My name is David," he looked strangely at the nun. "And this is my mother."

"Hello," said Sister Theresa nodding at David's mother.

"Your friend is very sick?" asked David.

"I'm afraid so," replied the nun.

"Oh," said David. That was not the answer he had expected. "I was just wondering that's all." Then he changed the subject quickly. "Two weeks ago I got a nail stuck in my foot," said David. "It didn't hurt."

"Yes I know," said the nun. "I'm afraid I heard you telling that other boy. You must be a very brave boy," she smiled at David.

"I'm sorry he's so talkative," said David's mother.

The nurse then called out "Mrs Baxter" and David's mother looked up. "Yes that's me," she said.

"Will you go to room seven?" said the nurse. "The doctor wishes to see you on your own for the minute. David you stay there," said the nurse.

David's mother went to room seven as the nurse had told her to and sat down at the desk.She had a strange feeling again and rubbed the back of her neck. The doctor then came in, with a nurse, who stood nearby.

"Mrs Baxter, I'm afraid we may have some bad news for you," said the doctor.

David's mother shivered as she remembered the last time she heard that. She had that dreadful sinking feeling, in the bottom of her stomach.

"Yes, what is it?" she asked.

"We want to keep your son in for some more tests," said the doctor, looking at her. "We feel that it is best under the circumstances to warn you that it doesn't look too good."

"Why, what do you mean?" asked David's mother. She was frightened at the look on the doctor's face. "What's wrong?" she asked.

"We are not quite sure but we will do some tests and try to find out," said the doctor. "I realise that this has come as a shock to you, as you lost your husband the same way. I'm sorry it's a million to one chance that he will live, some times miracles do happen."

"Oh my god," cried David's mother. "Not to him as well, but why? It can't be true." Tears began to roll down her cheeks and she tried to brush them away.

"Nurse," said the doctor. "Get some water for Mrs Baxter please."

The nurse left the room and in a short while returned with a glass of water. David's mother took it in her shaking hands; she drank some of it and placed the glass on the desk.

"Thank you," she said looking at the nurse. "Are you sure?" she asked again. "I just can't grasp it."

David's mother picked up her bag and took out her handkerchief and wiped away her tears. She really felt like fainting but she knew she couldn't because she didn't want David to see that anything was very wrong.

"I'll be all right," she said after a while. "I must not let David see I have been crying. When do you want him in?"

"Right away," said the doctor looking at her. He put his hand out and held hers. "We'll do everything we can," he said.

"You know that his father died of the same thing don't you?" she asked.

"Yes I know," said the doctor once again. "I am dreadfully sorry, but what can I say?"

"Nothing, nothing," said David's mother. "It's not your fault, don't worry I'll be all right".

David's mother got up to go and went with the nurse to get David who was still sitting with the nun.

David looked at his mother's face and could see she had been crying.

"Are you all right?" he asked her.

"Yes darling I'm fine. It's just that I'm a bit upset. They want to keep you in for a while," she said. "Who will I have to talk to at home? Still you will be out in a couple of days."

"But mum," said David. "You said we were going to see about saving up some money to go to Africa."

"Yes darling I know but I can do that while you are in here." She looked at him and saw the disappointed look in his face. "Now be a good boy and I will see what I can do", she said.

"All right mum," he said. "But you promise to come in and see me every day won't you?"

"Yes I will," she said, seeing the worried look on his face.

"Now go along to the ward with that nice nurse and be a good boy and I will bring you some comics in later," she said.

David took a quick look at his mother and then at the nurse and then turned to the nun.

"Bye, bye," said Sister Theresa. "It was nice talking to you, I hope you soon get better".

"I hope your friend soon gets better too," said David.

"If you like," said Sister Theresa "I will come in and see you if that's all right with your mother?"

"Why yes," replied David's mother.

"Come on David," said the nurse, as she led the way along the corridor. David waved goodbye to his mother after giving her a kiss.

"Bye, see you late,"she said.

"Bye son," she said her voice shaky. Her heart was crying out for help but she dare not let David see. The room began to sound hollow and her legs felt like jelly. The strain was too much and sister saw the colour drain from her face. Then her legs collapsed and she fell into the arms of the nun who called for some help.

"Please someone help this lady," called the nun. "She has fainted."

Sister Theresa laid her down on the seats and patted the back of her hand.

"Mrs Baxter, Mrs Baxter, are you all right now?"

The nurse who had brought the water to the office came over.

"Oh dear, we thought this might happen," she said. "But she seemed all right in the office."

"What's wrong with her?" asked the nun.

Later when David's mother left the hospital she had no doubts as to what to do next. She went straight to her solicitor's office and demanded to see him immediately. The secretary was most put out.

"I'm sorry Mrs Baxter, Mr Johnson is with someone at the moment, but you can make an appointment for tomorrow. He has a space left at about 11.30 am. That's the best I can do."

After much debating she saw her solicitor. She begged him to let her have some money putting up her house as part payment for the costs involved. She decided to take David on his trip to Africa.

Three days later she had confirmation from the hospital. David was dying of leukaemia and she knew she had done the right thing. Only God could tell her now if there would be enough time for him to do the other things he wanted to do. Small consolation for her dying son.

OUT IN AFRICA WE JOIN A FILM CREW SOME DAYS PREVIOUSLY

We join the crew making a film about lions. Everyone is busy doing their bit, One chap sits on a high tripod. Fixed to this is a seat and on that lights which are worked by a generator. Down below and on the front of that there is a camera; the camera is trained on a man and woman standing on a veranda made out of wood. It's a set made especially for the film. Nearby sits the director who is giving instructions to the stars, the producer is the husband of the female star. He sits and watches what is going on while the other three cameramen are positioned in various places, camouflaged so they cannot be seen.

The husband producer is a bit effeminate; he is about forty-two, slightly built and casually dressed. He has been married to the star for only a short while.

"Right is everyone ready, quiet please," the director called.

The clapper boy came out. "Scene six take one."

"Action, roll them," called the director.

The woman came out onto the veranda and she stood looking at the sunset, then slowly she lifted her hands to her hair and took out two grips and let her hair fall to her shoulders. She then took hold of her hair loose and brushed her hand up through it, and then she slowly undid the top button of her blouse.

"Cut, cut," called the director. "That's not good enough," he shouted. "Why the hell can't you put a bit more feeling into it? You're not advertising bloody bubble bath, you are supposed to be trying to turn a man on, not treat him to a wash. You bloody fool get on with it, and this time do it right, try to be a little more alluring, put more feeling into it."

The woman was angry at the way the director shouted at her and she showed it on her face. Then she went back inside and the make-up artist touched up her face.

"Oh leave it," she snapped at the make-up girl.

"Quiet please," said the director once again. He pointed to the cameraman and things began to move again.

The clapper boy came out once more. "Scene six, take two."

They go through the same scene again and this time it's right. She lets her hair fall to her shoulders, then a man emerges from within the hut and comes up behind her and gently puts his arms round her waist. She turns and they kiss passionately. She gazes into his eyes.

"Darling, we can't go on like this," he says.

"No I can't," she replies, moving away from him "He would never release me. Divorce is out of the question," she said.

"But why not? I don't understand. I can't see how he can refuse, when you tell him that …" he said.

He paused.

"Oh you are impossible," she interrupted. "I know I have been unfaithful to him, but that doesn't give you the right to rub it in." She turned her face to him when she said this, and she was very angry. "How dare you throw that in my face," she said.

"I'm sorry I didn't mean it to sound like that darling," he said.

Coming over to her side, he put his hands up round her face and kissed her gently and she responded.

"Let's leave well alone for the time being. Yes? There will be a right time and place to tell him, and only I know when that will be," she said.

"Cut, cut print," said the director. "That was perfect; Bob did you get all that?" he asked.

"Yes sir, the lighting was perfect," said Bob, as he patted his assistant on the shoulder. "Thanks, that bit of advice you gave me was good," said Bob.

The assistant nodded.

"Right, shall we try the next scene, Harry?" said Bob, and he turned to where a man was sitting. He had some cages in which there were two lions.

"How long will it take you to get them set up for the next shot?" he asked.

"Not long," said Harry.

He got up and went over to the cages. He picked up a stick and poked at them and they roared at him.

"Ah," Harry said to them. "Be quiet now, I want you to do your stuff."

"Harry," said the director. "You know your cue don't you? It is to come and let the lions free."

"Ready when you are," said Harry.

"Right Cindy, are you ready for this scene? Tony you too?" said the director.

"Yes," said Cindy.

They went to the same positions they had been in before.

"Right," said the director. "Roll them, I don't want any one to muck up this shot as we are behind with the schedule and I don't want to have to reshoot it."

The clapper boy came out and called the scene and the cameras were ready to roll. The beautiful woman kissed the man as before, then she pulled away.

"Shush," she said "Did you hear something?" She looked round.

"No," said the man "Why?"

"Well I thought I did," she said once more.

"I think it must be your imagination," he said.

The trainer let out his two lions and they dashed to where the couple were standing. Without any warning, a terrible darkness came across the sky like a plague of locusts. Thousands of birds of all shapes and sizes flew past in a huge mass. This caused the lions to panic and they dashed to the couple and knocked them down; then a noise from what seemed nowhere hit them all, causing a dreadful pain that made them all hold their ears. The woman screamed and they knocked her and the man off the veranda. She fell awkwardly and cut her leg and arm. She was trapped between the steps and a post had come away from the top of the veranda.

Suddenly the noise was gone, save for the sound of one of the crew who had been bitten by a lion.

"Shit, shit and damn," cried the director. "What the bloody hell is going on? Why can't you keep your animals under control?" he said. "What the hell caused all that to happen?"

"I don't know, you tell me," called out one of the men. "Someone come and help the woman," he said.

Then Tony saw her and went to help.

"Here," he said. "Are you all right?" He put out his hand to help her up.

"Thanks," she said. "Ouch, oh, that hurts."

She clutched her foot.

"What the hell's going on and where did all those birds come from?" she asked.

"I don't know," said Tony. "Here lean on me. You'll have to get that seen to or you will get an infection in it. How's that?"

"Thanks that's fine," she said, holding on to him.

"Here come and sit down, I'll get one of the men to look at that cut," said Tony.

"Three thousand dollars, and a load of crap. The whole film's been exposed to light," grumbled the director, picking up the ruined film from the ground. "Just take a look at his," he said.

He rubbed his hands through his hair, and then he threw the script to the floor.

"Sir, sir," said one of the men running over to him.

"Yes what is it?" asked the director.

"One of the men has been rather badly bitten by a lion, he'll have to go to hospital," said the man.

"That's all I bloody need,", said the producer, coming over to see what was wrong. "It's safe to say that I don't think my men are safe," he said.

"Sir," said the man. "The others are all shook up and refuse to go back to work. They have quit and want to go home."

"What? They can't, they've signed contracts. I'll sue them if any walk out on me," said the producer.

"I told you not to work them so hard," said the woman, as one of them bandaged up her leg.

"It's all your fault, if you didn't spend so much time with your so called," she paused "friend, then this whole thing would not have happened."

"You shut up," said her producer husband, and then he slapped her face. Just as he did that Tony put up his hand and stopped him giving her another slap.

"Now," said Tony. "There's no need for that is there? She's right you know. You have wasted two hours today I have counted them."

"Mind your own business," said her husband "She's my wife and I'll do as I please., If she had not been so fussy earlier on then we would have been well away from here and back in town, so don't poke your nose in where it's not wanted. Remember you are paid to act not to voice your opinions about my wife," he finished angrily.

"Shit man, if that's the way you want it then I quit, contract or no contract," said Tony. "You can sue me or do what the hell you like."

Tony stomped out of the area of the set.

"Oh no please, now come on all of you, we are all just losing our heads, just because of this upset, please cool down all of you,", pleaded the producer.

"Tony," said the woman. "He didn't mean it, he's only like this when we get behind with the schedule. Please keep calm all of you."

She looked at the men who by all accounts were ready for a punch up.

"Darling," she said to her husband. "Please help me to my room."

"How does it feel?" asked the man who bandaged her leg.

The woman got up and her husband came over to help her to her room, saying that he was sorry that he had hit her. Then he helped her to her portable room nearby.

Everyone was a bit edgy but they went back to work and the trainer took a couple of men and went in search of his lions, putting them back in their cage as soon as he had found them. Tony went and sat under a tree and thought for a while. The crew cleared up the mess and then packed the cameras away into boxes to prevent the dust getting into them.

The woman got to her dressing room and started to retouch her make-up. After a short while Tony could no longer contain his curiosity and went to her dressing room. After a moment's hesitation he knocked on the door.

"Come in," a voice called.

Tony entered and was relieved to find his co-star alone.

"Oh Tony it's you, come in and sit down. How are you feeling?" she asked, dabbing at her face. Then she picked up a lipstick from the table. As she put some on she looked at Tony's reflection in the mirror. "Why so glum?" she asked. "You are not still angry about what happened are you?"

"If you must know, yes," he said looking at her. "Yes."

He took out his cigarettes from his top pocket. "Want one?" he asked.

She took one. "Thanks," she said waiting for a light. He took out his lighter, flicked it, lit her cigarette and then lit his own.

"Thanks," she said as she held on to his hand to steady the lighter. "You shouldn't be," she said.

"Frankly, I don't understand you, letting him beat you like that," said Tony, putting away his lighter and cigarettes. "Why do you let him get away with it?"

"You don't understand," said the woman. "And if I told you, you would still think me weak."

"Try me," said Tony looking into her eyes. "The trouble with this job is that you think I'm a weakling and that this is the way I always behave, but it isn't, so there."

"Well ok, but if you don't like it, stop me, I don't wish it to go any further than you,"she said.

She glanced quickly at Tony and then began her story.

"I met Lee eighteen months ago in Miami. on a hot and sticky night, at about seven o'clock. I was just an up and coming stagestruck starlet at the time, just about willing to do anything to get on a film set." She turned away from Tony and looked at his reflection in the mirror. She was almost afraid to say the next thing but found the courage to do so.

"I mean anything," she said. "Regardless of what it was or cost. So, with my neck out I took the chance.".She stubbed out her cigarette in an ashtray and turned to face Tony. "The only trouble was, at this time one of the directors who goes by the name of, oh that doesn't matter," she paused. "Well, that's not really important. One of them decided to find out just how much talent I really had and I mean talent, just that. He only wanted to find out in one way." She found it hard to bring herself to say what she wanted in so many words. "Then," she said. "I thought, in for a penny in for a pound, and started to let him do as he wanted. It was then that Lee came into the room," she continued. "Things then got out of hand and he began to shout at the director. There was a terrible scene and later I saw Lee who apologised and said that the director had no right to make me go through that and I should have known better than to let him take advantage of me in that way and do as he had asked."

"Then what happened?" asked Tony stubbing out his cigarette.

"Well, later I married Lee, and for the last year or so we have been quite happy, that is up to the other month," she said. She seemed very nervous. "I came back from a shopping spree unexpectedly and caught him with the same director that had asked me to you know? He was kissing him full on the mouth," she said with a disapproving look at Tony. "You can well imagine the horror when I realised what he was, for the previous year I had been quite happy, believing that he had been fighting for me, but now I realised that he was jealous, and was fighting for the other guy and not me. Believe me it was a great shock, but I got to thinking that even though he had double crossed me he had been kind and helped my career, so since it did me a favour, I feel I owe him that much. Can you see that Tony?" she asked.

She looked at Tony for some form of approval but Tony was not about to pass any out.

"Didn't you ever suspect anything like that when you first met him?" Tony asked.

"No," said Cindy. "I suppose you think I'm a fool?"

She got up and went behind the screen where she took off her dressing gown and put on a dress.

"They say love is blind and I must have been as blind as a bat," said Cindy.

"You can say that again.", said Tony to himself.

"Pardon," said Cindy coming out from behind the screen.

"Nothing important," said Tony. "You don't have to stay with him though do you?" he asked.

"No, but I feel that as long as he hides the fact that he is homosexual then I'm needed. Only when he faces that fact will I be able to leave him," she said.

"Well, what happens to any poor devil who falls in love with you in the meantime?", asked Tony, studying her reply carefully.

He looked at her full in the face and hoped that she would see that he was in love with her.

"I don't know anyone who is in love with me," she said. Cindy was completely blind to Tony's feelings.

"I don't know how you can waste your life on someone who doesn't care one way or the other," said Tony. He felt very hurt but was not about to give up and tried once more. "Supposing I was in love with you?" he asked bravely. "Then what would you say?"

Cindy turned; she stared at Tony's face.

"You,",she said. She wasn't sure as to what to think. "No, you can't be."

"Yes," said Tony. "I have been for some time now, so what have you got to say to that?"

"I really don't know,", said Cindy. "It's strange."

"Why?" said Tony going over to her and putting his arm around her waist. He kissed her tenderly. It was not like it had been on the set. It sunk deep into her soul, and she pulled away, almost afraid to believe it to be true.

"Why haven't you said anything before, or even worse why couldn't I see or feel it when you kissed me? You must think I am an idiot."

She flapped her arms in the air and continued "Why does everything happen to me?" she said. "What am I going to do?"

"Nothing," said Tony. "Nothing, I admire your loyalty and love, maybe I should not have said anything, but I would like you to remember that I do love you and if you want I shall wait for the day to come when you can come to me."

He then took her into his arms and kissed her.

ONE DAY BEFORE IN THE USA

At the satellite and weather station at Cape Kennedy they are hard at work tracking a hurricane off the coast of Florida. In a small room is a man in charge at work.

He watches his screen intently; others are busy watching various other screens and equipment. Suddenly the man watching the small screen sees something strange and looks again; he stops the recording and goes back to have another look to make sure he was not seeing things, then presses the mike button connected to his chief's room. The chief can see all that is going on in the other office through a one-way mirror so he has a good view of everybody.

"Yes, what is it?" the met chief asks.

"Sir, I think you ought to come along and have a look at the screen in the viewing room, something funny is going on and it ought to be checked," said the man.

"Right," said the chief. "I'll be along in a few minutes, sure you can't deal with it yourself?"

"No sir," said Brian.

The chief called to a woman sitting at one of the desks and she came over.

"Sir," she asked.

"Here take these to Peter and get him to look at them, tell him I want the results as soon as possible," said the chief.

"Yes sir," said the woman picking up the papers off the desk. "Do you want any copies done?"

"No that is not necessary," said the chief. "Thanks."

The chief got up and went into the large room followed closely by the woman. He grinned as she walked away to do as he had asked, and saw the other men grinning also. As work continued on the course of the hurricane many photos were needed. As the chief walked into the office he began shouting many orders.

"Joe get some more copies of that area and bring them to my office and you Wendy bring them in as quickly as you can.," .

"Yes sir," answered Wendy.

"You get all the maps out and then get me the coastguard. After that see if you can get me the Governor. If that hurricane doesn't turn soon we shall have to evacuate the coast.".

"Yes sir," said Wendy as she set about her tasks.

The chief eventually got to where Brian was; he was still watching the screen.

"What's this all about then?" asked the chief as he walked to the screen.

"You had better come and check this for yourself sir. I have some very strange pictures on the screen. Here have a look for yourself," said Brian.

Brian rewound the tape and then started to run them through for the chief to see.

"Look sir, there," he said as he pointed to two small things on the screen. "What do you make of them?"

"That's our new satellite number sixteen isn't it?" asked the chief.

"Yes sir, we only launched it a couple of weeks ago," said Brian

"Well it looks to me as if someone has made a boob," said the chief scratching his head.

"They are not there all the time sir. Just now and again, look see what I mean? Now they've gone. What do you think it could be sir?" he asked.

"I'm not certain," said the chief. He went to the door and called Peter to come over and have a look.

Peter came over and the chief continued talking to Brian.

"Get me a still shot of that thing," he said. "I'm not sure but they look like insects to me, and if they are, how the devil did they get into that unit?"

"Sir," said Peter, as he came through the door. He was tall, and wore glasses and was dressed casually.

"Pete, get me U.S.U.D. on the phone right away will you?" asked the chief. "Got it Brian?" said the chief, as he pivoted in his seat and turned round.

Brian held the shot still for the chief to look at and he studied it carefully.

"Sir, they are on the line now," called Peter

"Thanks," said the chief to him. "There is only one person who can tell us what the hell's going on," he looked at Brian. "I hope he's got the answers because I'm lost as to what is causing this."

"Hello, hello, can I help you?" said a.voice.

"Yes," said the chief. "Can I speak to Commander Leslie Hagget please?"

"Would you hold the line please?" said the voice.

"Yes sure," said the chief. He put his hand over the phone and spoke to Brian again. "Maybe Leslie can throw some light on the subject, since his department is to blame," said the chief.

"Hello, Commander Hagget here.What can I do for you?"

"Hi, it's Norman here," said the chief. He sat down on the corner of the desk as he spoke.

"Hi Norman, to what do I owe the honour of this call? How are the family?" he asked.

"They are fine thanks and yours?" asked the chief.

"They are ok, Danny's gone to camp for a week, he liked it so much last year so we let him go again. Kids, they cost more money than my golf does. Anyway you didn't phone me up to talk about the kids, so what can I do for you?" he asked.

"I'm not sure," said Norman, and Les could detect a tone of annoyance in his voice. "We have a problem, and you may be able to help us, we are not sure," said Norman.

"Oh yes and what might that be, you sound annoyed about something?" asked Les.

"No, not you personally but your department., Anyway I think I had better ask you to come up and see for yourself. We have something strange on our satellite, and we don't know what they could be. To us they look like insects; now I don't wish to point fingers but until yours truly sees them we don't know, could be nothing and yet again it could be serious. Anyway I feel it ought to be sorted out right away, don't you?" Norman asked.

"Yes sure," said Les. "You sound pretty worried, and I feel you think that my department is to blame so to get it sorted out I'll be along right away."

"Thanks," said Norman as he put down the phone and turned back to Brian.

"Sir," said a woman who had come into the room. She was blonde and well built and had a flashing smile and a good figure. "Here are the latest reports on the hurricane Betty," she said as she saw the picture on the screen and frowned. "There are also reports of bird migration, sir."

"Thanks," said the chief and took them from her and smiled.

"Sir, I nearly forgot this," she said. She handed him a teleprint message that had just come in from Africa. "There's some sort of electrical storm coming up the coast and heading inland., The strange thing about it sir is, that there are no form of clouds and none can be detected. There is nothing that our charts are picking up," she said.

"Ok, thanks," said the chief, taking the message from her.

He raised an eyebrow as she went out through the door, then the chief and Brian put the reports on the desk and began to study them.

Les came through the door and then came over to the two men. The chief read the telex the woman had brought in.

"Now what's all this nonsense about?" asked Les.

The chief and Brian looked up and Les walked over to the desk and they shook hands.

"Come and have a look for yourself," said the chief, leading the way over to the screens. Brian had rewound the tape once again and showed him what they were talking about.

"Christ," said Les. "You could be right, someone has made a boob." He scratched his head. "How the devil did they get in there? Everything was carefully sterilised and top men are used to doing that job, so I don't see how they could possibly get in. It's impossible," he said.

Brian had now given up his seat to the commander and had been studying the report the girl had brought in. On one of the screens that they were not looking at two blotches appeared. One of the blotches then let out a shower of smaller objects. They were only on the screen a few seconds and then they were gone again. Then one of the larger objects went off in a different direction.

"Sir," said Brian. "Have you seen these reports yet?"

He looked up from the reports and they both came over to his side.

"Why, what's that?" said the chief looking at the screen.

The commander took a quick look at the reports and then went back to the screen. He was curious at what was on the screen and how it got there.

The chief and Brian looked at the photos that the woman had brought in.

"Take a look at this sir," said Brian. "Don't you think they look funny?" The chief looked at them carefully.

"Yes, they do look kind of strange don't they? Have you ever seen anything like this before?" the chief asked. "Brian, can you get me the details of that area? I'd like to find out a bit more about it. Les come and look at this."

Brian left the room and was back in seconds. In his arms he held a rolled-up map, and on reaching the table he held it out. The chief and Les picked up the photos that were already on the table and laid them on top of the map.

"There's your answer," said the commander, pointing to the centre of the map on one of the TVs. "What you saw was bird migration, that's all."

"Yes, but if that's the case that still doesn't tell us what those things were on the screens does it?" asked the chief. "Or how they got there."

"I don't think they are in the camera," said Brian who had gone back to the screens again.

"Look, I'm not going to spend all day arguing with you," said the commander. "I say they are only bird migration."

The commander suddenly had a funny feeling and rubbed the back of his neck, then without any warning a high pitched noise could be heard all over the city, so much so that everyone held on their ears as it hurt them so much. As quickly as it had come it was gone and everyone in the weather station thought it was something to do with the hurricane. Within seconds the phones started ringing with all sorts of complaints.

"True," said Brian as he broke the silence. "If all we see here are birds migrating then fair enough, but supposing that is that what we are meant to think, or have we other forces at work?"

"What?" said the commander. "Are you trying to tell me that the Russians have a new secret weapon, and that they are trying to sabotage our satellite? You better be knowing what you are saying my man or you will be in a lot of trouble."

"No, sir," said Brian, "but it's worth investigating isn't it?"

"Now hold on a minute there's no need for speculation, I say that we start again and make sure of the facts. Here, come and look at this again, there, take a good look."

He ran his fingers around the area on the map. "That's about a hundred square miles," said the chief, "of desert land only and with a few inhabitants; surrounded by a mountain range. That seems to be the place all those birds are heading. Here, take a look for yourself., Let's have another look at the film, right?"

They all went over to the screens and rewound the film. To their complete surprise they found more than they had bargained for. Shots taken when that noise had occurred came up on the screen. The three men stared in amazement at the screen. The two insects that had appeared before had dropped a shower of smaller egg type objects and these insects parted as soon as this happened and went off in different directions.

"Christ," said the chief. "What the hell is happening Brian?"

"Well you may ask sir," said Brian. "Do you want a projection on those things?"

"Yes," said the chief.

"Right, as fast as we can we may not have much time," said Brian.

"I'll get on to the war department," said the commander "and try to find out if they are testing out any new weapons. I don't like the look of all this at all. They could be trying to block our radar."

"Sir," said the woman coming back into the office. She seemed upset.

"Yes, what is it?" snapped the chief.

"I don't know what is going on sir," she said "but everyone is phoning up to complain and to find out where all the birds have gone and what that terrible noise was."

"Oh, don't worry me now with that for the moment," said the chief. "Tell them something, anything you like.".He waved his hand in the air. "Make up something, say it has something to do with the storm," said the chief.

"Yes sir,", she answered, shrugging her shoulders and leaving the room.

Brian pressed a whole lot of buttons to find the projectory?(trajectory) of the things and soon came up with the answer.

"Sir," said Brian. "You are not going to believe this, they shot in the direction of Africa. The larger ones," he hesitated...

"Well, come on tell us," said the chief.

"One into space sir, and the other to Africa,", said Brian.

In the meantime the woman had gone back to the chief's office to put some papers on his desk. The phone rang and she answered it. Her face went bright red when she realised who she was speaking to.

"I want to speak to the chief in command," said the voice in an angry tone. "Right, now do you hear?"

"Yes sir," said the woman who almost came to attention as she answered.

She put down the phone and ran down the corridor to where the chief was and went over to him; he was still talking to the commander.

"Sir, sir," she gasped. "Excuse me…"

"Not now," said the chief. He rubbed his hand across his chin still trying to work out the puzzle.

"But sir," she said again, very agitated by now.

"I said not now," said the chief and waved her away.

"But I insist," she said, getting angry.

"My, but you are a sassy little thing aren't you?" said the chief.

"Oh," said the girl in disgust, and went on "it's a case of having to be when the commissioner is on the phone and he wants to speak to the chief right away."

"Oh shit," said the chief. "Sorry, thanks," he said looking at the girl.

"Sorry," said the commander. "I should not have been so rude Will you accept my apologies?"

"Yes sir," said the girl as she left.

"Thanks," called out the commander who then took a quick look at Brian and shrugged his shoulders.

"Sometimes I should keep my big mouth shut," he said.

The chief had by now reached his office and had picked up the phone.

"Yes sir, sorry to have kept you waiting we have a…" He wiped his sweating forehead with a hanky taken from his pocket.

"What the hell is going on down there?", shouted the commissioner. "I've just had the Secretary of State on the hotline to find out what was that awful noise all about? What's going on? Now you had better have a really good excuse. He says that the President has had a call from the USSR to say that someone is trying to sabotage their satellites, and I want to know just what is going on. Do you hear me?" The commissioner continued shouting down the phone. "He says that they have been bombarded by something or other, says that we are trying to cause a political uprising. They have accused us of blocking out some of their messages and using bugging devices. So what have you to say to that? Well I'm waiting."

"Sir, I'm sorry but it isn't us. In fact we were beginning to think that it was them bugging us," said the chief, "but everything is in hand. The commander is on to the war department now to find out if anyone is testing a new device, which we don't know about".

"Right," said the commissioner. "Let me know the results as soon as you have them and one other thing, I understand you want my authority to evacuate the coast off Florida?"

"Yes sir there is a full alert on hurricane Betty, she's at her height in four hours," said the chief.

"Do you know the panic that will cause if I do that?" asked the commissioner.

"Yes sir, but the hurricane will do an immense amount of damage to houses and the people if nothing is done soon Thousands will be killed," said the chief.

"Ok, Ok, but be it on your own head," said the commissioner. "I'll give my authority to the guards to start the evacuation, but keep me informed at all times on everything."

"Yes sir," said the chief.

The phone went dead, and after a second the sound of buzzing could be heard.

MEANWHILE IN AFRICA

Meanwhile, David's mother had advertised for a private nurse and one had answered that she thought suitable. Little did she know that it was the nun, now free who had by now completely changed her appearance with a new hairstyle and clothes. Sister Theresa had not let on that she knew them. But she liked David for his bravery, admired him a great deal and looked upon him as her own son might be if she had one.

After she was found to be acceptable they were now en route and enjoying their trip stopping off at many places. Although weak, David was really enjoying himself. She found his faith a wondrous thing and wished she had what he had.

STEVE ANDERSON, TWO NIGHTS
BEFORE THE FLIGHT

We join Steve at a dinner party with a few friends in the city of Camgonga. The party is held in a club. Officers and their partner are sitting chatting at their tables in the candlelight. The hall is fitted with such tables and everyone is having a lovely time. Steve glanced at his watch, it's about eleven o'clock. Then he glanced at one of the two ladies sitting at his table. On the other side of him sat a man. The two ladies chatted to each other while Steve kept his eye on the woman, his girlfriend who was dancing. They danced to the band, and a singer was singing to the tune of "*Alintine Dale*".

"How are you and Steve getting on?" asked her partner.

"I don't see that is any of your business," she answered. "What's it got to do with you anyway?"

"There is no need to be so sharp about it," said her partner. "Come here and let me hold you closer. I like a woman with a bit of fire," and he pulled her closer and went to kiss her. She shoved him away.

"Get your hands off me you creep," she said. "How dare you!"

Just then the dance came to an end and she was glad to get off the floor and back to her seat. Steve had seen what had happened and was concerned about his girlfriend.

"You ok?", he asked.

"Yes," she answered. "Thanks."

She dropped her eyes.. She took up her hanky and wiped her eyes.

"Thank you, thank you," said a man who had come on to the stage. "Ladies and gentlemen," he said. "We hope you have enjoyed your evening, but now we come to the highlight." He went on to say "It has been my pleasure over the past forty years or more to work with the force and seeing that tonight is a special occasion I have two duties to perform. Once in every man's lifetime he is proud to meet a man who is both proud of his profession and of his men. It's not very often that we come across such a man but there is just one and tonight to show him that we really care, we ask Warren Bates, my friend and companion who is retiring from the force to come on to the stage, to help me perform one more duty," he finished, pointing to a man sitting at a table with his wife and friends.

"Ladies and gentlemen a big hand for Warren Bates," said the man.

Warren got up, bowed to the people and made his way to the stage. He smiled at everyone and got carefully on to the stage. The other man shook his hand.

"Right," said the other man. "I wonder if you could help me Warren? How much was it I borrowed off you when we put that bet on those horses? Let me see now, don't worry about that now, not here we can sort that out later".

"I don't understand all this," said Warren.

"Oh don't worry Warren I'll pay you back and I may as well do it now," said the man. "Oh, shit, I've only got empty pockets, there's plenty of coppers around but no silver".

They all laughed at the man who searched his pockets.

"Well, never mind," he said.

A beautiful young lady came on to the stage carrying a silver plaque.

"Excuse me," she said. "This is all the silver I could find. Is it any good?"

"Well yes, it's better than coppers, thank you," said the chief of police.

It was the chief of police who was doing all the talking. The assembled officers all laughed.

"Ladies and gentlemen, to Warren," said the chief. "This is presented to you with all the love from the officers and men of the sixteenth police force, in gratitude for forty years' hard work. Thank you."

They all stood up and clapped. This brought tears to Warren's eyes. He smiled broadly as he accepted the shield. They all stopped clapping. Warren looked at the shield

"I don't know what you are smiling at, does it say this shield is for you?" asked the chief.

Warren looked at it and shook his head. "No," he said. "It says to Steve Anderson, most outstanding officer for the fourth year running on the firing ranges at Camgonga national sports centre.

"Oh," said Steve's girlfriend. "You won darling, you won," she clapped.

"Steve will you please come up and collect your reward?"said the chief.

All Steve's friends clapped him as he went to collect the shield. Warren handed him the shield and Steve turned and aimed two fingers at his opponent sitting at his table. He also smiled and clapped.

Steve left the stage and returned to his table., His friend shook his hand.

"Thank you Warren," said the chief. "To think your last duty was to hand out this, thanks."

Warren was about to leave the stage when his friend called him back.

"Just where do you think you are going?" he asked.

Warren pointed to his table.

"You needn't think you are getting away with that do you?" the chief asked.

The crowd all laughed.

"Yes why? Can't I go?" asked Warren.

"No come here for once in your life man and do as you are told," said the chief.

Warren got back on stage.

"Now listen Warren, you have done all your work", said the chief.

"Yes thanks," said Warren. "Tomorrow I've just got to tidy up my garden a bit because I have neglected it somewhat. But I have got plenty of time now to do it haven't I?"

"Well, no you have not," said the chief. "The force have all chipped in and we have thrown all our coppers in one pile. We would like you to accept this, a good holiday for you and your good wife, for three months, travelling around the world, all expenses paid. Not a penny has to come out of your pocket; everything has been done for you. You can fly straight to the States, or whichever country you like starting the day after tomorrow. A big hand for Warren Bates, cop of the century."

They all went mad and Warren was so overwhelmed he brushed the tears away from his eyes. He had always dreamed of going round the world and now it had come true. Flowers were brought for his wife and there for the moment we fade out.

Later that night, Steve is dropping his girlfriend off at her house; Steve gives his girlfriend a goodnight kiss outside on the porch, when the next-door neighbour appears. It is almost midnight. The neighbour sees them on the porch.

"Good evening Cherry," said a man's voice. "How are you tonight?"

"Fine thanks Deator, how's the common cold coming on?" she asked.

"Who's that?" asked Steve.

He had his arm round her; it was so dark that he could not see much of Deator.

"Why that's Professor Deator Hayes," said Cherry. "Don't you know he's famous? He's said to be able to cure anything. I read his thesis on skin grafting, part of my curriculum at college a few years back. He's fantastically clever. I've heard that he uses himself as a guinea pig," she sighed.

Steve looked at her and realised she wasn't the one for him, far too young he thought. At twenty-two she wasn't a mature woman yet.

"Sounds as though you have a crush on him," said Steve

"Everyone gets a crush on him, especially if you are interested in your work and his, but he is married and has two teenage kids and a wife who nags him to death. Poor man, I failed though", said Cherry.

"Oh well never mind," said Steve. "Anyway I must go, got a busy day tomorrow. Have to pack. I'm off to the States the day after, so I won't be seeing you for a while."

"Oh really, never mind it was fun while it lasted wasn't it? We've had our moments haven't we? You did say no strings didn't you? Thanks for a lovely evening. I'm glad you won the shield." As Cherry said this she flashed a look at Steve.

"Yes," said Steve, as he kissed her. "Goodnight."

"Bye Steve," said Cherry as she went in and closed the door. Steve got back into his car and drove off.

Meanwhile Deator had parked his car and gone indoors.

THE DAY BEFORE THE FLIGHT IN CAMGONGA

Harry is a man who works mainly on his own; hard working and an expert at his job and that is mining. He is in his boss's office in the city after doing a job blasting a hole through part of a mountainside. He is about forty and very well spoken and well dressed.

"Harry, I have just received a call from London and your expertise is required there," said Harry's boss.

He sat in a large leather chair; he was about fifty-five and had greying hair and a moustache.

"I have arranged for you to be on the next grasshopper flight, that's first thing in the morning ten thirty, that's the boarding time," said the boss.

He looked at Harry who was sitting opposite him. Harry was surprised.

"I'm sorry I couldn't give you any warning," said the boss. "But that's the way it goes, you understand?"

"Yes sir," said Harry. "But tomorrow it's my kid's birthday, I was planning…"

The box of cigars was passed to Harry.

"No thanks," said Harry.

"Yes I know. I'm sorry. Maybe you can make it up a bit when you come back," said the boss. "I hate putting you out Harry but you are the only one who is expert enough to work with jelly."

"What's the job then?" asked Harry.

He fiddled with a pencil taken from the boss's desk. He was annoyed. He could hear his kid's voice asking him to stay at home for his sixth birthday. He could hear him in his head.

"Daddy why do you always have to go away? You make mummy cry, she says that you make things go bang and fall down. Mummy smacks me if I break my toys, when you're away I don't like it," said his son Danny.

"Does she?" asked Harry.

"Yes, so why can't I break things? You don't get told off when you break things," said Danny.

Harry brushed the boy's curly hair and looked into his big brown eyes.

"You are a bit too young to understand yet," said Harry. "But one day I promise I'll tell you all about it."

"Harry your tea's ready," said his beautiful wife

All this conversation was going on in Harry's mind when the boss's voice broke into his dream.

"Harry, did you hear what I said?" said the boss.

"Sorry, no I didn't," said Harry returning to reality.

"Seems you were a little preoccupied. You feeling all right? Heck I know you are tired," said the boss. "But a good job was done on that tunnel. Geographically speaking, they said it was impossible, but you proved them wrong didn't you?"

"What's the job I have to do in England?" asked Harry.

Getting up, he pointed to the coffee maker in the corner of the office.

"Yes, help yourself," said the boss, swivelling round in his chair. He stubbed out the remains of the cigar.

Harry offered the boss a coffee.

"Thanks," said the boss. "Some kids did a bank job in London, damn fools I don't know what the world's coming to these days. They caught two of them, but not before they managed to lock three of the tellers in the safe. It's one of those new time lock systems. Impossible to open until after the weekend. That being the case they will only be able to survive for seventy two hours. They have men working on it now so they could be out by the time you get there, but just in case they cannot manage it they have asked us to help them deal with it, and you are the only one who could possibly do the job. They have sent us a print of the locking system by telex and here it is. It's none too clear, due to some electrical storm building up on the coast, but I guess you can study it on the flight and you can then decide what's best when you get there."

He took the coffee from Harry.

"Thanks," he said.

He put the print down in front of Harry who sat down and looked at it carefully.

"Right, I reckon this one will be ok," said Harry. He picked up his coffee, drank some and put his cup down.

"Guess I'll have to try and make it up to Danny before I go. Better get down to the shops and see if I can get that bike I promised him, but it is a pretty poor substitute isn't it?" said Harry, getting up. "Thanks, I'll see you when I get back. Ok, don't worry. I ain't taking it out on you. I'm just bloody annoyed with the kids today and if I'm not too careful mine will be the same. Have you ever thought that it could be our fault? This so called democracy we live in is a load of crap. Sometimes this so called society we live in doesn't see or use the media that it's got. Take TV for instance."

"What do you mean?" asked the boss as he drank his coffee.

"Our kids," said Harry "spend hours sitting glued to the TV, yet their teachers at school don't use anything that they see. Do they? For instance why don't they get kids to do a thesis on programmes say like "*Tomorrow's Science*" or even on plays or films that they see. Try to get them to see the difference between fact and fiction for instance? There's such a lot kids should know but it's just left to sink into their brains and never used in the right text."

Harry sat on the edge off his boss's desk.

"I'm puzzled, I don't get your meaning," said the boss as he put his cup down.

"That's just it, now don't get me wrong," said Harry. "I'm not putting you down or anything and you have worked your way up in the world or you wouldn't be where you are now. So did I, but you and I had fathers to help us. I don't know what your father was like but mine was one hell of a guy. He was never cruel; he always asked questions first and never jumped to conclusions. If you know what I mean?"

"With me it was my mother, bless her. I hardly ever saw my dad. She was the business one in our family," said the boss. "Dad was away most of the time and she was left in charge of bringing me up. After sending me to business school she had doubts that I would make it, but I did with flying colours, thank god. Guess I must have inherited that from her as they later split up and I have had to do the lot myself."

"So perhaps you will understand what I mean, I always had my father to confide in," said Harry, as he got up and went over to the window and looked out. "Somehow it's not the same as a woman. I'm not saying your mother was wrong, but it was highly unfair to leave her to bring you up. My dad was a good talker and we used to go fishing and things like that and it was great fun. We were very close you know and as I grew older we became good friends as well as him being my father."

"Yes, guess you are right," said the boss. "I can remember being called a mother's boy at school and to be honest I was glad to get sent away, to get out of her clutches. Still Harry this is not getting you on your way now is it? So we will have to continue this at a later date when you get back."

"Yes, but let me tell you this," said Harry, "then you will be able to see what I mean. I remember seeing this film. At the time I never thought anything of it; it was about a boy who went on a trip to Africa with his father. On the way they developed engine trouble and eventually crashed. The boy's father was killed and the boy was left alone to die in the desert. Now how does one survive in that intense heat, it's hard and the only chance you have is to wait and see if you will be rescued, by someone. By some fluke chance he had seen a survival film on the television a few weeks before and had remembered what to do and that is what saved his life. Nowadays, the kids sit up and watch the so called box and their parents complain that they are not learning anything, but they are. It only needs the experience before it is applied, not when it is too late, don't you see? Even to me at first it was just a story until I came out here and found out it's real, and to survive you have to know everything or die. If my father, god bless him, hadn't made me see that I dread to think what would have happened to me. Anyway this won't get me to the shops in time to get my son the bike I promised him for his birthday now will it? So you see, I'll see you when I get back and I'll tell you the rest of the story. Oh, thanks for the coffee that refreshed me quite a lot," Harry said as he made a beeline for the door. "I shall only just make it in time now."

Harry closed the door behind him. His boss called to him as he opened the door.

"Hey Harry, I think you are in the wrong job."

"Yes," said Harry, smiling at his boss. "I know that's what Pusiller said, but nar, I enjoy my work even though it's dangerous, but one thing I do know I don't want Danny growing up and doing the same job as me., So far I've been lucky but it can't go on forever," he shrugged his shoulders. "When I get back I'll try putting my views forward and see what happens."

Harry waved to his boss who waved back. Harry left the building and went shopping to get a bike for his son, but he was not in the mood to take it home to him as he knew what he would have to face. As Harry left the children's shop he passed Mrs Heal as she was looking in the window, but he didn't know her and was not around to see what happened next. Harry reached home much earlier than he expected. He walked up the path of their fine detached house, and took a paper out of the door and went in.

"Danny, are you anywhere around? Honey?" he called.

He could smell a very nice steak cooking, his best meal. So he went on to the kitchen where his wife was. Pusiller was busy cooking.

"Hi honey," Harry said going over to her. He kissed her on the back of the neck. "Mmm, that smells good," he said sniffing.

"Me or dinner?" she asked turning and smiling at him. "You're home early."

Then she saw the brown paper parcel and the look on his face, the one she had seen time and time before.

"Oh no," she said, giving him a kiss. "Not another job," her face saddened.

"Afraid so love," said Harry; he kissed her again this time on the nose. "Sorry darling, that's the way of things. I have got to go first thing in the morning, but at least we will have tonight."

"But darling, it's Danny's birthday, and you promised you would be here this time." She looked at Harry's face and could see he was just as disappointed as she was. There was a moment of silence broken by the sound of a small boy's cry. It was Danny.

"Daddy, daddy you are home.", He then caught sight of the parcel. "Oh what's that dad?"

Then he saw his father's face and his eyes fell to the floor and he was very sad. Harry tried to brush it off.

"Hello sunshine," said Harry picking him up. "How's my best boy then?"

He sat him on the table and looked at him.

"Not on there darling," said Pursiller. "I'm always telling him off for doing that."

"Sorry love," said Harry.

He took Danny off the table. He knew that she was angry with him, but what could he do about it. It was his job and that was that.

"Dad's got your present Danny Would you like to open it now?" his mother asked.

The boy looked at his father's face then the look of excitement changed to one of displeasure.

"You are going away again, aren't you dad?" he asked.

Danny scuffed his feet from one side to the other. Harry bent down and put his hand on Danny's shoulder and looked straight into his face.

"Yes son, but only for a few days. I'll be back Monday," said Harry.

He never liked to involve his family in his work but for some reason that he couldn't understand he felt that he had to this time. He felt that he was breaking all the rules for some obscure reason.

Tears were now rolling down Danny's cheeks, as he sobbed quietly to himself.

"You see it's up to me to try to save some people who have got themselves locked in a safe," said Harry. "That's not really true. What happened is that some naughty boys got in to rob a bank and although two of them were caught, they locked three people in a safe and they can't get out." Harry looked at Pusiller. "If I don't go and get them out they will all die. That's why I can't stay for your birthday son."

Pursiller suddenly felt very small and she realised just how selfish she had been. She knelt down beside Harry and put her arms around him and kissed the back of his neck tenderly. Danny looked at his father and suddenly he felt very proud of him and in those few precious moments they were all very close.

"He is right you know son?" said Pursiller. "We must not be cross with daddy must we, when he is trying to save people's lives? After all if you fell down the stairs and mummy didn't patch you up you would think we didn't care wouldn't you?"

The boy looked at his father and then threw his arms around his neck. He stopped crying and, after saying sorry, asked "Can I open my present now?"

Pursiller got up with Harry.

"Whoops," she said. "With all this going on I have nearly spoilt the steaks." She went over to the stove as Harry handed his son his present.

"They are a little on the well done side," said Pursiller. "Ok?"

There was a knock on the door and Harry went to open it.

"Just how I like them," he said.

"Oh that will be Gordon," said Pursiller. "He said he would pop over with Danny's present today. I forgot to let you know he can't make it to the party tomorrow, something to do with a storm."

Harry opened the door.

"Hi Gordon, come on in," said Harry. "How's things?"

Gordon stepped into the house.

"Hi, everyone. Hi Danny," said Gordon.

Danny was still busy undoing his bike with great excitement.

"Hello uncle Gordon," he said, not bothering to look round. "Look what I've got, it's a bike. Isn't it smashing?"

"Yes I'd say it is," said his uncle.

He took Harry's hand and shook it.

"Hi," he said to Harry. "You look tired, hope I'm not interrupting anything."

"No, come on in," said Harry. "Nice to see you. Don't often get the chance now do I? You are always off somewhere and so am I, and never the twain shall meet."

"Hmm, some brother you are. Here Danny," said Gordon.

He handed Danny a brown paper parcel. It was not far off the size of the one his father had given him. Harry looked at his brother.

"You got what I said?" he asked.

"Yes and they match," said Gordon.

Danny came over and gave his uncle a kiss.

"Thank you uncle Gordon," he said.

He went over and busted himself opening the parcel.

"Oh," he said as he took the paper off. "Mummy, daddy," shouted Danny. "Look they match. My bike has got a trailer kit to fit the back. Oh how lovely."

Pursiller bent down to fix it on for him and winked at Gordon as he looked at him.

"What's this about a storm? Is it a bad one?" asked Harry. "Only I have to fly out tomorrow morning."

Harry went over to their small bar and poured a drink for his brother and handed it to him.

Gordon took the drink.

"Thanks," he said. "No, not too bad, that is to say it's not a hurricane or anything like that, it's just an electrical storm, a strange one that's all."

"What about that new rig that was supposed to have come? Any news of that yet?" asked Harry.

"No, but if it had then we would know a lot more about it, the storm I mean, so far the only exciting thing that has happened lately is a strange migration of birds from all sorts of places. It's just as if they have all suddenly gone mad and forgotten what they are doing, and of course this storm. Still not to worry, stranger things have happened, said Gordon.

Pursiller didn't like the sound of the storm or the news and for some unknown reason she began to rub the back of her neck. Then she shivered as if someone had walked over her grave. She looked at Harry at this point and saw that he was rubbing his neck as well.

"Dinner ready in two minutes," she said to both men. "You are staying aren't you Gordon?"

"Yes thanks," said Gordon looking at them both strangely. "Have I said something wrong? You both look so gloomy."

"Just a strange sensation that's all," said Pursiller

MEANWHILE WITH DAVID

David was awoken that night by a bad dream. "Mum, mum," David tossed and turned. "Mum, no, no, don't,"he yelled out "No I don't want to. Please I hate it, go away, no don't mum please they're pricking me. Get them to stop, it hurts."

He let out a yell, as Theresa and his mother entered the tent.

"Oh dear," said David's mother, "he's having another bad dream I feel so helpless, what can we do?"

"Nothing Mrs Baxter," said Theresa "Nothing, he's quietened down now let's leave him."

THE DAY BEFORE AT ABOUT FIVE THIRTY P.M.

We are now in the city shopping area; Mrs Heal who is seven months pregnant is looking in one of the children's shops where Harry passed her carrying his son's bike. Brenda is waiting for her husband who has gone into the sports shop opposite to get himself some shorts to play squash to get rid of the kink in his body after all the hours of flying he does. With the shorts in his hand he then decides to pop into the betting shop to put a bet on a tip he had been given. Brenda saw this and was annoyed so she paced up and down on the other side of the road. He went in and looked at the odds on the horse that he wanted to bet on when a voice said from behind.

"Hey Garry.". It was an old acquaintance of his whom he had not seen for years. "What horse are you betting on today?" he asked Garry.

"Christ, Ben isn't it? I haven't seen you for years. How are you?" said Garry.

"Me, I'm ok I guess. Well what are you going to bet on and how much are you going to put on?" asked Ben.

"I don't know yet, I see my wife is getting impatient across the road," said Garry. "She gave me a list of some horses but they don't look too good. I've been given a tip so I think I'll try that."

Ben looked at the list Brenda had given Garry.

"Well, she gave you plenty to choose from," he said. "Tell you what, have you ever done the accumulator, that's when you put one bet on top of another and so forth?"

"No," said Garry. "I don't have that sort of money to do that sort of thing."

"Well, tell you what how much were you going to put on today?" asked Ben looking at him.

"About ten dollars," said Garry.

"Well, if you're willing and I am we can do an accumulator together," said Ben. "Then we will double our chances. We can both sign the paper so that it's all fair. Besides I owe you anyhow, I ain't forgotten you saved my life.."

"Ok," said Garry. "Here's my ten dollars. Let's go and do this right."

The two men went over and signed the forms and put their bets, they chose their horse together, shook hands and left the shop.

What Garry didn't know was that standing in the betting shop door was a cop who was after his old mate Ben., He was just waiting for the right time to move in and get him, but Ben knew this and asked the guy behind the counter if he could use the loo. He made his escape through the window before the cop could get to him. In the car park he searched for a car with keys left in it, then jumped in and drove off. Just at that moment Garry came out of the betting shop. Brenda caught sight of him and waved at him. He went to cross the road just as the stolen car came out of the car park and the two cops in hot pursuit. If it had not been for a man who instinctively knocked Brenda to the ground as the car sped by she would have been killed but of course he did not realise she was pregnant and she fell heavily.

Garry saw all this from the other side of the road and felt helpless to get there in time but it was too late. In that fraction of a second he thought he recognised the man in the car as his friend he had been talking to a few seconds ago.

"You ok, ma'am," asked the man helping Brenda up off the ground.

Garry had by now managed to get across the road after the police cars had gone.

"I'm sorry," said the man. "I didn't realise you were pregnant, but if I had not grabbed you, you would have been killed, that's for sure."

"Darling, darling are you ok?" asked Garry. "The bloody fool nearly killed you."

"Sorry I had to knock her to the ground mate," said the man. "I didn't know she was pregnant."

"That's ok, thanks you saved her life," said Garry. "You did not happen to get the number did you?"

"No, sorry mate," said the man.

"All I got were the numbers five, seven, two, or was it three? Christ, if I get hold of that stupid fool I'll kill him."

"You all right Mrs?" asked the man.

He looked at Brenda who had gone pale and was holding her stomach. Garry looked at her and felt very worried about her.

"I think I had better get you home," he said to her. "I think I'll call the doctor right away darling."

She bent towards the man and said, "thanks for saving my life."

She then turned to Garry. "I think I've frightened the little bugger," she said.

Garry put his arms around her and led her back carefully to the car park and put her into the car and drove home. When he got there, he phoned for the doctor who came out right away. By the time the doctor had got there Brenda had gone into what Garry thought was premature labour.

Garry was so mad about the whole thing that he went to the phone after he had seen Brenda was being seen to and phoned the police to report the numbers he could remember and then he remembered that a police car gave chase. So he went back to tell Brenda that he was going to the police station.

Brenda by this time had been taken to the hospital. She was in the labour ward and the hospital staff were in control of the situation and they thought it best if Garry left and came back later. He kissed his wife who was crying out for him and reluctantly left the ward, very angry and wanting revenge.

All this had happened while Harry was giving his son his bike.

HEAD QUARTERS POLICE CAMAGONGA

Garry went straight to the police headquarters about half an hour after he left the hospital. He went straight to the main desk and asked to see the chief of police.

"Excuse me, may I speak to the head of the department?" Garry asked.

"In connection with what?" asked the girl at the desk.

She was tall and slim in her uniform and looked very smart. She was about forty.

"I wish to file a complaint," said Garry. "I'd also like to see someone at the top, this is no ordinary matter."

"I'm sorry sir," she said politely. "The commissioner does not deal with complaints of this nature himself. You will have to go through the usual channels the same as everyone else."

"I'm sorry about that," said Garry getting very angry. "I don't wish to be rude but I want to see someone in authority, if you don't mind. It's of a vital importance. Of course it doesn't matter to you that my wife is in hospital because of some nut who nearly ran her down; I've wasted enough time all ready while that son of a bitch is getting away."

At this point one of the police officers who was on the scene at the time came in. Garry recognised him even though his back was towards Garry. He was with another officer who were bringing in two prostitutes for obvious reasons.

"Keep your lousy hands off me," said one woman "or I'll have you for assault."

"Ok lady," said the officer. "Cool it and get a move on."

He watched his partner walk over to Garry. This officer then turned.

"Jones," he said. "Put them in number six, it's free. After you have booked them."

"Yes sir," said Jones.

He then directed the two girls to the desk opposite and booked them with the help of another officer.

"Can I help you?" he asked Garry, as he reached him.

Garry vaguely recognised him.

"Were you in the betting office earlier?" asked Garry.

"Yes," said the officer. "I saw you talking to the man we are after and we have been trying to trace you. We didn't know about the accident. How is your wife?"

"She's in the hospital having our baby two months before time," said Garry. "I just hope that she and the baby survive. Did you manage to catch the maniac?"

"Come into the office we can talk privately there," said the officer.

Garry was still very angry. They went into a nearby office and he and Garry sat down. The officer got out a cigarette and offered him.

"Thanks," said Garry.

"My name's Quinn," said the officer. "Tell me what you know about this man the one you were with in the betting office."

He showed Garry a photo of him.

"Why that's Benjamin Row," said Garry. "We were mates in the forces."

"We have been after him for years," said Quinn. "But he has always given us the slip."

"That's not unusual," said Garry. "Since he was trained for that job. I expect you have all that information already. Master of disguises is our Ben, and if it weren't for me he would not be alive today."

"How come?" asked Quinn.

"We were out on a reccy together and he disappeared. We, that's the boys and I thought he had done a bunk," said Garry. "Then we got a lot of shellfire and had to retreat and made it to a small village being blasted to bits. While we were there I saw this old lady who was wounded. It turned out to be Ben that's who in disguise. We found out later that he had been sent ahead to see if it was safe for us to go., Of course you can guess the rest. He got caught the same as the rest of us. If I had not bothered to pick up what I thought was an old lady he would have been a goner."

"Pity you did not leave him there," said Quinn. "The things he has done since: murder, rape, theft, well I could go on forever, but you can guess the rest. He's a nasty bit of work I can tell you."

"Are you trying to tell me he nearly killed my wife?" asked Garry.

"Yes, I'm afraid he won't be doing it any more," said Quinn. "That's the worst part if it."

"Why? The bastard got away again?" asked Garry. He was ready to give him what for.

"No, he's dead, that's the trouble," said Quinn. "We chased him into a dead end street and he piled up. Killed outright, the coroner said. There's no justice done in a case like this."

He put out his cigarette and Garry did the same. They looked at each other then Garry got up, shook Quinn's hand and left. He was still very angry at saving the life of someone so cruel. He wondered if he could ever forgive himself if anything should happen to Brenda. He made straight for the phone box, but had to wait as someone was using it. He waited for what seemed a lifetime as every word the woman using the phone seemed to take.

"Deator now listen here. I've had enough of this. You promised to take me out to lunch," the woman said. "The girls have gone to the pictures and I have been stuck in this damn restaurant for an hour waiting for you., When are you coming to meet me?"

"I'm sorry darling," said Deator on the other end of the line "I just can't make it. Look I promise to make it up to you at the weekend. The girls go off tomorrow and then we'll have the weekend to ourselves. I just can't drop everything that I'm doing at the lab or all the work that I have been doing all week will have been a waste of time."

"Well that's the limit," said the woman. "The common cold is more important than me."

She slammed the phone down, pushed open the door and pushed past him. She thought for a moment that he had heard her. She looked hard at him.

"Sorry," she said. "Men," she muttered as she walked away. "They make me sick."

Garry then stepped into the phone box to make a call.

IN THE CITY ON THE DAY BEFORE THE FLIGHT

We join a couple making love in a hotel room. They are very young, the girl eighteen and the boy a bit older.

"Beautiful, beautiful," said the boy to the girl as he caressed her tenderly, kissing her all over her body, down her back and between her breasts. She heaved a sigh as he did so and responded to his every touch. Then she whispered, "Oh darling I love you so much, you make me tingle all over. You know just how to please me, ah don't bite so hard," she said laughing.

"Do you think we did right?" she asked. "You know getting married without telling our parents. Oh what are they going to say when you tell them and do you think your mother and father will accept me into the family? Mmm, do that again," she said.

"They will have no choice now darling," said the young man. "You are my wife and I intend to stand by you no matter what they say. They have tried to part us before but they won't do it again."

"Do you mean it darling?" said the girl putting her arms round his neck kissing him again.

"I do," said the young man, responding. "They say that young people our age don't know the meaning of love, that's not true, besides what the hell do they know about our feelings towards each other. Just because it never happened to them they think it can't happen to others. We have loved each other since we were ten haven't we? Remember the pact we made, to love each other till death do us part. Even at ten I meant it you know, even sealed it with a kiss at that party, ha, postman's knock. God I was scared of that weren't you?"

"Ha, ha, yes I remember that and I meant it too. Then it was not long after that you moved away," said the girl. "And I thought I would never see you again. I cried for days and my mother thought I'd gone down with a fever."

"Yes, I know. You wrote later and told me," said the young man.

"You wrote and told me you were going out with another girl Silver," she said. "She was horrid. Even though you were hundreds of miles away I could just imagine her. That was when you left and started college, thank god at least it got rid of her. How I hated you then but well you could have knocked me down with a feather when we both ended up going to the same college. I fell in love with you all over again didn't I?"

"Yes," he said, cradling her in his arms. At this point she could not see his face, but behind her back he was making a face as if he were saying it was all lies for it was true she had fallen in love with him all over again and had never left him alone for a minute, spying on his every move. He patted her bottom.

"Ouch that hurts," she said laying back.

He also laid back and said, "It was good of Jimmy to arrange everything. God, I'm hot aren't you darling, our wedding and everything," he continued. "Our running away and that. He's very generous; he's always doing me favours, a good pal, best mate. You are still on the pill aren't you?"

This question came right out of the blue and took the girl by surprise.

"What on earth made you ask that all of a sudden?" she asked him.

She was angry and rightly so, but she didn't let on.

"Of course I am, stupid," she answered.

But she found as he lay there she was very puzzled over his last remark.

"Oh no reason", he said.

He gradually drifted off into a shallow sleep. His mind drifted back to what he had done. She was so persistent, always following him around everywhere, so much so that he had arranged it to look as if they had been married. Jim's mate had dressed up as a vicar when he was really an engineer in another part of the city. He and all his mates had known the score and had carried it off very well. Everything went like a dream, perfect.

"Now, how the hell do I get out of this?" he thought, as tomorrow they were going home, and all hell would be let loose.

"Darling are you asleep?" said the girl. She tickled his stomach with her hair.

"No, just thinking," said the young man.

"What about?" she asked. She thought he seemed very distant.

"Well darling," he said. "I didn't tell her I was coming away to get married I only said I was coming on holiday. She and father would go crazy if they knew I had got married as you know."

The young girl turned over and rested on her elbows looking at him. She asked, "Well, what can they do about it now? They can't do anything. We are wed and that's that. Besides aren't you proud of me? You don't sound as if you are."

"Of course I am. You know that," said the young man. "It's just that Dad would cut me off without a penny and I don't want that, do I?"

"Why?" said the girl. "I would not care if you had no money."

"Do you trust me?" he asked.

She gave him a queer look then answered, none too sure of what he was going to say next.

"Yes why?" she asked.

"Good," he said. "When we go home tomorrow I want you to do something for me."

"What's that?" she asked very puzzled.

"I want you to pretend we are still courting and that nothing has happened at all," he said. "After all you are supposed to be on holiday in Scotland and I'm in Africa, so this is what we can do. I'll get a bigger flat when I get back and you can come round as often as you want. We can to all intents and purposes still be courting, at least that's what it will look like and nobody will be any the wiser. I can then still get my allowance off my parents and that will help keep us going. Won't it?" he answered.

"That sounds despicable," said the girl. "It sounds as if you think more of money than you do of me. I didn't marry you for your money; I wouldn't care if you didn't have anything at all. I love you."

"Yes, that's all very well, but I'm used to a big cash flow," he said. "Besides you want some of the things it can buy don't you?"

"That's not really fair," said the girl. She was very hurt. "It sounds to me as if you love money more than me, besides haven't you learnt that there comes a time in every rich man's life that the money he owns, owns him not he it. But then I am stuck with it. All I hope is that Barbara and John did not forget to post the cards that I wrote before they went or our so-called plan is going to fall flat on its face and I say now that if your dad had not made so many millions then he would have been a happier man."

"I suppose your family is just as happy as mine," said the young man. "It was your mother who made you a ward of court because you ran away before."

He started to get dressed.

"You are angry with me," said the girl, and tears began to flow down her cheeks.

"No, I'm not; don't be silly, come on get up," he said. "We have to go shopping to get another suitcase."

"You are annoyed. I can tell," she said, wiping her eyes.

"Don't worry everything will work out fine," he said, sitting on the edge of the bed and putting his arms round her. "I'm sorry I didn't mean to throw that in your face."

He kissed her gently on the lips.

"Come on, cheer up," he said. "Tell you what, if you say it's ok then we will tell them on you eighteenth birthday which comes up in a few months, then we will get married again this time in front of the whole family. How's that?"

"Oh darling will you really? Do you think that they will accept the idea, you're not just saying that?"

"No, of course not," he said as he kissed her again.

The young man knew there and then there would be no wedding and what was more he knew that once and for all she would leave him alone when she found out that they were not really married at all. Because he was so selfish he had not thought of the consequences of his foolish game as long as he had his own way.

MEANWHILE BACK WITH DAVID

David, his mother and the nurse have just dressed, when a native who knows David is dying, comes to their tent.

"Master David," said the native, "my boss, he say come quick, you too misses he has a big surprise for you, come see quick."

They all followed the native who is very excited and find to their surprise two nearly born lion cubs and David had to name them.

THE NIGHT BEFORE AT
SEVEN O'CLOCK IN THE CITY

"Deator," called Sally up the stairs. "It's time, it's six o'clock. Are you coming?"

"Do I look ok mum?" asked a pretty, petite dark haired girl.

"Yes honey you look fine. Have you got your things altogether?" asked her mother.

"Yes thanks mum," she said. "Do I have to go? Why couldn't I have gone to Samantha's? She said I could."

"Now don't argue Lesley. You can always go and stay with Samantha another time, besides it is hardly a break for us," said her mother, "if we have to worry about you popping in all the time."

"I don't know what you mean," said Lesley, looking at her mother.

"Now don't argue with mum," said Lesley's sister. "You know she's right about last weekend. You were in at least sixteen times."

Her sister who was very much younger than Lesley stood brushing her hair.

"Oh, shut up you, you are always lying. I wasn't in and out all the time,", said Lesley.

"Oh no? First your jeans then your scarf, then you came back to get some clothes for the disco and then you said your feet hurt and you came in to get your shoes. What beats me is how you can keep a boyfriend?, You can imagine him trying to have a conversation with you. By the time he has finished you've heard nothing. If you ask me the whole thing's crazy and so are you."

"Shut up and why don't you mind you own business?" said Lesley, looking at her mother. "Why don't you tell her off mother she's heckling me again?"

"It's quite true," said her mother. "Maybe one day you will settle down a bit."

"Now you are siding with her, you always do," said Lesley, as she pulled away.

"Being impertinent is not going to improve on what we can see for ourselves," said her mother. "So I suggest you take a good look at yourself and see what you can come up with and less of the rudeness."

Sally then called out again to Deator. She was getting very impatient.

She went to the stairs.

"Are you coming?" she called. "The girls are still waiting."

She turned to the girls. "Now stop arguing and get off to gran's. Here give her this jam and tell her I have followed the recipe she gave me and this is the result," said Sally.

Deator by now had got to the top of the stairs.

"What's all this noise about?" he asked. "I could hear it up in the bathroom, sounded like a lot of cackling hens. Do we have to have this every time you go away? Do you know your mother and I spend the rest of the weekend worrying if you two are behaving yourselves at gran's house. Now pack it in, both of you."

"Sorry dad," said the girls looking at him.

"Right," he said pulling on his jacket. "I'll drop you two of at the station since I have to go that way myself."

"Where are you off to then?" asked Sally.

"Oh, nowhere, just got to pop into the lab and see if everything is ok. Got some specimens in the incubator to check on," he replied.

"Ok, you girls get into the car while I say cheerio to your father," said Sally. "And don't argue."

"Bye mum," said Lesley. "See you on Monday and if Samantha phones up…"

"Goodbye," said her mother. "And don't worry about Samantha. I don't know, you two girls are insufferable."

"Tell her I'll see her as soon as I get back. Ok mum?" said Lesley.

"Yes, yes go on out with you," said her mother.

"Bye mum," said her other daughter. "I'll give gran this jam." She looked at the jar. "I expect it will be all gone by Monday," and laughed. "She makes us eat it all."

She put the jar of jam in her holdall and both girls went out to the car and waited for their father.

"Now you," said Sally to her husband. "Don't you be too long down at that lab of yours or there will not be much of the weekend left."

She kissed him on the cheek and then whispered to him.

"Our weekend starts tonight not tomorrow."

"There's a time and a place for everything," said Deator smiling. "You find the place and I'll be there ok?"

"Now where have I heard that before?" said Sally.

She smiled and waved as she went up the path.

"Oh by the way dear," said Deator. "I'll pick up a bottle of wine on the way home ok?"

He raised his eyebrow at Sally, and the girls giggled to themselves in the car. Deator got into the car and drove off.

MEANWHILE WITH DAVID SOMEWHERE IN AFRICA

"Mum, I've had a really wonderful time and I'm grateful," said David. It was late afternoon as he leant up against his mother's shoulder. Pale faced and tired, he said, "I think we'll have to forget the USA, Abraham Lincoln and Hitler," he said softly. "I don't mind not seeing him anyway because he was a cruel man, Hitler I mean. At school they taught us about the bravery of men like Abraham Lincoln, men with ideas for the good of mankind, so my teacher said. But I can't see that he did much good can you?"

"No dear,",she replied.., The thought of losing David saddened her even more; he was so understanding, not like any other child she knew.

"I am tired mum, very tired, you know what I mean, I feel as if I want to sleep forever sometimes. I know I'm dying mum, I've known for some time but I did not want to hurt you."

David's mother swallowed hard when she heard him say this to her and tears began to swell up in her eyes.

"We haven't much time left mum," said David compassionately. "So let's go home. Please mum,. I want to say goodbye to all my friends."

"Yes son." She was so proud of David, for his bravery and his love and compassion for others. Also his thoughtfulness for her. She cradled him in her arms. "I love you son," she said. "I love you." "Yes I know mum, and I love you too."

THE NIGHT BEFORE AT A PARTY
IN THE TOWN OF ZIMBA

About fifteen boys and girls are at a party on the outskirts of town. They are all joking and dancing to records at one of the boy's houses. It's really wild and everyone is happy. One of the boys at the party brings in a box and puts it on the table.

"Hey Joe," said one of the boys. "Look what Andy has brought."

A bunch of boys went over to the box and emptied it. It was full of drinks. They were all really drunk.

"Way hey, that's bloody great," said someone. "Hey Charlie come and see what we have got; vodka; whiskey and gin. Hey where's my glass?"

"Hey Barry," he yelled. "Bring my glass over and yours and Nickki's she's got to try some of this stuff."

He stroked and kissed the bottle.

"Nothing but the best," said the young man as he patted it again.

"I don't want any," said Nickki to Barry. "Leave my glass here."

"Ok," said Barry as he walked over to his mates. "Be back in a jiffy."

Nickki looked on. She was only fifteen..

"You scared?" said a girl to Nickki.

Nickki tried to show that she was not as scared as she felt.

"First time you have been to one of our do's ain't it?" asked the girl. "I can tell. Oh hell, we all have to start somewhere."

"Probably my last too," she said. "Why does everyone have to drink so much? Look at him over there." She pointed with her glass in the direction of one of the boys. "It's not even ten thirty and he's out cold. If you ask me I can't see any point in it at all. I can't see the fun," finished Nickki.

"You will later," said Hazel.

She was a stunner, long black hair and a good figure.

"Hey Nickki,"called one of the girls. "Come on, that's no way to enjoy yourself. Come on, let's get on the floor and dance."

One of the boys grabbed one of the girls. He was somewhat the worse for wear for drink.

"Bug off, keep your hands to yourself," said the girl. "You pervert!"

It was Jason who was very drunk.

"You dirty bastard," said the girl. "Leave my bum alone. Go and screw yourself, you fink."

"How about me?" said Hazel to Jason. "Now I'm much more your style."

"No thanks," said Jason. "You piss off." He looked angrily at the other girl.

"Ok," said Hazel. "Suit yourself there are plenty more fish in the sea."

She let him see as she raised her little finger to him. He glanced at Nickki and thought she's more my type.

"Helen, oh Helen where are you my little darling?" Jason called.

"Hi Nickki!" He walked over to her as she leant against the wall and he tried to kiss her. "Have you seen Helen?" Jason asked Nickki. "My, you are a little beauty."

"You lay off Jas," said a voice from behind. It was Barry back with his drink.

"Come on Barry me old mate, I only asked if she had seen Helen," said Jason.

He flung his arms round Barry's back. "Come on," he said. "Let's have another drink."

"Ok, what was her answer?" asked Barry.

"She ain't bloody well answered me yet, have you sweetie?" said Jason. He looked at Barry as he said this and also at Nickki.

Barry looked at Nickki and could see she was very scared. On seeing this and to avoid a fight, he turned to Jason.

"What about this drink then?" Barry asked.

Then he suddenly changed his mind. "Let's dance," he said to Nickki. He took her hand and led her on to the dance floor.

"Thanks Barry," said Nickki, "for getting me away from him."

"Darren, hey man," said Jock. He had found his younger brother instead of Helen. "You still a virgin,? Of course you are," said Jock and he looked at the other lads in the room.

"Hey boys," he said. "It's initiation time, for fuck's sake."

He then turned to his younger brother.

"Tonight's the night my fair weathered friend," he said to Darren. "A night you will remember as long as you fucking well live."

He put his arms around his brother's shoulder.

"Angels will sing round your bed," he said. "Cupid's little arrow will stick through your heart. Well, not exactly but beggars can't be choosers can they?" he ended, drunkenly

"Hazel, Hazel, where are you my darling? We have a little job for you. Come and meet Darren. Darren meet the angel of your eye," Jock called.

Hazel came over. She smiled at Darren. "My you are a young un ain't you?" she said, as she looked coolly at Jock. "You want me to take him in hand?" she asked.

"Something like that," said Jock. "If he goes on the way he does he's apt to break it off, or his wrist."

Darren gave his brother a sharp look.

"You fuck off," said Darren. "I ain't going with her."

"Why, boy?" asked Hazel. "That's no way to talk to a lady."

She flicked his tie, which hit him in his eye.

"In half an hour I can make you into a man," she said, making kissing signs at him and flashing her eyes.

"Oh," said Nickki, as she danced with Barry.

Jason was behind her dancing with one of the other girls and had pinched her bottom, and she jumped.

"What's up?" asked Barry, looking at her.

"Nothing, nothing at all," replied Nickki.

They carried on dancing and Nickki watched Jason out of the corner of her eye.

"Off you go Darren," said Jock. "And don't be scared." He patted Darren on the shoulder.

Hazel grabbed hold of Darren and led him away reluctantly. While this was going on, Barry went to get some more drinks and someone else asked Nickki to dance. Over in the corner another girl was talking to a couple of guys.

"Am telling you now," said one of the girls in the group. "I saw it, I ain't lying I promise, Harry and I were out on the porch and he kissed me as it flew across the moon. Do you believe me?"

"You saw stars," said one of the boys who had been listening to the conversation. He was drunk like the rest of them.

"Maybe it was the cow they all chant about," he said drunkenly. They all laughed.

"I was not talking to you," said the girl, sharply. "Go away, this is private and nosy parkers like you should keep their noses out so piss off unless you want Harry to lay one on you."

"I think you have had too much to drink," said someone else.

"My, my who's a sassy one then?" said the lad who was talking first. Then he left and went off somewhere else.

"It was big I tell you, at least the size of three houses. I'm telling you I did see it, it was like a giant wasp thing," insisted the girl.

"Nar, more like a gnat. It weren't that big really just the light made you focus a bit more," said someone.

"Oh," said Nickki again. She turned to Barry. "Barry, I want to go home," she said. "It's late."

"Aw come on," said Barry. "Just one more dance that's all."

He flung his arm round her. "You like me, don't you?" he asked.

"You are drunk," said Nickki. "I want to go home and I don't want to go out with you again."

"Come on," said Barry. "Give us a kiss then."

"No," said Nickki and pushed him away. "Get off, piss off, you pig."

Some of the lads could see she was in trouble and came over to her.

"Come on Nickki," said one of the boys. "We'll take you and him home then we will come back, ok?" They surrounded Barry who by this time could hardly stand.

"Yes thanks," said Nickki.

They picked Barry up and as he went he saw Jason standing at the door.

"It's your fault," said Barry to Jason. "I saw you pinch her bum, you swine." He took a dive but fell.., Jason left while Nickki went to get her wrap.

"Pack it in Barry," said one of the boys.

The boys took them both so far and then left Nickki to go home just a few yards away. Barry passed out before he could say goodbye. Nickki was disgusted and walked down the alley to the back of the store. Before she had gone very far someone jumped out on her., She screamed but no one came to her aid. Someone had their hand across her mouth, and she fought like a demon but she could not escape. She felt something sharp cut her cheek and she made a grab at the man's throat trying to get away. Then she felt a stab as he forced himself into her body. She struggled and lashed out but it was no use. She could not see him in the dark and he was much too strong. She remembered bright colours flashing. She heard a window open but saw no one then she passed out. In the distance she remembered what her mother had always said, not to struggle or you will be killed.

Barry in his drunken stupor heard someone screaming from far away, got up and crawled down the alley but only saw a dark figure running past him. Then he passed out.

When Nickki woke up her dress was torn to shreds, her face was cut and bleeding. She could hardly see. She crawled along the alley as best she could and finally made it to the door. She banged on the door and fell into the arms of her father who had waited up for her. The time was twelve thirty am ; the bar had been closed earlier because of some trouble.

THE MORNING OF THE SAME DAY

We find the police chief in the bathroom having a shave. He sings to himself while doing so, rather loudly. Susan his daughter pops her head round the door after knocking first.

"Dad your breakfast is ready," she says but he doesn't hear her. "Dad, I said your breakfast is ready," she said again, and put her hand on his shoulder. He then turned to her.

"What, oh all right sweetie, thanks be with you in a moment," he said.

Susan left him and went into her bedroom to put away some clothes, and got out a new summer dress and laid it on the bed. Then she got out some shoes to match, and some clean underwear, pulled the cord of her housecoat tighter and returned to the kitchen. Her father came in and sat at the table.

"Morning sweetie," he said, picking up his drink. "How are you today, you finished with the paper?"

"Yes," said Susan. "Thanks, I'm fine." She poured out some more coffee and took it over and placed it in front of her father. She then went back to the oven and took out his breakfast.

"Here you are dad," she said. "Get this inside you and you will feel better." She looked at him and smiled then put her finger under his chin, and laughingly said. "I see you have delivered your usual amount of blood to the vampire today."

"What would I do without you?" said her father. "Go back to the wild beasts I suppose." He rubbed his chin. "Must have had a spot there or something and took the top off, anyway not too worry. I'll live, got seven more lives yet. What, haven't you got any breakfast?" he asked Susan.

"Me, yes thanks, only I'm just having toast. I don't want to ruin my day with Jamie and I'm going out to dinner later," she said. "He phoned last night while you were at work. He gets in on the midday Chinook, and I have to meet him later."

The chief got on with his breakfast.

"I'm sorry you had to wait so long for your time off, love," he said. "But still we've got someone to replace you. Well ,now you know what it is like. Anyhow what do you intend to do with yourself?"

"They say you should not count your chickens before they are hatched," said Susan. sipping her coffee. "So I'm not sure yet, but I do know Jamie has something up his sleeve besides his arm," she said Susan smiling, and putting down her cup. "I expect we will go and see a few of his mates at the base, and I would like to do some more shopping and then we will drop back and go out to dinner later."

The chief finished his breakfast, but just as he did so he put his hand to the back of his ear.

"Your ear playing you up a bit?" she asked sympathetically. "Why don't you go and see the doctor again, I'm sure he could give you something to help it?."

"Oh I'll be all right sweetie," he said. "These things take their time."

"I know," said Susan. "But it has been three months now and surely that op was all right, it got rid of the mastoid didn't it?"

"Yes," said her father. "But it's still inflamed inside; it's left my ear drum in a bad state." He picked up his coffee and finished it off. "Don't worry so much," he said. "You are as bad as your mother was."

Susan looked sadly at her father and put her arms gently on his shoulders from behind.

"You miss her terribly don't you?" she asked. "I've watched you now for the last four years, you hardly ever go out, you spend most of your time working. Dad, that isn't the answer you know, you can tell me to mind my own business if you wish, but remember I loved mum just as much as you did only in a different way, and I say it's time for you to relax a bit."

"Time for me to go to work too," said the chief, putting down his serviette. "I have a faint idea that you are nagging me. Now don't get me wrong Susan, duty calls," and he got up.

"Well, I say you are," she said compassionately and gently put her arms round his neck. "Ok," she said. "I won't nag you or give a sermon,", and she kissed his cheek.

"I doubt if we shall see much of each other for the next few days sweetie,", he said. "So be careful, I'll be able to rest up a bit soon and maybe take a few days off myself. Ok? We could go to the city and see Deater and Sally. Would you like that?" He kissed her forehead and looked down at her.

"Sounds great," said Susan and nodded. "I'd like that."

"Ok sweetie, I must go," he said and walked to the door. "Thanks for the lovely breakfast; it was great to have your company."

"Dad," said Susan She looked at him thoughtfully. "Let go just a little, ok.."

Her father knew what she meant and he nodded and drove off to work.

IN THE TOWN AT ABOUT
NINE O'CLOCK THE SAME DAY

In an old empty shed used for stores we find a bunch of kids.

"Have you done what I asked?" said Billy, a boy of about twelve who was, thin and scruffy. He sat on an old bench twisting a bit of string. "Did anyone see you do it? Knowing you, you always muck it up with your clumsiness," said Billy.

He stared hard into the eyes of the other boy who was about the same age as himself, only he was better dressed.

"Yes I did and no one saw me I swear," said the boy, looking at him.

"Right, I'll fix up with the others and we'll go and do some more," said Billy. He got down off the bench. "You scared?" he asked the other boy.

"No," said the other boy, but he was puffed out.

"You look scared, why don't you admit it?" Billy asked the other boy as he walked round him. "I ain't scared of anything and if you want to be in my gang, you'll do as I say, with no questions asked Do you hear?" said Billy.

"Yes," said the boy. "All right, but…"

"Don't but me," said Billy. "I said no questions. It's all part of your initiation."

Billy got out a small notebook from his pocket.

"The laws are all laid out in this book, and if you don't do all the things it says then you are out. Tommy Farmer gave me this book and he was the last leader of the gang until he went away. It says here that you have to put lollipops in petrol tanks, steal something gold, kill a snake and loads of other things like helping to build a tree den, and getting food,," said Billy.

"But I always end up doing the rotten jobs," said the boy.

"So," said Billy. "You can't have all the juniors lagging behind like babies, we ain't going to do everything for you., You know you make me laugh."

He tossed a gold chain in the air.

"Why?" said the boy. "I've done some of those things ain't I?"

"A gang is a very special thing to us, we don't play games like other kids. It's all for a reason. It's to make us tough, so nobody bullies us, and we can learn to look after ourselves," said Billy twisting the chain between his fingers. "You don't even know how to cook," he said. He looked at the boy, then turned away.

"No, but my mother doesn't like me to," the boy stuttered.

"See what I mean," said Billy. "By the time you have done all these things in the book you will be a man not a sissy like you are now. Come on let's go and see what the others are doing at the den. Somehow we have to get some tools to make a roof, first though we have to do some more of these things," he, said and he swung a lollipop on a piece of string that he had in his pocket.

"Do you really want me to do that?" asked the boy trembling.

"Come on," said Billy. "Don't be such a baby, stop moaning."

He opened the shed door and they left. They walked along the path and met up with four other boys.

"Ok, gang," said Billy. "This is Michael, he's joined our gang .As from today if he passes all the other tests he can become one of our future leaders, any objections?" he asked.

"Yes," said one of the boys. "He ain't nothing but a sissy."

"Yes," said another. "He's a poofter, look at him."

They all walked round him. Michael was very scared.

"Rule number two," said Billy, looking at him. The boy clenched his fist and dived in. They all fought together, but Billy was on Michael's side and he passed his second test.

LATE THAT DAY

Michael arrived home at dinner time with his clothes in a terrible state.

"What have you been doing Michael?" asked his mother, as she looked at his big black eye. "And how did you get that?

"Arthur," she called to her husband. "Take a look at this."

"It's nothing mum," said Michael sitting down at the dinner table, His dad sat at the other end reading his paper.

"Mmm," he said.

"Can I borrow your football tomorrow dad?" asked Michael.

"Why?" asked his dad. "If you do you had better take care of it or else."

"The boys want to see the names on the ball, and have a game," said Michael.

"Looks like you had one today," said his father. "I hope you won."

"Yeah dad," said Michael proudly. "I did and Billy helped me."

THE AFTERNOON OF THE SAME DAY IN ZIMBA

We join Jamie and Susan having a meal., he has hold of her hand as they sit at the table.

"Darling," said Susan. "From now until Monday we have three whole days to ourselves." She looked at him lovingly.

"Yes and I am looking forward to them honey," said Jamie as he smiled at her. "I could do with a rest. I have been on duty now for four days non-stop."

"Has it occurred to you darling that we have known each other for a year? It doesn't seem possible does it? Why only last week I had a letter from Vicky. She was that freckled faced girl at college with me."

Susan looked at Jamie and then a waitress came over to their table and handed them a menu, and asked if they would care for some wine.

"She's married now you know?" she said.

"Yes please," said Jamie. "A bottle of Rose, thank you."

The waitress left the table.

"What would you like to eat?" asked Jamie. "We may as well start off the weekend with a good meal. I think I'll have fillet of steak, that's my favourite."

"Oh thanks," said Susan, taking the menu handed to her by Jamie.

"I'll have, let's see mmm, oh yes I'll have the sirloin steak thanks," she said.

The waitress came over for their order.

"Yes," said Susan, "to some guy she met up with while he was here from the States. Somehow I can't imagine her staying married for long. She was such a scatter brain at college, always eyeing up the fellows and having numerous affairs."

"I say you were a bit jealous," said Jamie, offering Susan a cigarette. He held open the packet for her.

"No thanks darling," said Susan. She had not liked his remark.

"Mind if I do?" asked Jamie.

"Of course not, go ahead," said Susan. She picked up her serviette and opened it.

"You seem a little nervous tonight," said Jamie. "Everything all right?"

"Yes fine thanks," said Susan. She laid her serviette on her lap.

"You seem a little preoccupied with something," said Jamie. "Dad ok?" He lit his cigarette and moved the ashtray a little closer to him.

"Yes, he's fine though he wouldn't admit it, but he does miss mother a lot. He seems to have cut himself off from the world lately. He hardly ever goes out, except when it's something to do with work," answered Susan.

"And you?" asked Jamie. "How's the new job going? Do you like it, and working for your dad?"

"Oh yes I do, but it's very tiring you know. Each day John and I, that's one of the officers, have to type up all the reports that come in. Never a dull moment. At the moment dad's investigating four rapes that have happened in the town in the last four months," said Susan. She was using the 'get jealous' traffic but Jamie was not falling for it.

"Not guilty," said Jamie. "I wasn't anywhere near the place."

Susan was very surprised at this remark.

"I should bloody well hope not, and I don't find that remark very funny either," she snapped..

"Sorry, only joking," said Jamie. "Come on, what's made you so jumpy?"

The waitress brought their meals over and placed them in front of them. Jamie wished he had not been so flippant and corny. He knew she had been working long hours like himself.

"Thank you," said Susan looking up. "I'll have you know," she went on angrily "that some girls have been very badly beaten up. It could happen to me. Thankfully we were taught how to look after ourselves at college, that's all I can say."

Jamie took Susan's hand.

"I'm sorry," he said. "I didn't mean to upset you, come on cheer up don't let's spoil our weekend with a fight."

Susan looked at Jamie and could see that he meant it.

"Oh all right, sorry. I lost my temper. You are right, I expect it's been getting on top of me, but on Monday it will be better," she replied.

She picked up her knife and fork and began her meal and Jamie did likewise. The waitress brought over the wine so Jamie could taste it.

"That's fine," he said.

The waitress poured their drinks and left their table, and they began to eat again.

"Why's that?" asked Jamie.

"Amm.. Oh like I told you on the phone the other day. Dad's getting more staff. I've seen them on file, someone called Marlene Boxall, Robert Johnson and Colin Motley. We have had a definite yes from Marlene and Robert but not from Colin. He's coming from another part of Africa so I expect his answer is in the post somewhere. Mmm, this sirloin is lovely, how's your steak?" said Susan all in one breath.

"Fine, lovely, tell you what," said Jamie. "Tomorrow we'll go for a flight in one of our choppers. How would you like that? We could take in some of the spectacular sights around here. Joe at the base will take us up, if that's ok with you and tonight," he winked, "we'll curl up in front of a super coal fire. Imaginary fire, it all adds up to soft romantic mood. We'll put on some records and cuddle up for a truly stunning evening. How does that sound darling?" he said beaming at her.

"Like a bloody fairy tale," laughed Susan. "When are we going to grow up?" she smiled. She was joking of course.

"If it pleases your royal highness, then she will be very honoured to sit beside you," she smiled and said "as long as your highness does not get too fresh."

She tipped her glass at his.

"What do you mean?" said Jamie looking at her. "I'm always fresh." He sniffed at his armpits and Susan laughed even harder.

"Behave yourself," she said. "People are watching."

"Who cares?" said Jamie, as he pushed his plate to one side and took hold of Susan's hand.

"I love you," he said. "I love you," and kissed her hand.

"Excuse me sir," said the waitress standing by the table. "There's a phone call for you."

"Oh thanks," said Jamie, and looked at Susan.

"I wonder who that can be?" he said. "Excuse me darling. I'll be back in a minute."

Susan had finished her meal and was now finishing her drink. She watched Jamie on the phone and knew something was wrong right away.., Jamie left the phone and came back to her., He looked at her with a sad face.

"Oh no!" said Susan looking up. She tore her serviette from her lap.

"Sorry ,darling an emergency. Darren's wife has gone into premature labour, and I've got to take his flight, there's nothing I can do about it."

Susan stood up. She was furious.

"Well, there is something I can do," said Susan.

"What's that?" asked Jamie.

"Go back to bloody work," said Susan. "Goodbye."

She stormed out of the restaurant, leaving Jamie standing at the table.

MEANWHILE AT THE BUNGALOW
OUT IN THE SCRUBLAND

Three weeks had passed since their visit to the town and Frank was sitting on the veranda talking to Mark. He had enjoyed the company of Keith but he had failed to connect the visit with the disappearance of his boy JoJo.

"Hey you dossers, want some lemonade? I'm just making some," called Ann.

"Yes sure, thanks mum. Dad?" said Mark. "What does cloning mean?"

"What would we do without her?" said Frank, turning to Mark and smiling. Then he turned his gaze and his eyes towards the sunset.

"What?" said Mark's father, "that's what I like."

He took off his hat and rubbed his forehead after removing a hankie from his pocket, and then put his hat back on.

"Cloning, well, that's making more of exactly the same thing I think," said Mark's father.

"What's that dad?" said Mark looking up from his book. "Oh that."

He looked at his father; Mark was sitting in a large bamboo chair near his father who was sitting on the top of the porch. He could see he did not know.

"It's magnificent isn't it? I could not bear to live in town now not after this," said Frank. "It's wild and free and the air is great. I love it, I really do you know."

He turned back to Mark who frowned, and took a deep breath.

"You'll find all you want to know from the school library, if you look," said his father.

Ann came out on to the porch. She was very timid and petite. She had her hair swished up with grips, and was very pretty.

"Would you like a piece of cake with your drink?" she asked Mark and Frank. She stood, hand on hip looking around.

"Where is James?" she asked. "Has anyone seen him around, little devil? He always vanishes when I want him."

"Yes to the first question and no to the second, thanks," said Frank.

He turned to Ann and smiled and pushed his hat further back on his head. He patted the step for Ann to sit down beside him, but she didn't.

"I expect he is playing with Reaker somewhere," said Mark.

He was right. As Ann had gone out to the front, Reaker had entered the kitchen and found Ann's bun mixture and was crazily tucking into it. James was not short of helping himself either. Ann heard one of the bun tins fall to the floor and James hid behind the door..

"What the ... oh you little..." yelled Ann. "How the hell did you get in? James, James where are you? Come here."

She rushed to the corner of the kitchen and grabbed a broom. Then she lashed out at the scared but mischievous little chimp, who found it great fun to be chased. He was covered with sticky bun mixture and flour that he had knocked to the floor. He screeched loudly, and scurried to James's hiding place. James appeared from behind the door .He, too was covered in bun mix and flour.

"James what you too? Aren't you ashamed of yourself?" asked his mother. "How many times have I told you not to let that thing into the house?"

She pointed to the chimp who was sitting on top of a chair, kicking his feet. The chair was next to the kitchen table.

"If I've told you once I've told you a thousand times," said his mother angrily. "Oh you kids make me mad, it's like talking to a brick wall."

James stood for a second, thought a minute or so then went and stood facing the wall muttering to himself.

"What are you doing now?" she asked him, as she went to the basin on the side and got a cloth. After putting the broom away, she damped the cloth and started to clear up the mess.

"Seeing what it's like," said James.

"Seeing what, what is like?" she asked.

"Talking to a brick wall," said James.

"Don't be so impertinent," she said, as she slapped James's legs. "Go to your room at once. Do you hear me?, Right now and take him out first. You naughty boy."

James bent down and rubbed his sore legs. He did not expect that slap. Ann pointed to Reaker and James's legs.

"Out," she said, to the pair of them.

He bent down and rubbed his legs again, then he walked over to Reaker and put him on his shoulder.

"Ouch that hurt, ok I'm sorry mum it won't happen again, honest," said James.

He took the chimp out through the door and passed Frank and Mark on the steps. His father spoke to him.

"What have you been up to this time?" he asked.

"Sorry dad, I upset mum again. Reaker got in and ate mum's bun mix, and tipped it all over the floor so I …" said James.

"Yes I can imagine," interrupted his father. "Wipe your face while you are at it, you look like a ghost. I don't know"

"I'm going to put him in his favourite tree and see if he will stay there, ok dad?" said James.

"All right son," said the father. "But you don't half ask for it don't you?"

James nodded and walked over to a nearby tree, its leaves dulled by the dust of the parched land around the bungalow. When James reached it he carefully climbed up, thinking it best to stay out of his mother's way for a while. The chimp clung to his shoulders, his eyes following the path of the ants on the ground below.

"Hey you," James yelled at the chimp. "You are always getting me into trouble. Better stay here and get lost for a while or you will end up in a cage. Mum was right about one thing. Talking to you is like talking to a brick wall," said James.

The chimp looked at James who also sat on a branch.

"He's a right nutcase that little brother of mine, can't trust him for five minutes you know?" said Mark; he looked at James up the tree.

"Oh, why's that?" asked his father

"If he does it again I am going to hit him hard," said Mark.

"Does what?" said his father. "Do you two always have to argue?"

"Last night he was playing with something under the bed clothes, under the blankets. All I know it was gone midnight," said Mark.

"Why do you say that then, and what was he playing with?" asked his father. "No wonder he's too tired to get up in the mornings."

"One of his cars or some aeroplane, a friction toy I expect, because all I could hear was a hissing sound," said Mark.

"I'll have a word about that with him later son, all right?" answered his father.

At this point Mark caught sight of a fly that landed on his knee and he cupped his hand ready to try to hit it. His eyes never left it. It settled on his knee and Frank sitting nearby watched him. Suddenly Mark's hand came down.

"Got you, son of a bitch," he said triumphantly.

The fly managed to get away and flew to a post nearby and settled there.

"Got to be a lot faster than that son," said his father. "When I was your age I used to be tops at catching them. Then when we caught them we used to tie cotton on their wings and tie them up so they couldn't get away. Same with cranefly and with beetles. Some of the lads even used to race them at school, until one day the teacher caught us and we got a hiding. Cruel little buggers we were now I come to think back."

"Did you dad?" said Mark laughing. "Now you've got this job, what would you do if you hadn't got it? Anything special, or would you take anything that came along?"

"Nowadays son, beggars can't be choosers, it's far better to have a job rather than none at all. In the old days of the twenties or thirties so many people were trained to do a certain type of job that when it came down to it and leaving school, they'd only plug for that one job, and not try anything else," said his father. "They became frustrated and apathetic and finally they just didn't try or want to work at all. This caused unemployment because they wouldn't do jobs that were below their dignity to do. So many forgot that it is necessary to have some type of experience behind them, even if it's cleaning out loos or collecting rubbish. It will happen again in years to come, you can bet on that."

"It's important to try other things then?" asked Mark.

"Oh yes, anything, no matter what, so you have some stored conversation. Who knows one day you could meet up with an old pal, and he did the same job. Right away you have something in common with him. In the army, you get to do everything," replied his father. "That's why you all get on well together., Why do you think the royals do everything together?"

"I don't really know dad, never thought of it that way before," Mark replied.

Frank got up from the step and moved to the small table with his son, and sat on a small stool.

"Come on son, just think what I've said and put it all together. What do you come up with?" asked his father.

Mark bent forward and put his hands up round his face, elbows on the table. He thought carefully and frowned, and then after a while it suddenly came to him. He beamed.

"Oh yes I see what you mean dad," he said. He put his hands down on the table. "It wouldn't look good, would it if say a prince who goes round meeting people didn't know something about what they were talking about? It would embarrass him to think that they knew more than he did, but he doesn't have to know everything does he dad? Because if he did he could become a bighead couldn't he?"

"No son, that wouldn't be right either, but he must know just enough not to be made a fool of when he's out. The rest, if he's interested enough ,he can learn by asking questions in such a way, thus gaining more knowledge of what he already knows, and that's what you must do,".

Frank then took off his hat and placed it on the table.

"Now that wasn't hard, was it?" he asked Mark.

"Dad, mum, someone's coming," shouted James from the tree.

He pointed to a ball of dust in the distance and Frank picked up his hat and walked down the two steps with his hat in his hand. He shaded his eyes to see if he could see who and what it was but whatever it was it was too far away, so he waited for it to come closer.

"It's not a land rover or truck, it's going far too slowly for that," said Frank.

He then turned to the house and called to Ann.

"Ann, you had better make another drink."

They watched the dust turn into a figure as it neared the house.

"Ok darling," replied Ann. "Who do you think it is?"

She placed another glass on the tray, and put out the jug of lemonade she had finished making and a plate with some cakes on it, then carried it out to the porch. She put it on the small table and wiped her hands in her pinny. She shielded her eyes and tried to see who it was.

Mark stood next to her.

James sat in the tree, his legs dangling from his perch, and the chimp sat close by, watching everything. In his hand he had a twig and he was busy stripping it and eating its leaves.

"It's a man dad, I can see him now," said James. "He's quite old too."

"I thought I told you young man to go to your room. Get down from that tree at once and do as you are told," said Ann crossly.

James climbed out of the tree, just as an old and tattered herdsman scuffled by. His clothes were torn and dirty; his face black and aged with the nomadic existence he had endured in the wild desolate land.

"Hello mister," said James. The old man paused but he took no notice of James and James mimicked his steps as he walked behind him. He didn't smell none too pleasant either, and James made a face as he caught a whiff of him.

"Where do you come from?" asked James in the native tongue. He thought perhaps the old man would answer.

"Have you seen him before darling?" asked Ann.

"No, but he could be one of the locals from a nearby village, we'll see in a minute. Maybe it's JoJo coming back. I wish I knew why he ran off," said Frank.

"Looks like one of the Wappa tribe to me, dad," said Mark.

"How do you know that son?" said Frank, frowning.

"By the beads round his neck and arms, dad .It's about a hundred and fifty miles from the missionary to the south, a couple of the boys live in as it's too far to go each day," Mark told his father.

"I wonder what he's doing here then, he's miles away from home," said Frank.

James scurried to Ann's side and stood watching, while the old man lowered his frail body to the ground in front of the bungalow. He sat crossed-legged on the ground and waited for Frank to come down the steps to greet him.

"Get the drinks Mark and follow me," said Frank, frowning.

Mark picked up the tray and followed his father, while Ann sat down in the chair on the porch. James stood beside her.

"What can I do for you?" said Frank, making a friendship sign.

With that, the old man began to babble in his native tongue, and throw his arms in the air. Frank turned to Mark, who was listening carefully to what the old man said.

"He's too fast for me son, what's he saying?" asked Frank.

"From what I can make out dad, he says that someone in his village has put a voodoo spell on his animal and him. He isn't very happy about it and wants to know if white man's medicine can help. He's saying that some of his animals have decided to settle down and not move any more. He knew something was wrong yesterday when he saw they were motionless. He was afraid to go near them, for fear the spell would be fixed on him. Also many birds sat near his animals waiting," translated Mark for his father.

"James," Frank called. "Bring my notebook from inside. It's the one on the desk in the office. Oh yes, and a pencil, so I can write down the old man's story."

James turned and went into the bungalow and got his father's notebook. Ann looked on nervously. A strange feeling came over her and she found herself shivering as if someone had walked over her grave. She ran her hand up her arm to quieten down all the goose pimples. James came out and ran down the steps to hand his father his notebook. Frank wrote down the old man's tale and James went back to Ann.

Mark handed the old man a drink after he had finished talking. The old boy took a sip and spat it out. He didn't like the taste so threw the rest away. It soaked into the dust immediately. Then he got up and walked away in the direction from which he had come and was gone just as quickly.

"Well how strange," said Ann as she put her arms around James and pushed him into the house. "What do you make of all that?" asked Ann. "James you go to your room, ok?"

Frank and Mark got up from the ground as the old boy disappeared into the distance and dusted their clothes down. Frank picked up his hat and bunged it down on the side of his right knee.

"Don't really know," he said, as he studied his notes. "Seems he's got a right nasty problem there, and I'm not qualified to handle it really."

He walked back up the steps. Mark followed closely by his side.

Frank put his hat back on the table after reaching the top of the steps.

"I don't like the sound of it, that particular problem at all, so honey. I shall have to go out and see for myself," said Frank to Ann. "It will mean getting the landrover loaded first thing."

"Can I come dad?" asked Mark.

"That's up to your mother, son as you know already. When I'm away you are the man of the house and the only one left to help her," said Frank to Mark. "James is too young, right James? Fetch the tray! It looks stupid there on the ground all by itself doesn't it, and bring the other glass," said Frank.

"Right dad," said James.

James tore down the steps after leaving his mother's side, anything to get out of being sent to his room. Mark turned to his father, and then to his mother with a pleading look in his eyes.

"No, Mark," said his mother. "You can't go, and get that look off your face. If JoJo had not left us in such a predicament then you could have gone, but he has gone off, and that's that."

"Oh, please mum," said Mark in a pleading voice, as he picked up a drink from the tray that James was bringing back and sipped at it. James put the tray on the table.

"No," said his mother. "And that's final." She handed the cakes round.

"Dinner will be ready in about half an hour," she said. "James will you get washed up and Mark will you put the ostriches in their pen for the night, and then clean up the porch? Reaker's made a mess again."

"I'm going to check the landrover over, make sure it's got enough fuel and all that, then I'll get washed up too," said Frank to Ann. "No, thanks," he said to the cake she was handing round, but he did take a drink from the tray.

Reaker watched from the tree that James had left him in. As he went inside James turned and winked at the chimp.

"That's the strangest visitor we have ever had," said Ann to Frank. She turned and went back into the house. "He made me shiver, you know darling."

"What, in this heat? You'd better make an appointment to see the doctor when we next go into town," said Frank.

"Whatever for?" she asked. "I feel all right."

"You have got a short memory haven't you?" Frank winked at her.

"What are you on about?".

"Eight years and nine months ago, remember?" said Frank.

Ann looked down at her stomach then put her hands on it.

"You mean, oh no, not that, you told me," she went on to say then stopped.

"Dad's thinking you are pregnant again isn't he mum?" Mark asked..

"And what would a lad of your age know about that then?" said his mother.

"Well, I do read a lot mum, and I see enough of nature around me to know that much and I am coming up to fifteen, aren't I?" was Mark's reply.

Ann smoothed down her pinny and held her head to one side., She had not thought of that before.

"True, true, but I'm not, so there. Babies that's all I need," said Ann.

"All right mum, I believe you," said Mark laughing.

So did Frank as he went down the steps towards the landrover, that stood outside the shed, which was built a short way from the house. Mark left the porch to attend to his jobs, and James went to his bedroom. While Mark was putting the animals away, Frank filled the landrover with fuel and checked the engine, tyres and put a large can of water ready to load with the other gear for the vehicle.

When he got to his room James poured some water from a large jug, and washed his hands ready for dinner.

Ann put away the buns she had made, and then started getting the dinner ready.

MEANWHILE BACK IN THE BUSH.

Meanwhile, back where the old man had left his herd of wildebeest, two poachers were nearing in their landrover. They were both in their late twenties. One was quite well dressed, in a safari suit, nice looking and clean-shaven, and had on his lap a brand new rifle. His name was Sam Tyler, a hunter by trade who enjoyed the game of chase and kill, the modern way. The other man who sat next to him was a born killer who didn't just kill for the sake of it. He had morals deep down in his head, that conversation couldn't drag out of him. But both men had something in common, the love of and life in Africa.

Both were out that day, and the night before to celebrate for some apparent reason and carried in front of the landrover a box containing a case of beer and some whiskey. Both the worse for drink, they drove erratically over the rough ground, Sam holding onto his rifle with one hand, in the other he held a can of beer. They were on their way from the village of Wappa where Bennett had spent a couple of nights in one of the huts with a native girl, who considered herself by natives to be married. Her son had come home after hunting and caught her at it. This was all related to the boy's father who punished him for lying and then he beat up his wife for going with Bennett. The boy was put down a large hole in the ground and made to fill up buckets of water for the villagers; he was to spend three days and nights doing his penance. The two men talked as they went along.

"You are nothing but a dirty old man aren't you?" said Sam. "Nearly got caught last night didn't you? Shit man you could have at least found one for me too, couldn't you?"

Sam took a swig of whiskey after he placed the beer can between his legs. They bumped up and down on the road. He put the bottle back in the box at his feet and then turned back to his beer. Bennett, a half caste American Indian was driving the landrover, one hand on the steering wheel. He raked the can from Sam's hand and took a long swig.

"Ah, ah, that was good," said Bennett, and gave Sam a cheeky wink. "That's asking a bit too much ain't it?" He crushed the can.

"What do you mean by that?" asked Sam looking at his crushed can.

"Why do you think?" said Bennett as he threw away the can into the box behind him on the floor. The canvas was open and tied back.

"I'd heard rumours," said Bennett, looking at Sam's worried face.

"And what might they be?" asked Sam, picking up another tin from the box between his legs and taking off the tag.

"That you are a fag," said Bennett.

Sam's mouth dropped open.

"That ain't true, where did you hear that anyway?" said Sam, as he took a drink. "At some shitty bar I suppose, do you believe everything you hear? I ain't no fag that's for sure."

"Well, I wouldn't be surprised at all," said Bennett. "You don't exactly behave like most folk I come into contact with."

"And what may I ask do you mean by that kind of remark?" asked Sam.

Both men were getting very drunk and the land rover was swerving from side to side.

"What, pass me another drink," said Bennett as he pointed to the box.

Sam bent forward and picked out another can and handed it to Bennett who took it and removed the tag with his teeth.

"You tell me where you were last night. While I was well you know being someone's bum boy. Were you? Ha ha, oh man, come on give me an answer," said Bennett.

"If you want your nose pushed in just stop this crate and you'll get it ok?" said Sam angrily. "Beats me how you can go with those native women, who mostly stink to high hell, yelk what's the matter ain't you good enough for whites?"

It was now Bennett's turn to get angry and that remark set deep into his gut. He was sweating profusely, his long black hair was stuck to his face.

"Fuck it man, you'll get what you are asking for in a minute if you aren't quiet. Do you hear?" said Bennett. "Hell, you can't tell me that you know what it's like to have a woman between your legs, to feel her body pulsating like a horse running wild?".

Bennett finished his drink and crushed the can as before. While they drove, many wild animals scattered in front of them for fear they would become their next target. Their conversation was cut short when Sam saw something in front.

"Hey stop man, stop I say," yelled Sam. He held on tightly to his rifle.

"Ok, if that's what you want, but I'll knock hell out of you," said Bennett.

"No, no, not to fight, shit man we are both too drunk to do that, don't you know that, no, take a look over there," said Sam.

He pointed to a group of wildebeest in the distance. Some of the animals moved away while five others stood motionless. Bennett let the landrover come to a halt. By now they were both very drunk indeed, and Bennett could hardly see out of his bloodshot eyes, sore with the heat of the land, and tired by his night of passion, even worse by the drink consumed on their journey.

"Fancy a few shots just for the hell of it?" asked Sam.

"Shoot what?" asked Bennett. "I can't see anything."

Sam went to the back of the landrover and got out Bennett's rifle and brought it to him as Bennett got out of the driving seat. For a second he staggered and then leant against a tree. His knees felt like rubber.

"Shit, I've had a bit too much," said Bennett. "You wanna go shoot man, go. I'm staying here," and he got back into the seat.

"Oh come on man, it'll be good for you. Good fun, get some of that aggression out of your system," said Sam.

"No, you go, I'll never kill just for the hell of it not even when I'm pissed," said Bennett as he pushed Sam away. "But I'll come and cover just in case, not that I can see anything." The whole? shimmered in the heat.

He took his rifle and checked to see if it was loaded and checked his pocket for shells. Sam and Bennett staggered towards the wildebeest. Most moved off but five stood motionless as if too afraid too move.

"That group don't seem to know we are here," said Sam.

"Keep your voice down," whispered Bennett.

Sam's eyes were transfixed on the five beasts. Rifle at the ready, sweat pouring off his face and dripping down his nose, the drink had made his eyes blurry and he shook his head now and again as if to clear it. Bent low, he slowly stalked forwards and then he slowly raised his rifle. By now they were no more than twenty feet away. Bennett somehow knew something was wrong being the more professional of the two. He shook his head again and blinked. The stillness was uncanny and through blurred eyes Bennett saw birds sitting on the tattered bushes.

"Don't like this a bit," he whispered to himself. "Something's up."

He could see Sam had not noticed the strange quietness around him. The drink had blurred his brain. Sam clutched the barrel of his rifle and sweat began to make his palms sticky. He steadied his sight. Pulling the butt tightly to his shoulder he took aim. Bennett's fear increased.

"No," shouted Bennett. The silence became a mass of noise.

He lunged forward at Sam but he was too late. Bennett was on his way crashing to the ground. He missed Sam, the rifle let off three shots, the castings fell just to the side of Bennett. A tenth of a second past and the red hot bullet found its target. Suddenly as Bennett lay aching on the ground the beast Sam had shot, literally exploded.

"Jesus Christ," said Bennett. "What the hell is happening?"

Sam, who was standing up, could hardly believe what he was seeing. Bone, gristle and skin flew in every direction. In just a matter of seconds, the three other beasts blew themselves up, in the same way.

Sam stood paralysed, as he felt a splatter on his head, then on his shoulders and neck, and for a second he thought it was raining, but immediately he realised he was being covered with blood and pieces of gut from the animals. Birds swooped at them pecking off the bits brought down by the explosion. They pecked at Sam's motionless body almost covering him completely, but he did nothing. He tried to run. Bennett did likewise. They weren't going to hang around and see what would happen next. Bennett's tanned face turned yellow with fear and his legs buckled and swayed under him. Sam felt something stinging his neck and rubbed his hand on it., When he looked at his hand it was covered with blood and in the middle was a small maggot. He quickly brushed it off and it fell to the ground. The fevered and blood-stained Bennett came to his senses, and he stumbled and ran to the landrover. He threw his gun in the back, got into the driving seat, turned the key and started the engine. Sam was still standing. He had seen everything, but was still in half a trance. Bennett drove straight to him and pulled him into the vehicle. He could see Sam's face stained with blood and his suit wasn't as clean as it was before. Both men were scared out of their wits, and went racing past the spot where the beasts had been. Now the area was stained and crawling alive with maggots.

Birds of all shapes and sizes swooped down for the maggots on the ground. Bennett turned and looked at Sam's face. His eyes were glazed and shock had set in. It was up to Bennett what happened next. Never had he sobered up so fast in his life. Sam's rifle was still fixed and held tightly in his hands. They drove for a while and then Bennett stopped the jeep.

"You ok?" asked Bennett. And he slapped Sam's face.

The engine idled while Bennett tried to shake Sam out of his stupor.

"Come on man come on. Hell, man you are scaring me," said Bennett.

"What ahhh ..." moaned Sam.

Bennett reached for a can of water that was in a box behind the seat. He unscrewed the top and poured some on to a hanky taken from his pocket. It was oily, and soon some of the water soaked in. Then he started to clean Sam's face and neck. The hanky soon became red with blood.

"Come on mate," Bennett almost shouted at him.

Sam slowly lifted his head.

"Holy mother of Christ, what the hell happened?" yelled Sam.

"You tell me," said Bennett. "You froze, you bloody fool."

"Never mind what I did, what the hell was that all about?" said Sam.

"How the hell do I know?" said Bennett, as he poured some more water on the hanky and wrung it out.

"Hey, go steady with that we need it for the truck and for us. We must tell someone what has just happened," said Sam.

"Not bloody likely mate," said Bennett as he wiped some of the mess from his own face and hands.

"How the hell do we explain what we were doing?" grumbled Bennett, and hissed into Sam's face. "Besides, I don't want to spend any more time in that hell hole."

He contorted his face when he saw the mess he had removed.

"What do you mean, you been inside then?" asked Sam. "You never told me."

"Why was that then?" asked Sam. "You'd better switch off the engine."

"I don't have to answer to you for nothing," said Bennett.

He bent down and pulled another oily rag from behind the seat.

"Here," said Bennett to Sam. "Better use beer to remove some of this stuff. By the time we hit town it will be dry and a different colour. Boy we don't half stink." He handed the cloth to Sam, who took it.

"Yeah, ok, thanks. Jesus what the hell's going on? I ain't seen nothing like that ever before. Have you?"

The two men opened cans of beer and cleaned themselves up. As they got back into their seats Sam rubbed the back of his neck and felt a small swelling, Bennett noticed it too.

"No, what's that and I don't want to again". Bennett pulled Sam's hand away and looked closer. "You ok now then, shall we go?"

"Oh nothing, a piece of bone or something must have hit me," said Sam. "Nothing to worry about, I'll survive, heck what's the fuss about?"

The sun was sinking low in the sky. Sam looked for his hat in the back of the jeep, found it and passed Bennett's hat to him at the same time.

"Now don't tell anyone what we saw. Do you hear?" said Bennett.

He then started the engine and the two men drove to the nearest town, which was a good eighty miles away from where they were.

It would be late by the time they reached Zimba.

BACK AT THE BUNGALOW

It was now seven thirty pm and Frank was busy making sure everything that was needed to be taken with him was at hand, ready to be loaded into the landrover: butane stoves, cooking utensils, rifles, a camp bed and a tent and enough food for three or four days. Suddenly from nowhere Frank had a feeling he was being watched. He stood up from what he was doing but couldn't see anything. From inside the shed came Mark carrying two jerry cans of fuel for the truck.

"What's up dad?" asked Mark. "Worrying about tomorrow?" He put the cans down in front of Frank, who by now had removed his hat, then taking the scarf from round his neck wiped his face and lips.

"No, no, but I must admit there is something going on, something strange," said Frank.

"Why do you think that dad?" asked Mark. He stood up and looked around.

"It's too quiet, just listen," said Frank.

"I can't hear anything dad," said Mark, as he made sure the clips were on tight.

"That's it son, don't you see, not even a bird is making a noise," said Frank.

Mark looked across at the young lion cub; even she seemed to be ill at ease.

"See what you mean dad, creepy ain't it, ever since the old man came," said Mark. "Do you believe in all that voodoo stuff?"

"Makes you wonder son, I certainly don't like this stillness," answered frank.

Mark stood back as he heard some bushes move nearby.

"What's that?" he asked. He stood still and scared, the bushes moved and his eyes opened wide.

The silence was broken when Ann called from the house. "Frank, Mark, supper's ready. Has anyone seen James?"

She came out on to the veranda.

"Mark, have you seen James? He's not in his room, he always disappears when it's time to get washed and ready for bed," said Ann.

"Not sure," said Frank as he winked at Mark and pointed to the bushes.

"Ok, dad I did see him," said Mark pointing to the bushes, to where he thought James was hiding.

"James I'm going to count to five. If you are not here by that time there's going to be trouble," said Ann. "One, two, three…"

She moved to the bottom of the steps looking at the bushes. James who was hiding under the veranda crawled out with Reaker following, close behind him. Ann stood at the bottom of the steps as she watched the bushes move and was scared stiff when James suddenly pulled her dress.

"Oh you little devil," screamed Ann.

Both Frank and Mark were totally surprised when they heard her scream out. Frank instinctively bent down and slowly picked up his rifle, which stood nearby with the packed camping equipment. If it wasn't James in the bushes then who was it, he wondered.

"Come out, whoever you are or I'll shoot., Do you hear me? Come on," said Frank.

The bushes moved again, Frank aimed his rifle, and stared into the sights. Ann stood motionless with James and Mark, not daring to move an inch. Reaker stood high on his legs. He, too was scared.

"Don't shoot, it's only me," said a voice.

Then a black face appeared from within the bushes.

"It's me, bossy," said JoJo.

"JoJo, what the hell do you mean by scaring us like that? You nearly scared the pants off me," said Frank.

"Me too," said Mark, whose knees gave out and he fell to the floor.

"You had me scared for a minute," said Ann. "What's the meaning of this? First you run off and leave us for no apparent reason, then you come back and nearly scare us all to death."

"James, you get ready for your shower, do you hear me?" said Ann, angrily as she pushed him towards the side of the house.

"I sorry boss, I not mean to scare you, I really sorry," said JoJo as he put his hands in the air when he saw Frank's gun.

Frank lowered the gun, and stood alongside and placed it by his left leg.

"Don't ever do a dang silly thing like that again," said Frank angrily. "Makes me feel like James Bond. Shoot first and ask questions later. Only there won't be a later if you carry on like that, you stupid fool."

"Sorry bossy, sorry master Mark." JoJo went over and helped Mark to his feet. "You ok master, I mean no harm to you, honest," said JoJo.

"Well, why did you come back, and where have you been JoJo, what have you been up to?" queried Ann, as she walked slowly round him. "There's something different about you, what is it? Are you going to tell us or aren't you, you've been gone for three weeks now."

"Ok, ok, don't get all pecked up, I ain't done nothing wrong."

"Just hark at him, all of a sudden there's a man talking," said Ann, as she turned and looked at Frank. "You know he sounds just like you, when you are riled, if that's what five years does, he'll soon be telling me what to do. I don't know."

"Now darling," said Frank coming over and putting his arm round her shoulder. "Give him a chance, let JoJo tell us in his own time. Well, JoJo."

"Fifteen, that's all he was when he came to us, when you first hired him," said Ann. "Now look at him. He's got muscles where there shouldn't be any. Well, why did you run off then? Aren't we good enough for you, aren't we good to you? I always treated you like one of the family. Never beaten you have I?" she finished in desperation, as she slapped her hands on her side. "Well," she said to Frank. "You find out ok, then let me know Frank Why did you run off then?"

She went off in the direction of the house muttering. "Kids, they always…"

"Well JoJo, we're waiting," said Frank.

"Well boss, it's like this, when a boy becomes a man he gets a little lonesome," said JoJo.

Frank put his rifle down against the tents and cans. Mark's knees felt better and he dusted them down.

"He gets a hankering for female company, and I seed this pretty gal last time we was in town, and I figured out by the looks she gave me that she'd be a fancying me, so I runned off to see if it were right," said JoJo.

"Well you did, did you and were you right?" asked Frank.

"What do you think boss?" said JoJo, turning and beckoning towards the bushes. A girl appeared. She was dark, with long, black shiny hair. Her eyes were big and a smile like the sun came from her glowing lips. "This is Suchana, my wife, we got married before we leave town. I took the liberty, I know because maybe you not want her here," said JoJo. "But we go back to town if you not like us both, she's a very good cook, maybe help missy Ann in the house.".

"Can she speak English?" asked Frank, smiling at Suchana.

"Yes bossy she very good," said JoJo.

"Yes, I speak very good, many tongues, my father chief of village of Wappa Missionary. Teach many of my family," said Suchana for herself.

Frank continued the conversation with JoJo and Suchana.

Ann was trying to get James to have his shower.

"Get your clothes off and put them outside. I'll fetch some clean ones," said Ann. "You may as well put your pyjamas on as it is much later than I thought."

"Do you think JoJo will stay with us again mum?" asked James as he undressed.

"Oh good, he's such fun, and he knows all about the animals, doesn't he mum?"

"Yes that's true," said his mother, as she pulled a piece of string connected to the inside bottom of a wooden tub. "You ready then? Here's the first lot," said Ann, as she pulled the string.

"Wha, wha," yelled James. "That's cold."

"Stop moaning, soap yourself down and yell when you are ready for the next lot. Wash you hair too, all right? I'll be back in a minute."

Reaker stood nearby on the fence.

"You want a wash too?" Ann asked Reaker as she passed. She patted him and Reaker scurried away. Not if he could, the chimp thought to himself.

Ann stopped at the bottom of the steps. She called out to the two men. "Supper's ready in five minutes. She was puzzled at the fourth person, but couldn't quite make out who it could be. Who's that with you?" called Ann.

"Ann, darling, come here, you'll never guess what?" said Frank.

Ann came down the steps, after she had put James's dirty clothes down and picked up his pyjamas that she had left by the door.

"What's that darling?" she said as she started down the path.

"JoJo's got himself a wife," said Frank.

"Well, I'll be," she said, as she came nearer the group and at a glance she could tell that she would get on fine with Suchana.

"Hi," said Ann. "Well, what a surprise," turning to JoJo who stood by watching apprehensively.

Suchana bowed and smiled.

"Hello," said Suchana to Ann.

"Sorry if I snapped at you JoJo," said Ann.

"That's ok, missy, it's my fault I should say," said JoJo.

"I'm ready mum," called James from the shower. Ann half turned.

"Coming in a minute son," said Ann.

"Maybe I help with boy, all right please," asked Suchana.

"Ok, fine," Ann smiled at Frank then she turned and she and Suchana moved off towards the house.

"Looks like you have got yourself a nice girl there, and a nice job here. Come on and give us a hand ok?" said Frank to JoJo.

"I'd better get washed up," said Mark.

"We'd better do the same, all right? Here, cop hold of this," said Frank, handing JoJo his gun. "Bring it into the house."

"Ok, bossy you make JoJo very happy," as he took the gun and followed Frank.

"You may not say that tomorrow," said Frank. "We have got a job to go out to. Come on, let's get washed up and I'll tell you all about it."

They all moved towards the house.

"Brrr, that's colder than the last lot," squealed James.

He stood behind the wooden framed shower.

"Pass me a towel please mum. Thanks," said James, taking the towel..

"When you are nice and dry, get your pyjamas on and dressing gown, then come in for supper," said Ann, as she moved off into the house.

"I'd better lay two more places, as now we have two more added to the family," Ann smiled at Suchana.

"I see to boy," said Suchana, as she smiled at James.

"Hi," he chirped looking over the top of the door. "Do you like lions?"

"Why?" asked Suchana, as she held up his pyjamas.

"I've got one, and if you like I'll show you her tomorrow," said James who was now dry. He came out and shut the door.

"I'd like that., I once had a pet snake," replied Suchana.

The men washed and tidied themselves for supper. It was now about eighty thirty pm and the sun was setting and all the night noises had begun to start up.

"Did you really have a snake?" James asked Suchana.

Food was passed round the table and the conversation was light hearted, as JoJo told Ann and Frank about his marriage toSuchana. They all laughed at some of the things he told them; how he had had a fight with Suchana's boss man, where she had worked.

"I laugh now, but not then," said JoJo. "He say I may not take her away because she good cook, and he also say that he had no one to take her place so quick, and he not manage so good on his own."

"So you end up in his bad books eh?" said Frank.

"I bit his ear till it bled," said JoJo.

"He hit my JoJo very hard. If I had a knife I would have cut him," said Suchana. "He very big man." Suchana made a sign with her hands to show he was fat.

"Oh no, you wouldn't, would you?" asked Ann laughing.

"I wish I'd seen that," said James, stuffing his face with food.

"Haven't you finished yet?" asked Ann, pointing to James's glass of milk. "Come on young man, you drink that and then get to bed, it's almost nine thirty".

"Oh, do I have to mum? Can't I stay up a little longer?" pleaded James.

"No, bed, now go on, and don't let that beast into your room," said his mother.

"Right mum, goodnight dad, night JoJo and Suchana, see you in the morning, Goodnight Mark.,"

"Goodnight Rat, and go to sleep, no playing with your toys under the bedclothes either," said Mark.

"What are you on about, I didn't play with anything last night, I went right to sleep. He's lying mum, honest," said James, denying Mark's accusation.

"Oh yeah, what may I ask was all that noise last night then? Pretending to be a spaceship again, were we?" said Mark.

James got up from the table and went round and gave his mother a kiss, then Frank then nodded to JoJo and Suchana.

"I didn't play with any toys last night under my blankets, honest dad. Night," said James. He kissed his dad on the cheek.

"Then who, or what made that buzzing sound in the middle of the night," said Mark.

"I don't know, but it wasn't me," said James indignantly, poking out his tongue at Mark.

"Go on stop arguing and off to bed with you young man," said his father.

"Something made that noise then, and if it wasn't him who was it then, or what was it?" asked a confused Mark. "Didn't you hear it mum?"

"I'm sorry I didn't hear anything, I was too tired to hear anything last night," said Ann, and, turning to James "go to bed". She then looked at Mark. "You had better go too in a minute," she said to him.

"Ok, good night everyone," said James and disappeared up the stairs.

"Well, is everyone finished? If so, I'll clear up the plates," said Ann.

"I'll help," said Suchana, as she got up.

They all left the table, leaving the two women to clear away the plates and fetch water from outside to wash the dishes, while Mark made his excuses to go and do some modelling in his bedroom.

"Night mum," called Mark.

"Night Mark," answered everyone.

Frank and JoJo sat by a small fire, as it gets much colder at nights in the African countryside. Mosquitoes were flying around the wire mesh door and moths were trying to get in. Reaker had settled down on a blanket outside on the floor. Frank sat in his chair and lit his cigarette and JoJo sat on a stool.

"You'll come tomorrow?" said Frank. "We have to investigate a story an old man came in with this morning. He said someone had put a spell on his animals. You scared of voodoo JoJo?"

"Yes, sir bossy, me once saw a man in my tribe foaming at the mouth like a wild dog. Next thing he ok, like nothing happened. Two days later he found with split gut," said JoJo. "My father say he mess around with woman in tribe not his own, so spell was put on by father. She was promised to someone else."

"Horrid, who did it?" asked Frank. "The son or the father?"

"No bossy, he did it to himself, voodoo make him take his own life. Like the Chinese men do in your country and the East I hear," answered JoJo.

"It's time for bed I think don't you?" said Ann. "as you have an early start in the morning. But, JoJo you have it wrong, the Chinese do that for honour."

"Yes, sure darling, said Frank, and he got up and put out his cigarette.

"Suchana and JoJo will you be all right in the cot tonight? It's not very wide, but it's comfortable," asked Ann.

"Sure thing missy boss lady, we be ok," said JoJo as he went over to Suchana, who handed him some blankets. "She small and I cuddle up to her. We be fine, goodnight," said JoJo.

"Goodnight Ann," said Suchana. "I like your little boy, he kind, in the morning I help you cook breakfast, later see baby lion Sophie."

She nodded to Ann and Frank as they left and went upstairs. JoJo and Suchana made themselves comfortable in the cot.

"I like lady Ann," said Suchana. "She kind too I think I be happy with her, and she with me." She took off her native robe and settled down.

"Go sleep now," said JoJo and he kissed her goodnight. "We have a long day, walk many miles. Sleep now, ok?" They both settled in the cot.

"Three days will seem like three years without you darling," moaned Ann as she got undressed and climbed into bed. She watched as Frank undressed. "What a fine figure of a man you are darling, even if you have got muscles where muscles shouldn't be," she said teasingly.

"Well now," said Frank smiling at her. "I know just where one muscle is going to be in about half an hour or so, so watch out girl, here comes 007. Only remember, this guy don't shoot first, he waits".

Frank climbed into bed and cradled Ann in his arms.

"Ooh Frank," said Ann.

"What's up darling?" said Frank. He looked into her face and laughed.

"Your gun's cold,.What will Moneypenny say?" joked Ann.

"It won't be cold for long," said Frank, and they both rolled over laughing.

"Shush, shush you'll wake the boys and they will hear us downstairs," said Ann.

"Nar, no they won't they are soundo. To hell with Moneypenny, she's got nothing to complain about. I've hung my hat up ain't I? Ha ha!" said Frank.

Later that night Frank woke up. From where he lay he could see the dark purple sky. His mind was filled with questions; they kept running through his head. He thought about the old man's story, and how he should tackle it. He was pleased that

JoJo had come back. He felt for his cigarettes and then realised that he had left them in his pocket. He got up slowly so that he didn't disturb Ann, then carefully pulling back the sheets he got out of bed. He could hear Ann's heavy breathing and as she lay she looked lovely. Thoughts came back to him as he remembered what had happened earlier. When she had rolled over and kissed him on the cheek, how her warm body had felt beneath his and her responses as his hands slipped slowly down her body until he reached her thighs. How he had bent towards her caressing her body till it shook with excitement. Then they kissed and his fingers fluttered down her body again. Frank remembered how he felt all his physical parts tingle when she lay cradled beside him in his arms, how when love reached its climax they lay side by side still touching, tenderly whispering things of love to each other. He stood up, and felt in his pocket and found his cigarettes. He sat back on the bed and lit up, and putting his lighter down on the table took a deep drag.

Suddenly all the night noises had ceased. It was so sudden that for a second or so he did not realise what had happened. He picked up his watch on the side of the table next to him and looked at the time.

"What the, one o'clock," he exclaimed.

He got up off the bed and went over to the window and looked out. He shook his head, as his ears began to hurt. Suddenly Ann woke up as she could hear this strange noise.

"What's happening, what's that noise?" asked Ann as she got out of bed. She put her robe on.

"I don't know, but sure hurts my ears," said Frank, holding her.

"Oh it's terrible, whatever it is,"

They were soon joined by JoJo and Suchana, who knocked at the door. Suchana screamed out and held her hands to her ears.

"What's happening boss man?" asked JoJo "What be that awful sound? I can't take much more."

JoJo went to the window and joined Frank. Ann turned too and they all gazed out, and in the distance could see a red cloud. Ann comforted Suchana, and then as they looked into the night, they could see in the distance a fierce red glow on the horizon.

"What's that?" asked Suchana. She pointed, "Oh it's my village burning I must go."

She made a panic move for the door. Frank made a lunge at her.

"No, no," he said as he grabbed her. "Don't get hysterical, you can't go rushing off into the middle of the night, that's over a hundred and sixty miles away. It will take hours to get there, besides we haven't even got the truck loaded."

"I must go," moaned Suchana, as she pulled towards the door. Ann pulled her back. "Frank knows best, come on come and sit down," said Ann.

JoJo looked worried. As soon as the noise came it was gone.

"What do you think it was boss?" asked JoJo.

"I really don't know," said Frank staring out into the blackness.

They all went slowly back to their beds none the wiser for what had happened. For the time being they were safe.

THE TOWN OF ZIMBE

One hundred miles away lay the small town of Zimba, which was Frank's home base and also the headquarters of the small police force of about twenty men. It was considered quite large for the area, and had for some years been the base where people from all parts could come and pick up a helicopter, that would take them to the main city for any reason under the sun.

The chief of police had his own helicopter to do searches and surveys anywhere if any reports came in, and this was often a great help to Frank. A useful sort of back up system.

The time was six thirty pm and the time for the day shift to be relieved and the night shift to take over. Six men stood in a row waiting for their orders, the night roster and information for the day. The sergeant came in; he was six foot tall and seemed just as wide. He was a man, who stood no nonsense from any of his men, but on the other hand he was well liked and a pretty fair cop as things go.

Three whites and three black native police stood in a line motionless waiting while the sergeant walked around them, checking to see that they were all properly dressed for their duty.

He came and stood next to one of the white policemen and eyed him up and down.

"You," he said, "to my office as soon as we have finished here."

"Right sir," said the officer, coming to attention.

"Right men," said the sergeant. "Take it easy. There is only one thing I have to say to you tonight. I don't like sloppy uniforms. We may be out here in this god forsaken land of heat and sand, but there is no need for you to go round looking as if you have just been through hell and high water if you'll pardon the expression. Tomorrow night if you come in looking like you do tonight then you are going to know just how nasty I can be."

"Anyone found with an untidy uniform will get double duties, do you all understand?"

"Yes sir," said the men.

They respected their sergeant even though he came on a bit strong at times.

"Furthermore, I don't like shoddy reports. Some of these I can hardly decipher let alone understand," said the sergeant. He stood rocking on his heels, hands behind his back.

"I don't like the chief breathing down my neck because of shoddy work you men bring in, so now I have got that off my chest let's get down to the nitty gritty of tonight's work. I want results and good ones. Do you understand?"

"Yes sir," said the men.

"When the chief gets frustrated and angry, I get it in the neck and I don't like that one little bit," he shouted. "So you can be sure that if I get it in the neck then you will get it the same."

He rubbed the back of his neck.

"I think it's going to be one of those days today so men let's get on with tonight's work.

"It has been reported to me tonight that another girl has been raped. That makes this the fourth in the last four months. This one is in the care of the doctor. He's, carried out a full examination, and she has been brutally beaten up and is in shock., She is unable to give any information about who attacked her. So far all he has managed to get out of her is that the man had on something bright. Then she passed out and couldn't remember anything else. If you saw what he did to her, you would be shocked. She is badly cut about and has lost lots of blood and will have to be taken to the city for treatment. It matches up with all the other cases we have had and it's obviously the same guy, so men, you must be on the lookout for the fiend. I want every man to take a good look round at anything suspicious. You!" he looked at one of the officers. "You cover all the alleys where all the other rapes took place, check each of them, the places are all on the report sheets." He passed the sheets to the officer. "Thank you sir," he said as he studied the sheets and handed copies to the others.

"I want this bastard caught," said the sergeant.

He walked up and down the room. Behind his back he held a small stick in his hand and banged it up and down. He eyed each man up and down as he did so.

"On each of his and all of these attacks so far he has eluded us and left no clues. I'd consider him a very lucky man so far or a very clever one, but he's bound to slip up soon, and then we have got him. I think there is a lesson to be learnt here." He looked at one of the men and went on, "what am I talking about?" snapped the sergeant.

"Sir," said one of the men. "The rapist."

The sergeant came and stood in front of the officer. He looked closely into his face.

"Funny," he said, spitting., "Now tell me something I don't know. You stupid fool."

"Sir," said the officer. "I don't understand."

"You never will if you don't listen to what is said," shouted the sergeant.

"Do I have to do all the thinking for you too?"

"No sir," said the officer.

"Well then," said the sergeant. "Please," he squinted at the officer who was scared of the sergeant.

"Do you mean sir?" said the officer.

"Yes, yes," said the sergeant nodding his head. "Come on, come on out with it."

"Sir, I think you meant to say crime doesn't pay," said the officer.

"Correct," said the sergeant.

At last it made sense. He looked at the other men.

"The only trouble is," said the sergeant "that this bum thinks it does. This time we are going to get this chump who thinks he is better than us. Do you hear?"

"Yes sir", said the men.

"In the reports that you men have in your hands you will find many things listed about the rapist. One witness says he is coloured, about twenty years old and on his attacks he is known to have worn a very colourful short-sleeved shirt. The other witness who was raped was lucky enough not to be beaten, compared with this poor kid who is just fifteen. Next,, the question of the raid on the ammunition hut at the other end of town. Seems that poachers took some shells and dynamite. Can't think what they would want dynamite for, shells yes, well they'd be good for hunting. Do your job and keep a sharp eye out," commanded the sergeant..

"Yes sir," said the men.

"But for Christ's sake, be careful," he ended.

He dismissed the men and they went off to do their duties. One to the desk, while the others left by the main door, after checking their equipment -, small pistols packed in their side holsters. Two officers the sergeant had asked to go to the chief's office headed that way. While they walked down the corridor they chatted to each other. Keith spoke first.

"He's a bit tetchy tonight," said Keith.

He was referring to the sergeant.

"I wonder who upset him?" asked Keith.

"I don't know," said Dale, the other officer, "but that's not going to be my worry. Tomorrow I am off. Off to the cool snows of Switzerland." He stopped, bent down, pulled up his socks and straightened his tie.

"How do I look?" Dale asked Keith.

"Maybe we are getting promoted, ha ha," laughed Dale.

"Christ," said Keith. "You must be joking. Since when have we done anything to deserve that, hey?"

"What do you mean? Wasn't it us who caught that old buzzard feeding whiskey to the natives, and how about that chap, you know the one who had all that dope stashed, up his you know what?," said Dale.

"Ass," said Keith to Dale. "Why don't you speak your mind boy? That's what my father always said no matter what."

Keith pulled down his jacket, pale green in colour and safari style and turned to Dale.

"Why do you have to be so damn well, provincial?" asked Keith.

"Oh shut up," said Dale giving Keith a quick witty smile. "Why do you have to be so African? You went to the same recruiting school as me."

They reached the door of the chief's office and knocked on it.

"When you are born in Rome you do as the Romans do," said Keith. "When in Africa you do as Africans do boss boy. Ha ha." He slapped Dale on the back.

"You fool," said Dale "Stop mucking about and get in there or we will both be in the doghouse."

"Come in," said a voice from inside the office.

"All right boss, don't beat me master please," said Keith.

"Oh, shut up," said Dale pushing through the door.

"Come in and sit down," said the chief to the two men. They sat down while the chief fumbled with the papers on his desk, and signed some of them, putting them in a wooden tray marked "out", and then looked up at the two sitting there.

"Something funny or can anyone join in?" asked the chief.

The two men wiped the grins off their faces immediately.

"Sorry sir," said Dale "just something Keith said outside."

"Oh," said the chief, "not about me I trust."

"No sir," said Keith.

He swallowed hard and ran his hand through his hair.

"Dale," said the chief. "I prefer it if you took your job a little more seriously."

"Yes sir," said Dale.

"Don't interrupt," said the chief., "When do you go on vacation?"

He sat back in his chair, resting his hands at the back of his head.

"In the morning sir," said Dale.

Dale was very surprised to be asked this.

"Good," said the chief. "Where are you going?"

"Switzerland sir," replied Dale, "with my wife and kid brother Barry."

"Well," said the chief, "we'll miss you. This last few months you and officer Keith Marshall have been doing very well. When you get back there will be a surprise for both of you. I've put you in for your promotions and you get it on your return."

Both men looked very surprised, because just before they entered the office they had been joking about that very subject.

"Really great sir, thanks," said Keith. "I thought we were in for a grilling."

"Don't thank me," said the chief. "It's only your effort and hard work that has got you this far. Well, what do you think?" He looked at Dale.

Dale Parker, the senior of the two, had been in the force about nine years and had been an inspector for almost five. He had spent some of his time in the main city of Camgonga, some two hundred miles from Zimba. His home was Switzerland, but he had not seen it since he was a boy. He had completely lost his accent and had grown to love Africa as though it was the land of his birth. His sister had come out some years ago and met and married Frank, the game warden, who was now in charge of the safari park and game reserve, but Dale didn't see any of his family very much.

"I wouldn't be lying, sir, when I say, I, we, are very surprised," said Dale, as he turned to Keith and smiled.

"Flabbergasted, would be a better way of expressing it sir," said Keith.

The chief stood up and so did they. He put out his hand to them "Here," he said, "both of you deserve it, believe me."

He shook both men by the hand and then sat down again. He took out a packet of cigarettes from the drawer of his desk and offered them the packet. They each took one; Dale got out his lighter from his top pocket and lit them and also the chief's.

"About this business," said the chief. "These girls who are being raped. A nasty thing that, the worst case I've seen for years."

"Yes sir," said Dale. "The sergeant said outside. Have you any hunches about this sir, or who did it I mean?"

"Not any, the only thing is he's got to be local,," said the chief.

He put his hand to the side of his head to indicate that the man must be nuts. The window was open behind him.

"How the hell he's got away with it, four, of them I don't know, I suspect he lives on one of the outlying farms but we've checked and found nothing," said the chief. "There's no evidence at all. He's too quick. I'll give him that, and fast. He leaves the scene and gets away before anyone can get to it."

"I'd like to get my hands on the bastard," said Keith getting angry at the thought of the man getting away with it. He stubbed out his cigarette remains in the ashtray on the chief's desk.

Keith was a bit younger than Dale by about two years. He had met Dale at the police training school in the main city and they were quite good pals, but of the two Dale was the more expert.

"Me too," said Dale. "By the way, you haven't said who it is sir. On my report. It says female, fifteen." Dale put out his cigarette.

"It's Nickki Quartermaine, the doctor's grand daughter, and I only want you two to know it, ok?" said the chief. "If we say she's at the doc's house then we can keep it quiet. The mother is far too upset to see anyone, so she's been given a sedative and her husband is looking after her. There is another child, Kim, she's only five and it's best that she knows nothing about it."

"Oh my god, poor kid," said Dale. "I see what you mean."

"Yes," said Keith. "They haven't been here long either, what a thing to happen." Keith shook his head and looked at Dale whose face expressed the same thought.

The chief then went on to say to the two men about many other things. As he did, he walked up and down behind his desk. Then suddenly Dale began to laugh, so did Keith. There was a lollipop stuck to the chief's behind. The chief caught sight of the two men trying hard not to laugh.

"I don't see anything funny to laugh about, this is serious," he said.

"Sorry sir, yes I know but …" said Keith.

"Well what's so bloody funny then?" the chief asked rudely.

"Sir?" asked Dale.

"For Christ's sake man," said the chief. "Come on, get it out."

"Sir, there's a lollipop stuck to your pants," said Dale.

The chief, white-faced at first, turned to look, then his face went bright red with embarrassment.

"If I get my hands on that little bastard, I'll kill him. This is the third time today, the little brat. Oh, I'll get him," said the chief.

"What?" said Dale, still laughing.

"Yes, he buggered up my car," he said, taking the lollipop off his pants and throwing it in the bin. "He's put one in my petrol tank and one in my shoe, and now this," said the chief.

He took his hanky from his pocket and wiped his forehead. He walked over to the drinks container and picked up a plastic beaker. He pressed the beaker to the top and got a drink of water, and damping his hanky he tried to get some of the mess off his pants. At this point he glanced at a photo on his desk. It was of his wife and he wished for a second that she was still alive and able to clean his pants, but she was not.

"He's got a hell of a lot of spunk doing that to you," said Keith.

"He won't have, not if I have my way," said the chief, putting the damp hanky on his desk.

"Go on you two, get out and keep your eyes peeled, ok? If you see anything suspicious, report it to me," said the chief as he waved them out of the office. Then he beckoned and said to them, "Keep this to yourselves." He pointed to the seat of his pants. "Ok, I'll deal with them myself in my own way. I don't want to be the laughing stock of the place."

"Ok sir," said Dale.

They left the office.

"Phew," said Keith and he laughed quietly to himself. "Now we know what's upsetting him and why the sarge got it in the neck."

They continued on down the corridor and they carried on talking.

"Just wait till I tell Jenny the good news," said Dale. "She will be pleased as this will mean a lot to Barry and her."

"Why's that?" asked Keith.

"Well, she's always wanted her mother out here to visit, but we've never been able to afford it and now with a rise we'll be able to pay for her to come out., As for Barry, he will be able to buy a new wardrobe of clothes and he will be happy."

At this point they reached the notice board.

"Anything interesting?" asked Keith.

"Just think," said Dale, "this last night duty and we will be off on two weeks holiday. Boy, am I looking forward to it."

"Why does Barry want new clothes all of a sudden?" asked Keith.

He was still looking at the notice board. Keith pointed at something.

"Look," he said to Dale. "It's here and we never noticed it."

"What?" asked Dale?

"Our promotion," said Keith. They both laughed.

"Hey, take a look at that," said Dale.

"What?" said Keith.

"Would you believe it?" said Dale.

"Steve Anderson's got the top award again for shooting. He must be bloody good to carry it off for three years in a row. Man, if I could shoot like him I'd be made."

"You ever met him?" asked Keith.

"No, but I'd like to, maybe he'd give me a few tips. I'm not too hot at the moment, there's certainly room for improvement," said Dale.

"I wish it were me," said Keith.

Turning away, they continued along the corridor.

"What shooting you mean?" asked Dale.

"No," said Keith. "Going on holiday. Anyway what time do you go off in the morning, and will there be time for me to pop in and say cheerio to Jenny and Barry?"

"Why sure," said Dale. "The Chinook goes at nine, that takes us to the city airport and then we will catch the flight. We are going via the grasshopper route."

"What the hell does that mean?" asked Keith smiling.

They were now nearing the end of the corridor and in front of the main desk and through a pair of doors. Through the doors and standing by the front desk was a tattered forlorn figure of a native boy aged about ten. He was waving his hands about and mumbling in his native tongue, but the chap behind the desk was not having much joy. He could not understand him.

"Oh," said Dale. "That's where we go from Camagonga, to Spain, then to Zurich and from there the plane goes to London and the States. It's a lot slower than the new vanguard service but it's much cheaper."

Dale opened the swing doors.

"It's also called that because on one ticket you can drop off anywhere and stay overnight or even a couple of days and then catch the next grasshopper flight to the next place," said Dale.

"Oh," said Keith. "Mind if I ask you what the price is?"

"Eight hundred pounds a piece," said Dale.

He let Keith through the door first.

"In fact," said Dale, "we may pop over to London and spend a couple of days there. Jenny has an old school friend there she hasn't seen for years."

The doors closed behind them and they walked over to the main desk.

"Having problems?" asked Dale, to the officers behind the desk.

He looked at the boy who continued to babble on. He was very upset and crying. Native boys did not cry. They were always much tougher than the whites, Dale thought. Keith looked at the boy. He noticed his torn clothes, shorts worn through and hand-me downs from white folk. His shirt too was torn and in holes. Keith also noticed that the boy had something in his clenched fist, but he couldn't make out what it was.

"Yes," said John, leaning over the top of the desk. "One, he's speaking much too fast, and two I can't understand him. Can you try and slow him down a little?"

"Yes sure," said Keith. "I'll try if that's all right with you Dale?"

"Yes go ahead," said Dale. "Remember I'm off in the morning and you will have to sort it out anyway."

Dale looked at the boy while Keith questioned him. Keith bent down to the boy and asked the lad to slow down in his own tongue and then he listened to his story.

"Well," said John. "What's it all about?" He got his pen and pad ready to write it all down.

"Well," said Keith, standing up. He held on to the lad by his side, and gently put his hands on the boy's lank long hair. "It's a very strange story. It appears that two whites came to his village some days ago. Hunters they were, one was clean and the other was not. He says that for three days one of them had his mother almost as a prisoner in their hut. After a while they left. He went off to find his father to whom he told what had been going on. His father was furious and thought he was lying so he dragged his son home to find out the truth. So mad was he that he beat the boy for not looking after his mother. His penance was to be put down the water hole for three days and to fill the water buckets for the villagers, but no buckets came down to be filled and the whites had long been gone after being chased out. The boy would normally have been brought to the top after three days in one of the buckets, but the night before this was to happen he saw a strange red cloud that hovered over the village. He said he heard a buzzing bird., That's their name for a helicopter. This was because of the buzzing in his ears."

"What's that?" asked Dale.

He bent down to take the object from the boy, but he put his hand behind his back and started to mumble again. Keith who now had the boy's confidence, bent down to see what he had in his hand.

"What have you got there son?" asked Keith.

The boy eased his hand slowly open and in it was a cone-shaped object. He looked at Keith's face and pointed to the cone. Keith listened with great care and his face showed surprise at what the boy was saying. Keith looked at Dale and John.

"John," said Keith. "This is all that remains in his village There are many more scattered round like this. This one was outside his parents' hut. He says it is his parents' spirit and that it tells him to keep it."

"What?" said Dale. "No, I can't believe that story. Do you believe it Keith?"

"I don't know," answered Keith. "To do that we will have to examine that thing and we have not got the equipment here in Zimba to do that."

"Well," said Dale, "what are you going to do about it then?"

"If he will let us have a look at it," said John "we could have it photographed and x-rayed and then send the results to the city. Sounds as if they have just packed up and moved off. The natives often do that."

John wrote something in his notebook at the desk.

"Sounds like some kind of voodoo, but this bit about everyone missing is strange. Where did they all go?" asked Dale

"I'll try your idea John," said Keith, bending down to the boy and asking him to see the object.

The boy reluctantly handed over the cone to Keith. It was mauve and orange in parts, and shaped slightly like a pine cone but smaller and seemed to have no weight at all. Keith handed it to Dale.

"What do you make of that?" asked Keith.

"I don't know," said Dale, holding it up to the light. "It seems to be almost transparent. I've never seen anything like it before, anywhere, it seems almost like a kind of seed."

"Could it be an egg?" asked John. "One of those prehistoric ones?"

"Don't be daft," said Dale. "It doesn't even look like an egg."

He showed it to John who took it in his hand.

"Very strange," said John. "Here, you have it, it gives me the creeps."

"Perhaps it is seed," said Keith. "In this dried up land it could have been buried for years."

"I don't know," said Dale. "Anyway you had better check with the helicopter base and see if anyone has been that way. The natives don't understand these things. Maybe some crazy bastard has been scaring the hell out of them just for the fun of it, just testing the chief's helicopter."

"That doesn't explain though," said Keith "where this cone came from does it, or the others that the lad tells us are out there?"

"I don't know, maybe the rotor blades took off the top layer of soil, but something like this lad's story should be thoroughly investigated," said Keith. He held out his hand to the boy who carefully put his own hand into Keith's. "I'll let the chief know as soon as possible. You see to the report John and get it ready for the chief and I'll take this lad to the forensics lab and hand this object over to Susan. She'll know what to do with it," said Keith

"Right Keith," said John. "I'll get on to that right away."

John picked up the phone and asked to be put through to the helicopter immediately. A voice answered.

"Yes sir," it said, "could you hold on please?" It was a female voice.

"I'll wait outside," said Dale. "I've got a few bits and pieces to pick up for Jenny ok?"

"Yes sure," said Keith.

He walked on through the corridor with the boy.

Dale waved to John who wished him a good holiday. He had finished his phone call.

"Lucky bugger," called out John. "How I would like to be you."

"Yes sure," said Dale. "Anyway thanks, I'll be seeing you when I get back. Maybe I'll even bring you a snowball. Bye, I'll report in later tonight."

Dale went out through the front door and ran into Fletcher who was going off duty.

"Dale," said Fletcher. "I hear you are off in the morning?" The two men stood on the steps talking. Nearby was a gunsmith's shop and store. Dale half looked in the window and half looked at Fletcher.

"Yes that's true," said Dale, as he stood there. His thoughts were on what he had to get for Jenny, and half on what Fletcher was saying.

After a while he saw the boy leave the police station still clutching the cone in his hand. Inside the building Keith was putting the photos and x-ray into an envelope ready to give to the chief. Dale watched the sad boy walk down the street and was still half listening to Fletcher. The boy then sat down by the gunsmith's shop.

"Yes, sorry, what were you saying?" asked Dale.

"I hear you are off in the morning," said Fletcher. "Hey, what's up? You look puzzled."

"Oh, nothing, yes you're right I am," said Dale.

"Well," said Fletcher. "I wish you a good holiday."

"Hmm, thanks. I think I need it," answered Dale, thinking that he had been rather rude to Fletcher.

"When are you off then? Dale asked him.

"I'm going home, to have a shower a good meal and then, who knows?" said Fletcher.

"Anyone I know?" asked Dale.

"I sincerely hope not," said Fletcher laughing, "because I don't think Jenny would like it if you did."

Dale laughed and gently punched Fletcher on the arm.

"I see what you mean," said Dale. "Anyway it's time I was off. I have to pick up a few things so I'll see you when I get back .Ok, sorry I can't stop any longer and talk, you understand?"

"Yeah sure," said Fletcher.

The two men parted company as Dale went to pick up his shopping. He stopped by the boy and spoke to him and asked if he was ok.

"I've got two sisters in another village and I shall go to them," the boy told Dale. "Perhaps my parents forgot I down a hole and go there maybe buzz bird make them scare and they run away. I don't know."

Dale smiled down at the boy. "In our language they are called helicopters, you say helicopter ok?" said Dale.

The boy twisted his mouth. "Helicopter," he said.

"That's right," said Dale. He patted him on the hand.

Dale then continued on down the road to get the shopping for Jenny. Keith still had not come out of the station so when Dale had finished his shopping he went back for him. Inside Keith had by now put the photographs in the envelope and had given them to John to deliver the chief.

"Have you seen Keith?" called Dale, as he came through the door. "Ah, there you are," he said. "I was wondering where you had got to. Come on, we were supposed to be on patrol at least half an hour ago. Are you ready?"

"Yes," said Keith, passing through the swing doors. "Thank god that's done, the poor kid, he's gone now."

"Yeah, in fact I saw him; he's sitting on the steps of the smithy. Says he's going to his sister's home or something," said Dale.

"Hey what have you got there?" asked Keith.

"Just a few things for Jenny," replied Dale. "Why".

"Oh nothing," said Keith. "What are you going to do with them? You can't carry them around with you all night."

"No, don't be silly," said Dale. "We can drop them off on our way round and maybe we might even get a cup of coffee. Have you put that report into the chief's office yet?"

"Yes, don't worry about it," said Keith. "John is dealing with that right now."

"Right then, off we go on my last night's duty," said Dale.

He felt elated that he only had a few hours work and then he would be off on holiday.

"Come on," he said to Keith. "Let's drop these off with Jenny and then be on our way. Ok? She would love to see you anyway before we go. She asked about you only the other morning, and I said you would call in."

Keith was still worried and it showed by the look on his face.

"Oh did you?, Good?" replied Keith

"What's bothering you now?" asked Dale. "You don't seem to be your usual bright self tonight."

"Oh nothing really," said Keith. "I'm sorry, it's just that lad, poor little bugger. Don't take any notice of me it will wear off when we are out working. I'm a bit superstitious that's all. I can't get his story out of my mind. You know, he said something very strange."

"What was that?" asked Dale, as they walked down the street.

"He said he saw and heard many birds, plus of course the red cloud. It just doesn't make sense, that's all."

"Well, I shouldn't let it worry you, not tonight. Come on let's get rid of these parcels," said Dale. "Jenny will want to get these few last things packed so come on in and have a drink."

While the two men had been walking down the street they had been keeping a sharp look out as requested by the sergeant for anything suspicious, but as they reached Dale's house they had seen nothing unusual, just a few people walking up and down and the boy sitting on the smithy's back step.

"Come in," said Dale. "We won't be more than a few minutes."

The two men entered the house but there was no sign of Jenny, so Dale called.

"Jenny, Jenny, where are you? We're home." He was a bit worried.

"Down in a sec," she called. "I've got my hands full."

Dale unzipped his gun from his holster and put it on the table and then looked at Keith.

"You'd better do the same," he said. "Jenny does not like them worn in the house.".

Keith looked at his watch. "We shall only be here about five minutes, and then we must get back on our beat," replied Keith. "Well ok, just this once," and he unclipped his gun and put it on the table next to Dale's.

At this point Jenny came into the room with a pile of clothes in her arms.

"Hi, you two," she said, as she came over to the table and placed the clothes on a small coffee table. She moved an ashtray out of the way.

"Hello Keith," said Jenny, as she stood up and caught his eye. "How are you? You look well. Would you like some coffee?"

"Hi darling," she said to Dale and went over and kissed him. "Did you get everything I asked for?"

"Yes love," said Dale. "Where's Barry tonight? He should be helping you."

"I don't know," said Jenny. "I'm getting a bit worried. He never came home last night. Said yesterday morning he was going to a party at his mate's house and by the way he got himself up I think he had a date or something. He wore that dreadful coloured t-shirt you bought him."

Keith raised an eyebrow and looked at Dale. He said nothing and let is pass.

"Yeah sure that's what we came for, coffee," said Dale. "Then we must be on our way."

She took the parcel from Dale and kissed him at the same time. Then she turned to Keith.

"One has to take advantage of the situation," she said with a smile then went on to say, "doesn't one?"

Keith blushed, as he remembered that he had once dated Jenny before Dale married her. Then he had introduced her to Dale. It had been a stupid thing to do after only two dates. Dale and Jenny had hit it off right away and seemed right for each other but Keith had lost a good girl and he knew it now.

"Yes, I suppose you are right," said Keith

"I'll get the coffee," said Jenny.

She left the room and in next to no time was back with a tray. Dale got out his comb and went over to the mirror and could see what Jenny did next. She knew she had embarrassed Keith. She kissed Keith on the cheek.

"I'm sorry," said Jenny. "It's a bad habit of mine, I'm always embarrassing you aren't I?"

Dale didn't mind, as he knew Jenny loved him and not Keith. He smiled at Jenny through the mirror. Jenny put the tray down on the table, and then poured coffee for the three of them.

Dale turned to Keith. "She's not a bad kid really, but god knows why you didn't snap her up first before I got my hands on her?" said Dale. "You were a bit of a fool there, weren't you Keith?"

"Yes, you can say that again," said Keith "Still it's obvious that you two were meant for each other, and that's not my fault is it?"

Dale put away his comb and came over to the table and picked up his coffee and began to drink it. Jenny smiled at Dale and she knew that she really loved him as much as he loved her. Keith picked up his coffee and drank it and thought of the things Jenny had said on their two dates. Now he thought of what she had said about Barry wearing a brightly coloured t-shirt for the party and wondered. His thoughts were broken into by Jenny.

"Do you want to take your brown shirt on holiday with you?" Jenny asked Dale. Keith looked at his watch.

"Hey come on," said Keith, "we must get back on duty or we will be in trouble. We have to do another tour of the town tonight ok?"

He looked at Jenny and gave her a kiss, this time with Dale's permission.

"Have a super holiday Jenny," said Keith. "I'll see you when you get back. God bless and thanks for the coffee. Bye."

Dale and Keith then went over to the table by the door and picked up their guns. Dale gave Jenny another kiss. "See you about seven love," said Dale.

They put on their guns and were ready for duty. The two men walked down the street and continued talking. As they did so they checked the doors of the stores and looked in windows. The street was almost deserted and looked not unlike those old cowboy towns. As they walked along they saw the doctor come out of one of the houses after making a visit. He saw them and stopped by his landrover and waited for them to get nearer.

"Hi, lads," he called out.

The doctor was in his fifties, slightly greying hair and had a nice kind homely face, but tonight he was worried and almost heartbroken.

"Hi," said Keith

Keith looked round to see if anyone was near and then spoke to the doctor.

"He's told you then," said the doctor. "I said he could, but no one else, you understand?"

"Yes," said Dale. "I'm sorry, don't worry it wont go any further than us."

"That's ok. I asked the chief to put you two on the case. She's in a bad way, gone into complete shock now, can't even get her to speak about it, she's just lying there staring into space," said the doctor.

He paused and took out his hankie and rubbed his head.

"I just don't know what to do for the best. So I'm sending her to the city for treatment. There I know they will help. The thing is, he stole everything. Her earrings, necklace and what little money she had, poor kid, just a kid. I'd like to get my hands on that bastard." said the doctor angrily.

"The son of a bitch," he went on. "Instead she has to carry the scars for the rest of her life as well as what he did to her, as if that's not enough."

The doctor put away his hankie and got into the landrover, turned on the engine and bade farewell to the two officers. Just as he drove off, he turned.

"Get the bastard for me will you?" pleaded the doctor.

"Sure doc," said Dale. "We will."

They watched as he drove off to his house in the centre of the town.

About nine miles away from town Sam and Bennett approached at breakneck speed. They were very glad to see the nearing buildings of Zimba. The town zoomed closer. Bennett slowly brought the landrover to a halt, and turned off the engine.

"We've got to get rid of these shirts," said Bennett. "They stink like hell."

He removed his hat and brushed his hand through his hair.

"Yes I agree with you on that score," said Sam. "Have you been to this town before?" He looked at Bennett's sweaty face.

"Naw, not for many years," said Bennett, taking a squashed packet of fags from his pocket.

"Do you know anyone here?" asked Sam.

"Nar, mmm, hang on a minute, I reckon I do know someone," said Bennett.

"Yeah who?" asked Sam, taking a cigarette from his pocket., It was somewhat dirty.

"Shit," said Bennett "even my fags are bloody done in."

He threw the packet to the ground in disgust.

"If my memory serves me right, there is an old native living on the outskirts of the town who I once knew," said Bennett. "Yeah I know I used to have him to help me on hunting trips, pretty good he was; now I think back to it." He got out of the jeep.

He kicked the fag packet away from where it had landed, just in front of his feet, and then picked it up.

"Do you reckon he will help us?" asked Sam.

He broke his cigarette in half and flicked it away with his index finger.

"He owes me," said Bennett.

"Does he?" said Sam.

He got out of the jeep, after throwing the fag packet away in the box in the back of the vehicle. He then went over to a small patch of bushes, unzipped his pants and had a pee. He continued talking to Bennett.

"Why's that, and what for?" asked Sam.

Bennett joined him in the bushes. The sound of water had made him get the urge, plus the amount of drink he had consumed.

"I saved his life for what it's worth. Some bull elephant charged him one day, if I hadn't been quick he'd have been squashed to hell, so I reckon he will help us." They both zipped up their pants.

"Come on. Let's get going," said Bennett. "They will smell us coming from a mile off."

They got in the landrover., Sam picked up the whiskey bottle that was in the box next to the others but it was next to empty, so he put it back. All the beer had gone as well.

"We'll be in town by ten, if we hurry," said Bennett as he eased himself into the driving seat and turned on the engine.

Sam was thrown backwards as Bennett slammed it into gear and rammed his foot down hard.

"The sooner we get cleaned up the better", said Sam.

"Yeah," said Bennett. He held on hard to the steering wheel.

MEANWHILE BACK IN TOWN.

The chief switched on his desk light, as it was getting dark. His head was beginning to ache with all the work he was doing..

"I'm getting too old for this lark," he said to the photo on his desk.

His thoughts were interrupted and brought to an abrupt halt by a knock on his office door; the knock was repeated, louder this time.

"Come in," he called.

Susan entered the room. She was about nineteen, slim and blonde. She had stunning green eyes and a worried look on her face. The chief did not notice the look at first. In her hand she carried a folder.

"Ah Susan, I didn't know you were working tonight, why are you here?" asked the chief.

Susan gave a sharp look of anger.

"Well," she said angrily. "I don't have anything else to do or anywhere else to go."

She pushed her hand forward with the folder as if hoping to change the subject.

"Forensic have just sent these down for you to look at," she said.

She put down the folder on the desk in front of the chief.

"Why is that then?" asked the chief as he picked it up. He took out the photos and x-rays; he flicked through them with a puzzled look on his face. He eyed Susan up and down from behind his desk.

"Mmm, they look like a lot of tree cones," said the chief as he read the report.

Susan came round the desk and looked at the photo from the side.

"What are those small dots and those tiny fish-shaped things?" she asked.

"I don't know," said the chief. "I've never seen anything like that before; mind you these photos are blown up a lot from the real size, Take a look at this one."

"I've just typed the report," said Susan. "I find it very hard to believe."

"We haven't got the equipment here to do more tests on these things," said the chief.

"In other words you don't know what it is really?" said Susan.

The chief put down the photos and sat back in his chair.

"No, that's perfectly true," he said, looking up at Susan's worried face. "Look, tell me why you are so snappy tonight?" said the chief. "Didn't your dinner go down well or even go at all because I would say you are about to bite my head off? What's happened to Jamie?"

He put his arms on his desk while Susan turned back and folded her arms; she put her hand up after a second or two and wiped away a tear. The chief pretended not to notice.

"Oh, well," he said. "There's nothing else to do but to send this lot off to the city, right?"

Susan nodded.

"Yes, do you want me to arrange it?" she asked.

"No," said the chief. "I'll do that."

He dropped his hands to his desk and asked, "By the way what happened to your date?"

"Oh," said Susan. "He's gone, seems he had to go to work in the city."

"Oh," said the chief and said no more.

He put the photos and x-rays back in the folder, then he jotted a few words on a piece of paper and put it in the folder. He put the lot into a large envelope and sealed it. He looked again at Susan's glum face and he suddenly became very sympathetic. He reached into his top pocket and pulled out a clean hanky.

"What's up Susan?" he asked.

He got up from his seat and went over to where she was standing. Her back was still turned away from him.

"Come on love, tell me all about it." He put his arms around her shoulder. "Another lover's tiff? Only this one hurts a bit more than the last one. Why's that then? asked the chief. "Come on Susan, do tell me after all I am your father," he said.

Susan put her head gently on his chest and began to sob quietly.

"Yes dad," she said.

She rubbed her eyes as tears cascaded down her tanned face like glittering pearls running over a waterfall. Sympathy filled his heart as he stood holding her in his arms; again he glanced at the photo on his desk. Girls are so different he thought, so difficult to bring up and he wished Sally, his wife, was still alive. Susan pulled back her shoulders and wiped away some of the tears and stood looking into his face.

"I'm sorry about this dad," she said.

She breathed deeply and sighed, her wet lashes gleamed as she looked at him.

"I'm not usually like this, am I? It's nothing really."

The chief took a chair from behind the door, and placed it near to his own, then he pressed his intercom button.

"No calls for the next ten minutes," he told the desk.

"Right sir," came the answering woman's voice.

"Thanks dad," said Susan, smiling at him.

"It's about Jamie isn't it?" asked her father, sitting down next to her.

"Yes," Susan said, as she twisted the damp hanky between her fingers. "Oh, I don't know what to think. You see we had three days leave starting yesterday." She lifted her head and looked at her father. "He promised to spend those days with me because tomorrow we would have been together for a whole year; it's a sort of anniversary." She wiped away a few more tears that kept welling in her eyes. "Now he's gone and come up with some cock and bull story that he has to work. Dad, I was so looking forward to those days, I'd even got it in my mind he might even ask me to marry him. We have talked about it. Now it has all gone to pot. I was so mad

I shouted at him and went off in a huff. I love him so much, dad. Why do things always get spoilt by me?"

"Oh come on love," said her father. "Things can't be that bad can they? I'm sure he will come and see you before tomorrow, he may even phone you here. If he loves you and can't take one argument from you then he's not the man I thought he was."

"Oh," said Susan. "It's just that he's always fobbing me off with some story or other, but this one was the limit. He said one of the pilot's wives is in premature labour so he had to take over his flight schedule, and when he said that I just saw red. He must think I'm an idiot to fall for that one."

Susan lifted the hanky to her nose and sniffed back some more tears.

"Do you know Susan, you are just like your mother? The way I remember her when I first met her," said her father sadly, looking at her.

Susan suddenly felt very guilty, pouring out all her troubles to her dad who had no one to pour out his troubles too.

Before she had realised what she had said, she added, "He's got another woman, I know it, I just know it."

A tear came and clung for dear life to the corner of her eye and finally fell. The chief sat and looked at his daughter for a minute, and then he took her hand.

"Right my girl," he said, in a firm but gentle voice. "I know you have worked with me now for quite some time and I may say you do a damned good job. You can hold your own, but you are also stubborn."

Susan looked sharply at her father and pulled her hand away but he took it again.

"Now, now don't be like that, it isn't true," he said. "I know what Jamie means to you."

He held on fast to her as she tried to get up.

"If ever two people were meant for each other, it's you two," he continued.

Susan stopped pulling away and stared at her father's face. It was full of compassion.

"Come on," he said. "I'm willing to bet that Jamie told you the truth and if he had any choice in the matter whatsoever he would be spending his time with you. Why ever should he bring up a story like that? It's so easy to check, don't you see honey? Look Susan, all you have to do is pick up that phone and ask. I'm not going to because I believe Jamie." He picked up the phone. "You do it if you don't believe him, but love, real love starts with trusting someone."

Susan hesitated; she put her hand towards the phone.

"If you think that for just a few seconds, you will see I'm right, just imagine, Jamie trying to avoid seeing you. Don't you think he could have thought of a better story than that, one that could have been checked? Anyone could check it," said her father.

He replaced the phone, and Susan thought about it for a moment, then her face brightened up.

"I was really going to phone, wasn't I?" she said, putting her hands in her lap. "I'm such a fool aren't I? However do you put up with me?" she fumbled for an excuse and turned away ashamed of herself.

"Susan," said her father. "If I didn't know you better I'd say you had a bit of jealousy inside that pretty head of yours."

"It's only because I think so much of him dad," she said as she turned and got up smiling at him. By now his head was aching and he opened the drawer and took out some tablets.

"You've got one of your bad heads again dad?" asked Susan. "I'm just scared that he will meet someone else on the plane and forget all about me."

"Now, now," said her father. He walked over to the fountain and pulled down a cup, and pushed it under the bottle and got some water. He threw the two tablets into his mouth and took a drink, and then he threw the cup into the nearby bin.

"Stop, now my girl, don't be silly.," He came and sat down on the corner of the desk, and kissed her hand. "If he was going to do that he would have done it a long time ago. You'll have to learn my girl that part of a love relationship is trusting a person explicitly, and my girl I think you have learnt that today." He looked into her eyes and went on, "As you and Jamie get older you will begin to learn that two people can love so deeply that it hurts. Jamie maybe can see that because he is older than you. It's the sort of test that both of you are going through and remember you don't go through it alone."

"It feels like it sometimes though dad," said Susan.. "But why does it always hurt so much?"

"Yes I know, but no one gets something for nothing, one has to work at it, very hard sometimes to achieve it. Money is of no real importance if you have each other. That should be enough, ok?"

He patted her hand to reassure her.

"Sorry dad," said Susan.

She got up and went towards the door. She smiled but her eyes were still red from crying. She turned and went back for the chair. She stopped and put her arms around her father's neck and kissed him on the cheek and then let go.

"How's your headache, is it going?" she asked. "I'm a selfish bitch aren't I? Sorry, here's me babbling all my troubles to you and you have no one to tell yours to, since mum died four years ago. Haven't you ever thought of getting married again dad?" she finished, with a questioning look.

She looked tenderly into his tired eyes.

He smiled; he was pleased to see she had cheered up at last.

"Yes I have," he said. "But I haven't found the right lady yet, and I'm too tied up with the job at the moment and well you know I seldom have time to socialise."

Susan smiled and placed her hand in his.

"Well," she said. "I'll have to see what I can do about that then won't I? Anyway I must get back to work."

She put the chair away behind the door, waved goodbye and left.

"See you later," she called.

"Yes sure, bye," answered her father.

Bennett was right about the time. It was just two minutes past ten o'clock when he brought the landrover to a halt outside the bar. With them they had the old native that Bennett had spoken about earlier. He had done them proud; by their appearance he had cleaned up their pants and had given them clean short-sleeved t-shirts, although they were very brightly coloured. The native had also hidden their rifles behind the back number plate in an oblong box that stretched the whole length of the bumper. This was well hidden and looked like part of the vehicle. They were safe and they were not worried. Neither of them had seen anything or anybody since hitting the town. They were seen by a pair of white staring eyes that watched them for a few minutes as they arrived. From the minute of their arrival they had been watched by Jason who was once more roaming the town.

The two men and the native entered the bar. They were confident about their appearance as they entered the double storey building next to the Quartermaine stores. It was dimly lit with oil lamps and a smoky haze hung over the place. As the three men entered the bar they were immediately stared at because of the native who was with them. In the corner sat Cindy the actress, smartly dressed in an off white safari suit. With her sat her producer husband. He was very dark haired and slim. He also was very smart. By the side of them was a stack of suitcases. Three were dark brown, the others were too small hand cases. There were also two cream coloured ones and a black handbag. On the other side of the room sat a deeply tanned white woman wearing a bright red low cut dress showing all. She smoked a cigarette held in a long holder and was somewhat under the influence of drink. She was about thirty-five and the town's whore; anyone's for the asking for a small fee. She eyed the native with flashes of her eyes. She had obviously had him before and knew what to expect. She also eyed Bennett, a stranger to her and Sam.

Chubby, the man behind the bar and also the boss saw the native and eyed the two men up and down.

"I ain't serving that pig," said Chubby referring to the native as the men reached the bar.

"Why my good fellow?" said Sam. "He's with us."

Chubby, because of his size, leaned over the bar and grabbed Sam by the shirt collar and pulled him towards him. Chubby was well named. He was a mean bastard and his size was gruesome and anyone in their right mind wouldn't be wise to take him on. Sweat began to run down Sam's face. It was bright red, and he felt very hot. Chubby noticed the swelling on the side of Sam's neck.

"Any more from you young man," said Chubby, spitting into Sam's face "and I'll beat your brains out you big poofter."

Bennett, who was more of a man than Sam, gambled on Chubby being a bluffer and grabbed hold of his wrists. He didn't want any more trouble so staring Chubby deep in the eyes he squeezed hard and Chubby let go of Sam.

Looking at Bennett, he said, "Get that filthy bastard out of my sight. He makes me sick." Chubby looked at the native and stared hard at Sam who was straightening his clothes

Chubby wiped his hands.

At the other end of the bar stood a man in his early thirties who was looking at Bennett. He was a half-caste. For a second, Bennett thought he knew him but couldn't remember from where.

His eyes met those of the man for a minute and he paid no heed to him. The man paid for his drink and left the bar. Bennett was still trying to remember where he had seen him before. He turned and asked the native, if they should leave. Then the woman in the red dress came over to the bar and draped herself around Bennett's shoulders.

Bennett raised his eyebrows.

"Hi, stranger," said the woman.

"I'm going to sit down over there in the corner," said Sam. He had seen the way Bennett tackled his women many times before.

"Here's your drinks," said Chubby passing them across the bar, still eyeing the native and Sam.

Sam took his drink and walked away to the corner of the bar.

"I'm going to get my drink down and get some sleep," he said. "I feel knackered."

"Two more please Chubby," came a call from the other corner; it was the other woman's husband. He held up his glass as he called to Chubby.

"Yeah, you do that," said Bennett to Sam. Bennett had now turned and saw the other woman, her long slim legs showed from a slit in her pencil slim skirt. Bennett tipped his glass at her, the woman turned away in disgust. Bennett's eyes never left her for a second and he pushed the whore away. "I've got other things on my mind," he said to her.

"Suit yourself," she said laughing at him. "Plenty more fish in the sea," she paused. "That's if you know where the sea is," she ended sarcastically. Bennett made a disgusting sign and she got very annoyed and took a swipe at him.

"I wouldn't do that if I was you," said the native as he grabbed her arm. "Surely we can find something to do," he grinned at her.

"Why not?" said the whore. "It seems that I recall that we have had fun before. Yes well, are you going to get me another drink?" she asked. "Ok, all right," said the native smiling. He ordered a drink.., Chubby stared at Bennett as he served him, and then the native led her out of the bar.

She turned as she reached the door and looked at Bennett.

"Who the hell does he think he is anyway, Christ or something? Even he doesn't have a say in what I do or not," she said.

"Sure," said the native. "Not here, at your place, eh?"

Sam went over and sat down and the two other people came into the bar., Bennett was still stood at the bar staring at the woman and her husband in the corner and Chubby tried to make light conversation with Bennett.

"Ain't I seen you around these parts before?" said Chubby, pouring out drinks for the couple in the corner and putting them on a rusty tray.

"Ain't none of your business either," said Bennett. "Give me another drink ok?" He slid his glass to Chubby who refilled it with whiskey.

"What's wrong with your pal's neck?" asked Chubby, pushing the drink along the counter.

"Oh, nothing." "Is it a birth mark or something like that?" he asked again.

Bennett then remembered the horror he had seen before and turned to look at Sam who by now had wedged himself in a far corner seat, put his hat over his head and folded his arms and was fast asleep.

"Yeah, that's right," said Bennett. "It's a birth mark."

"Maybe that's why he is a bit strange and the way he is," said Chubby. He picked up the tray and opened the bar top to get out.

"Anyone ever tell you?" said Bennett, putting down his glass.

"Tell me what?" asked Chubby.

He still had the tray of drinks in his hand as he looked at Bennett again.

"That you talk a load of bullshit," said Bennett.

Chubby did not reply and took the drinks over to the couple in the corner. As he came back he asked the newcomers what they wanted to drink.

MEANWHILE BACK AT POLICE HEADQUARTERS

The chief walked briskly back to his office. The time was about ten thirty five am.. After a word with the technician in the forensic lab about the photos and x-rays he opened his office door, went in and sat at his desk. He was still perplexed about his daughter's love life. He could still see her face as he sat with his back towards the opened window. He wondered if in any way he was to blame for his daughter's insecurity. He had asked himself this question so many times before. He looked at the photo of his wife on his desk and leaned back and looked at the ceiling. His eyes followed the wall and he wondered "why did you have to take her away from me.'? He wasn't even sure if it had been his fault. The coroner said she died from an accident she had had some years before and nobody could have foreseen that because of that she would die so suddenly a few years later from a brain tumour. He leaned forward and pressed the intercom button.

"Get Fletcher for me, and before you say anything, yeah I know he is off duty, but wherever he is get him for me," ordered the chief.

"Yes sir," said a female voice.

"Try his home first, see if he's there, ring me when you have got him,", said the chief.

"Right away sir," said the woman.

The chief then spotted the handkerchief that Susan had used to dry her tears, the one he had lent her. He picked it up. It was still damp, and he put it in his pocket. His head still ached so he took two more tablets from the bottle in his desk, then he sat back in his chair. After taking the tablets he closed his eyes for a few minutes. He put his hands behind his head and let his mind drift back to when he first met his wife and that fateful morning when she had died. He had woken earlier than usual and had decided to get up quietly and make Sally a nice cup of tea. He was on duty at seven am and it was only when he took the tea up to her he realised something was very wrong and that she would never wake up again. She was in the deepest sleep of all, the sleep that lasted forever. His thoughts were interrupted by the buzzing of the intercom. He put his finger on the button.

"Sir," a voice said.

"Yes," he said.

"Fletcher is on his way," said the woman.

"Thanks," he said.

He let the intercom button go and picked up some papers and started to read them and then sat back once more. On the wall opposite the window hung a mirror. It was fixed just at about his height. As he sat at his desk his attention was caught by a movement in the mirror and he could see a boy's head. He pretended not to have noticed and picked up the phone.

"Get me a free line in about ten minutes," he said.

"Yes sir," said a female voice.

"Thanks," said the chief.

He put the phone down and pressed the intercom button.

"Sir?" asked a voice.

"Send John Smith in for a moment will you?" asked the chief.

"Yes sir," said the voice.

Within a few minutes there was a knock and John entered the office. He stood by the desk while the chief wrote something on a scrap of paper.

He wrote, "There is a young boy outside my window. Will you please go and fetch him quietly without any fuss? He's apt to leave sticky things around." He handed the note to John and John made to leave the office. As he did so, the chief stopped him.

"Oh John," said the chief. "I want you to carry out this order straight away, it's very important, do you understand? We could be in a very sticky situation if you don't."

John looked puzzled as he was given the piece of paper, as this was not the usual thing he was asked to do. He was not going to ask why as his job was to obey orders and that was that so he took the paper and went out of the office.

Just then the phone rang. The chief picked it up.

"Sir, your line is clear now," said a voice.

The chief then rang the number 778349. He waited for the ringing tone to stop.

"Camaconga University of Science," said a voice.

"Put me through to Professor Deater Hayes, please," asked the chief.

"Hold the line please," said the voice. "Putting you through now."

"Thank you," said the chief.

He was still looking in the mirror and he could still see the top half of the boy's head.

"Hello, can I help you?" said a male voice.

"Deater, is that you? said the chief. "George here."

"Hi George, what a surprise, what can I do for you? By the way how is Susan?" Deater asked.

"She's fine," said the chief, and then the phone began to crackle.

"Damn awful line we've got here," said Deater. "Anyway what's up? Why are you phoning? Is it to say that you are coming to the city? You know you are welcome to come and stay any time. Hey, can you hear me all right? Damn awful line we have here."

"Yes," said the chief. "How's Sally and those pretty daughters of yours?"

"They are all fine," said Deater. "Maybe Susan would like to come with you. Sally would like that I'm sure. Well, when are you coming up? We haven't seen you for ages."

"Listen Deater, I haven't phoned you about that, I have a bit of a problem down here and I was wondering if you could help," said the chief.

"Yes sure, what's the matter?" asked Deater.

"I'm sending you some photos and x-rays of what can best be described as a sort of seed. We can't send the seed thing itself because of special circumstances but I won' t go into that now. What we have done is to blow up the x-rays and photos of the thing, both of the original size and colour, and I'm sending them to you on the midnight Chinook, so they should reach the airport about one thirty. If you could arrange for them to be picked up I will be most grateful."

"Yes sure George, anything to help," said Deater. "What's so special about these photos?"

"I don't know," said the chief.

There was a scuffle and a yell from outside the window.

"What the hell is that?" asked Deater, who had heard the noise on the phone.

"Oh nothing," said the chief. "Just some kid who is going to get himself into a mess."

"What do you mean mess?" asked Deater.

"Oh nothing really, some kid who has been buggering up my car," said the chief.

"Yeah, I know what you mean," said Deater, laughing. "We've had a lot of it in the city. All right George, you get those things off to me and I'll have a look at them ok? I don't know what I can do unless I see the real thing."

"Thanks" said George. "I'll get them off right away, let's see it's nearly eleven fifteen, so I had better get a move on. I may see you later if necessary, but do get your specialist to try to find out what the thing is. I'll send Fletcher to the airport right away. You'll see the report inside; I think it's important, thanks." He put the phone down.

AT THIS MOMENT BACK AT THE POLICE H.Q.

The desk sergeant, John Smith had hold of the boy, and he had slung him over his shoulder and was carrying him into the office. He knocked on the door.

"Do come in, John," said the chief.

He entered the office and shut the door behind him. Two or three people had come out into the corridor to see what all the commotion was about. They all laughed when they saw what was happening.

"Someone's in for a tanning," said a nice looking forty year old woman who had come out of her office near the reception desk.

"Yes," said Susan who had come out of her office to go to the toilet. "I can remember getting a few of those," she said as she patted her bottom. "I can still feel them sometimes," she went on.

"Really?" said the woman, who laughed. "Is he that bad?"

"Oh no," said Susan. "Not now." She looked at the woman and said, "You are new here aren't you?"

"Yes, does it show that much?" the woman asked Susan.

"No, don't be silly," Susan laughed. "That's my father in there."

"Oh I see," said the woman. "I'm sorry, I didn't know." She put her hand on Susan's arm. "I've not said anything out of place have I?"

"No, of course not," said Susan. Besides, it's not ethical to talk about it, that's all."

BACK IN THE CHIEF'S OFFICE

"Good man," said the chief. "Set him down there and empty his pockets, after all we don't want to punish the wrong boy, do we?"

"You leave me alone mister," said the boy struggling. "I ain't done nothing wrong."

"I'll leave you to get on with it sir," said John.

"No," said the chief as John was about to leave. "I may need a witness for what I'm about to do."

"Who? Me sir?" asked John. "Right sir."

John went over to the window and closed it so no one could hear the noise.

"You ain't going to beat me are you mister?" asked the boy, who was by now very scared. He was a scruffy little devil with jeans that had patches on the knees. "If you do," he said pouting, "then I'm going to tell my pa."

His name was Bill., He stood with his legs slightly apart, hands on his hips, and stared at the chief.

"And, who might that be?" he asked the chief, who was facing him.

"I ain't going to tell you, so there," said the boy, stiffly.

John returned to the boy and made him turn out his pockets. In them he found a whistle, a piece of string and on the end of it a lollipop, also some cigarette ends and a gold chain with a bead in the centre. The chief noticed this and picked it up. It was too good for the boy to own himself.

"Where did you get this from?" the chief asked the lad, picking it up. "You been stealing?"

"I ain't saying," said Billy.

The chief then picked up the lollipop. "And whose tank were you going to dangle this in tonight?" he asked the boy.

"I ain't saying," said Billy defiantly again.

"So," said the chief. "You know the consequences of you not speaking then, don't you?"

So saying, he took the boy over his knee and, holding him tight, gave him the hiding of his life. The boy let out a yell; the chief's hand came down time and time again. Just as he finished, a tired and bemused Fletcher came through the door. After knocking first to no avail, the boy's cries had made it impossible for the chief to hear him. He had been to the main desk before and had asked the woman what the chief wanted, but she didn't know. He also asked where John was because he was supposed to be on duty. Now he had found both John and the chief in the office. When he saw what the chief was doing he looked at John and winked.

"Sorry sir," said Fletcher. "I did knock."

"That's all right," said the chief. "Come on in."

He turned to the boy. "You won't be doing that again in a hurry will you?"

"You great big bully," said Billy, rubbing his backside. "You wait till I tell my dad, he's bigger and stronger than you and he'll be round to beat you up. Wait till I tell him, that's all, just wait."

"Why I never laid a finger on you, did I, men?" asked the chief.

"What sir, did you speak to us?" they asked.

"He said I hit him and beat him up. Did you see me do that?" asked the chief. He winked and the boy saw him.

"It's a trick," said Billy. "I saw you wink, you did beat me."

"Sorry sir," said the two men. "We didn't see anything."

"Off you go," said the chief to Billy. "And don't let me catch you doing anything like that again."

The boy flew out of the office and down the corridor after calling the three men a few choice names, words that a boy of his age should not have really known.

OUTSIDE IN THE RECEPTION AREA

Out in the hall there was a lot of commotion going on. Dale carried in a young native boy, his small limp body swinging from side to side. Keith followed close behind with a prisoner. It was the man who had been in the bar earlier.

"Get in there, you son of a bitch," said Keith.

He pushed the man through the door.

"And don't try anything either."

The chief ,on hearing the commotion, came out into the hall with Fletcher just behind him.

"What the hell's going on here?" asked the chief as he reached the main desk.

"Book him," said Keith. "Murder one, he's killed the kid."

Dale laid the boy carefully across two seats that were side by side in the main hall. He checked for a pulse but could not find one; he then checked the boy's eyes. John came out from behind the desk and the woman came out also.

"John, get the doc quickly, he's barely breathing," said Dale, looking up.

"Right," said John. He left the desk and rushed through the door.

"What's happening?" the woman asked., She bent down beside Dale; she looked at Dale then at the still body of the boy.

"Is there anything I can do?" she asked. She took hold of one of the boy's hands, and still clenched in it was the strange cone-shaped object.

"Look," she said, "It's a seed or something."

Fletcher bent down and took it from her. The chief nodded and Fletcher put it in the folder in the brown envelope for the city.

"You get off, I'll see to him," said the chief as he walked over to Keith.

"Right sir," said Fletcher and he left the station.

"How did this happen?" the chief asked Keith.

The prisoner continued to struggle and tried to get away.

"We were passing the store downtown, sir, when Dale remembered he had to pick up some things for Jenny," said Keith.

The chief eyed the prisoner.

"Stand still you pig!" he said.

Earlier Dale had done some shopping for Jenny..

"Well sir, you know he is off in the morning," said Keith.

"Come on, come on," said the chief. "Get it out, I want a report not a bloody notebook."

"Well, Dale had seen a rifle in the window," said Keith.

"So," said the chief, wiping his brow with a hanky.

"It wasn't there when we passed just a while ago, so we checked again, and found the kid by the back door, and the door was ajar. Well you can guess the rest. We caught him inside trying to steal the lot," said Keith.

Keith threw a box of cartridges on the desk and handed the rifle to the chief.

"I can see this is going to be one of those nights," said the chief. "Heaven knows why it's always got to be you two."

"Ok, go and lock him up," said the chief to another officer who had come on the scene.

At this point the doctor came through the door.

"You need me sir?" he asked the chief.

"Oh no, not another one?" he asked.

He thought it was another rape case only worse than the last one. The woman got up, she caught the eye of the chief just for a second then she went back to her office and slowly closed the door behind her.

She looked through the glass, unbeknown to the chief, who was talking to the doctor. He bent down to examine the boy.

"Sorry," said the doc., He got up, took his stethoscope from his ears and said, "he's dead."

"Poor little bugger," said Dale as he stood up. He was very angry. Keith was also very upset.

Keith made a grab at the prisoner.

"You bastard," he yelled, and hit him full in the face.

"Aw shit man," said the prisoner, holding his nose, which was bleeding profusely now.

The officer held him fast, arms behind his back.

"He's only a fucking native, why the fuss?" asked the prisoner. "They are two a penny out there; they die like pigs every day." He spat at Keith who was being restrained by Dale.

"You son of a bitch," said Keith.

"Cool it man," said Dale. "It's too late, you'll do no good. You are no better than he is. Let the law deal with him".

"Get him out of my sight," said the chief. "You two get a report done and then resume your duties."

The chief tapped Keith on the shoulder, and turned to John.

"Better get him fingerprinted and a mug shot too," he said.

"Yes sir," said Keith He picked up the boy's body and took it to the morgue.

"You get that report to my office as soon as possible. Then we can send along the line of information about that man," said the chief.

"Yes sir, right away," said John.

"I'll be in my office," said the chief.

He turned and walked down the corridor., He put his hand to the back of his neck, sweat was making his collar wet.

"Christ, that's all I need now is an attack of malaria."

He opened the office door and went in. He slammed the door behind him. He took a drink from the fountain, went to his desk drawer and took another two pills from the bottle. He sat down at his desk, pulled off his shoes and put his feet comfortably on the desk. He sat there with his eyes closed for a second. The night breeze coming in the window was very pleasant, he thought, to himself 'if I take many more of these damn tablets I shall give myself an overdose.'

MEANWHILE OUTSIDE THE TOWN

The two eyes that had previously watched the two men and the native enter the town had returned with their owner to one of the outlying farms. These were mostly rundown places, not much more than shanty type huts of wood, a few fenced off areas with one or two horses, a couple of rough looking cows, tough as old boots that yielded little or no milk, but enough to suffice.

In one of the huts sits an old half caste native woman with a shawl around her feeble shoulders. She sits scratching at the hearth where there is a small fire to keep her old bones warm. Around the hut are dirty curtains at each window, some crockery on the old wooden dresser, and a loaf of bread going mouldy. She has no shoes on her feet; her dress is torn, once it had been decent, brown with printed flowers all over it. The whole place, although old could do with a damn good clean., It had a quaintness about it and it had once been quite nice. The old woman was now too old to keep it clean.

She sits humming an old song that she once learnt when she was a slave years ago when she suddenly hears a noise in the dark. Only her face is lit by the light from the fire.

"Be that you boy?" she called out, not even bothering to look up.

"I said be that you boy?" she squinted her eyes and turned to see who it was.

"Ain't you in a talking mood then boy?" she asked.

"Oh I know, you's in one of them moods ain't ya, where you been this time of night, to the town again eh?" she asked.

From out of the darkness of the door where he had just entered the hut stepped a native, his big eyes shining.

"Yer gran, it's me," said the native He was dressed in white man's jeans and a brightly coloured shirt.

"You bedding down for the night then?" she asked him.

"No, why?" he asked standing in the shadow.

"You been lying to me ain't you?" she asked.

She turned to look at him. She was in a wheelchair; she put her hand down and tried to turn the chair round.

"Why do you say that?" he asked, "I ain't lied to no one."

"You's lie to me now boy." she said looking at his eyes in the darkness.

"Cos I found your boxes hidden under the stairs," she went on. "An where does you think you's going then boy?"

She held the poker in her hand, then she ran her cuff up across her nose and sniffed.

"I'm leaving this rat hole for good," said the boy.

He was about twenty., He put down the brown paper bag he was carrying.

"Oh you is, is you?" she said.

"This ere place not good enough for you? It was good enough for your mother, and it should be good enough for you, why ain't you satisfied then. There's food in your belly ain't there?"

"We ain't starving," the boy sneered at her. "It's the only reason because I gets everything, you old bag."

She was surprised to hear him speak to her like that.

"Now you talk to me with a bit of respect boy, does you hear, always snivelling cause you got to do a bit of work. You had it easy lad, you don't know the half of it," she went on. "Why, in my days twas nothing but work from five in the morning til sun set at night, picking berries till your hands bled and run all over, why by the end of the day I'd had more thorns than a porcupine. You wasn't allowed to rest up either, the next day we was back doing the some chores. You's nothing better than a swivelling rat."

"Well, I ain't about to spend the rest of my life in this ere dung heap," said the boy.

He then stepped toward the cupboard under the stairs.

"You been in my boxes?" asked the boy.

"Nope, ain't but what's the betting? I can tell ya everything that's in them," the old woman said, pulling back her chair.

"What do you mean?" he asked.

He opened the catch and took out the box from the cupboard.

"I said to you what you been doing boy?" she said as she spat in the fire, like a snake spitting venom at its victim.

"I heard rumours about young uns being dealt with whites too, seems you'd been leaving your spunk about boy. It whitens and gets you into trouble; you ain't nothing but a pervert as they say. You's a stinking swine mounting them and coming home stinking of they's perfume," the old woman said.

The boy's brain began to fill with fear for the old woman seemed to know everything.

"Stealing and messing around boy will soon get ya caught, that's what it will do, I can see you's in for a hanging boy," she said.

"Oh yeah," said the boy.

He looked through his things in the box.

"Who'd be telling them then?" he asked, looking up.

He was now beginning to sweat profusely; he picked up a handful of money.

"What you got there boy?" she asked, hearing the notes crackling.

He got up quickly and went over to where she sat at the fire and thrust a handful of money in her face. She gasped as he did this. She could see he was very angry, but she was not about to show her fear.

"I've enough here," the boy said, "to start a new life and one where the likes of you ain't around."

"You's thinking of leaving boy?" she asked.

"Yeah," he answered, shaking his hand with the money in it.

"Then who's going to look after me?" she asked. "I ain't about to stay here on my own."

She was by now really scared and pulled her shawl around her shoulders.

"I'm going to make it look like you been robbed and there's nothing you can do about it," said the boy.

He went back to the box and replaced the money in it with the other things. He picked up the parcel and picked up the box. He then rushed up the stairs and began to turn everything out, tearing everything up that he didn't need. He then picked up all his things and put them into a suitcase. He pulled off his bright shirt and tore it in half. He opened the parcel and took out a clean white shirt and put it on, and a new jacket. Downstairs, the old lady heard all the noise and she tried to make it to the door, but as she edged her way slowly across the room, using every bit of power in her frail old body, the boy came down the stairs.

"Get out of my way you old hag," he yelled, his temper was really up now.

"No, no you ain't going to leave me on my own my son," she said. She held up the poker, which she had laid across her lap.

"Stay back here, so you will. Get back up to your room, how dare you?" she said to him.

"Oh, shut up you silly old woman," shouted the boy. "Get out of my way."

He rushed at the wheelchair and pushed it hard after dropping his case. Suddenly it tipped and one of the wheels stuck in a crack in the floorboards. Over went the old lady and she struck her head on the corner of the old wooden dresser. Blood poured from her temple and she lay there bleeding. The boy got up as he also had fallen as he pushed the wheelchair away. He looked at her limp body as it lay bleeding. Suddenly he came to his senses and rushed round the room knocking everything over, and hoping it looked as if someone had been there and upset the place. He picked up his case then replaced it. Seeing himself in a broken mirror , he decided to change his appearance. He cropped his hair short, put on a false moustache and left.

IN THE TOWN OF ZIMBA

Dale and Keith have now resumed their tour of duty and are on their way down the street when they meet the doc on his way out of the store next door to the bar. They stop and chat to him.

"How's the girl doc?" asked Dale.

He unclipped his pistol and checked to see if it was loaded.

"Not so good," said the doc. "She's gone into severe shock and Joe is going to fly her to hospital as soon as possible."

"Will she be ok, though doc, when she comes out of it?" asked Dale.

The doc thought the same and said to Dale, "that's something I can't tell, some do, some don't. I've known cases where they are never the same again."

"Oh no," said Dale, as he put his pistol away.

"It all depends on the amount of shock a kid of her age can take. Then there is a lot of nursing and understanding to come or she will never get better," said the doc.

"Jesus," said Keith.

He took out his cigarettes and offered them. Doc refused the offer.

"How's Nick taking it?" asked Keith.

"I've got to get on now. Nick will have my guts for garters if I don't get some supper down me," said the doctor. "Very badly I'm afraid."

"Right doc," said Dale.

He leant back against the landrover; the three men had driven from the police station into town. Dale and Keith could see one or two people milling around. Two people left the bar; they all knew Dale and Keith.

"Hi you two, still on your rounds?" yelled one of them.

Dale and Keith lit their cigarettes.

"Yes," said Keith, he laughed. "It looks like you're still on yours too."

"What?" said one of them. "You jealous, cause you ain't had any?"

The man waved at them with the palm of his hand facing them.

"Hey," said one of the others to Dale. "Have a nice holiday."

"Yes thanks," said Dale "Cheers."

The group went off down the road singing loudly as they went. Keith stood with his back to the bumper of the land over; he and Dale watched the men and the street as they finished their cigarettes.

MEANWHILE BACK IN THE CHIEF'S OFFICE

The chief sat with his eyes closed. He was remembering how he had first met his wife. It was at a party held once every week for trainee police officers. He had only been there a few weeks when everyone received an invitation.

At first he hadn't wanted to go as his younger brother had told him he had got a girl friend. So he didn't feel like being the one to upset his brother's plans, but after some debate he went along that night, and it turned out to be a grand do. All the trainees were like peacocks, strutting around and dressed to kill. Some came with lady friends and others alone in the hope that they might meet the lady of their dreams. He was one of the hopefuls.

As soon as he sat down he set eyes on a young lady waiting for her partner to come back from the bar with a drink for her. He did not know her name or who her partner was until he saw his brother return with the drinks. He hadn't wanted to interfere in his brother's night so he just watched as he wined and dined her all night long. He wondered if she was aware that he was looking at her. Every so often she put her hand behind her neck and turned round, but he always turned away just at that point. George could also see that his brother was getting slowly drunk. He wondered if she was aware of this.

Sadly, the evening came to an end and he had not been introduced to his brother's girlfriend, and then she was gone.

Suddenly, for some unknown reason he felt empty inside, as if part of him were missing. He climbed into his car thinking at least his brother could have introduced him to her. He could have done that much. Then he started the engine and drove off back to base. As he came to one of the many corners he caught sight of a car's headlights; the car had crashed. It was, to his horror, his brother's car. He had been thrown clear but the girl was trapped inside and unconscious. He looked at his brother who seemed to be unharmed and ran over to the girl in the hope of getting her out, but not knowing quite what to do, or what he would find. He dragged her out of the car and she was out cold. On her temple to one side was a nasty cut from which blood was pouring out. He put her gently on the back seat of his car, then picking up his brother he drove like fury to the hospital and as he left the scene the car burst into flames. Later he found out that she had very severe concussion and waited around to see if she was ok. When his brother came round he severely reprimanded him for his bad behaviour.

George was furious with his brother and a terrible row broke out. It was his date with the girl and George's brother didn't care one way or the other how she was. So from that day they never spoke to each other again. As she got better George became friendly with her and from there love blossomed. Much later, George forgave his brother and was well until that fateful morning some years later. She was rushed to hospital to have a small cyst removed from her neck. He thought of the anxious time he had been through, then he thought of all the good times they had had together. He sighed and this roused him from his memories. His head felt a little better now. This was replaced by a pounding hunger in his stomach. He put his feet down from his desk and bent forward and pressed the intercom button on his desk.

"Yes sir?" asked John, who had now returned to duty.

"Arrange for someone to get some sandwiches and beer bought in for me can you please?" asked the chief.

"Yes sir," said John.

"Got that report done yet?" he asked John.

"Being typed up now sir," said John "and Keith and Dale have gone back on duty."

"Thanks," said the chief. He took his finger off the button.

John asked Marlene to get the food for the chief from the canteen.

MEANWHILE AT THE BAR

Inside the bar, Cindy and her husband had just finished a meal that Chubby had fixed them. Cindy was very tired.

"Have we got to sit here all night?" she asked her husband.

"Why?" he said, wiping his face with a hand towel and then putting it down.

"I'm comfortable, what's wrong with this place?" he asked.

"I feel shitty," she replied.

"Is that unusual?" he asked.

"I've had just about all I can take from you," she answered; she slammed her serviette down on the table. "Why do you have to be so bloody selfish?"

"Oh, my dear," he said, "coming from you of all people, the star of many films. There are people around who might recognise your face, and let's face it you are used to a far bigger audience."

He grabbed hold of her arm and squeezed it hard.

"We could have made three million dollars if you had not been so fussy, me selfish, ha, ha," she said. "Let me out of here."

She tried to pull away. She looked hard into his eyes.

"Let go of my arm, you are hurting me," she whined.

"I haven't finished drinking yet. Now sit down," he commanded.

"I won't," she snapped back at him. "If you had paid the crew more money they would not have called it off."

Some of the other people in the bar were now watching them.

"You will sit down or I'll break your arm," he said.

Outside the bar the two officers Dale and Keith were still smoking and talking.

"What airport do you land at?" asked Keith.

"Zurich," answered Dale.

Inside the bar Bennett had now drunk himself to sleep and had slumped over the bar. His mate Sam was still asleep in the corner with his hat over his face. His arms were folded and he was wedged in the seat.

Keith put his foot on the bumper of the landrover to rest it. Oh how his feet ached. He felt a slight movement on the bumper.

"Why ain't you and Jenny had any kids yet?" he asked Dale.

"I don't see that's any of your business, really is it?" said Dale, stiffly.

He was annoyed that Keith had brought the subject up.

"Now don't get on your high horse, I only asked a question. I don't need a debate about it," said Keith. "But since it's a tetchy question, you are forgiven for giving a spikey answer. No more said, sorry ok?"

Dale felt guilty at the way he had answered Keith.

"I'm sorry," said Dale. "Why did you ask that all of a sudden?"

"I've heard it said in many a film script that to say sorry is a sign of weakness in a man," said Keith, "but I don't agree on that score, it's a load of bullshit you know."

"Why?" asked Dale, throwing away his dog end.

"Because in everyone's life there comes a time he may have to say sorry to save his own life, such as it is, and I ain't talking about dying," said Keith.

He pressed his foot down harder on the bumper and felt it move again. It was soft and springy.

"Such a thing happened to me once," went on Keith. "That's why."

"Oh yeah when was that?" Dale asked his friend as he smiled at him.

"Why?" asked Keith. "If I tell you something you will not tell a living soul."

"Sure, all ears that's me," replied Dale.

"I am a father you know, I got a kid," said Keith.

"Who? When you tell 'em you tell 'em well," said Dale laughing.

"It ain't no laughing matter. It's true," said Keith.

"I'm sorry. You are serious aren't you?" said Dale standing in front of him.

"Yeah," said Keith "I am."

"When did this happen?" asked Dale. "How long ago?"

"Two years ago, my little girl is two next month," said Keith.

He threw his cigarette end away.

"Shit, it's a long story and I won't go into it all now, but what I do know is that if I had had the courage to say sorry I'd still be with that woman and my daughter now," said Keith. "Dad said it was a sign of weakness to say sorry, I suppose he got that from his father."

"Maybe he saw the same films," said Dale.

A grin spread over his face as he saw the funny side of the situation. The two men burst out laughing; Dale grabbed hold of Keith and gave him a friendly hug. Keith's foot slipped and hit the catch and the box flew open, displaying the hidden rifles, and also loads of cartridges. There was also two straightish ivory tusks.

"What have we got here then?" asked Dale who saw the contents first.

"Take a look at this little bundle then. Phew, just take a look," said Dale.

Together they took the rifles out and looked at them and then looked towards the bar. They put them back in the box and clipped it up again. They found empty bottles and cans in the back. They walked over to the bar door and peeped in. There were two people left in the bar besides the man and the woman, Sam in the corner and Bennett sleeping at the bar.

AT THE AIRPPORT

It was five to twelve when Fletcher handed over the folder to the pilot of the Chinook and he was now on his way to get some sleep. He had decided to stay in the vicinity of the airport with a woman he knew, but when he reached her apartment she was out of town, so he returned to the town.

AT THIS POINT IN TIME

The two officers surveyed the occupants of the bar before entering.

"Right," said Dale

"Come on Dale," said Keith.

Keith waved Dale over to the door on the left hand side.

"What can you see?" asked Keith.

"Just one man in the corner and one man at the bar," replied Dale.

"You?" Dale asked Keith. He looked across at Keith.

"Two men and a woman," Keith replied, smiling. They have been making a film about lions in the vicinity," Keith went on.

"What?" said Dale.

"We shouldn't have too much trouble," said Keith, pointing to the couple.

"I know those two," he told Dale.

"We must somehow get them out first," said Dale.

Dale looked towards Bennett and noticed a bulge at his belt.

"Just in case he decides to use that," said Dale.

Dale thought Bennett was carrying a gun, but the bulge was Bennett's whiskey bottle.

"I think the one at the bar has a gun," said Dale.

"I see," said Keith. "So we will walk into the bar just as if we go there every night?"

Keith looked at his watch. "It's almost closing time anyway," he said.

The time was almost midnight. Dale unclipped his pistol and Keith did the same, ready in case of any trouble. Keith pushed open the door and both officers entered the bar.

"Hi Chubby," said Keith, as he came into the bar.

Dale followed Keith closely. Chubby looked up. He was cleaning the last of the glasses before closing the place.

"Any problems tonight?" asked Dale.

"No, hi fellows, want a drink?" asked Chubby.

"No thanks," said Dale. "On duty and all that stuff."

"Sorry," said Chubby. "I wasn't trying to get you to break the rules you understand?"

"Yeah sure," said Keith. He looked across the room at the couple he knew.

"It's been quite a night tonight," said Chubby. "Apart from a few mates of yours earlier on, god knows what they were celebrating, but they all left pissed."

"Yes," said Dale. "We saw them some time ago."

"Still standing, were they?" asked Chubby, smiling.

Dale leaned against the bar and looked at Bennett who was out cold.

"Any trouble from him?" asked Dale.

"He's had it," answered Chubby. "Out for the count, keeps mumbling about something he's seen, keeps saying it was horrible, that's all I've had from him for the last half hour."

"Oh," said Dale.

Keith was looking at the woman. She recognised him and smiled.

"Hi," said Keith as he walked over to her. Now was his chance to get her and her husband out of the bar. He stopped short of the table, the husband looked up at Keith. He was smoking a large cigar.

"Not so hot tonight," he said, as he picked up his drink and stared hard at Keith. He was being sarcastic but Keith could not think why.

"Oh," said the woman. "Take no notice of him he's in a bad mood, and anyone's the target tonight including you. It's just because he's feeling very insecure at the moment. Anyway how are you Keith?"

"Oh me, I'm fine. Why's that?" said Keith.

He was just about to take out a cigarette when he remembered what he was supposed to be doing.

"We lost all our crew," said the woman, looking displeased.

Her husband was making it very obvious that he did not want Keith to stay and talk.

"They, the crew that is, got scared of the lions for some unknown reason. The lions got scared when some noise frightened them. They scared the hell out of all of us come to that," said the woman.

He looked at the bandages on her leg and arm.

"Yes, she's turned into a right bitch," said her husband.

"See what I mean?" said the woman. She turned to her husband. "There's no need to take it out on Keith, or anyone else., Keith might get the wrong idea and think we are unhappy."

"Boy can she act," said her husband sarcastically, again putting down his drink.

Keith didn't want to get involved in any argument.

All he wanted was to get them out of the bar if he could. Besides he had heard rumours about them anyway.

"Do you know anywhere we can stay the night?" asked the woman suddenly. Keith couldn't believe his ears at first.

"I'm really tired and all the hotels seem to be full," she said. "Seems a lot of people turned up on the Chinook for some safari party."

Keith tried to think of somewhere they could stay.

"It's just for one night," she said.

"You god damn it," said her husband. "We are off in the morning. Chinook back to the States, get another film crew and back to the bright lights of the good old USA, of A, and get some people who are not scared of a few lions."

"Why not try Mrs Thomson, just down the road?" said Keith. He pointed and beckoned the woman to the door. "Look," he said. "I'm sorry you are in a mess."

She got up and went to the door with Keith.

"If you go down there and knock on the door, the one with the light outside. I'm sure she will be able to put you up," said Keith. "I'll give you a hand with your cases if you like," said Keith.

"No, thanks, we can manage," said her husband. He got up and came over to the door.

"Manners darling," said the woman. "He's only trying to help. Thanks Keith."

She looked back at him; Keith went towards the cases and was about to pick one up when there was a shout.

"Mind my camera," yelled the woman's husband.

They were helped to the door by Keith and then they left. Over in the other corner was a man who obviously had had too much and had passed out. Suddenly he got to his feet and started shouting that his head hurt.

"Oh, oh," he moaned. "What the hell's happened?"

Keith who had gone outside with the couple had not noticed him there. Dale went over to the man.

"I think it's time you went home and slept it off don't you?" said Dale.

The man nearly stumbled over backwards and headed for the door.

Outside, the woman turned as she reached the other side of the road.

"Can you hear something funny?" she asked her husband and Keith.

"No," said Keith. "Why, what do you mean?"

"A sort of buzzing noise, it's in my ears," she replied. She shook her head.

"Don't be silly darling," said her husband. "It's just that you are tired. I think you have had too many and in the morning you'll have a nasty hangover, and so will I now I come to think of it. Now you've got me hearing things."

"Oh dear," she laughed. "It's the fresh air."

They reached the bottom of the steps as the other fellow rolled past and headed for the houses. The other two headed for the house to which Keith had directed them. Keith watched them go down the road; the other two in the bar were still out for the count.

Dale stood at the bar watching Chubby finish the glasses and waiting for Keith to return.

"What do you intend to do with those two?" asked Chubby "You can't leave them there till morning can you? He's been asleep ever since he came in and he's …"

"No," said Dale. "We have reason to believe that they are poachers, so we are taking them in".

He looked towards the door but Keith still had not come back.

"Right," said Dale. "If you take the one in the corner, I'll take the one at the bar ok?"

"Did you ever see them before?" asked Chubby. "They are strangers to me. I'll get the one in the corner he's a bit lighter than that one"

Dale got up, for by now he had sat and started to keep an eye on Bennett. He put his arm round Bennett's middle and started to drag him to the door.

While Chubby put down his cloth and strolled over to the other man, Sam was still fast asleep. His hat was covering his face and looking down, Chubby called out,

"Oi you, wake up."

He knew Sam had not had so much to drink as Bennett so he assumed he was just asleep rather than drunk.

"Hey you," he called again. "We are closing."

He did not fancy handling him, as earlier he had thought him to be a poof.

"Hey do you hear me, wake up!" he said as he bent forward and poked him. Sam's hat fell from his eyes. Underneath, to the barman's horror, was a massed monster that had enclosed Sam's eyes, nose and mouth and also his ears, with a crust of honeycomb-like material. In absolute horror the barman let out a scream, Sam exploded right in front of him, covering him and all the room with maggots that almost as they touched him began to eat him alive. They stuck to his clothes and skin as they blasted themselves in all directions.

Dale, as he saw what happened, shielded himself and Bennett behind the seating that was all round the room. He dropped Bennett to the floor while blood, guts and pieces of Sam rained all round the room. Some of the maggots landed on his clothes and he brushed them off quickly. He could see what they were doing to the barman who was screaming for help as he rolled in agony on the floor trying to get them off, but it was no use. Soon his cries could be heard no more as they consumed his body, and he became a heap of honeycomb now twice the size it was before. Dale had heard himself screaming as he saw what happened and something hit him on the leg. But because of the panic he did not notice. Bennett had been saved because of the place Dale had dropped him.

Keith heard all the screaming and came rushing into the bar to see what had happened. He stood dumbstruck and looked at the scene with horror.

"Go and get the chief and the doc," screamed Dale, "quickly."

Keith's hand touched the table and when he looked, one of the maggots was on his hand, which was now covered in blood. He quickly wiped it off, twisting and contorting his face as he did so. Then turning, he rushed down the steps and tore down the road to get the chief and the doc. When he reached the doc's house he was puffed out and could hardly talk. Heaving and choking he managed to get doc up. He was in his dressing gown and he headed towards the bar, bag and all.

"What's up?" asked the doc. "Another bar brawl?"

Keith was too dumbstruck to explain and just pointed towards the way he had come. The doc put his coat on and did as he was asked.

"The bar, doc," gasped Keith. "I haven't time to explain, quick."

Keith then rushed down the road to the chief's office.

"Where's the chief?" he yelled out at the woman at the desk.

She was astonished to see the state he was in.

"He's in his office," she said as Keith rushed through the door and without knocking, burst into the office.

He threw open the door, his face was as white as a sheet., The chief was about to ask what was up when he saw the terror and horror on Keith's face.

"Chief," gasped Keith, panting and sweating. "You'd better come quickly, something terrible has happened."

"What, has there been an accident? Has Dale been shot?" asked the chief.

"No no," said Keith. "I don't know what the hell it is, it's horrible that's all I know and there are maggots everywhere. They've eaten the barman."

"You're having me on," said the chief. He got up from his desk and went over to him.

"No sir, come on for Christ's sake quickly," said Keith. "You had better get some men down there quickly, as fast as you can."

"Right, you get back and I'll get down there and see just what's going on," said the chief. "I'll grab the boys from the forensic lab while you're at it."

Keith left the office to go to the lab and return to the bar.

.He left as quickly as he had arrived.

The chief leapt into his landrover and then remembered that the boy had buggered it up.

'Shit,' he said to himself, hitting the wheel.

He got out and rushed down the road as fast as he could. He would have been very embarrassed if anyone had seen him. Hot footing it down the street would have done little for his image. When he got to the bar he found Dale outside, his face almost white with fear. He had dragged Bennett outside and was leaning up against the post at the top of the bar steps.

"What the hell's going on here?" screamed the chief. "Have you two got me here for a drunken brawl or something?"

"No," said doc. "He's just part of it."

"Part of what?" asked the chief.

He climbed to the top of the steps and went towards the bar door.

"How much damage did he do?" asked the chief.

"No sir, you've got it all wrong," said Dale.

The doc came out of the bar; he was standing just inside the porch. He came out backwards and bumped into the chief, who by now was trying to get in. The doc stopped the chief.

"No, if I were you I wouldn't go in there," he said, as he grabbed the chief tightly.

"Why, what's wrong? What's going on?" asked the chief. "What the hell happened?"

"Whatever it is you had better burn it quickly and take no chances, it's eaten Chubby," said the doc.

"What the hell are you talking about?" asked the chief. "You don't expect me to believe that do you?"

He entered the bar to find only a few remains of the barman and a mass of creatures that had eaten him; he stared in horror and backed slowly out. The boys from the lab had now turned up and the chief, white and pale, told them what to expect.

"Don't touch anything and only pick up one or two of those things and then get the hell out of here. You understand?" said the chief.

"Yes sir," they said.

They were only in the bar a few seconds and then they came out. One had managed to get two maggots and the other a piece of Chubby's remains. The chief walked down the steps, saw Bennett and grabbed hold of his collar.

"What the hell happened in there?" he yelled at him. "You bastard, I know you know something about it; I can feel it in my bones. If you do you had better tell me about it or you are for it."

He let go of Bennett, hit the post and rubbed the back of his hand and shrugged his shoulders. Dale had been hit in the leg by a piece of something. He had not noticed it before and now it started to swell.

"I don't know nothing," said Bennett. He was still drunk. "Leave me be."

"Take him back to the station," said the chief. "Book him for being drunk and disorderly."

"For poaching as well," said Dale. He showed the chief the rifle and the box.

The other men came out of the bar and puked over the steps. With them they brought a small black box containing the samples and gave them to the doc who put them carefully in his land rover.

The chief thought about doc's advice and started to give orders to the men. The doc's daughter and son-in-law and two children lived in the house next to the bar. This was also the store. Fortunately, the doc's grand daughter was at the doc's house. She was the one who had been raped. Several more people who had heard the commotion had come to see what was going on.

Stacey, the doc's son-in-law came to the window. He had been awakened by the noise and screaming. After looking out he came downstairs with his housecoat on.

"What the hell's going on?" he called to doc, who saw him and came over to him.

"Stacey, Stacey, get Marie and Kim out quickly and bring everything you need with you and be quick about it," cried the doc.

"Why, what's up?" he asked.

"Don't argue," said the doc. "I haven't got time to explain now just do it ,ok?"

"You men," shouted the chief, "break the window of the store as soon as everyone's out, get all the fuel you can find, pour it round the bar and make sure everything is soaked, and then set fire to it."

Stacey came out after wakening Marie and Kim with a few things they would need and when he saw what was happening he tried to stop them.

"What are you doing?" he yelled, as they broke the windows and poured fuel all round.

"We must burn it to the ground, some monster or something is in there and it's ..." said the chief.

Then he saw Kim and he had no wish to frighten her any more than she had been already. The doc went over to Marie and Kim and shepherded them away to a safer place than where they were standing. The chief then told the men to set light to the bar. This they did without question and then they all stood back and watched it burn down., Screams came from inside as if the monster from within cried out in pain. Stacey had wrapped blankets round Marie and Kim before taking them from the house. Kim was crying, she was very sad to see her house burning down. Marie suddenly came to her senses. Earlier she had been given a sedative and when she saw what was happening she began to cry too.

"Oh no they are burning our store," she cried.

It was getting too hot to stand anywhere near the fire and as the bar and store burned tins of paint from the store began to explode.

"Get everyone away from the area," said the chief. "You men get all the land rovers away from here."

As he called out the orders, the men rushed about doing as he said.

"Dale, you and the men keep an eye on this place until it's finished. Keith, you get back to the office and write out a report and then get back on duty with Dale ok?" said the chief.

"Yes sir," said Keith.

Keith delivered Bennett to the station and put him in a cell with the other prisoner.

"Here John," said Keith. "He needs fingerprinting in a minute. The chief wants information about that guy right away."

John did as he was asked and returned Bennett to the cells. He closed the door and Bennett sat down on the edge of the bed, only to come face to face with the man he had seen earlier.

Bennett dropped his head on the pillow. He was just beginning to realise what had happened, but he wasn't going to tell any more. Keith, after filling out the report, went back on duty with Dale. By now Dale's leg was beginning to swell.

Two hours had passed since Fletcher had got up from his sleep. He had had nothing to eat, so he got himself a coffee and a sandwich and went outside. He stretched and checked that he had everything he needed for his trip. After second thoughts, he had stayed at the airport. He remembered like the good cop he was to check with the chief before he left the bush. He had seen no one so he knew nothing of the goings on in the town. As he drove in, he saw the long pillar of smoke and wondered what was up. Fletcher got out of his landrover after turning off the engine, and then he waited a moment and went into the main hall. John was sat at the desk reading a paper; it was the report the chief had requested.

"What the hell has happened down town?" asked Fletcher, stopping short at the desk.

John told him.

"I'd better go and check with the chief," said Fletcher, as he started down the corridor.

"Here take this with you," said John.

"Yes sure," said Fletcher.

"Thanks," said John.

Fletcher opened the swing doors and headed towards the chief's office. As he did so he passed two more officers carrying some papers.

"Hi," he said.

"Oh hi, still on duty?" they asked.

Fletcher did no more than shrug his shoulders as if to say 'yes'. He soon reached the chief's office and knocked on the door.

"Come in," called the chief.

He was sat at his desk reading the file and fingerprints of Bennett.

Fletcher came in and the chief motioned him to sit down.

"Oh, yes Fletcher, I'm glad you came in, instead of calling in by radio. Did you get those things off?" asked the chief.

"Yes sir," said Fletcher. "I also got my head down for a while as well."

"Good," said the chief.

"So, I'll be off then," said Fletcher.

"Ok, for a moment I thought it was my sandwich and drink I asked for," said the chief. "It takes forever to get some food in this place, doesn't it? Did you hear about the happenings earlier?" asked the chief.

"Yes sir, I did, John from the desk told me. By the way he sent this report along," said Fletcher.

"Yes thanks, it appears that this is more serious than we thought," said the chief. "First the story from the boy and now this, it's getting quite worrying I must admit."

He stood up and went across to the map on the wall Pointing to it, he looked at Fletcher.

"It's all got something to do with this village. I've tried to get information from this guy Bennett, but he's tight lipped, but I'm getting him checked out double quick," said the chief.

"You'd better take someone with you," said the chief.

"Yes sir," said Fletcher.

He looked at the chief who was studying the prints.

"Most of the men are going off duty soon, but Peter Seddons has only been on duty a short while. At the moment he is charge of the prisoners. Get someone to relieve him, and take over his duty." He snapped his fingers. "I know, get John to take over from him and get that new woman who joined us this morning to take over the desk, she'll do. I've not met her yet so a desk job should not be too difficult for her to handle."

Fletcher got up from his seat with a worried look on his face. The chief noticed it.

"What's up?" he asked as he returned to his desk.

"Sir," said Fletcher, "he's not been in the force very long".

"You mean he's not very experienced eh?" said the chief, sitting down.

"Yes sir," said Fletcher, standing with his back to the door.

"Nor, were you once," said the chief.

He leaned over and pressed the intercom button and it crackled.

"Yes sir," said John at the other end of the line.

"John, get Peter from the guardroom can you please? Get that new woman to take your place, and you take Peter's, ok? Get him to wait at the main desk for Fletcher. Oh, but before you do that get me the heliport please," said the chief.

Fletcher left the office and went to pick up Peter.

While the chief waited in the office for his phone call, the phone rang and he picked it up.

"The heliport," said a female voice. It was the one he liked. Even though he could not see her, he knew who she was.

"Thanks," he answered.

"Base here sir, can I help you?" said a man's voice.

The chief did not know but he was talking to the father of the boy who he had given the hiding..

"I'd like a chopper in five minutes please. Thanks," said the chief.

He put the phone down after getting a 'yes sir' from the other end of the line.

There was a knock at the door and in walked doc without waiting for an answer. He and the chief were good friends and both men liked and respected the other.

"Hi, just the man I wanted to see," said the chief.

"I've done the tests you asked for on some of these things, but what I've done is not really enough," said doc. "Besides, I don't like working in the dark, and after what I saw happen at the bar I was scared, so like you said I put them in a sealed box ready for you to take to the city."

"It's my fault, it's just that we have not got the right equipment here," said the chief.

The doc rubbed his ear and scratched it, then rubbed the back of his neck.

"Well, what are we going to do about it?" asked the doc.

"I'm just going to remedy that," said the chief. "I've ordered the helicopter and I'm taking them to the city myself."

He pressed the intercom button.

"Yes sir?" said a female voice.

The chief raised an eyebrow at doc who was watching him closely.

"Did John give you a message?" asked the chief.

"Yes sir," she answered.

"Give John a message for me," the chief said.

"Yes sir," she said.

"Tell him to get someone to take over Dale's duties; I want him in charge here while I'm away. I'm off to Camagonga and will be back in two hours," said the chief.

"Yes sir, I'll do that right away. Do you want transport to the base?" she asked.

"Thanks yes," said the chief.

He let go of the button.

"Now that's what I like," he said to the doc.

"Someone who doesn't ask too many questions and gets right on with the job, none of this so called inefficiency."

"Remind me," he said giving the doc a grin "to find out who she is."

The chief picked up the samples carefully off the table and stubbed out his cigarette and got up ready to leave. As they both went to the door he turned to the doctor.

"How's Nickk? i Any more news?" he asked.

"No," said the doctor. "What about the rapist? Anything on him yet?"

"No," said the chief as they both walked along the corridor and through the swing doors and towards the main desk. The chief headed to the main desk and caught sight of the woman and liked what he saw.

"Your transport's ready sir," she said to him, "and waiting outside."

"Thanks," he said, raising his eyebrow. Then he turned to the doc.

"I want you to contact Deater Hayes, and tell him I'm on my way," said the chief.

They opened the door and went out into the yard. The chief got into the land rover.

"Right," said the doc. "I'll get onto that right away. Bye, see you in two hours."

The officer started the engine and, waving to the doc, the chief was driven to the heliport.

BACK AT THE BUNGALOW

Both Ann and Frank are up and dressed. The time is five o'clock in the morning. Ann went into James's room and sat on his bed.

"Come on you sleepy head," she said. She patted his arm that hung over the edge; this was accompanied by a foot as well. On his big toe was drawn a face. He twitched as he started to wake., He growled and rolled over. "Come on," said Ann, as she slapped his bottom.

"Ouch," said James from within his sleep. "Aw, do I have to mum? It's so early." Slowly, he sat up in bed and rubbed his sleepy eyes.

"You do want to say goodbye to your dad, don't you?" asked Ann, looking down at him.

She bent forward and gave him a kiss on his head, then grabbed his hands and pulled him fully up sitting in his bed. James looked sleepily round the room; his eye caught the window, where Reaker was sitting up in a nearby tree house.

"Yes ok mum," said James. "Ouch, this mat pricks.," He rubbed his foot. Ann got up and went to the door.

"Right then," she said as she reached the door. "I'll wake Mark and you get dressed and washed. There's still some water in the jug., She pointed to a jug on a small table next to the window. Ann still held on to the door as she said this to James. "Besides Reaker will want some breakfast," she smiled." Won't he?"

James walked to the table and lifted the jug. He poured out some water, then he opened the window and Reaker climbed in.

"Hello, baby," said James. "How are you this morning?"

The little animal almost dived into his arms, and licked his face as if he had not seen him for years, and not just the night before.

"Now pack it in," said James laughing. "Here," he said "you stay there while I get washed and dressed and don't knock anything down or mum will hear you."

Reaker did no more than to attack an old stuffed teddy bear over in the corner. It was sitting on a bamboo chair that Frank had made. James washed his face, hands and neck and then dried himself; while he was trying to do so Reaker took a bite out of the toothpaste. There was a shout from downstairs.

"James are you dressed yet? Mark are you up?" called their mother. "Breakfast is ready."

"Coming mum," called James.

James noticed what Reaker was doing.

"Aw come on," he said "you'll get me in trouble."

James took the toothpaste away from Reaker who sat there with it all round his face. He began to lick it off.

BUZZ

"I'm ashamed of you, you naughty thing, you," said James, pushing Reaker out through the window as he heard his mother coming back upstairs. She came into the room.

"How many times do I have to call you?" she asked.

James rapidly pulled on his pants and shirt.

"Why you aren't even dressed yet, and just look at your hair. It's all over the place," said Ann.

She walked over to a small chest of drawers and picked up a hairbrush that lay there.

"Come on, come here," she said, "I'll do it."

James went across to her pulling on leather flip-flops, and did up his shirt too. Ann brushed his hair

"That hurts," said James.

"Keep still," said Ann, trying to break a knot in his hair. "Don't be such a baby."

"Will dad be away long mum?" asked James. He looked up at her and squinted.

"No, only a couple of days., He's got to find out if what that man said was true," replied his mother.

"It is important then, mum?" asked James.

"James I'm surprised at you," said Ann. "You know your father has to check all things, no matter what the cost in the way of travelling. That's his duty." She finished his hair and looked to see if he was tidy.

"Go downstairs," she said, as she hit his backside. "You know the truth is always important, unless of course it rebounds back and bites you, just like my hand did."

James frowned, as he wasn't sure what she meant by that remark. Then he went downstairs. As he did so Mark came out on to the top stair. He leaned over the rail.

"Mum have you seen my jeans?" he called.

"Yes," said Ann, coming out of James's room after making his bed.

"And my clean shirt too?" asked Mark. He was standing in his underpants.

"How old are they?" asked Ann, pointing at his pants.

"About two years, why?" Mark replied.

"I didn't mean that," said Ann laughing. "I meant how long have you been wearing them?"

"Oh, about two days, that's all," said Mark with a grin.

"I'll believe four," said Ann. "Get them off, there's clean ones on the shelf with your other things ok?"

She opened the door and pulled out the things he needed.

"Here," said Ann, handing the things to Mark. "I don't know," she muttered under her breath. "When will the day come that you men will ever think for yourselves?"

Ann went back downstairs and Mark returned to his room to get dressed. As he did so. he remembered he had finished his model.

"Mum," he yelled, "I've finished my model."

"Have you?" said Ann, and returned to the kitchen.

"Hi everyone," said Ann.

JoJo, Suchana and Frank all replied. Then Mark appeared and they all said good morning to Mark.

"You want some cereals master Mark?" asked Suchana.

He picked up some orange juice that had been poured out. "Yes please," he said.

Frank looked at JoJo and the others. "Did you have a good night?" Frank asked the boys.

"Not bad," said Mark.

James just sat and read his comic.

"James what about you?" asked his father. James looked up.

"Sorry dad, what did you say?".

"Did you sleep ok …last night?" asked Frank, drinking his tea.

"Ok I guess, I did have a dream though," said James, and he looked at Ann who sat down at the table with her tea and toast.

"What was that all about this time?" she asked.

"Oh, no," said Mark. "Not another epic story." He made a face.

"Be quiet," said Frank. "Don't be rude."

"Sorry dad, it's just that his dreams drive me up the wall," said Mark.

"I was up this big tree," said James. "It was very dark and suddenly a great big wave comes and washes me out of the tree. I screamed, didn't you hear me?"

"No," said Ann, looking at Suchana, who was smiling at James.

"I saw this log, so I grabbed hold of it, and I was washed downstream,".said James.

"How long is this dream?" asked Mark, sarcastically.

"You shut up," said James. "Mum says everyone dreams, so there."

"That's right," said Frank.

The others nodded.

"It's true," said JoJo.

"What are dreams for?" asked James, turning to his dad for an answer.

"Not sure," said Frank, "but I think it's some sort of way the brain chucks out information, or they could be a warning of some sort."

"Oh yes," said Ann. "At college we were taught that that's what the saying mindless information means."

"I see what you mean," said Mark. "Can I have some more tea please mum?" He passed his cup to Ann.

"Sure, anyone else want some?" asked Ann.

"Like things we do from day to day, see and think, they all get muddled up and then get chucked out again when you are asleep," said Mark.

"That's right," said Ann.

"Do you know?" said Suchana. "I've never thought of it that way before."

She passed Mark his tea.

"Thanks," he said.

"See, it's not silly, like you said," said James, sticking his tongue out at Mark. "You can't drive up a wall either, so there."

"That's enough you two, get on with your breakfast," said Ann.

"I'll go and pack the landrover for you boss," said JoJo.

"Right," said Frank. "I'll be with you in a minute, then I'll give you a hand."

Ann handed Mark and James some eggs and bacon. "Come on, get on with this," she said.

"Ok mum," said Mark. "Sorry."

James picked up his bacon in one whole piece on his fork and started to eat it. Frank stared at him in disbelief.

"James," he said, scowling at the boy. "Not like that. How many times do I have to tell you to cut your food up?"

He clouted James across the head, James ducked, but he still felt his father's firm hand.

"Sorry dad," said James, putting the bacon back on his plate and cutting it.

"By the way," asked Ann. "How long would it take you to go to town after you've been about the old man's tale?"

"Why?" asked Frank, picking up his tea that Ann had already poured out.

"We are getting low on some of our stock," said Ann. She started packing up some of the things on the table.

"I'll see to that," said Suchana. "You see master off."

"I wondered if you could pick up some more things," said Ann.

Frank put down his cup on the table. "Sure, I'll order it over the radio in the truck, then they will have it ready for me to pick up," said Frank.

"Good," said Ann "Thank you darling."

"Right," said Frank. He looked at his watch. It was now nearly six o'clock. "We'd better be off soon, I'll help JoJo finish off the packing," said Frank. "Come on you kids I'm off in a few minutes."

"Ok dad," said Mark looking at his dad in a pleading sort of way.

"Sorry son," said Frank getting up. "Next time ok?"

"Yes ok dad," replied Mark.

Frank went out with the boys while Ann finished clearing the table. Suchana helped her. Ann wiped her hands on her pinny and she and Suchana walked to the door., Both women felt unhappy to see their menfolk going off, but more so Suchana. She realised she was pregnant, but she had not told JoJo.

They both went to the landrover and stood watching the men check everything once again before they left.

"That's what I like," said Ann, looking around the countryside.

"What's that, miss Ann?" asked Suchana.

"The smell of the land first thing in the morning. It has a definite smell that just isn't there later in the day, don't you think?" said Ann.

"Yes Miss Ann," said Suchana. She smiled shyly at JoJo and looked back at the landrover.

"As a child, my mother called it Comm Shurra," said Suchana.

"What does that mean?" asked Ann. "It sounds like the title of a song."

James was playing with the chimp, trying to teach it to play hopscotch, but James ended up falling over it and landing in the dust. He laughed and the chimp jumped up and down. Frank went over to the landrover; he picked up the intercom and tried to call town.

"Zimba, Zimba, this is Cakurie Home base, can you hear me? Come in Zimba. This is Cakurie Home Base …" He let go of the button at the side of the mike and waited. All he could hear was a crackling sound.

JoJo came to his side. "What's up boss?" he asked.

"I don't know," said Frank, "there's something wrong with the radio."

He looked at the two boys who had by now stopped what they were doing and looked at their father.

"You boys been mucking around with the radio?" he asked.

"No dad," they chorused.

"I can't raise anyone. I'll try again on the way, ok?" he said.

"Yes all right love," said Ann, coming to Frank's side. "You off then?" she asked, kissing him tenderly. Frank looked at Ann and smiled.

"All ready JoJo?" he asked, not taking his eyes off Ann.

"Yes boss," replied JoJo.

JoJo looked at Suchana and smiled. She came across and hugged him and JoJo kissed her on the nose.

"Mind you not cheek Miss Ann now. Won't you?" he said to her.

"Sure JoJo, I be very good," Suchana replied.

Frank looked at Mark. "You make sure you look after these women now won't you, you hear me?" said Frank. He nodded to him. "You take good care of them."

"Yes dad," said Mark proudly.

"James," said Frank. James went over to his father as he got into the vehicle. "You be a good boy, do you understand?" said his father.

"Yes dad," answered James. "Why can't we come with you?" James stood on the fender and held on to the door as JoJo went round to the other side and got in.

"Maybe next time," said Frank. "Ok? Bye now."

James put his arms round his father's neck. "Ok," he said. "But you promise now or I won't get down." Ann smiled and so did the others.

"Ok," said Frank. "I promise. Now will you get off?" James did as he was told.

"Bye dad, see you soon," said James.

"See you honey," said Frank. They all waved and Frank drove off.

"Bye, be careful," Ann called to them.

MEANWHILE IN THE TOWN OF ZIMBA

Under the burned out floor of the bar half a dozen maggots had escaped the conflagration. They were beginning to grow and live off the small creatures that came over their way. Each one glowed in the dark and were not unlike the glimmerings of the fire itself.

THE CHIEF OF POLICE'S HOUSE IN ZIMBA. DAVID AND HIS MOTHER HAD BEEN IN AFRICA SOMETIME

At about the same time as Frank and Ann had woken up, the chief of the Zimba police had arrived at the city of Camagonga heliport. Waiting there was Deater and Ken. Deater left Ken by the car and went over to the chopper after it had landed

"Hi," said Deater, shaking hands with the chief.

They left the tarmac and walked to the car via the terminal. Three or four groups of people were waiting for other planes to go out and some of the planes were delayed.

Deater and George walked past them Deater could see the worried look on George's face.

David and his mother who had been in Africa with his private nurse were there. The plane they had arrived in was only a small one, so now they were waiting for their flight back home.

David was very pale, but still had strength of character to look after his mother. He was determined to do everything for her and himself. He helped her onto the moving platform, while the nurse kept an eye on him. It took them to the area where they had to see to their tickets and check they were all right for the flight home. He looked up at his mother and smiled but it was apparent that he had not much time to live; his mother knew this and so did the nurse.

"You are tired mum, aren't you?" asked David.

They had done a fair amount of travelling over the past three weeks.

"Yes darling," she replied. "But don't worry about me; I'm fine as long as you have fun, that's all that matters."

"Hey, you're the one we should be looking after," said the nurse smiling at him. "Anyway I'll go and book a hotel for us all,", she said. "All right?"

"Thank you," said David's mother. "That's very kind of you."

"Leave the cases. I'll get a porter to pick them up later," said the nurse.

"Yes thanks, they will be all right, they'll be safe won't they?" said David's mother.

IN THE MEANTIME IN THE CITY

Deater came through the main hall where another man was waiting by his car.

"Hi George," said Deater. "I never expected to see you here."

"I tried to contact you," said George.

"George" said Deater. "This is my assistant Ken. Ken meet George, he's the chief of police in Zimba," Ken put out his hand and shook the other's hand.

"Nice to meet you," said Ken.

"Hope you don't mind first names?" said Deater.

He opened the car door.

"No sure," said George.

He got in the car, Ken and Deater followed him. The three men sat in the back. The driver was partitioned off by a thick glass screen and it was firmly closed. George put the small box firmly on the back seat with him and held it tight with one hand.

"Can he hear?" said the chief to both men.

"No why?" Deater replied, making himself comfortable. He was very tired.

"I wouldn't want him to hear what I am going to tell you, that's all," said George.

He then proceeded to tell them the whole story while they were driving along; soon they reached the main city's university. When they arrived they all got out of the car and made their way to the laboratories. As they walked along Ken spoke to the chief, so did Deater.

"I have done some more tests on that thing you sent us," said Deater. "Now we have to put it into deeper x-rays. So far we have not found out anything very much."

"See what you can do with these things," said George, handing the box to him. "I feel that they somehow could be connected but I'm not sure how," said George.

He handed the container carefully to Deater. They reached the lab and Deater put the box carefully on the bench and opened it, taking out a small wooden rack, which contained the samples.

"Christ," said the chief, as he looked at the samples.

"What's the matter?" asked Ken.

"When those things were collected," said the chief, "there were only one or two of them. Now there are many more, and that piece of skin ..."

"What about it?" asked Deater.

"I'm sure it wasn't as big as that. It's grown," said the chief. He peered at the samples. "I'll leave it all to you; you are the experts, ok, see what you can come up with. You keep in touch and let me know when you have any information," said the chief.

"Right George," said Deater.

"Let's see," said the chief, scratching his chin, pausing for thought for a minute or two. "Between you and me is Frank Parker, Although he is quite new to the job he is the game warden. The lines to the town are so bad," said the chief, "the best thing to do is to get in touch and then he can relay your message to us. He will probably receive it ok, on the landrover radio."

"Fine," said Deater.

"Right I must go, nice meeting you Ken," said the chief, holding out his hand. "Good luck both of you and thanks," he said, after shaking hands with them both.

The chief left the lab and went back to the waiting helicopter, and returned to Zimba.

ONE HOUR LATER

The chief arrived back in his office at about the same time Frank and JoJo left the bungalow. He reached his office and slumped down in his chair and pressed the intercom button., His stomach felt really empty.

"Yes sir," said a female voice.

"Bring in my beer and sandwiches please, will you?" he asked. "By the way is Fletcher back yet?"

"Yes sir," she said. "No sir."

"What do you mean yes or no, make up your mind, which is it?" snapped the chief.

"Sorry sir," she said. "Yes to the first question, and no to the second."

He left his finger on the intercom and rubbed his chin.

"Send in Dale," said the chief.

"Yes sir," replied the woman.

The chief rather liked the sound of her voice.

'Bloody hell,' came a voice from inside his head.

The chief removed his shoes wriggled his toes up and down and then took out another pair of more comfortable shoes from the bottom drawer of his desk. He rubbed his feet again.

'God that hurts,' he muttered to himself.

He put on his other shoes and stood up.

"Ouch, ow," he said.

He got himself a drink of water. As he drank it, he caught sight of a photo of himself on the wall. It was the one taken when he was being awarded a medal for bravery. Standing proudly next to him was his old chief. Alongside that photo was a certificate of recommendation from the police force. George smiled and tipped his cup to his old boss.

"If I had known then what I know now, I'd have never joined," he said. "The hours I have to work. I think it's about time I gave it up Nancy," he said, looking at the other photo. "But then I would never have met you would I?" he sighed. "Maybe I'm wrong," he continued, "but they were good years weren't they, and I wouldn't have missed them for the world." He sat down in his chair. "I've got to let go honey," he said smiling at the photograph. "Sorry, I've been so lonely lately you understand?"

He turned towards the window and let the night breeze blow on his face. There was a knock at the door.

"Come in," called the chief. It was Dale.

"Sir" he said, standing by the desk.

"Anything else to report?" he asked.

"No, nothing sir," replied Dale.

"Sit down," said the chief. "You're making me nervous."

"The doc's family are all leaving in the morning," said Dale.

He took a chair from behind the door and sat down.

"They are going to take the girl to the main hospital," he continued.

"Right," said the chief.

He lit a cigarette and offered one to Dale.

"No thanks," said Dale.

"Rum do this," said the chief. "Are you ok?"

"Yes thanks," Dale replied. "I was a bit shocked, but I'm ok now, although I still can't forget the awful sight."

"Me neither," said the chief. "Any ideas on how or what happened?"

Dale bent forward and rubbed his leg; he then leaned across the desk looking hard at the chief.

"God, I'll be glad when tonight is over," he said, rubbing his leg again.

"No," said the chief. "I've not the faintest idea."

There was a knock at the door.

"Come in," said the chief.

"Sir" said the officer. "This has just come in, sorry it's not complete, only something's wrong with the teleprinter."

"Thanks," said the chief. and

Dale took the report and handed it to the chief. The officer left and closed the door behind him. The chief opened the report.

"Oh that's all I need," he said. He glanced at the sheets quickly and handed them to Dale.

"Three years in Alcatraz, the pen in nineteen sixty to sixty three, a year in Camagonga state prison more recently" said the chief as he flicked through the pages. "He's got a record as long as your arm as our Bennett. Handling of arms, grievous bodily harm, damn it he has the lot. We can chuck the book at him," the chief gloated.

"How long has he been in Africa then?" asked Dale. "Is he married?"

"Mmm, let's see," said the chief.

He flicked through the rest of the papers.

"From what I can make out he stopped at one, about five years," he said. "Married now divorced, no wonder she divorced him," he said dropping the papers on the desk.

"She's probably had enough of him," said the chief.

"There's no accounting for taste," said Dale.

"Yes I guess you're right," said the chief, leaning back in his chair. He put his hand to his stomach.

"Christ I'm hungry. So then what about this other fellow, what's on him I wonder?" said the chief.

Dale had already picked up the other folder and was reading it.

"Well, I give credit where it's due," said Dale. "Seems Pete managed to get the other information ok, here take a look at this."

"Thanks," said the chief. He took the papers from Dale.

"Hmm, that's good, very good. Mind you as far as I'm concerned there is only one thing to do with bastards like this you know, and that's lock them up for good," said the chief. "It seems they leave a trail of chaos behind them wherever they go."

"Yes, I know what you mean," said Dale.

Dale got up and got himself a drink of water and sat down again. He was feeling a bit hot.

"Well, at least Bennett gave us his name, I suppose that's something," said Dale.

"You ok?" asked the chief, looking at Dale.

"Yeah fine," Dale replied. "A bit tired that's all, don't worry I can make it up on the plane."

"Right," said the chief. "Let's see now. Name. Same Kidd alias?, That's the one who bought it in the bar. Christ what a name. Seems he and Bennett palled up about a year ago. Born in the States, San Francisco, 1948. That's when he came out of prison, Bennett I mean," said Dale.

"Correct," said the chief, looking up. "Seems Sam spent time too in the cells, importuning young males. He was a hustler, a freak that no one wanted to know," said the chief.

"The kind you wouldn't want to meet on a dark night," said Dale.

"Not if you've got any sense that is," said the chief. "Did I ever tell you about the one that made a pass at me?"

"No," said Dale. "What did you do?"

Dale looked across at the chief who took out some cigarettes from the packet on his desk. He offered one to Dale. Dale took one and lit it. The chief then lit his.

"What do you expect?" said the chief. "I kicked him in the balls."

"Christ," said Dale. He shook his head slowly and laughed to himself.

"Where's the report on this other guy, what's his name?" asked the chief, snapping his fingers.

He put his cigarette down and fumbled through his papers.

"God, I wish I were a tidy person, used to be once, but not now. Ah, here it is," said the chief. "There's something I want you to take a look at.."

He passed the paper across to Dale.

"What's this then?" asked Dale, looking at it. "Well, I'll be damned; it's a recommendation from the war office."

He picked up his cigarette and took another drag. He also picked up the gold chain that had been left on his desk.

"No, you mean it's one of those men?" asked Dale, as he replaced it on the chief's desk.

"Yep, you're right, the other guy in with Bennett," said the chief.

"Well I'll be damned. He saved four of his mates in his unit in Vietnam," said Dale.

He watched the chief slithering the gold chain up and down.

"Oh yeah, it seems that he had a good side also," said the chief.

"Bit late now," said Dale, "no way he can save himself, can he, not after tonight? Sir, where did you find that?"

"Not now, not ever," said the chief. He put down his cigarette. "This is the second one he has killed, only last time it was a bank job. He blew a safe with one of his mates as well; the cops were informed someone grassed."

"Well, I'm glad it was one of their own," said Dale. "But whatever made a good guy turn bad?"

Dale looked at the chief. Where did he get that, he wondered.

The chief got up and closed the window.

"They will both have to go to the city prison, so you can... oh shit I've just remembered you are on vacation from today aren't you?" said the chief. "Ah never mind," he said as he put the chain down on the desk.

"Yes sir," said Dale.

He bent down and once more scratched his leg. By now, there was a small mauve swelling. He got up after pulling down his trouser leg, scratched his head and looked up at the chief.

"I am sure I've seen something like that on someone before, only round some one's neck" Dale said to the chief.

"What's that?" asked the chief, as he saw Dale look. "Oh half the kids go round with marks on their necks these days," said the chief. "Probably a bite from a mosquito. Yes, you are probably right Jenny's not to blame, you haven't had enough time off lately,?" said the chief. "Now let me see where were we?" the chief went on.

"Oh yes, Sied Mandle, the guy in with Bennett. His mother was part British, part French. Sied was born on Portland, a place called Tophill. Case you've never heard of it, it's a place in England, a small peninsula off the coast of Dorset. Father was a white African, mixed race himself. Both are now dead. Drowned on the Umbarla while on a safari trip. He was then an orphan and sent to a missionary school. He then became a tough little bugger by the sound of it, got told off for stealing and many times reprimanded. He ran away and lived rough for years. I could go on but you get the picture don't you? Something must have happened because he joined up and his experience helped him to become good with dynamite and explosives. Since he made that bad start, he's a natural, far more at home out here than on Portland," ended the chief.

The chief grinned when Dale made his earlier remark. He had been reading the report. He now looked up at Dale and smiled.

"Don't worry, you can make it up to her next week," said the chief. "This guy Sied Mandle, he's clever, he doesn't look for fights, but appears to be the type who gets picked on rather than do the picking, if you get what I mean?"

The chief yawned and stretched his arms and got up and made his way to the drink stand and got himself another one.

"What were you about to say sir?" asked Dale. "That I should change my leave. That was what you were thinking wasn't it sir?"

"Yes, I was thinking of doing just that, but then I had a change of mind. It won't be necessary," said the chief.

He pushed down the intercom button and a voice said in answer to his question. "Yes sir."

"Yes sir," said Dale.

"I don't know why I told you all that stuff, with luck …" said the chief.

He stopped what he was saying to Dale and answered the voice on the intercom. 'That voice again,' thought the chief.

"Send Susan into me please," said the chief.

"Yes sir," said the voice.

"We shall have him safely away by the time you get back, thanks" the chief said to Dale.

He let go of the intercom button.

While he waited for Susan to come to the office he looked at the chain he had taken from the boy. He turned to Dale. "What's this?"

"If you do remember where you have seen this chain before let me know" said the chief. He picked it up again and twiddled it between his fingers. "What time is your flight?" he asked Dale. "Do you know?"

"Yep sure I do," said Dale as he looked at his watch, the time was seven thirty. "Let's see, the Chinook gets here about eight fifteen, then we load and get on board at nine thirty say, taking off from the city at about eleven thirty. From there we have just a few minutes wait while our luggage is transferred to the flight we take out We are going on the grasshopper," said Dale, looking at the chief. "Why?"

"Ah good that's all I wanted to know," the chief said with a cheeky grin, as if he had something up his sleeve and that seemed to be the case.

"What's that sir?" asked Dale

There was a knock at the door and Susan came into the office.

"Oh never mind," said the chief.

"Come on, come on in," he shouted. "You won't have time to get the prisoners to the city jail, will you Dale?" asked the chief.

"No sir," said Dale as Susan came right into the office.

"But I could get the next flight out if you wanted me to. Jenny would not mind I'm sure," said Dale.

"Right," said the chief. "No it's ok, anyway you'll miss your other connections, you had better get off, or you will not have enough time. I'll deal with this."

As Susan came into the office, Dale stood up.

"Thanks, I'll just have enough time for a quick shower," he said. "Hi Susan."

"Hello Dale, you off then? Have a nice time, see you when you get back ok?" said Susan. "Regards to Jenny," she added.

"Thanks," replied Dale smiling at Susan. "Don't work too hard."

"Bye," said the chief. "Enjoy yourselves."

"Ah Susan,"" said the chief as the door closed behind Dale. "Sit down. I have a job for you and what's more I want you to do it, and what's more I think you are going to like it very much."

MEANWHILE BACK AT THE DOCTOR'S HOUSE

Marie popped into her daughter's bedroom where Nickki lay in bed. She was very still.

Her eyes were wide open. Sitting on her bed, she gently brushed her daughter's hair back off her face. Nickki did not even flinch.

"Hi honey, how are you?" asked Marie. There was no response. Her anxiety was at its greatest.

There was no reply from the still figure in the bed. Tears began to well up in her mother's eyes. "Oh my god, what do I do?" her eyes gazed towards heaven.

"My poor baby. How cruel life can be sometimes, but don't worry too much, we are going to take you away from this awful place, to the city, where nothing can hurt you again my poor love," said Nickki's mother to her silent daughter. "I promise nothing like this will ever happen again to you."

There was still no sign of response from Nickki. Marie wiped her tears.

"Back in a minute honey, all right?" she said as she looked down at Nickki.

She got up from the bed and left the room and returned downstairs. The doc's wife Mabel was washing some things at the sink when Marie came in. She had already made some tea as Marie sat down at the table with her other daughter Kim. Mabel poured a cup for her. They were all dressed. It was now breakfast time but none of them felt like eating after what had happened overnight. All the family had been affected by Nickki's rape and the burning of the store because of the incident in the bar. They were all devastated, all except Kim that was, she didn't really understand.

Stacey, Marie's husband, looked across at his wife as Marie sat down. Mabel brought over the tea, and she then brought over the breakfast for them.

"Still no change," said Marie. "Thanks."

She picked up her cup of tea and looked at her husband and mother.

"Thanks mum," said Marie again.

She stared at the breakfast her mother had cooked.

"I'm not hungry," she said. "I'm just scared for Nickki's sake. I feel so useless, nothing seems to get through. Stacey what are we going to do?"

"You eat that my girl," said her mother. "These things take time, you should listen to your father. Remember what he used to tell you when you were a child? Time is a good healer."

She patted her daughter's arm.

"Come on now, just a little bit?" she asked.

"Oh all right then, I'll just eat the toast, let dad have the rest," said Marie.

"Can I have some more milk please nanny?" asked Kim, who had been sitting quietly as she stared at all the grown up faces.

"Yes darling," answered her nan.

She poured Kim some milk into her glass.

"Thank you nanny," said Kim.

"Would you like some more tea Stacey?" asked Mabel.

The doc came in and sat down. Mabel poured the tea and got up to get doc's breakfast.

"Yes, thank you," said Stacey.

"Thanks," said doc, as he picked up his napkin. "Just give Nickki a little more time. Don't try and rush things, and above all don't ever tell her what she has gone through is dirty. Don't protect her from the nasty things in this world, help her to try to understand, try to get her to accept what happened. If you don't you'll have on your hands a child who is always afraid of sex. When she grows up she will become frigid and withdrawn, into a world of her own, maybe even fantasise, and that can cause even more problems than you have now," said the doc to his daughter and her husband.

"I don't really understand," said Marie. "I'll not question what you are saying, but it does seem hard for someone so young to have to go through it like that, doesn't it darling?" she turned to her husband.

He remained very quiet and looked very worried.

"Don't you think so darling?" asked Marie; she nudged Stacey on the arm.

"I don't know," he replied, sipping his tea. "I can't take much more of this." , He was really shaken up at the whole situation. It still hadn't really hit home that they had nothing left except their lives and each other. Mabel and doc sensed that an argument was pending and looked at them both.

"Mum, what's wrong with Nickki?" asked Kim. "She won't even speak to me now. Have I done something wrong? I never told you anything did I? I never said she had any make-up, did I? I think she's not talking to me because she thinks I told you. Please tell her it wasn't my fault. I don't like her when she's like this. She's horrid."

"How would you like to help nan with the washing up?" Marie asked Kim. "I'm sure she would be very proud to see that you can do it now you are a big girl."

"Oh yes please," said Kim. "I want to wash the dishes in those bubbles like you do, can I please, can I?"

"Well, I don't know about that," said Mabel. "Can you really wash up properly?"

"Yes I can nan and when I get bigger mummy is going to teach me how to cook. I've already cooked pretend cakes you know," said Kim.

"All right then," said her nan. "Come on, into the kitchen and when we've done that we shall go to the shops and get a few things for mummy."

The doc got up from the table and patted Stacey on the shoulder as if to say sorry. He then left the room, and left Stacey and Marie to have their talk.

"Mummy," interrupted Kim suddenly. "I left Rebecca at home, my dolly has gone. I shan't ever see her again will I?"

That remark summed it all up for Stacey what he was already thinking in his mind. Because he now saw for the first time that the young daughter he had the night before would no longer be the one he had known. It was as if she had suddenly had all the fun of growing up taken away from her and would no longer be the innocent girl he had grown to love. It was that that had been taunting him all night long. Suddenly she was a woman. Out there in this god forsaken country it was accepted for the native children to be all grown up at fourteen, but never in a thousand years had he expected his own daughter to be like one of them.

"What's up darling?" asked Marie.

She picked up Kim and cuddled her.

"My dolly, mummy? queried Kim. "She's dead, she got burned in that dreadful fire, and we have no home left to live in do we?" asked Kim.

"Oh darling, I thought you had her with you. I'm sorry," said Marie.

She looked across at Stacey; he seemed unaffected by her remark.

Mabel took off her pinny and put it down.

"I don't know," she said. "Let's leave mummy and daddy to have a talk and go down to the shops, shall we Kim?" she asked. "Then," she went on. "We can see if we can find you a new baby all right? How does that sound to you? Mummy and daddy have a lot to say to each other. Come on then, here's your cardigan."

Mabel and Kim left the house to go to the shops. While they were gone the doc went upstairs to have a wash and shave. He also told Marie that he would get Nickki ready for the journey.

"Thanks dad," said Marie. She gave half a smile as he went up the stairs. "Thank god we left a few clothes here," she said "or we would have had nothing, though I must admit, having just two dresses and a few bits of underwear leaves much to be desired now doesn't it?"

She got up from the table. It was bad enough to have had their daughter lose her innocence, and even worse their home, but now it looked as if she was about to lose her husband as well. For he seemed to be taking it worse than anyone. She left the table and went round to Stacey who sat with his arms resting on the table.

"Anyway, what's this business of 'I can't take any more?' What exactly do you mean?" Marie asked Stacey

Stacey turned to her.

"Look, I've put every penny I earned and more besides into that store and now it's gone, we've nothing left, not even a pot of paint," said Stacey.

"Yes I know darling," said Marie, as she brushed her hand through his hair.

"Then this," he could hardly bring himself to say it. "What he did to Nickki."

"Yes I know love, but we mustn't give up, we started with nothing and can do so again," said Marie. "Everyone goes through a bad patch in life. It's just our turn. I know it will be tough, but deep down inside I know it will all work out fine if we stick together. Come on you'll see, first things first. We must go back to the city and get Nickki well. We'll take her to the specialist that dad said to see. He of all people should know who can help her and who is the best."

Marie put her arms round Stacey's neck. He turned on the chair and held her tightly.

"God, I only hope she comes out of this all right," said Stacey. "She's so young."

"She will, she will," said Marie, and they kissed each other.

Then the tears ran down Stacey's cheeks. The shock of it all had finally been released.

"I know this is the wrong time but did you manage to get the insurance papers in time?" asked Marie.

Stacey stopped crying.

"Yes," he said, "but they are only worth three thousand."

"Well darling," said Marie. "It's not much, but it's a start." She let go of his neck.

"We had better think of getting going. We'll get the tickets on board. Dad's given us enough money to get to the city, and he said that when we get sorted out we can pay him back. It's ok, he knows what a proud man you are," said Marie. She smiled at him and he knew what she meant.

Suddenly there was a great deal of excitement; Mabel and Kim were back from the shops.

"Mummy, mummy, look," called Kim, as she came through the door carrying a new stuffed doll. "Isn't she beautiful? Nanny's friend gave her to me," she said as she cradled the doll just like a real baby. "She's just like a real one."

Marie looked at her mother who came through the door followed by a small boy she knew. He was a bit older than Kim, and carried a drawing book.

"Allen's come to say good bye, mummy," said Kim. "Isn't that nice?"

"Why yes," said Marie. "Hello Allen, you are up early today aren't you?"

Allen nodded shyly.

"Thanks mum," said Marie. She was picking up a small suitcase her mother was lending her.

"Well, it's the least I can do," said her mother. She leaned forwards and kissed her daughter and Kim.

Kim threw her arms around her nan's neck and hugged her for a few seconds.

"Why don't you and grand dad come and live with us? You can always share my room, I only sleep in a small bed you know," said Kim.

Then she turned to Allen.

"Will you come and see me one day too?" she asked.

"We'll see," said Mabel.

"You promise," said Kim.

She then let go of her nan's hand and held on to her mother's hand. As they stood there Nickki was brought carefully down the stairs by her grandfather. Her eyes were swollen and bruised and two cuts on both cheeks were hidden behind clear tape. Her ears were swollen where the rapist had pulled her earrings off. Her left arm was broken. Allen looked at Nickki being carried down the stairs by her grandfather.

"What's wrong with you sister? Has she fallen down the stairs or something?" he asked.

"Yes," said Marie, quick to answer his question.

"I don't know," said Kim. "She won't speak to me and I don't know what I have done unless she blames me. Perhaps she hurt herself in the fire and it wasn't my fault at all."

Nickki, helped by doc and Stacey, was taken out through the door. Allen dropped his drawing book that he had been carrying, and Kim helped him pick up the drawings that had fallen out, but the doc was not there to see them. Kim handed the drawings back to Allen. As she did so, she said goodbye to him.

"Now don't forget Allen you promised to come and see me," said Kim.

One of Allen's drawings was of a cone-shaped object, just like the one the native boy had in his hand.

The family all left to go to the place where a mini bus was to collect them and take them to the base so they could get the Chinook. After the bus had gone doc went out on some more house calls, and Mabel went back to finish the dishes.

MEANWHILE BACK IN ANOTHER PART OF AFRICA

David was looking very pale and listless as he rested with his mother and Theresa, while the native guide gave orders to pack up the camp and load into the landrover. His mother looked on sadly at David .She, like her friend, knew that he had not long to live and like he had asked began? after a couple of hours to make their way back to the city's airport. This meant they would be travelling overnight before reaching their early morning destination. It was time for them all to have a rest before the flight at least. David especially needed it more and more each day.

BACK AT DALE'S HOUSE

Dale has arrived back home and is halfway through a shower. His muscular body gleams and is covered with soap. He calls out to Jenny from the shower.

"Where's Barry?" he called, getting out of the shower. "I thought he was supposed to be helping you?"

He grabbed hold of a towel and began to dry himself.

"I don't know," said Jenny.

She was getting dressed in their bedroom.

"That's what I tried to tell you," said Jenny, "when you first came in, but you were in such a rush. He didn't come home last night."

Jenny fluffed up her hair and put on some lipstick.

"The night before last he said he had a date with someone. Remember ,he said he was going to stay with some friends, and then going to a party in the evening?" said Jenny.

"Did he say who?" asked Dale frowning.

"No," said Jenny. "He was all coy about that part of it. Well, you know Barry. When I asked him he just said someone, he said no one in particular. But if you ask me it was a date".

"Ah," said Dale. "Christ, that hurts." He touched his leg. "Why do you say a date?" he asked as he pulled on his socks.

"Never seen him so fussy. Do you know he even put on some after shave," said Jenny.

"Mine I suppose," said Dale.

"Yes, the one mum sent you last year, ha, ha," laughed Jenny.

"So you don't know where he is?" asked Dale. He came into the room. "Damn, just when he is needed, that brother of mine is not around, he always lets me down," said Dale.

By now Dale had got his underpants on. He pulled on his trousers and put on a clean shirt and did it up.

"How do I look?" asked Jenny, turning from side to side and smoothing her skirt.

"Fine," said Dale, doing up his shirt sleeves.

He bent down and picked up his watch and looked at the time.

"Seven minutes to get down to the bus stop," said Dale. He put on his tie and gave Jenny a quick kiss.

"You look stunning," he said to her.

"Thanks," said Jenny, smiling at him.

"Have you sorted things out with Mrs Jones, darling?" asked Dale.

"Yes," said Jenny. "I've got to leave the key under the mat, and she is coming in to clean and keep an eye on things for us."

"Right," said Dale. "You all ready? Perhaps Barry will be at the bus stop. One thing's for sure, and that's we are not waiting for him. We will go without him if he doesn't turn up. I'm not cancelling our trip because of him; he's old enough to look after himself now."

"Right," said Jenny. "If he's not here we'll leave his suitcases."

She picked up two small suitcases and her handbag.

"You are right," she said to Dale.

Dale put on his jacket and picked up two more cases and just as he did so he saw Barry running down the road.

"Where the hell have you been?" Dale yelled at him as he came through the door.

"Sorry," said Barry; his face was very red with running and his clothes looked as if he had slept in them.

"Here," said Dale. "You take these cases, we have four minutes to get to the bus stop. You look dreadful, bloody awful in fact. You'll have to change on the flight ok?"

"Ok," said Barry.

Still puffing from his run, he picked up the cases and they all left the house. Dale's leg was still hurting him and he rubbed it again.

When they reached the bus stop the doc's family was also waiting, so were the film couple Cindy and Hugo, as was Jason whose face turned a shade of pale when he saw Nickki. But she was in shock so that she didn't even know he was the one who had raped her. She was too ill even to put two and two together. Marie and Stacey helped her to board the bus, along with her other daughter Kim and her new doll.

"Is this the bus we are going on daddy?" asked Kim. "And that thing that flies with them twisting things?"

"Yes darling," said Stacey. "They are called rotors."

"I don't want to go on one of them, they make too much noise and I don't like it," said Kim. She clung to her father's neck. "Allen said they would cut off my head no, no won't go."

"Of course they won't do that, daddy wouldn't let anything happen anything nasty to you, now would he?" said Marie.

Stacey gave a look of disapproval at that last remark but let it slide. Then Marie remembered her father's words.

"Oh do be quiet," she said to Kim.

She was beginning to get angry, as if she had not had enough trouble over the past few hours. She felt she was the only one who had kept a cool head and now it was all beginning to boil over.

They all boarded the bus.

MEANWHILE BACK AT THE POLICE STATION

Back at the police station, Susan had done as her father had asked. She had been home and packed her overnight bag and had now been delivered to the helicopter base, where the bus was just pulling in with her and her two prisoners. They had been driven there in a special van.

Dale was to be her safeguard while they were on the Chinook. After they reached the city her job would be done. The prisoners and Susan were put on board the Chinook first. Both men were handcuffed together as a safety precaution. Then the bus drew up and came to a standstill.

Jamie who was already there caught sight of Susan, and as she boarded he looked round for her.., He seemed annoyed that she was there at all.

"Hello," he said to her, when he finally caught up with her on the right hand side of the chopper. She sat just behind the two prisoners.

"What are you doing here?" he asked her.

Susan could see he was annoyed and held her head in the air. She could feel his eyes on her and his indifference towards her.

"Well it's like this," said Susan.

"Don't tell me. You didn't believe my story. Ha, I thought as much," said Jamie.

"Oh, how dare you?" said Susan, "of all the impertinence."

She was defending herself, and felt very guilty about it.

"If that's what you think then why don't you go away, go and get on with you …?" She stopped as tears welled up in her eyes. He could see he had hurt her deeply, but not as much as she had hurt herself.

"Sorry, I didn't mean it to sound the way it did," said Jamie. "It's just that I'm shattered, that's all."

He sat down beside her and tried to take hold of her hand.

"You leave me alone," said Susan. "I've never been so embarrassed in my life."

"I'm sorry," said Jamie. "Come on, tell me please."

Susan was shaking with temper, her father was right, now she understood what he had meant, and everything was hitting back at her. This was one lesson she would never forget.

"Here," said Jamie "have one of these."

He took out his cigarettes and offered one to Susan.

"You look as if you need one," he said to her.

Susan took one and Jamie lit hers and then his own.

With everyone now seated on the Chinook, it took off.

"Would you like some coffee?" asked one of the hostesses to Jamie and Susan.

"Yes please, two," said Jamie. "You'll have one, won't you darling?"

Susan nodded, her eyes still red with crying.

"Thanks," she whispered.

Jamie looked hard at Susan.

"Now come on tell me what this is all about, tell me everything," he said.

"Well, all right," said Susan. "I was about to say before, well never mind about that bit. Dad gave me the chance to talk to you by giving me this job. I've got to take these two prisoners to the city jail. Dale up front is my back up to see that nothing goes wrong, though they of course don't know that. It's a terrific responsibility you know?"

"Whatever have they done to warrant such treatment? It's unusual for your father to go to such lengths, isn't it?" asked Dale.

"Oh," said Susan. "It's a long story. Bennett, the one in the bright shirt, had something to do with what happened downtown. I think he burned down the bar or something".

"What? Christ," said Jamie, looking round at them.

"Yes it seems something happened to his mate, but dad wouldn't say.

Anyway I do know what the other one did," said Susan.

She stubbed out her cigarette.

"He killed a native kid, I was there when Dale brought him in," she said. She sniffed and looked at Sied who was picking his teeth.

"Here's your coffee," said the hostess, coming back and handing them two cups.

"Thank you," said Susan, giving her a quick half smile. "Could you give this to the captain please?"

"Shall I get one for them for you?" asked the hostess. She took the note from Susan.

"No," said Susan. "You had better stay away from those two, they are both very dangerous, thank you."

"Right that's ok, I just thought I'd ask," said the hostess. She was blonde and had an attractive face.

"Anyway ,on with the story," said Susan.

"What happened? How did the bar catch fire? Did he really do it?" asked Jamie.

"I'm not sure," said Susan frowning. "It's all down in the report but it's sealed. I have to hand it to the commissioner in Camagonga."

"Now I really do feel rotten," said Jamie. "I'm sorry darling for disbelieving you."

"Don't be," said Susan, for the moment of truth had come just as her father had said it would. She held her breath and then went on, "It's all my fault, I'm a self centred bitch," she said. "Today dad has made me see quite a few things that I couldn't see before. He told me I as good as go round with my eyes shut and my nose stuck up in the air, and I've realised he is right. And another thing is that my job has been getting on top of me. It tends to make me distant towards people. He said that it was about time I sat down and thought about things. He's good and what's more he's right. He said that this job tends to make you both judge and jury and to take sides, but one shouldn't. He even quoted the law to me. He said a man is never …" Susan caught sight of the hostess and saw she still had her note.

"What's that then?" asked Jamie.

"Oh," said Susan. "Why the law states that a man is innocent until proven guilty, and not vice versa. We must trust to reason until we have proof".

"Oh why's that?" asked Jamie.

"Dad said that it is better to trust one another, which means trust everyone until our sense tells us otherwise. Besides if you don't trust anyone then you yourself do not get trusted, for other people are not fools either. Don't you see a sort of trial and error thing," said Susan.

"I suppose there is some sense in that," said Jamie. "But how does that solve our particular problem?"

"It doesn't," said Susan. "But dad has made me see that I'm not ready for marriage yet, to settle down I mean. I've still got a lot to learn darling, you understand don't you? Now if you are prepared to wait, then maybe we have a chance to work things out."

She looked at Jamie's face to see if she could see a ray of hope. Impatiently, she asked," Am I worth all that trouble darling?"

Jamie put his hand on hers.

"Somehow," said Jamie. "I don't think I have a very long wait."

He bent forward and kissed her, and then they drank their coffee.

Not long passed when Kim came up and tugged Susan's sleeve.

"Excuse me," said Kim. "Are you a lady policeman?" she asked. She was still holding her new stuffed doll.

Susan bent forward and smiled at her. The hostess took their coffee cups away.

"Thank you," said Susan.

She turned and continued to talk to Kim. Jamie was still smiling.

"Why yes, I certainly am, why do you ask?" said Susan. She glanced anxiously at Jamie as if to say what's all this about.

"I don't like policemen," said Kim with a defiant look on her face.

Kim seemed sort of angry and distant..

"Why's that?" asked Susan.

"You people burned my home down and you made my daddy cry and my sister won't speak to me," said Kim. "Now we have nowhere to live and mummy is unhappy. She's only got one dress left and my Rebecca is dead, I hate you... I hate you..." she ended screaming at Susan.

Susan felt awful and tears welled up in her eyes again.

"Kim don't be so rude," said Marie, coming to fetch her. "Come and sit down you naughty girl, you are not supposed to run about the gangway. I'm sorry," said Marie. "I didn't think she would take it out on you, we've been half expecting this, you know shock and everything, it was my daughter who..." She thought better of what she was going to say and then went on, "I'm truly sorry, excuse me."

Marie turned to Kim.

"Now, just you come and sit down., Do you hear? Whatever has come over you?" said Marie as she tried to pull Kim away. "Come on now."

"No, no, no," cried Kim.

She gripped the side of the seat as her mother took her hand, and then she caught sight of Dale.

"You did it, you horrid man, I hate you, I hate you," Kim screamed hysterically. "You did it, you did it," she went on.

Stacey heard all the commotion and came back to help his wife.

"Now just stop it," cried Marie.

She tugged at Kim's hands to make her let go. She saw Stacey coming.

"Please darling, do something quickly, this is getting out of hand," cried Marie.

Stacey did no more than to slap Kim very hard as he got hold of her, then she let out another scream and buried her head in her father's shoulder. Then he carried her back to her seat.

"I'm sorry," said Marie to everyone as she walked back to her seat.

"I don't know," said one of the passengers in disgust.

"This would have never have happened if she had not had such a shock. It wasn't her fault at all, honestly," said Marie, by the way of an explanation.

"Oh now I've heard everything," said another passenger. "The brutality of the police force these days. I'm telling you now there's nothing but fascists running it, well that's what I say anyway."

The other passengers began their own versions of what they thought had happened, talking among themselves.

All through this, Nickki sat staring at nothing, no outward sign of life. It was all going on in her head. She kept going over and over again the day before the party and she could hear her sister talking to her. Although she did not realise it she was trying to stop herself believing that anything had happened to her.

NICKKI'S MEMORIES OF THE DAY
BEFORE THE PARTY

We join Nickki's mind the day before the party. Nickki a young girl of fifteen is up in her bedroom with her younger sister of five. Nickki is sitting at her dressing table brushing her hair, her sister is doing the same thing with her own brush and is counting out loud.

"One hundred and one, one hundred and two, one hundred and thre…,Oh, how long do I have to keep this up?" asked Kim. "My arms are aching."

"Not until I say so," said Nickki.

She looked at her reflection in the mirror.

"It's not necessary to count out loud Kim," said Nickki. "You can count in your head."

"If I do that I forget," said her sister. "Then I have to start again."

"Oh all right baby," said Nickki. "That will do for today."

Nickki put her own brush down on the table.

"Come here," she said to Kim. "Mum wants me to plait it for you."

"No," Kim replied. "I don't want my hair done like that, I want it all loose like yours, like you do."

"Mum said I was to plait it so there., Come and sit here and shut up making a fuss," said Nickki. "I'll make you look beautiful"

"Yes please, and can you put some lipstick on me too?" asked Kim.

"Lipstick, why I haven't got any lipstick you know that," said Nickki pushing her down.

"Oh yes you have," said Kim. "I saw it the other day, I saw you buy some in the shop. It's in your drawer."

"So you've been snooping again have you? I've told you before not to go to my drawers," said Nickki. "I'll be glad when I have a room of my own then you won't be able to do that."

Nickki was very angry with her sister.

"Why?" asked her sister, looking up at her. She had a very cheeky glint in her eye.

"Because I shall lock it, that's why," said Nickki.

She picked up the hairbrush and removed some hairs.

"It's about time mum gave you a tanning," Nickki said to Kim. "I'm going to tell her."

"Oh no don't do that, you can't," cried Kim.

"Oh and why not?" asked Nickki. "What else have you been doing you little sneak?"

"Lots," said her sister. "I found some powder, some stuff you make your cheeks red with and some things made out of cotton wool., I don't know what they are for, but best of all a letter from a boy, the one who has been standing at the gate all week. I bet it's from him. Seems silly to me, him standing there mooning over every little thing little you do. Boys are daft."

"Ha, ha, you won't be saying that in a few years," said Nickki. "You'll be doing just the same as me, only heaven help the boy you get, he won't be able to trust you as far as he can throw you. How do you expect me to get a nice plait if you don't sit still? Right nosey since you know where everything is, then get out the lipstick and things and I'll put some on you ok?"

The little girl opened the drawer and got out the things and placed them on the dressing table.

"Have you told mum you got that letter?" asked Kim.

"Yes, why? Are you thinking of trying to blackmail me into letting you keep something?" asked Nickki

"No," said Kim. "Why do you say that?"

"A brooch is missing from my jewel box, come on hand it over," she said to Kim.

Nickki stood with one hand on her hip and held the other on to Kim.

"Come on," she said to Kim. "Let's have it back."

"Are you two girls ready yet?" called their mother from downstairs. "I want the breakfast finished and done with before I open the store."

Nickki turned again to Kim.

"Come on, come on, no brooch, no lipstick," said Nickki to Kim.

"Oh all right," said her sister. "You win."

She pulled the brooch from her dress pocket, and gave it to Nickki, who then put on some lipstick for her. All the time the older girl had a grin on her face, as if she knew something her sister didn't.

"Kim," said her mother as she sat down at the table. "What on earth do you think you are doing with that mess on at the table?" She looked at Nickki.

"Why do you let her do such things?" asked her mother.

"But I didn't, mother," said Nickki. "She took it and put it on herself; she found it in my drawer."

"Well dear," said her mother. "If you are going to take to wearing make-up at your age, why don't you get your sister to put it on for you? Then perhaps you will have it on straight," she laughed at Kim's face. "Go and look at yourself, it's awful darling ..."

Nickki laughed at Kim as well. Kim went over to the mirror and looked in it. Then she turned and poked her tongue out at Nickki who grinned back. She had got her own back.

"She did it mum," said Kim. "It's not fair, she always gets away with it. I hate her."

Kim left the room and went upstairs to wash the mess off.

"Fasten your seat belts please," said the hostess. "We shall be landing in a few minutes."

Then she came forward to Stacey.

"Everything all right?" she asked him.

Dale bent forward and scratched his leg and looked at it. The swelling had got bigger.

Jenny looked hard at Dale.

"That's a bit strange isn't it? Why did she shout at you too? What the hell happened downtown last night? You haven't told me anything about that. Have you?" asked Jenny.

"Oh nothing," said Dale.

He thought it best that Jenny should not know about the happenings in the town.

"Just police work, that's all. I'll tell you about it later," Dale said. "Besides I don't really want to talk about it."

He picked up Jenny's hand and kissed it.

"Darling, we are on holiday, so let's forget work," said Dale, and then went on to say. "Do you know honey, as soon as we land here and board the other plane we really start our holiday? But now I can tell you one thing."

He turned towards the back of the chopper. So did Jenny.

"You see those two at the back," he said to her.

"Ah, ah," said Jenny, looking at them. Bennett saw her looking and winked at her.

"What about them?" she stammered.

"I've had to keep my eye on them the whole time I've been on board in case Susan needed me," Dale told Jenny.

"Why?" asked Jenny. "They don't seem dangerous."

"That's beside the point. I was told to and that's what I've done," said Dale.

"Oh the signs are up," said Jenny. "We are down."

"Yes," said Barry, who had been sitting quietly with his eyes shut.

"I thought you were asleep?" said Dale.

He unclipped his belt and Jenny did the same.

"I was," said Barry. "But not now."

"Well that's obvious, you idiot," said Dale. "Come on out."

Barry got up with Jason and went towards the door.

"Something is wrong," Jenny said to Dale.

"Why? What makes you say that?" said Dale.

"I don't know, it's just a feeling I have. Do you know only just a while ago he had a real worried look on his face even though he was asleep and his eyes closed. He's hiding something," said Jenny. "You know that don't you?"

"I don't know," replied Dale. "Maybe his date didn't turn up after all, or turn out as he expected."

"You could be right," said Jenny.

They all got off the Chinook.

"But then he didn't say anything to you about being late, did he? Has he said anything to you at all?" asked Jenny.

"No," said Dale. "You go ahead and I'll see those two get off ok. Right?"

"Yes sure," said Jenny. "See you in a minute."

She went down the steps. All the passengers were taken to a waiting room to wait for their other plane.

Jamie stood by Susan and kissed her.

"See you in three days," he said.

"Yes, bye darling," answered Susan.

The two prisoners were led to a waiting car, as the note that Susan had given the hostess had requested the captain to arrange while they had been on board.

Mrs Heal had been taken to a private room with her baby in an incubator. The doctor went along with her as Warren, her husband had to report for the flight out.

Jason kept well away from Nickki in case she regained her memory. Nickki didn't, she was taken out of the building in a wheelchair, with Stacey, Marie and Kim beside her.

While they waited there for the change of planes Jenny noticed that something was still worrying Barry. When Dale returned to her he was limping a little. Jenny also noticed how tired Dale looked He had been awake for nearly twenty four hours. The other passengers were joined by those already waiting there from the other flights in. They were from all parts of the city and Africa. They had by now sat themselves down and were reading books and papers, and eating sweets and such like. One was a professor of human behaviour, the other was Harry and the couple who had just got married, and they had made the mistake of telling someone they were engaged.

SAME DAY BACK IN THE STATES

We find Brian still in his room looking at the screen; he then contacts his chief in his office.

"Sir," said Brian. "We have some more information on that hurricane. She has decided to turn and is heading out to sea again, so Florida will only get the whiplash of it so to speak."

"Thank Christ for that," said the chief. "They would have never forgiven me. They would never have had time to evacuate half the State. Anyway you had better contact the coastguard and tell them the good news. Let's hope it stays like that. Better tell them to stay on alert for twenty four hours just in case. Oh, and what about the other thing?, Any more trouble?"

"No sir, no more strange pictures, everything seems clear," said Brian.

The commander had been on to the war department.

"They don't know what it is," said the commander. "And the USSR is just as bemused as we are when we contacted them a few hours ago.."

"Since then I've tried to contact Camgonga,'" said the chief. "That's in Africa. I'm afraid the electrical storm has caused havoc on the coast and from there all communications have been dreadful. I wanted to tell them about it, but I can't so they will have to do something about it themselves."

"Sir," said a woman, coming into the office.

"Yes" said the chief. "What is it?"

"This has just come in," she said and handed him a teletext.

"Reports on UFOs," said the chief. "Oh no, now you know that is not my department."

"Yes sir" said the woman.

"Contact Blue Book and let them deal with it," said the chief, and he smiled at her. "It's ok, it's just been a bad day."

"That's all right sir," she said. "We all get them sometimes."

She turned and left the office.

IN THE MEANTIME AT THE PRISON IN CAMAGONGA

Susan had delivered her two prisoners and was expecting to leave the police headquarters when something happened to stop her. So now she found herself in the commissioner's office.

"I'm sorry Officer Cleaton, but we can't accept these prisoners," the commissioner said.

"Why in heaven's name not?" asked Susan. She was stunned. "I don't understand. What's happened and what do you expect me to do with them? My job was …"

The commissioner interrupted her.

"We have done a complete check on these two men, while you were on your way here. We tried to contact you before you left," said the commissioner.

"And?" asked Susan as she stood by his desk. He was seated.

The commissioner looked through some papers on his desk., He then looked up at her.

"They are here illegally, they have forged passports and papers. There is no record of them entering this country at all, as far as we can make out the one called Bennett was deported some years back to the States. I've just found out that he spent some time in one of the prisons in this country and was deported back out again, and that's where the story ends," said the commissioner. "Our only guess is that the other guy Sied Mandel had something to do with the escape."

"Then in so many words sir," said Susan. "What does that mean? What have I got to do now?"

"It means Officer Cleaton that you must take them back to Zimba or take them all the way back to the States. If we can get you a seat on the next flight out then I suggest that you take them. It would be the best plan, and that's the best I can offer you," said the commissioner.

"But I can't sir," said Susan indignantly. "As much as I'd like to, my boyfriend is the co-pilot on the next flight out." answered Susan.

"And why not? May I ask?" asked the commissioner. "It's been done before and probably will be done again."

He was being somewhat rude, Susan thought. She looked disgusted at him. She was very angry.

"I haven't got my things sir," she said.

"That's your problem, not mine," said the commissioner rudely.

Susan got very angry, her face was bright red. 'How dare he,' she thought.

"Excuse me sir," she said. "I beg to differ on that point, if you don't mind."

"Why?" asked the commissioner, looking up at her again.

"It's not my responsibility to go trekking off halfway round the world with just my overnight case. Now is it? Well not on my pay it isn't," said Susan.

The commissioner looked astounded at her cheek.

"By god, you're a sassy little bitch aren't you?" he said.

He got up and went out and walked round her. His hand was on his chin as he walked up and down looking at her thoughtfully.

"How dare you speak to me like that!" said Susan.

She lashed out with her hand without thinking and caught the commissioner full on the face. Head of department or not, she was not going to take a remark like that from him or anyone else. She thought for a second of resigning from her job.

The commissioner rubbed his face.

"I could have you dismissed for that," he informed her.

"Oh," said Susan. "We shall see about that, first you will have to answer to my father, he'll want to know why?"

She turned her back on him and folded her arms just as she had when her father told her off.

"And what has your father got to do with the way I discipline my staff?" asked the commissioner.

"He's the chief of police at Zimba, that's who," said Susan angrily.

"Oh is he now?" said the commissioner.

He rubbed his chin once more and looked at Susan, and then he burst out laughing.

"No, ho, ho, ooooo ha, ha," went the commissioner.

"I don't think it's funny," said Susan. "If it amuses you to insult your staff, then I suggest you change your job," she said to him.

"To what?" asked the commissioner.

He paced up and down. He stopped his pacing and looked at Susan, who now felt as strong as an ox and as defiant as a bull elephant.

"Well," he said. "I'm waiting."

"If you tried smiling hard enough, perhaps you'd make a good clown," she said.

As she said this to him she looked him straight in the face. 'In for a penny in for a pound', she thought. 'If I'm going to lose my job I may as well get it off my chest'.

"Frankly, I couldn't care less at this moment," said Susan. "I've never been so insulted in my life. This week I've just about had it up to here," she raised her hand. "Just because I'm a woman people think they can walk all over you. I'm a woman trying to do a man's job, but that doesn't mean I can't have my say just as any man would. I demand respect the same. It's about time I stood up for myself, and sometimes you men make me sick, always shouting and screaming how good you are, and saying that we women are the weaker sex. Bullshit! Now how about that? I can be just as tough as you …"

"Oh no, now hold on a minute," said the commissioner. "This has gone too far."

"Oh no it hasn't," shouted Susan.

She was quite enjoying her last fling.

"That's typical of you men," she said. "Just when we have something to say you throw your authority by trying to quieten us down., Well, it won't work not with me any more. I quit, so there. To me you are just a plain sick old man, sick you hear?"

"By jingo, George was right about you," said the commissioner. "He said if you were riled you'd let me have it. Come and sit down," he beckoned to Susan. "Come on, sit down have a cigarette and calm down," he said, taking a packet out and offering her one.

Susan didn't understand but did as she was told and sat anyway. She was really uptight, she was still shaking with temper but she took a cigarette and let out a sigh.

"Your father and I had a talk weeks ago. He thought you weren't ready to take on responsibilities yet, but I can tell him differently now," said the commissioner.

"You know my father then?" asked Susan.

She still could not look him in the eye after all the things she had said, so her eyes were diverted to other parts of the room.

"That's your father," said the commissioner.

He pointed to a photo on the wall.

"And that's me, we both started off here" he said.

He pointed to a large map on the wall. Then he pointed to another place.

"Did our training there," he said, indicating the place with his finger.

He then walked over to Susan and lit her cigarette.

"Thanks," said Susan. "You are sounding like someone dad told me about. He's told me about you."

The commissioner nodded.

"He's a bit older than me of course," he said. "But only a couple of years."

"Are you? No you can't be," Susan said.

"Yes I'm afraid so, your dad's brother, and may I add I admire your guts, ha, ha," he said laughing. "You knew the consequences of what you were saying, but still you said it, no matter what."

"But you and dad fell out years ago," said Susan. "Haven't spoken for years, so he said."

"True," said the commissioner "but that was caused by the same defiance you have in you my girl. We patched it up weeks ago."

He held out his hand. "Here," he said. "It seems that I made a bit of a fool of you. Will you accept my apologies?"

At first Susan didn't know what to do, and thought about it and then realised that her own father had tried to give her a bit of warning but she hadn't twigged it.

"Ok" said Susan. "Friends," she said and added, "I do feel a right fool."

She stubbed out her cigarette in the ashtray.

"My fault, you know I'm used to talking to men, but we all have to change don't we?" said the commissioner. "Tell me, until today how have you been getting on with the duties you have had?"

"Oh I do whatever dad tells me, mostly office work," she smiled. "That's until today. Until last week I was the only one who could do it, but now we have some new staff so ..."

"So, this is your first real assignment?" asked the commissioner.

"Yes," she replied.

Susan began to feel more relaxed; she crossed her long slender legs.

"To be quite honest I should have loved to have gone to the States. You already know my reasons," said Susan. "But…"

"Oh yes, your boyfriend is one of the pilots," he said.

He sat on the edge of the desk.

"Now how do we get over this one?" he said, half to himself.

He pressed the intercom button on his desk.

"Yes sir," said a voice.

"Have we anyone going to the States?" he asked.

"I'll check sir," said the voice.

"Yes, do that right away," said the commissioner.

Dale Summers, one of our officers, is going to Zurich and is going to be on board sir," said Susan. "But he is only going to Zurich."

"Ah that helps a bit. Anyway, let's see what our good lady comes up with," said the commissioner.

He shook his head at Susan.

"Glad she's not a spitfire like you," he laughed. So did Susan.

"What are you going to do?" he asked Susan.

He picked up some files on his desk and put them carefully in the 'out' tray.

"Well," sighed Susan. "I'm going home in the morning."

She got up and wandered round the room, and then she looked at her watch. She wondered if she could find time to see Jamie off, but it was getting late.

There was a buzzing on the desk.

"Yes," said the commissioner.

"Sir, it appears that Steve Anderson is off to the States, booked on the next flight out," said the voice. "He's going for the championships there or something like that."

"Right, thanks," said the commissioner.

He looked at his watch. Fifteen minutes to go. He wrote down a few notes on a piece of paper, picked up the files on the two men and pressed the intercom button again.

"Yes sir," said the voice.

"Get the prisoners to my car right away, I'll be there in five minutes. Then get on to the airport and get them to hold that plane on my orders all right," said the commissioner.

"Yes sir," replied the woman. "Oh by the way, Chief Warren Bates is on that flight so I did as you asked sir?"

"Thanks, come on Susan, maybe we'll get a glimpse of that boyfriend of yours," he said.

They left to go to the car. When they sat down the commissioner told Susan he had ordered flowers for the retired chief's wife.

"Steve Anderson is the man for this job," he told Susan. "He won't take any chances, he's a professional, Once, he saved the lives of three of his men, but we won't go into that now."

The prisoners sat in the back of the car guarded by another officer.

"It's a long story," said the commissioner. "Briefly, he dragged three men from a burning car that later blew up. They were chasing some youngsters but got piled up instead - into a fence.

MEANWHILE AT THE AIRPORT HOTEL

David and his mother and nurse were getting ready to leave. It would soon be time to board the plane.

"David," called his mother. "Are you up and ready yet?"

She was in her bedroom putting the final touches to her make-up. In the next room the nurse was closing the suitcases.

"Don't you go carrying those suitcases David," she called out to him. "They are too heavy for you."

"There, that's all done," said the nurse. She put the cases down on the floor. "Ready and waiting for you," she said.

"Thanks," said David's mother She came over and patted the nurse on the arm. "Without you here I don't know what I would have done," she said. "Thank you for being so kind and understanding."

"No woman should have to face what you have to face alone," said the nurse. "It's my job and my..." She was going to say more, but stopped. "You just take it easy, this is the worst part, and I'm here to help you That's all you need to worry about."

"You think a lot of David don't you?" asked his mother.

"Yes I do," said the nurse. "If ever I'm lucky enough to have children of my own..."She paused because to hear herself saying such a thing seemed strange. "I hope to one day," she went on. "I'd like them to be like David, to be just as fine and brave as he is. He's a fine boy."

"It's not put you off then?" asked David's mother. "I mean having children. It's just that it seems all pointless that's all, first his father and now this ..."

"No, it hasn't," the nurse answered.

It was in fact the first time she had even thought of having children. She had kept it a complete secret that she had been the nun that David had spoken to at the hospital.

"Ah, there you are David," said his mother, as she looked across at him.

He came in with his suitcase.

"I thought I told you not to carry them," she said to him.

"I'm ok, honest mum," said David, as he came into the room. "It's not too heavy, honestly."

David looked very pale, but he had so much pride and that made him strong.

"We must be away or we shall miss our flight; come on darling," said his mother. She and the nurse picked up their cases and they left the hotel together. David kept looking at the nurse strangely for he had a feeling at the back of his mind all through the trip that he had seen her before, but he could not place where it had been. But it didn't matter because as long as she was there then everything was all right. It was as if she were his own personal angel.

"I'm sure I have seen you before," he remarked to her again, "haven't I?"

MEANWHILE IN THE AIRPORT

Jamie had now reported in for his flight and was getting his flight orders ready when another pilot came hurrying in.

"Ah good, there you are, glad I caught you in time," said the pilot. He was a man in his thirties.

"Why, what's up?" asked Jamie, puzzled.

"You are wanted down in sick bay, you're to go there right away," he told Jamie.

"Whatever for?" asked Jamie. "I've only fifteen minutes to take off." Then, for a split second, he thought something might have happened to Susan. He looked at the other pilot's face.

"Oh my god," he said, "I'll be right there."

He was gone in a flash, leaving the other pilot staring after him in surprise.

'Boy, that's the fastest I've ever seen him move in years', he said to himself.

Jamie rushed down the halls trying not to knock into anyone, but he bumped into one man in his forties. In his hand he carried a small black box, which he was holding carefully. It was Harry.

"For Christ's sake, watch where you are going," said Harry, clutching the box. For a few seconds Harry sweated as he looked down at the box he was clutching and made sure the lid was on ok.

"Sorry," shouted Jamie, looking back. "An emergency, sorry."

"You would have been," remarked Harry, looking at him angrily.

Jamie reached the sick bay, knocked frantically on the door, and then went in after he heard a faint 'come in'.

"What's up?" he asked breathlessly.

He could see someone lying on the bed. The doctor moved to one side and he could see it was not Susan. He let out a sigh of relief. He stood next to the pilot who was to have taken the flight, the one he was now taking. It was Brenda who was on the bed. Alongside her was a small incubator and in it was Brenda's baby.

"Oh no," said Jamie. He looked at his friend. "What's up?, What's going on? What happened?" Jamie asked.

"I'm glad we caught you before you boarded, Jamie," said the doctor.

"Why?" asked Jamie.

"It won't be necessary for you to take that flight after all," said his friend. "I'm going instead; Brenda has had her baby and it's not well. There are other complications. She's fine though under sedation, but the baby is not."

"What's the matter with her?" asked Jamie sympathetically, as he looked at his friend, Warren's face.

"The baby has no feeding gullet," said Warren. "Doc says if we can get her to the States she will live."

"Oh my god," said Jamie. He put his arm round his mate and rubbed his hand through his hair. "I'm sorry, how did it happen? No. Don't tell me. Just get on that flight and get her and the baby there as quickly as possible, ok," said Jamie.

The doctor then explained as Brenda was wheeled out with the baby in its small incubator. Warren went too.

"She won't live long as she has no way of feeding. Twenty four hours from now, and it could be too late. I'm going along to keep an eye on the baby's progress and Mrs Heal," said the doctor to Jamie. "She's so dreadfully upset. Anyway I must run …"

Warren had taken the flight schedule from Jamie and now everyone was boarding the plane. Warren was to be co-pilot on the flight. The doctor asked if they had a back up system for the incubator to be plugged into.

"Yes" said the pilot, "we carry a spare generator on board, in the hold. Warren, you had better get it up here, ok?" He looked at him as if to say sorry. Warren left his wife and went down to bring up the generator. When he came back he looked at the baby with tears in his eyes.

"Hang on in there girl, everything will be all right," he said., "You'll see."

Jamie now relieved of his duty had time to think about Susan. If he hurried he'd catch her and tell her he wasn't going. He was about to go through the door when over the intercom he heard his name called.

"Damn" said Jamie.

He knew that like so many times before, once on the base never off duty and he had to go out on another assignment.

IN THE MEANTIME, IN THE HEADQUARTERS AND ON THE WAY TO THE AIRPORT

The commissioner and Susan had arrived back at the airport with, of course, the two prisoners, and they drove straight to the waiting plane. It was now waiting for the passengers to board.

"Get out, you two," said the officer guarding the two men.

Reluctantly, Sied and Bennett slid out. They were still handcuffed together and they were taken to the tail end of the plane where the steps had been put down, while inside Mrs Heal was being made comfortable and the incubator was being joined to the generator. Mrs Heal was laid across two seats. Bennett and Sied looked along the gangway of the plane as they boarded. Steve handcuffed them to their seats. They watched as two crates were loaded. They belonged to one of the passengers. They both eyed the coloured man who still clutched his small box. Then the other passengers were allowed to board.

"Welcome aboard sir," said the hostess as they got on.

"Tickets please," said another.

"Thank you sir," she said. "Your seat is down in the rear section next to the gentleman." She pointed to Harry.

Then the film couple came on board and were seated and the rest were allocated theirs seats. Soon Jason was on board along with Barry, Jenny, Dale and the retired police chief and his wife. Steve had to leave his seat for a minute as he caught sight of the commissioner outside. He went to see what he had to say.

"Steve," said the commissioner. "Sorry to put you in this spot."

Susan looked eagerly from the car to see if she could see Jamie.

'Damn and blast', she said to herself, 'he must be all belted up now and I've missed him.'.

"You might need this," said the commissioner. He handed Steve a pistol.

"Sir, thanks," said Steve, as he clipped it to his side.

"Here's all the information on them. Be careful ok, oh, and keep an eye on Harry Aimes, that's the coloured guy near the back of you. He's there for a good reason, don't make it obvious ok, just keep an eye," said the commissioner. Steve took the things from the commissioner and went back on board. He glanced at Susan.

Dale sat next to Jenny, his wife, and close behind them was Jason,. Barry sat next to Jason. Now everyone was seated, the lights came on for everyone to fasten their seat belts and to stop smoking. It was time for take off. In the cockpit the pilots made their final checks, the captain in his seat for the ready. Next to him sat Brenda's husband, not Jamie. He sat running his checks as the captain called them out.

"Sir," said the co-pilot., "Everything ok but there is a lot of interference on the radio, mostly static electricity I'd say."

"Better check on that, ok," said the captain, as he looked at all the dials. "These seem to be ok."

"Right sir," said Warren.

The captain said to him, "I know your mind's not on the flight but…" He put his hand on Warren's arm, "…she's in good hands you know and soon your daughter will be."

"Thank you sir," said Warren "Thanks."

"Right, we have ground clearance for takeoff, so let's get this crate off the ground," said the captain.

OUT IN THE SCRUBLAND

Frank and JoJo reached the spot where the old herdsman had told them about animals.

When they were nearly there Frank stopped the landrover, got out his binoculars and looked all around. All he could see were a few animals roaming freely in the distance and nothing seemed to be wrong with them. Over to one side he then caught sight of a few buzzards. He pointed to them.

"Over there," he said to JoJo.

He sat down and put the landrover into gear and drove as quickly as he could in that direction. He had let the binoculars fall to his chest. As they neared he thought he could see something moving. It moved away from the place where the birds were.

"Boss, look," said JoJo. "Over there," he pointed.

Whatever it was had disappeared for a few seconds and Frank continued to drive.

"I'm sure I saw something, boss," said JoJo.

"What was it?" asked Frank.

"I'm not sure boss," said JoJo, "it were too far away."

As they drove on once again JoJo saw something move again as they went over a rise in the ground. Frank caught sight of two natives. They were running off with two ivory tusks. They had killed an elephant. They were sixty miles from their village; to a white man that's a fair way to be from home but to them it was nothing.

In the heat of the morning Frank and JoJo heard the cry – a high-pitched noise. He rammed on the brakes as he was confronted by a young bull elephant, about six months old. Its pitiful cry for its dead mother echoed in the ears of Frank and JoJo. Now the landrover was its enemy. With it head held high, its trunk fully extended and ears flipping it stood threatening the vehicle. For a few minutes Frank didn't know what to do. Then he and JoJo leapt out of the vehicle and, waving their arms, their hands outstretched, they closed in on the animal and calmed him down. Soon he became passive and friendly and with his trunk he gently pushed JoJo to the side of the landrover. The young elephant became very curious about the vehicle and sniffed it all over.

"Well, well, me old mate," said Frank, "what are we going to do with you now?" he looked at JoJo.

"We can't leave him here. He will surely die if we do and he's too big to put in the back," said Frank. "JoJo you'll have to take him back home, ok? It shouldn't take you long and I'll go ahead."

Frank got out of the landrover and went round to the back and pulled out a bed pack for JoJo and then got out one of the two rifles he had brought them.

"Here, you had better take this. I think you may need it. Ok,, I think you'll be all right," said Frank.

JoJo nodded. He understood. He picked up a box of shells.

"Sure boss, I be fine, no trouble. I used to walking long way, many miles" said JoJo. He took the pack and rifle from Frank. "Thanks boss, I look after baby, she be fine with me," said JoJo.

"Good," said Frank. "It's not so many miles back. I'll check the village first and then if I find nothing I'll head towards the town. There's nothing here at all. The birds have finished off what was left. I'll try the radio while I'm on my way and tell them I'm coming."

"Ok boss," said JoJo.

He carefully took hold of the baby elephant's ear and led it in the direction they had come from. JoJo knew a faster way back but it could only be used if one was on foot, a landrover couldn't go the way he was going.

Frank watched as they disappeared, waving as they went. Then Frank drove on.

MEANWHILE BACK IN ZIMBA

Susan's father, the police chief, was sitting at his desk. There was a knock on the door.

"Come in," he called.

He looked quickly at his watch. The time was nine fifteen. An officer came in. He had just come on duty and carried a small box.

"Sir," said the officer. "Here's some more information about the area where the girl got raped. We have searched and found next to nothing. This is just junk," He put the box down on the desk.

"I'm afraid it doesn't amount to much, does it sir?" asked the officer.

"Thanks," said the chief looking up at him.

"Have you had any reports in from Keith Marchelle and Peter Seddon? yet?" asked the chief.

He looked into the box.

"No sir," said the officer. "I'll check on that."

"Do that then," said the chief.

He picked among the items in the box. He found a very small gold clasp. It had been labelled and noted where it was found. Then he opened his drawer and took out the gold chain that the young boy had on his person. It matched.

"Where did you say you found this?" he asked the officer.

"It's on the label sir, in the sleeve of the girl's dress sir," replied the officer.

He handed the chief his report on it and pointed to the piece in the report.

"There sir, left upper side of the shoulder," he said.

"Yes you're right. Then how the devil did that kid…?" said the chief.

"What's the matter sir?" asked the officer.

"Nothing, nothing at all. In fact we may have come up with something. Look they match," said the chief.

"Yes sir, but where did you get that chain from," he asked.

"Oh never mind, that's my business," said the chief; he flicked through the files on the desk.

"Let's see, what time does it say she was raped, ah, here it is, between eleven thirty and twelve," said the chief.

The chief rubbed his chin and looked puzzled.

"I wonder?" he said.

"What sir?" inquired the officer.

"Oh, nothing, well I'm not sure," said the chief.

He pressed the intercom button.

"Yes sir," said John on the other end..

"John?" asked the chief.

"Yes sir," said John.

"What time would you say we had that little bit of trouble last night?"

"Which one sir, the native kid or the other one?" asked John.

"The other," said the chief.

He was still looking at the chain and its clip.

"I'd say about eleven thirty sir," said John.

"Thanks, do you know where he lives? Can you get hold of him again?" asked the chief.

"Yes sir, I think so," said John "He's one of your chopper pilot's sons. Jock boy, and he's also one of our mechanics at the base."

"See if you can get someone to go round and pick him up. I want to ask him some more questions, ok?" said the chief.

"Yes sir. I'm off duty now. I'll go round and get him myself," said John

"Thanks," said the chief.

He turned to the officer and asked him to take the things back to the store. He left the office. The chief then pinned the clasp and chain to the file and put them back in his desk. He then picked up his phone. A woman answered.

"Yes sir?" she asked.

"Where's my beer and sandwiches?" he asked.

"Haven't they arrived yet sir?" she asked.

"No they haven't," he replied.

"Sorry sir. I did leave a message at the canteen. I'll get on it right away and see what's happened," she said.

"Thanks," said the chief. "Are you new here?"

"Very," said the woman.

"That accounts for it then" said the chief.

"For what sir?" the woman asked.

"The fact they have taken no notice of your request," said the chief.

"Yes sir I suppose so, but don't worry," she said., "I'll make up for it even if I have to go and get them myself."

"That's possibly a better idea," he said to her.

"When do you get off duty?" he asked.

"About now sir," she answered.

"How about breakfast then?" he asked her. "I trust you will not think me flamboyant in asking you."

"I need a ray of sunshine at the moment and you may just be it," he said.

He thought for a while wondering if he had done the right thing, if he had made a right choice by asking her.

"Well what about it then?" he asked her.

There was a few minutes' silence as she thought about his offer; she couldn't believe her ears because it was not every day that the chief asked a member of his staff.

"I'd like that very much," she said.

"Good," said the chief. He let out a sigh of relief. "See you soon then."

He put down the phone and raised an eyebrow., He liked the sound of her voice.

MEANWHILE OUT IN THE SCRUB LAND

Frank, who is now on his own, is very near to where the old man had said his animals were standing very still. He knew nothing of what had happened in the town. He brings the landrover to a halt, gets out and looks around. He searches the area and finds next to nothing, only a few bits of bones which he thinks poachers have left anyway. Then after a while he feels that something is wrong. He stands, hands on hips, looking at the ground. He realises suddenly that he is standing in what appears to be a small crater of dark stained earth. Each patch is a perfect circle as if all the blood has been sucked to one spot in the middle. He removes his hat and scratches his head. Frank also noticed how silent it was and looked around only to see birds sitting on the branches looking at him as if waiting for their next meal. He shivered as if someone had walked over his grave. He placed his hat back on his head.

'What the hell is going on here?' he thought.

Slowly he began to be afraid, and backed towards the landrover. He got in and his confidence began to return as he started the engine to life. With the roar of the motor, the birds flew away. Frank continued to the village, which was some miles from where he was.

MEANWHILE WE JOIN FLETCHER AND PETER

Fletcher and Pete have almost reached the village of Wappa. As they drive along, they talk about things in general.

"Seriously, it's true," said Fletcher. "I'm not lying, she really did."

"No, I don't believe you," said Pete who was driving.

"Without a word of a lie, she really did," said Fletcher.

"What, she must be crazy. I don't believe it, her mother really wanted to go on your honeymoon with you both? Insisted on it even," said Pete.

"Yep," said Fletcher laughing.

"Now I've heard everything., What did you do?" asked Pete.

"Well, I certainly didn't agree. I said most definitely not," answered Fletcher.

"Then what happened?" asked Pete laughing.

"She fucking well attacked me," said Fletcher.

"What? Do you mean the mother?" asked Pete.

"No the daughter, dafty," said Fletcher.

"Don't be ridiculous, she didn't. You having me on," said Pete.

"No, true she came at me like a mad thing, kicking and scratching and screaming, I thought what the hell," said Fletcher.

"Christ," said Pete. "What happened then?"

"What do you think? One I can handle, but two never. I hit the daughter, and then her mother started on me. I wasn't going to wait around after that. That is the only time I have ever run away from a woman, Pete. I could have made it up with her when her mother died," said Fletcher.

"Jesus Christ," said Pete. "I think I would have done the same thing."

"She… ah, here we are," said Fletcher changing the subject and looking strange.

He pointed to the village huts coming into view about seven hundred yards away. Pete slowed down..

"Can't see anyone, can you?" he asked Fletcher.

"No, not yet, but there must be someone there. Look!" said Fetcher.

He pointed to the column of smoke in the middle of the huts, five in all now getting nearer.

"We had better do as the chief said," said Fletcher. "I'll go in from one side of the village and you go in from the other., Remember what I told you, don't touch anything, nothing at all, ok?"

"Yes ok," said Pete. "But I don't know why."

"Better unclip your pistol, but don't fire unless you have to, three shots in the air if you need help," said Fletcher.

He got out of the landrover, took out his hanky and wiped his face.

Pete turned off the engine and also got out.

"Just leave the keys in the ignition, just in case," said Fletcher.

"Right," said Pete.

The men left the landrover and walked slowly towards the village.

MEANWHILE BACK AT THE POLICE HEADQUARTERS

There is a knock on the door of the chief's office.

"Come in," he called.

In came the woman who had bumped into Susan earlier. She carried with her a tray. On it were two cans of beer, two glasses and two packs of sandwiches.

"Ah, food at last," said the chief.

He got up from his desk, quickly came round and picked up the chair from behind the door and put in front of his desk.

"You sit there," he told her.

"Thanks," said the woman.

She put the tray on his desk, and then glanced at the clock on his desk.

"What would you like?" she asked the chief. "Beef or cheese and tomato."

The chief went and sat down again. He quickly brushed his hand through his hair.

"Oh I'm not fussy," he said. "As long as it's food I don't mind"

He glanced at the woman. She was in her forties and her hair was permed in an Afro style.

'Hmmm,' he thought; now he could see her close up.

'Nice.'

"I'll have the cheese and tomato, if that's all right with you," she said.

She passed the beef ones to the chief. She caught his eye and for a second they stared at one another.

"Oh fine," said the chief. "Sorry."

"What for?" asked the woman.

"My manners," said the chief. "My name's George Cleaton." He put down his sandwiches.

He held out his hand to her.

"You have me at a disadvantage," he said, "although I'm in charge."

"Why?" said the woman who took his hand hesitantly.

"I have no idea what your name is. I expect it is on file, but I have not got round to it, it's been one of those nights," said George, laughing.

"Marlene Boxall," said the woman.

Her hand met and right away they knew they were meant for each other.

"Pleased to meet you," said George.

"Me too," said Marlene. She stared into the chief's dark eyes.

They concentrated on each other and were interrupted when the phone rang. The chief fumbled for it, too scared to take his eyes off Marlene for a minute, lest the dream went away.

190

"Hallo, George Cleaton here," said the chief.

He sat down and so did Marlene., She opened the cans and poured their beer into the glasses.

"George? Deater here," said the voice.

The phone crackled even worse than before.

"Who?" asked the chief. "You will have to speak louder, I can hardly hear you."

"Deater Hayes, about these things you sent me. We've done a few tests, got quite a few more to do, had it scanned. It's radioactive," said Deater.

"Speak up," said the chief. He smiled at Marlene.

"It's definitely not a seed, we've looked through all the libraries, and I've phoned up Ken Mutter, the professor from Munich. He's coming in on the next flight, should be here in half an hour. He's a gem in archaeology finds, so see what happens then. I'll let you know by late evening. I'll phone you again then, hope by then there will be a clearer line, ok, George must go. Bye," said Deater.

"Right thanks," said the chief. "Thanks for phoning, get you again later, bye."

He put down the phone and looked at Marlene.

"Here's your drink," she said smiling.

"Thanks, now where were we?" said the chief.

MEANTIME IN THE TOWN

Coming down the dusty road was a woman walking her dog, a large mongrel crossbred collie called Ben.

Playing further down the street near to where the bar was burned out is the boy the chief gave a lashing; he is with another boy, a friend of his, who has a football and is bouncing it up and down. Standing not too far away from the bar is a policeman. He is there to make sure that no one touches anything. On the other side of the street is a dog without a collar, He is wandering round and sniffing as dogs do.

"What are you going to do today Billy?" asked the boy with the football.

"Dunno," said Billy.

He stood with one foot on the bottom step of the shop opposite the bar and one hand hanging over the rail outside.

"If that bugger goes away we can go and see what's left in the store," said Billy. "But we can't until he's gone." "Yeah, that's a good idea, we may find some tools. How about getting on building our tree house?. If we had a saw we could make lots of things," said the boy with the football.

They both looked at the copper down the road.

"Maybe if I kicked the ball in there you could go and fetch it," said the boy.

"Now why didn't I think of that?" said Billy.

He stopped swinging on the post.

"Do you know something Darren?" he said.

"What?" asked his friend.

"The longer you stay mates with me, the more you learn. You'd never have thought of that a few weeks ago," said Billy.

Darren looked at Billy in surprise, and felt proud.

"Do you reckon I am getting good enough to join your gang?" he asked hopefully.

"We'll see. We'll have to wait and see about that, it depends on how good you are at sawing up some wood for the roof. Here, give me that ball," said Billy

He took it from Darren.

"When he ain't looking, I'll kick it in the middle, then I'll go and fetch it, while you talk to the cop," said Billy.

"Oh can't I go?" asked Darren.

"No," said Billy. "I'm the boss, you just follow orders if you want to join my gang ok?"

"Oh, all right," said Darren.

He looked at the cop and waited for him to turn his back. The copper recognised the woman coming down the street and turned to wave to her. Billy gave the ball a terrific kick down the street and it flew through the air and landed in part of the bar instead of the store.

"Shit!" said Billy. "It would have to land there. Never mind, we'll try again later."

"You ain't going to leave it there are you?" asked Darren. "My dad will kill me if I don't take it home. My auntie sent me that all the way from England."

"Oh shut up you daft bugger, don't be such a baby. Anyway, what's so special about an old football?" asked Billy.

"What do you mean? You go and get it or I'll bash you," said Darren.

"Oh yeah, just over a stupid ball, you wouldn't dare," said Billy.

"My uncle got it signed by David Burnside, that's who," said Darren.

"Who the hell is he?" asked Billy.

He put up his fists ready for a fight.

"Someone who played for a famous football team, in fact the first division," said Darren.

He poked his tongue out at Billy.

"Ok, if you're that fussed about it," said Billy. "Wait here and I'll get it for you."

Billy saw the policeman was watching him.

"Can I get my ball?" Billy asked the cop. "It's gone in there."

"You clear off, do you hear me?" said the cop.

"But my ball mister, it's in there," said Billy.

"Clear off. Do you hear me? Get out of here," said the cop.

Darren got scared and ran off round the corner, while Billy hung back. The copper saw the woman with the dog.

"Hi there, Mrs Smith, how are you?"

In that fraction of a second, Billy dived under the remains of the foundations of the bar and tucked himself in out of sight.

It was dirty and black in there but thank goodness the fire was out. In the darkness Billy caught sight of the ball and began to crawl towards it. He had only crawled a few feet when his ears began to hurt. A buzzing sound was close by. He felt compelled to go towards it, but he also sensed danger. He shook with fear. The noise got stronger and louder until he could no longer stop himself screaming out, but no one heard him. For as he let out a cry, the dogs who were apart at first had clashed and a terrible fight had begun in the street.

"Help, help," cried the old woman. "Someone do something."

"Ah, ah," screamed Billy as he was engulfed by the monster. Thousands of hungry maggots tore at his body. He was helpless but his cries were in vain. The copper rushed forward to help with the dogs and after a few minutes he parted them and all was well again. Darren came back from where he was hiding. The copper looked at him.

"What do you want?" he asked. "I thought I told you to clear off."

"My ball," said Darren. "He said he was going to get it out."

"Well, I ain't seen no one," said the copper. "I suppose he's gone home. Anyway he's not here. You can see that for yourself can't you?" said the copper.

Darren could not see Billy anywhere so he went off to find him. He wondered what his father would say when he got home without the ball.

MEANWHILE AT WAPPA THE NATIVE VILLAGE

Fletcher and Pete entered the village and immediately sensed the silence.
There was no one about. Pete went round one side of the village while Fletcher searched the huts. He noticed four or five cones on the ground and was careful not to touch them. Pete however let his curiosity get the better of him and he picked one up. He could see no harm in them after all. He had not witnessed what had happened at the bar like Dale and Fletcher had. Suddenly, as he held it in his hand, it began to make a buzzing noise or so he thought. He put it to his ear and listened. Fletcher who was at the other end of the village had seen him bend down and went to yell 'stop.' Suddenly from nowhere, he saw something large moving up on Pete. He quickly aimed his pistol at it but like a crazy fool he had the safety catch still on. He pulled it back as fast as he could, but it was jammed. Sweat was pouring from his head, and that awful noise was getting louder and louder. It was getting nearer and it deafened him and he was paralysed. He was unable to move, but he could see Pete.

"Ah," he screamed out but it was hopeless. Pete was completely engulfed by the monster. It was as if he was being devoured whole. He was almost spreadeagled across the thing. It was about fifteen feet high and a thousand small eye-type things and suckers had fixed Pete to itself. Pete's blood was being sucked out and his flesh changed colour, from flesh pink to a natural white. Fletcher's brain couldn't comprehend what he saw and he blacked out.

MEANWHILE BACK AT THE FARM......TIME TEN FIFTEEN

Mark and James got on with their chores. Mark fed the two ostriches and cleaned out their compounds. Their funny antics made Mark laugh. Each time he stacked the pile of straw it became dislodged because their big feet kept knocking it over.

"Oh shut up you two," called out Mark. "Keep still can't you. I'll be all day doing this if you don't".

He held a pitchfork in his hand and waved it at them.

"Ha, ha, go on get out of the way," he said.

"Aw, come on be fair, how would you like it if I did that?" said Mark.

Anyway he eventually got finished, then he went over to where he was making a birdcage.

Ann prepared the lunch, while Suchana did some washing. James was out playing with Reaker by his favourite tree. Reaker had learnt to do a somersault and was performing while James watched him.

"Come on," said James. "Ready, steady go. Way hey, that's good."

He kept shouting and the chimp jumped up and down and clapped himself and showed his large white teeth.

"Ow, ow ow, ow," mouthed the chimp.

"There's a clever boy," said James.

He patted the chimp on the back. The chimp sat himself on James' leg as he sat crossed-legged on the ground. Afterwards he licked his face. Then the chimp puckered his lips for a kiss. James gave him one.

"Come on," said James. "Last one up the tree is a monkey."

The chimp put his hands on James' head and began to pump up and down screeching at the same time.

"Sorry, sorry, sorry," said James. He laughed.

Reaker rolled over.

"Let me know when you have finished that washing Suchana," said Ann from the porch way.

"I'll help you hang it out," said Ann to Suchana.

Ann looked down from the top of the steps. Suchana held onto an old scrubbing board that had one end in an old tin bathtub. This was full of soapy water.

"Ok, Miss Ann," said Suchana. "I nearly finished."

On the ground was a bucket full of washing she had almost finished. Mark had changed jobs and was hammering away at the cage he was making. On the ground around him were rolls of chicken wire. He had fixed most of the pieces together as Ann came down the steps to help Suchana with the washing. The mynah bird sat in a makeshift cage, a box used for apples once upon a time, with chicken net over the front.

James was now playing with Sophie, the lion cub, as well as the monkey. All three rolled round in some old landrover tyres left by his dad. Sophie and Reaker got on well together. They were playing at chase my tail and biting the tyres. Ann looked at James. She nudged Suchana.

"Look," she said. "Is it really worth it?"

She laughed and looked at the washing and then at James whose clothes by now were covered in dust.

"Ouch," yelled Mark as he hit his finger with the hammer.

"What's the matter" called Ann.

"Nothing mum," said Mark shaking his hand. He put it under his armpit. He pulled it out and sucked it.

'Bloody thing,' said Mark to himself. ' I'm determined to get it done before dad gets back.'

"Oh dear, oh dear, who's a clever boy then?" screeched the mynah bird in a loud voice.

"You can shut up too," said Mark.

He threw a cloth at the cage.

"I hope you realise this is all for your benefit. I've had enough of your chatter for one day. I bet if you could speak proper English you would tell me what to do next," said Mark to the mynah bird.

"Can't a guy get any peace and quiet around here?" said Mark.

"Who are you talking to master Mark?" asked Suchana.

She came over to him.

"Oh, no one really," said Mark. "Just that stupid bird that's' all."

He looked up at Suchana.

"I would not say stupid master Mark," said Suchana.

"Why's that?" asked Mark, looking up from what he was doing.

"When I was a little girl," said Suchana. "One of those birds saved my life so my mother told me."

"How?" asked Mark standing up straight.

"I was three and in my village were many huts. My father found one of these mynah birds with broken wings and leg, so he brought it home and he taught it to say many things and make many noises," she said.

"Go on," said Ann who had now joined them "What happened?"

"A dingo came to our village one night. It was with many others. Our village was not fenced in with spiky bushes as it is now," said Suchana.

"Then what?" asked Mark.

"Well, my father was out hunting and my mother was asleep. The mynah bird saw the dingo enter the hut. My mother said afterwards that if it hadn't made a noise like a rattlesnake, I would have been carried off," said Suchana.

"Wow, what an escape," said Mark.

Mark looked at his mother. The cage was nearly finished and he had just one piece to fix. The bird wolf whistled at Ann.

"I won't call you stupid again," said Mark. "Hey mum, I think Joe's gone wrong somewhere. Where does this piece go?" He held up the last piece.

"Why?" asked Ann.

She bent down and studied what Mark had done. She laughed, so did Suchana.

"Do you intend to put him in there?" asked Ann.

"Why yes," said Mark. "What's wrong?"

"Try putting a bottom on it then," said his mother laughing loudly.

"Now who's stupid?" asked Suchana.

James had now stopped playing with the chimp and Sophie and had settled into a tyre. He was tired out after his romp. He looked around. He first studied the bungalow and the porch, and then he peered at his favourite hiding place under the step., Then he looked at the small table on the porch, and noticed that Mark had left his book on the table. The wind was playing tricks with the pages. He flicked them over one at a time and then caught sight of his once full fish tank. It was now empty. It had contained a few chunks of rock samples that he had collected over the years, like fool's gold, iron and a few fossils. Then his eyes came to ground level where he noticed a fly had settled on Sophie's droppings.

Both Sophie and the chimp were in their compound and had lap and had fallen asleep.

James suddenly caught sight of something he had not seen before. Where he was standing it looked like a cone. He got up and went over and picked it up. It wasn't so heavy so he threw it in the air and caught it and then looked at it again.

"Mum," he said. "Look at what I've found."

He ran towards her, but his once clean clothes were now filthy dirty. They consisted of torn jeans and a t-shirt.

"What's that?" asked Ann. She turned to Suchana. "Want some coffee? It's only dried milk though."

"Bring it here James and show me," said Ann.

"Yes please," said Suchana looking up. "I'll help, if I may Missy Ann."

"All right mum," said James.

"What's he found now?" asked Mark. "Something weird and wonderful I suppose., He's stupid. He even thinks an old tin can is made out of gold."

Mark turned the cage upside down and fixed the last piece in place.

"Don't be so horrid to your brother," said Ann. "You were just the same once. Come on, let's have a drink on the porch."

"I was never as daft as he is," said Mark, frowning. "Was I?"

"Look mum, what is it?" asked James as he ran up the steps.

"Now, how the hell do I know what it is? I haven't seen it properly yet," said Ann. "Here give it to me. Hmm," said Ann.

"It looks like a cone from a fir tree, but how the devil did it get there?" Ann asked.

"I'll get your book mum," said Mark.

Suchana went in to get a saucepan. She brought it out and filled it from a nearby barrel, and then went back up the stairs.

"What is it?" asked Suchana. She reached the porch table where Ann and James had sat themselves down. Mark came out with the book.

"Here it is," said Mark.

He took the book and James tossed the cone in the air.

"Put it down James," said Ann.

She was searching through the pages as James put the cone down on the table. Mark stood waiting.

"I'll put this on," said Suchana, taking the saucepan of water inside.

"Ok, thanks," said Ann. "Here," she pointed to the cones of a fir tree and showed the boys.

"But it's nothing like those in the book mum," said Mark.

"Where could it have come from?" asked James excitedly.

"I don't know," said Ann.

She rubbed her hand up round her neck., She had a strange feeling about it but she did not know why.

"Maybe it's one of those things I read about in my book," said Mark.

"What book is that?" asked Ann. She looked at him.

"This one," said Mark; he picked up the book that was lying on the table.

"Look it says here, that snakes, frogs and all sorts of things rain down from the sky and no one knows why or how they get there. Here you look," said Mark. "Here's the page, see, even people turn up themselves and are never see again."

"You and your imagination, Mark," said Ann. "How long have you been reading books like that? And where did you get it anyway?"

"I got it from school. They said I could have it for the hols. It's true they got it from the city, it's old but it's ok," said Mark.

"The word is holiday not hols," said Ann. "I don't know," she shook her head.

"Anyway James, I suggest you put it in your old fish tank, until we sort it out. You know with your other things, so that you know where it is," said Ann looking around.

"Behind you mum," said James.

"Oh yes I knew I'd seen it somewhere," said Ann.

Suchana brought out some coffee and put it on the table.

"Here we are then Miss Ann."

"Why thank you Suchana" said Ann. "I was just about to come and help you. You found the coffee all right?"

"Yes Miss Ann, it not take me long to remember where everything is," said Suchana.

"James," said Ann. "You let Suchana sit on the stool and put that thing away like I said."

"Yes mum," said James.

"Any cakes left?" asked Mark.

"Yes, go and fetch them," said Ann.

"No I go," said Suchana. "You stay." She disappeared into the house.

Mark sat on the top step, and James picked up the cone and placed it in his fish tank putting a sheet of glass over the top to stop the dust from getting in.

Ann suddenly heard a buzzing noise, and immediately looked up into the sky. She shielded her eyes expecting to see something, but she didn't know what, but having lived out here for some years she knew that just about anything could happen without any warning.

"In the house quick," she yelled out. "Shut all the windows. Suchana close the mesh frames and hurry inside."

"Why what's up?" asked Mark and James.

"Don't ask questions, just do it," said Ann.

She pushed them through the door and then ran around closing the doors and windows swiftly then she went inside. Suchana was the last to go in. Suddenly the buzzing grew much louder.

"Birds," screamed Ann.

All the animals scattered to the safety of their huts, as a black cloud of birds bashed and scattered the wire mesh doors. The sounds were horrific. For a few seconds what seemed like hours they clung together as they passed by, causing havoc and devastation and leaving some dead. As fast as they appeared they were gone. James who had hidden himself behind Ann's skirt slowly came out from his hiding place.

"I didn't like them mummy, take them away they are horrible, Why did they fly at us like that?" asked James.

"It's ok, now darling," said Ann, as she held on to James. "They are all gone now, it's all right, and I don't know," said Ann.

They all went outside and found many dead birds.

MEANWHILE BACK AT THE OFFICE OF THE POLICE CHIEF

The intercom on the chief's desk buzzed. He answered it.

"Yes, what is it?" he asked.

"Sir, I can't get through to Frank Parker at the game reserve," said the officer.

"Shit!" said the chief. "Why's that?"

He ran his hand over his chin.

"We have terrible interference sir, maybe an electrical storm or something. I've been on to the air base and they have the same problems, but they are not sure why. They've tried the weather station but no go," said the officer.

"How's that, what are you trying to tell me?" asked the chief.

"There's nothing on the radar sir, no clouds, nothing," replied the man.

"Christ," said the chief. "Has the whole world gone bloody crazy or something?"

"Sorry sir," said the officer and with that the line began to crackle.

"Ah, never mind, keep me posted on that situation, ok?" said the chief.

"Yes sir," replied the officer. "Will do."

There was a knock on the office door.

"Come in," yelled the chief, as he paced up and down behind the desk.

"George, got a minute?" asked the doc.

"Sure, come in and sit down. What can I do for you?" asked the chief.

"What's up?" asked the doc, taking a seat.

He watched George pacing up and down. He put his bag on the desk and opened it.

"Here," said doc. "Take a couple of these." He took two tablets from his bag.

"Nar, thanks, but I've got a clear head," said the chief. He waved his hand as if to say no.

"Orders," said the doc.

He went over to the drinking fountain and got some water. He held it and the tablets out to the chief. He took them and threw them down his throat.

"What are they?" he asked the doc.

He stopped pacing up and down and sat down at his desk.

"Tranquillisers, that's all, just to slow you down a bit," said the doc.

"There's something going on," said the chief, "and I'm damned if I know what it is."

"Why do you say that then?" asked the doc.

He sat back down.

"Ah, I don't know, just a feeling," said the chief. He put his hand to his stomach. "It's here, I feel it deep down in my gut, but Christ knows what it is. My ear is killing me and making my head hurt."

"Funny you should say that," said the doc.

"Why?" asked the chief almost jumping on the doc for information.

"Seems a lot of people these days are suffering from behind the ears., Some say they hear buzzing sounds, mostly at nights, and I've had a message that I've not been able to carry out yet, to go and see Jason's gran, poor old thing. Seems a might upset about something these last few weeks. You know what old people are like. They tend to hear all sorts of noises, mostly it's their own hearts and intestines making them," said the doc. He closed his bag and went on,. "Mrs Deacon down the road, she's the old dear who is driving me crazy. God knows what Mabel would say if she knew. I'm sure she fancies me or something. I feel she only gets me out to examine her chest, dirty old buzzard, but there's nothing wrong with her. She's lonesome and old, and that's a bad combination. Oh by the way I hear that you gave someone a licking last night?"

The doc smiled.

"Oh shit, who told you that?" asked the chief. "Can't keep anything secret in this town can I?"

"No," said the doc, shrugging his shoulders and smiling. "But from what I hear I doubt whether he will do that again, it was probably what he needed, poor old thing. They seem ..."

The chief picked up a new packet of cigarettes and, offered the doc one.

"No thanks," said the doc. "I'm here to save you and not help you kill yourself, and me in the process." The doc looked at his watch. "Ten thirty five, I've got to go, must get out to the farm and see Jason's gran. If there's anything I can do keep me posted, I'll be back in about an hour. Ok, bye."

"Yeah sure," said the chief. "See you later."

He took out his lighter, paying no heed to what the doc had said and lit his cigarette. He was trying to make sense of what was happening.

As the doc left, Robert Wood, another officer, who had relieved John came into the chief's office after he had first tapped on the door. He had in his hand a folder.

"Yes?" asked the chief.

"Sir, we have tried to locate this kid Billy Johnson. John said you were looking for him, and he's been looking too," said Robert.

"Yeah I know," said the chief. He got up from his seat.

"Well, he was last seen down by the burnt-out store but no one has seen him since. John's out trying to contact his brothers to find out if he has been home or not. He left a message because there was no answer. John has gone to look for them. I've tried the air base because that's where his father works, he's not seen him there either," said Robert.

"So he could possibly be with his brothers then?" asked the chief.

"Yes sir, I expect so," said Robert. "Anyway we won't know until they get back from wherever they have gone. Here's the report you wanted."

"Ok," said the chief. He took the file from the officer.

"Anything else?" he asked.

"Nothing much sir except the old drunk down the road said his dogs have disappeared. I said they had run away but he said…." The officer paused.

"What?" said the chief. "Well, come on what did he say?" he asked angrily.

"He said that if those sons of bitches ran away he'd kill them," said Robert.

"Forget it, never mind we've more important work to do than look out for bloody missing dogs," said the chief, pacing the office floor.

"The stupid b…" he mumbled.

"Right sir," said Robert.

"Next?" asked the chief stubbing out his cigarette in the ashtray.

"Nothing sir except what you know already," answered Robert.

"Right keep me informed," said the chief. "And get Keith Marchele back on duty; tell him I want him right away."

"Yes sir," said Robert.

He left the office to carry out the chief's orders.

The phone rang and the chief picked it up. It was crackling. It was Susan trying to get through to her dad.

"Yes," said the chief. "What is with this damn awful line? Speak up, will you?"

"Da… d I'm not coming home… tonight. I've…ied…to…ay with Deater and …allycan .ou…ere me," she asked.

"Speak slower," said the chief. "What's the matter with this bloody thing?"

But it was no good. He still could not make out what she was saying and slammed down the phone.

"Damn bloody phone lines. Why can't they …" He grumbled and went on with his work.

Some ten minutes passed and Keith arrived. He knocked on the office door and went in. He was very tired. He had only had two hours' sleep.

"Sir you wanted me?" he asked yawning, "excuse me."

"Yes, come in and sit down," said the chief.

Keith did as he was told.

"I want you to go out to Frank Parker's place. Yeah, I know he's your brother-in law, but this isn't a social call. We need to get in contact with him but can't, so take- with you two extra radios, fifteen or sixteen are available. Take whichever you want, set up a radio link if you can, between Frank and Camagonga and one back here to base," said the chief.

"Right sir," said Keith. "What's wrong with the phones?"

The chief did now answer him. He was too annoyed.

"Better take along someone in case of trouble, take some dynamite, shells and anything you might need," said the chief.

Then he scratched his chin and rubbed the back of his neck.

"Something's wrong and I'm not sure what., Could be some sort of an uprising, better be safe than sorry," said the chief.

"Right sir," said Keith as he remembered what had happened in the bar.

"Ok, then you get going. It will take you at least two hours or more to cover the trip, better take the fastest truck we've got left," said the chief.

"Yes sir," said Keith looking worried.

"Right get going and contact us as soon as you can," said the chief.

BACK IN THE CITY

Ken Mutter has now arrived and is in the laboratory. He and Deater have started many more tests on the cone and tests have been set up on the remains of the barman, and Sam the other hunter. The two men study the samples under the microscope.

"Take a look at this," said Ken to Deater. He moved away to let him look.

Ben, another assistant ,was busy doing more tests in another part of the room.

"What's up?" asked Deater, as he came across the room.

"That substance is not unlike beeswax, only it has a different property. As you can see it's dividing and growing again like any other ordinary cells do. It appears to be like blood," said Ken. "Look it's actually attracted by it."

"What exactly is it?" asked Deater.

"I'm not sure what it is. Some more tests will have to be done so we can find out all its properties and why it works that way. Take a look at this one. I put it with the remains of a piece of tissue from one of the two men and this is what happened." He slid the slide under the microscope so Deator could see it.

"Jesus Christ," said Deator "What the hell is it? It's devouring it."

"Yes, it's frightening isn't it? See, in the short time it's been on the slide, it has doubled its size after eating those remains," said Ken.

"What's happening? For god's sake, I've never seen anything grow like that before and so fast," said Deator.

"It can be killed." said Ken.

He picked up a very hot needle and placed it on the slide. The needle consisted of a very fine laser beam. The thing seemed to die straight away.

"It's only a small amount of heat in comparison to what it would take if we let it grow any bigger. We'd have to heat it twenty thousand times more if it grew to any size and heaven knows what it would look like then, I think those tiny dots have something to do with its growth but I'm not sure," said Ken.

"Are you trying to tell me something that I don't want to hear or believe that I'm hearing?" asked Deator. "That it's capable of ..."

Ken nodded.

"If it grew to any great size then an atom bomb will be the only thing that will kill it off," said Ken.

"Holy shit!" said Deator. "Where the hell did it come from?"

"I'm going to do an analysis now," said Deator. "It's obviously not of our planet."

He turned and called Ben over to him.

"Ben, put this slide into some saline and see what happens in a few hours." Deator said, "Add two cups of blood, ok?"

Ben took the slide and put it into a small bottle of saline and placed it in a wire mesh casing and put it to the back of the bench. Deator and Ken did not see this happening. They were busy with their conversation.

"About those maggots?" asked Ken. "How many did George bring?"

"Just two," said Deator. "I'll fetch them, they are in the incubator. Oh and by the way, I've put the cone behind glass till we know what it is., It's better to be safe than sorry."

"Those maggots and the cone could be connected in some way," said Deator. "One could explain the other if only one knew how."

"Right," said Ken. "You could be right".

Deator beckoned to Ben to get the maggots out. He did so and when he opened the door his face registered surprise. He was only a young man and had not worked there long with Deator.

"Sir, take a look at this," he said turning to both men.

He carefully removed the glass jar and placed it on the bench. Inside the two maggots had become four.

"Strange, how many did you say were in here Deator?" asked Ken.

"Two," replied Deator.

"How the hell… better get your gloves on," said Ken to Deator.

The two men put their gloves on. Inside the incubator some of the jelly dishes were now clear instead of red while others were red in the middle and clear on the outside., They were not covered up as the other ones were.

"What are they?" asked Ken. "That they could do this, or who did this?"

"They," said Deator, pointing to the dishes, "were some tests on the common cold. Why weren't they covered up then?"

Deator looked very annoyed as he turned to Ben.

"All samples must be covered up. Do you understand?" asked Deator.

"Yes sir, sorry sir," said Ben.

"You will lose your job my young man," said Deator. "Total incompetence."

"Nothing short of ignorance I'd say," said Ken.

He gave Deator a disapproving look on his choice of staff.

Deator looked at the maggots, and he glanced at Ben who shrugged his shoulders almost to say he didn't care.

"Put one of those on the slide I want to see what it is," said Ken.

Deator picked up one of the things with a pair of tweezers. It seemed strong. He put it on the slide., As he did so he pressed a bit hard and it split in two. At first he was annoyed, then Ken looked at the two halves. Instead of dying like Deator thought it would, it seemed to grow another head.

"Heavens," said Ken. "Take a look at that." He stepped aside so Deator could take a look.

"Christ, what do we do now?" asked Deator. "Seems we have two mini monsters on our hands, only this one's worse than the other."

Ben who had put the other samples into saline still hadn't put them away and now they appeared to have disintegrated into nothing. He had however placed the lid firmly on the top of the bottle and it was marked 'dangerous, handle with care', after adding the blood.

"Here," said Ken "Let's try something, where are those jells with the cold germs on them? No better still get me some of those others. I'll have a look at some of these."

"Deator handed the jells to Ken and he had a look at them.

"Ever seen cold germs act like this before?" asked Ken.

"No, can't say I have," replied Deator "And I've worked on them long enough."

"Let's see now," said Ken as he picked up a dish of jell and placed a maggot inside.

"We will leave it for a while and see what happens," said Ken.

He placed the lid carefully on the dish. "I'm not taking any chances. Ben get me some sticky tape quickly, please."

"Yes sir," said Ben, and he was back with the tape in seconds.

Ken taped down the lid and then put it in a small incubator and closed the lid.

"Better destroy those others in acid, I think. Don't you? We'll take this and seal it in the super intensified laser room and seal it in," said Ken.

"Yes I guess you are right," said Deator, and he did it right away.

"We've got some more tests to do on that cone so let's get to work," said Ken.

"If it's attracted to blood why not put some in the room with it and see what happens. That way we'll know exactly what we are up against," suggested Deator. "I have an awful feeling that something terrible will happen when we do."

"Good idea," replied Ken. "If we keep it contained then nothing undue could happen. But at least we'll know the truth won't we and its capabilities?"

"Ben have you done as I asked?" said Deator.

"Yes sir."

"Right good, we have lots more tests to do, so you had better contact anyone you may have made arrangements with and let them know you won't be able to leave."

"But sir," Ben was annoyed, not because he had to work but because he hadn't been asked, only told. It was a very bad failing on Deator's behalf for he naturally thought everyone should be as dedicated as he was. But he was wrong. He should have asked Ben not told him.

In his annoyance with Deator he forgot to put away the samples in the wire mesh case.

MEANWHILE UP IN THE AIRPORT

The take-off went smoothly and everyone settled down. Mrs Heal was fast asleep and the baby was settled in its incubator. The film couple sat talking to each other, as were the others though all was not well with one woman.

The nurse, David and his mother had made themselves comfortable, Jason was sat next to Barry, Dale's kid brother. Jenny and Dale were sat next to each other and parallel with Jason and Barry. In between were a number of other passengers.

A very young couple sat side by side, it was the two from the hotel. The retired chief of police sat with his wife further down the gangway. The grey haired professor sat next to Harry, the man Jamie had bumped into earlier on.

Although there were passengers, the plane was not quite full and there were at least ten empty seats near the back. Two of these seats were occupied by the two prisoners, Sied and Bennett. Steve Anderson sat on his own on the other side of the gangway. Most of the passengers had stowed their hand luggage about themselves.

Jenny noticed while packing that Dale had packed his pistol on top of her hand luggage. Two hostesses were on board to assist in the serving of drinks and meals and also to answer questions, and attend to the crew. One was a pleasant, neat, slim woman of about twenty-two with a nice smile. Another, a blonde hostess walked down the gangway. As she passed she smiled at the passengers, the other hostess checked all the passengers' tickets. The blonde hostess then went to the back of the plane where there was a small compartment where she could make coffee. She picked up a small hand intercom confidently.

"Good morning, ladies and gentlemen," she said. "The captain wishes to welcome you all on board. He hopes that you are all comfortable and that we all have a safe journey. We shall be flying at twenty five thousand feet and three hundred and fifty miles an hour. If you wish to keep a check on our trip there is a pamphlet in the seat hold in front of you. May I recommend that all passengers read the safety rules that are in the same pocket. Above your heads if you look, there are oxygen masks in case of accidents. Instructions on how to use them are also in the booklet. Should you wish to ask any questions, or want anything to drink then we shall be here to help you. Thank you, enjoy your trip, at about twelve thirty we shall start to serve drinks and coffee," she smiled, "should any of you feel so inclined to sample some".

The other hostess now took over. She was about five foot four and had a good figure. She took the intercom from the blonde hostess and repeated the message in French, replacing it afterwards. Then, she thanked her partner. The captain by now had made sure everything was safe and after instructions from a somewhat crackled ground control, put the plane on automatic pilot. Then he stretched and looked at his co-pilot.

"You ok?" the captain asked Warren.

"Yes sure," answered Warren as he went on with his final checks.

"Go back and see if your wife's all right., I expect you want to check everything's all right," said the captain. He understood his anxiety.

The captain gave his co-pilot a reassuring look and tapped him on the arm.

"Everything will be fine you'll see," he said to Warren.

The co-pilot unclipped himself and took off his headphones.

"Thanks, I hope to god it will. I'll only be happy when we get this baby to the hospital in the States where she will get the specialist treatment she needs. Back in a minute," said Warren. "Better see if my wife's ok too?"

"Yes sure, no hurry," said the captain.

One of the hostesses popped her head round the cabin door, the dark haired one.

"Coffee for you two?" she asked, smiling broadly at them..

The co-pilot passed her and went through the door and into the gangway.

"Yes sure, save mine till later. I'll be back in a minute or two," said Warren.

"Ok," she said. "Oh Warren, I'm sorry to hear about your baby. I've just looked at her. She's lovely. The surgeon told me a little about her. I hope she will be all right."

"Thanks," said Warren as he left. He was grateful for everyone's kindness.

"Right then," said the hostess "Coffee and biscuits for you two?"

She was referring to the captain and the navigator,

"If I remember rightly," she pointed at the captain "yours is black and no sugar."

"Correct," said the captain. "By the way how's that boy friend of yours?"

"Gone just like the rest I'm afraid," she replied. "The spark's gone out."

"Oh it's like that is it?" said the navigator, smiling at her.

"Yes," she sighed "seems like my magnetic personality drives them away. Instead of staying with me, they run a mile. Can't think why?"

"Never mind I can handle that problem," said the navigator grinning. "I'm an expert on electronics. I could turn you on anytime."

"Now there's an offer you shouldn't pass up," said the captain smiling.

"What?" said the hostess "Wired up to him would be like being the owner of a power station. He'd soon fizzle out and be on the run just like the rest of them. Oh no," she laughed. "I've had enough of men for the time being."

As she said this she brushed the navigator's hair with her hand. "Cheeky!"

"You won't know unless you try," he said as he beamed up at her. "Will you?"

She put her head on one side and raised her eyebrow. 'Nice,' she thought.

"Oh well back to work, see you later," she said. "I'll let you know, ok?" she said.

She left the cabin and returned to her duties. As she went past the co-pilot, he was sat with his wife, holding her hand but she was still sedated and fast asleep. The hostess thought 'god, I hope she will be all right.'

David, the young boy, had left his seat and was standing a few feet away from the baby and his face full of amazement. Warren looked at David and then at the baby.

"Would you like to come closer?" Warren asked David. "You can if you like..

"Yes please," said David, and they began to talk.

Dale sat next to Jenny and Barry sat in the opposite aisle next to Kevin. Kevin seemed very worried and nervous. He kept peering down the gangway to a point behind the prisoners. Barry just sat there with a worried look on his pale face.. He was very tired and also he had something on his mind.

The hostess walked along the aisle to Steve's seat.

"Excuse me," she said to him. She looked very smart in her red and white uniform. Steve looked up from the book he was reading, a book on guns.

"Yes," he said to her, right away. He liked her looks.

She hesitated for a second as their eyes met for the first time she had been in the middle of the plane and hadn't seen him board Stuttering, she said to him. "Er, er, sorry to disturb you sir, but the captain wishes to see you in the cabin in about five minutes, all right?"

"Thanks," said Steve.

He felt something was wrong but he wasn't sure what. He smiled at the hostess and checked that the two prisoners were still handcuffed to their seats and then walked up the gangway.

Dale caught sight of him as he walked past and he recognised him and his eyes too followed him as he walked towards the cockpit.

"Who's that?" asked Jenny. "Quite a dish, mmm," and then went on to say, "if I wasn't mar…"

"Well, I'll be damned. I've seen his pictures enough but I've never seen him. I believe that's Steve Anderson, he's a crack shot on the range," said Dale.

"Who?" asked Jenny. "Who did you say it was?"

"Hey, you just watch it," said Dale. He laughed. "That's no way a lady should act, going round fancying anything in a pair of pants."

"Who said I was a lady?" asked Jenny. She crossed her eyes and made a face.

She smiled at Dale and then she watched Steve enter the cabin.

Barry by now was feeling a bit more confident so he looked across at Jason who clung tightly to his bag. He noticed Jason was uneasy.

"Why don't you put your bag up there?" asked Barry. "You would be more comfortable."

He pointed to the rack but Jason clung on even tighter.

"None of your business," said Jason. "I'll keep it if you don't mind."

His big dark eyes were wide open and his dark skin shone. He was sweating profusely.

"Oh I get it," said Barry. "First time flying, ah, you don't have to worry about it. You'll find it smoother than riding on a bus. , Sorry, there I go again, me and my big mouth. You've never been on a bus have you?"

Barry looked at Jason sternly. "Haven't I seen you somewhere before?"

"What you on about boy?" said Jason. "Why don't you mind your own business aye, get off my back and stop bugging me." Jason's appearance had completely changed.

"Pardon me sir," said Barry. "Seems there are some coloured folk who don't want to be friends."

Jenny heard all this going on and looked across at Barry. Dale had his eyes closed.

"Why don't you leave him alone?" Jenny asked Barry, in a whisper.

"Do you have to read?" asked the film lady. She slapped her hand down on her lap. "Jesus Christ, am I that boring?" she asked, looking at her husband.

He pretended he never took any notice of what she said and went on reading.

"Don't let it worry you dear," he said and patted the back of her hand. "It never did before. You'll get over it." He was being sarcastic of course.

"Why can't we talk anymore? What the hell's going wrong? Please talk to me. If only you'd tell me what I've done wrong then maybe I could do something about it," she said. "I know you still blame me for what's happened don't you?"

"You've done nothing, nothing at all," he said still reading his book.

"Then if it isn't me, what are you trying to hide?" she asked.

"Hide?" asked her husband. "What are you implying, that I have? You seem scared? I won't run away if that's what's worrying you. You're my star aren't you?"

"You wanted to see me?" asked Steve as he entered the cockpit after he had knocked the door.

"Oh yes," said the captain. "The commissioner asked me to get through to the States as soon as we get to London. Something about transport, did you know that?"

"Yes I did," said Steve. "Thanks. Any problems?"

"Good, I'll do that as soon as I can," said the captain. "By the way we have an hour's stop at each refuelling point so I'll order an armed van to be waiting then you can take the prisoners off at each stop."

"Right thanks," said Steve. He nodded to the navigator. "Quite a headache isn't it? All this lot I mean." Steve looked round at all the dials.

"Not when you know your job," said the navigator, smiling up at him.

"Rather you than me," laughed Steve.

"The reason I'm doing it this way is that I'd rather they didn't mix with the other passengers. We don't want to give them the opportunity to cause trouble," said the captain.

"Thanks," said Steve. "A good idea, I appreciate it."

"Oh, I hear you are one of the best shots in the world, is that true?" asked the captain.

"I am," replied Steve. "I've heard rumours to the same effect," he smiled.

"Christ, no one can accuse you of being big headed can they?" asked the captain.

"I wouldn't know," said Steve.

He looked at the navigator and winked and smiled at him. He smiled back.

"If you have any problems with those two let me know," said the captain. "Try and keep them away from the others. I'd appreciate that as we don't want any trouble at the altitude, ok?"

"Yes thanks, see you later then," said Steve. "I understand."

He then left the cockpit and made his way back to his seat, sitting behind the two prisoners.

"I love my ring darling," said the pretty teenage girl sitting next to her boyfriend. She turned and whispered, "I've taken the other one off." Then she said loudly, "isn't it beautiful?" She held out her hand to show him.

"Just wait until our secret is out, I'm sure we'll get along fine. It's not every day a girl gets engaged," she said.

"It suits you darling," said the boy holding her hand lovingly. Then he whispered, "Remember you are not supposed to be here so don't make it obvious."

"What's the matter Warren?" said the elderly lady to her husband, the retired chief.

He was looking a bit pale and tired, and was having trouble breathing.

"Are you all right?" she asked him. "You look quite pale."

"Yes, don't fuss," he said. "You know I don't like it when you fuss."

"It's my job to fuss over you, you silly thing who else is there? After all those years you spent in the force I can now take proper care of you," said his wife.

"Would you like some coffee?" asked the hostess leaning over the seat.

"Well, yes all right," said the old lady. "But my husband is not feeling too good .could he have a whiskey please?"

She turned to her husband and patted his hand.

"That will make you feel better," said his wife. "It usually does."

"Yes I'll fetch it straight away," said the hostess.

She went back along the gangway, taking orders as she went.

"Dale," asked Jenny. "Are you all right?"

Dale still had his eyes closed.

"What's up? You sound worried?" asked Dale opening his eyes.

"I am," said Jenny. She flicked back her hair from behind her neck.

"Why?" asked Dale. "Are you still fretting about the fact that Barry didn't come home last night?"

"Something like that. Your brother is worried about something, but I don't know what it is," said Jenny. "And he looks ill doesn't he?"

"Have you asked him?" asked Dale whose eyes were slowly closing again.

"No I haven't but I intend to, so should you he's so bloody sensitive these days., It's strange. He was out the night before last as well," she replied. She noticed Dale was falling asleep.

"Then I'd say he was now fully grown up," said Dale. "Able to sort out his own problems, don't you think?"

"I'm only obeying my instincts," said Jenny. "I feel something is very wrong. Like you darling, for instance."

"I think it's time he left home," said Dale opening his eyes again.

"Oh dear, you look awfully tired darling, and here's me babbling on and you've been up all night," said Jenny. "I'm sorry. Why don't you go and have a good sleep, go on. I don't mean to nag? Sorry."

"That's ok," said Dale. He bent forward and kissed her. "I've got plenty of time. I'll catch up tomorrow. Maybe I'll have some sleep later if that's ok with you?"

"Of course darling. Barry can keep me company."

"That being the case I'll definitely get my head down but not here., I'll go down the back where I can stretch out," said Dale.

"That's fine darling. You'd think me very selfish if I didn't now wouldn't you?" said Jenny. "Go on, off you go."

She kissed him on the lips. They felt very hot. She frowned as he got up and knocked his head. "Anything wrong, you are very hot aren't you?"

"Ouch," said Dale. "That hurt."

"Sorry darling, I didn't mean to do that. Let me look at it," said Jenny.

"No, don't worry," said Dale. He turned to Barry "Here you sit next to Jenny and keep her company while I have a sleep."

"Sure," said Barry. "Anything's better than sitting next to this one I'm sitting next to now. He's a regular tiger about to bite my head off any minute. He reminds me of someone."

"Barry," said Jenny, "there's no call to be rude. I don't know."

"Tell him that," said Barry, "not me." He got up. "I only tried to be friendly."

He went over and sat next to Jenny.

"Bye darling," said Jenny.

She waved a few fingers at Dale. He just shrugged his shoulders.

"See you later," she said. "I'll try and see what's up with him."

Dale went down the gangway and he stopped when he reached Steve's seat.

"Everything all right?" he asked Steve and leaned over the seat.., The seat next to Steve was empty. Dale felt very hot. He rubbed his hand over the back of his neck. To him things began to sound as if they were a long way away.

"You ok?" asked an echoey voice.

It was the hostess, the dark one. She wanted to get by with some drinks.

"I just feel a bit dizzy," said Dale. "I worked all last night."

"Sit down mate," said Steve looking up. "You look awful."

"Thanks," said Dale. "I don't usually get as tired as this."

He lowered himself down in the seat beside Steve and he then felt a little better.

"You are Steve Anderson?" Dale asked.

Dale was not going to miss a chance to speak to his idol.

"You have me at a disadvantage," said Steve looking at him.

"Dale Sommers," said Dale holding out his hand. He shook it.

"Excuse me captain," said the blonde hostess. "One of the passengers says that her husband isn't feeling too well, a Mr Bates. He's about sixty five. What shall I do about it?"

"Keep a check on him," said the captain. "We may have to turn back."

He turned to her and went on, "let me know if anything else develops. By the way how's the baby doing?" he asked.

"Yes sir," she said as she made to leave the cockpit. "Oh she's wonderful, sir."

"Thanks," said the captain., He smiled at the navigator. "See what you might be letting yourself in for?" He winked. "It could be one of those flights."

The co-pilot had now come back to the cockpit and smiled at the captain and the navigator and got on with his work. "You think so?"

"Where are we now?" asked the captain.

"Look Barry," said Jenny looking out of the window "down there."

Barry leaned over and looked out of the porthole.

"Hmm, doesn't look much from up here does it? We're flying right over Zimba. Doesn't it look small? The houses are like little dots on a child's board," said Barry. Jenny could smell drink. She was about to ask.

Then suddenly he noticed something else.

"Hey what's that?" asked Barry. "Look down there."

"What?" asked Jenny. "I can't see anything, Barry have you …?"

"Oh nothing really I thought I saw a red light or something. Probably the beacon on the police station that's all," said Barry.

"Can't be," said Jenny. "An ordinary light wouldn't show this far up would it?" Perhaps Dale was right, thought Jenny.

Steve got out his cigarettes and offered them to Dale.

"No thanks," said Dale. "Not now. I just can't face them."

"You were saying?" said Steve, studying Dale's reactions.

"Yes I was reading about you in my report sheet last night funnily enough, must have been quite an honour to travel round the world. When did you start?" asked Dale. He kept rubbing his leg.

"Oh, it seems like years now," said Steve lighting his cigarette. "Eighteen yeah, that's about it I joined the force when I was barely old enough to be a cop, lied about my age, still got in regardless. They were going to chuck me out but I must have a good friend up there," he pointed skywards.

"When did you realise you were good on the firing range?" asked Dale.

He put his hand on his leg and rubbed it and yawned.

"Sorry," he said to Steve. "Not bored with the conversation, just that I've been up all night."

"It's ok with me," said Steve. "You don't have to apologise, I know the routine. Besides, anyone in their right mind wouldn't dream of becoming a cop if they knew the consequences."

"Why do you say that then?" asked Dale, looking at Steve quizzically.

"Well I wouldn't say it's ruined my life, but it sure has a hell of a way of bringing people down. Me for instance, a crack shot able to go anywhere, practically do what I want. I met and fell in love with a girl, got married then had two kids, then got divorced all in three years, and now I hardly ever see my two girls," said Steve.

"Why don't you leave the force then?" asked Dale, and try again.

His face was getting very red and he began to feel very hot.

"Hey, are you ok? Look why don't you talk again later?" said Steve. "Maybe we can have a drink together all right?"

"Yes, maybe you're right. Phew. It's hot, are you hot?" Dale asked Steve. He got up.

"Thanks, see you later," said Dale.

As he moved away he pointed his finger in the direction of the prisoners.

"Watch those two guys, especially that one," said Dale., He pointed to Sied. "He's mean."

Dale waved to Steve and went further down the plane.

"See you later" he said. He began to limp.

When he reached the back of the plane he stretched out across two seats and after settling down he raised his arm and switched on the cooling system, because he was so hot. He covered his face with his arms and went to sleep. David sat down and studied a photo of his dad taken from his pocket and remembered the good times he had.

The young girl put on some more make-up while her young man caught up with some sleep.

MEANWHILE BACK IN THE CITY

Back at the lab Ken and Deator looked at the specimens they had left earlier to find the maggots had devoured the blood on the plate along with what was left in the jar Ben had placed there. Now more than sixty maggots had transformed themselves into a blob, a small healthy mass. They were too dangerous to touch. Deator and Ken looked on, but neither knew quite what to do. They needed to keep it for a while to see what the connection was between them and the other things they had discovered.

OUT IN THE SCRUBLAND

Frank brought the landrover to a standstill just outside the village and got out. He noticed almost immediately his engine died just how quiet it was. He stood for a moment and looked all round him. Sitting like people after an accident were lots of birds, vultures, and others, large and small sitting silent and looking. Frank rubbed the back of his neck. It felt queer., He shivered in the morning heat yet he was sweating. He walked towards the hut and as he did so he saw many cones on the ground., He bent and picked one up. He put it to his ear not knowing the danger he was in, then threw it to the ground as he caught sight of the old herdsman. He was sitting by a long extinguished fire. He was about seventy and Frank was several yards away.

"Hey you," called out Frank in the native tongue. "Where is everyone? What are all these things on the ground and where did they come from?"

Frank got no answer and he began to walk towards the old man. As he got nearer his ears began to hurt like they did before at the bungalow. He shook his head to clear the noise but it grew louder. He began to feel very scared for some unknown reason and he tried to stop walking forward but he couldn't. Slowly his legs propelled him forward and now he was only a few feet away from the old man. His body shook violently as he tried with all his might to stop. Through beads of sweat he saw the old herdsman's face. He let out a cry for help when his eyes focused on the horror before him. The whole of the top half of the man was a mass of honeycombed type cells which contained a small maggot with tiny eyes that seemed to penetrate right through Frank's body. The noise was now deafening. Each maggot monster from within its home seemed to call to Frank 'come, come, come' they seemed to say to him. Frank could no longer control his own body as it was being taken over. He knew instinctively that if he touched it he would be dead.

"Ah, ah, ah," yelled Frank.

The buzzing was becoming more than he could tolerate. Suddenly from nowhere Frank was tossed aside, his knees now like jelly as he flew through the air. He thought for a split second that his end had come. First he felt a sharp pain as he fell on his left shoulder then he saw stars., He went out cold.

BACK IN TOWN

The doc is just finishing his house call on Miss Deacon and is trying to get away gracefully without upsetting the old buzzard.

"All right Miss Deacon take those pills I gave you three times a day," said the doc. "And make sure you do." He pointed his finger at her.

"Why doctor supposing I forget to take one I can take two the next time?" said Miss Deacon. "Why don't you stay for a drink? You know you are more than welcome."

The doc frowned as he held on to the top rail of the porch.

"No, thanks a million I must get on," said the doc.

He patted his bag and walked down the steps.

"I've got to do some more calls. I've gotta go and see old Ma Leggo...Jason told Stacey at the store a couple of days ago that she has been poorly and I've been so busy that I haven't had time to see to her in the last twenty four hours."

"Oh yes I know," said Miss Deacon. "I heard that Mrs Beckwith had a fine baby boy, and Trace, dear Tracey Saunders has broken her big toe. She fell down stairs or something. Then there's your poor Stacey and Maria and the kids, poor things. The store burned to the ground last night I heard," she hesitated as she looked at doc. "Never mind where I heard it from. Then there's that awful bar place a proper den of no goods in there. Why the night before last I was just going to bed when I heard an awful screaming and commotion coming from there. Awful, it was just awful. I'm glad that place has gone. Anyhow, then there was that kid stealing ..." While Miss Deacon said all this she slowly came out of her door and doc backed towards his car and got in.

"Oh, is that so," said doc. "Where did you say it came from?"

"Why over there of course," she said and pointed to the street that led to the back of the bar and store.

"Thanks Miss Deacon," said doc.

He started up his engine.

"Bye," he said, and drove away.

Thinking about what Miss Deacon had said the doc remembered reading the report about Nickki, his grand daughter. It said it could have happened at the time and place that Miss Deacon had mentioned.

OUT IN THE SCRUBLAND

JoJo was still on his way back to the farm, when he came across six natives out on a hunting trip. They were hunting for snakes. They were from another part of the region not the Wappa area but they were heading for the village. JoJo made signs of friendship and chatted to them for a few minutes and they in turn admired the baby elephant, patting him first. Then they were asked by JoJo where they were going. They told him that they were out to catch snakes and were taking them to the village as a present, a wedding gift for the bride's father. The one who was talking turned and pointed and beckoned to one of the men to come forward. He was about fifteen..

"My son," the man told JoJo. "He going to fetch wife from village and take snakes for girl's father, good eating," he said, rubbing his stomach.

The native then pointed at the elephant.

"You give to me, my son be honoured," he said to JoJo.

JoJo looked at the others and held on fast to his gun. He pulled it slowly up and rested it on his shoulders.

"No," said JoJo.

The native stepped forward and JoJo stared hard into his face. Then suddenly they left after the older native mumbled something to them. JoJo continued on his way. As he did so he heard the sound of a landrover and looked through his binoculars when he saw Keith's vehicle on its way to Frank's place with one of the other officers. Suddenly from out of the bush came a rhino. He stood in front of the landrover and refused to move an inch. Keith was now about six miles from Frank's place by now. He swerved when he heard his mate yell out.

"What the hell," yelled Keith's mate. "Watch out!"

The landrover hit a rock and turned over. The driver was thrown through the windscreen and killed outright. Keith found himself wedged under the landrover door and couldn't move; the pain was too great. His gun was just out of reach. JoJo saw what happened and ran as fast as he could to help, leaving the baby elephant behind. He held on fast to his gun.

The rhino stood threatening the upturned landrover. Keith feared it would attack. Slowly, he tried to reach for his gun. The sweat poured off his face, but he couldn't reach it. The door wouldn't let him.

Suddenly a shot rang out and the rhino dropped dead. JoJo had taken aim and fired just as the rhino charged. Keith fell to the ground with exhaustion. His eyes closed, but after a few seconds he came to. JoJo had fetched the baby elephant and had tied some rope around its neck and was pulling the landrover off Keith.

"Christ, I thought I'd had it," Keith said to JoJo.

"Pull, pull, pull," said JoJo to the elephant, holding on to the rope around the baby's neck. Slowly the vehicle moved and Keith pulled at his leg. JoJo came over and bent down.

"You ok boss?" he asked. "The other man dead, he hadn't a chance."

"Thanks, for a minute I thought I'd had it too," said Keith.

"Can you walk?" asked JoJo. "Is your leg broken?"

He helped Keith to his feet. He managed to get up, as he did so he pointed to the radios that had been thrown out.

"See if they are any good," said Keith. "What's your name? Haven't I met you somewhere before?"

"My name is JoJo boss, not lessen it been in town I don't rightly know that sir," said JoJo.

"Ah," groaned Keith, as he put pressure on his leg. "God, that hurts. Ah, at the bar now I remember".

"You badly bruised I'd say," said JoJo. "Don't look broken to me."

"Guess you are right" said Keith. "Anyway what are you doing out here?"

He watched JoJo go over and pick up the radios.

"This one's broken," said JoJo and he threw it to the ground. "This one's ok."

"Never mind that," said Keith. "Help me fetch those boxes." He looked at the baby elephant.

"Pack them on his back will you? I've got to get to Frank Parker's place. We have got trouble out at the village of Wappa and I've got to get there," said Keith.

"Why his already on his way out there bossman, he went off right early in his land rover," said JoJo.

"How do you know that?" asked Keith.

"Why isa with him till nine o'clock when we come across this little bundle. Seems some poachers kill this fella's ma, so boss said to me to take him back to farm," said JoJo.

"Thank god he did," said Keith. "Or I wouldn't be here either. Come on we can use Frank's other landrover, I know he's got two".

"You know boss man Frank then?" asked JoJo.

He looked up at the baby elephant, after tying on the radios.

"Yes, yes I do," said Keith. "He's married to my sister, why do you ask?"

"Oh nothing I knows who you are now," said JoJo.

He helped Keith on to the back of the baby elephant.

"I'd often heard them talking about you that's all," said JoJo.

"I can't say this is going to be a comfortable ride but never mind," said Keith as JoJo helped him on to the elephant's back.

Then they all headed in the direction of Frank's place. They were unable to bring the officer who had been killed.

MEANWHILE OUTSIDE THE TOWN

The doc drove up the dirt track road just a few miles outside the town. He came across many wild animals for it was quite wild where the old lady lived. In the distance he spotted one or two zebras and the odd slender necked giraffe. There just a few hundred yards in front of him as he drove along the road he caught sight of hyenas. He wondered for a second or two why they were so close. He came to a fenced off area and stopped when he noticed the old mare had tipped its bucket over. He brought his landrover to a halt and got out.

"Hello girl," he said to her.

It was now gone midday and the sun was high in the sky.

"Jason not give you a drink today?" he asked.

He bent over and picked up the bucket and patted the horse.

"Where's Jason then? Here, I'll get you some. Perhaps you had some this morning and it's all gone," said doc.

He felt the inside of the bucket.

"Jason usually sees to such things, bone dry what's going on round here?" said the doc to the horse.

Doc went to the back of the landrover, opened it, pulled out a large water canister and put some in the bucket for the horse.

"There you are my girl," said the doc. "That should keep you happy. Bye now, I'll see you later."

The horse looked on and then had a drink. Doc put the canister back in the vehicle and got back in the driving seat after wiping his face with his hanky. When he reached the house he was longing for a cup of herbal tea that the old lady used to make him. All was silent; he got out of the vehicle and noticed the door half ajar.

"Jason, Jason, where are you?" he called out.

He looked all round but saw no one but hyenas on the parched land nearby. He walked up the steps and opened the door. He heard the buzzing of hundreds of flies and smelt a horrible stench. There on the floor lay the dead, old lady. Jason had been very clever. He had made it look like the place had been torn apart by natives. The doc covered his mouth and nose with his hanky and felt instinctively for a pulse but there was none.

"Damn, damn, damn," said doc.

He suddenly felt as if he had killed her himself. He looked around. If only he had come out sooner; yesterday perhaps she might have still been alive.

"What the hell, Jason," he called.

He got up from the old lady and went to the bottom of the stairs.

"Jason, Jason," he called again.

There was no answer to his calls; afraid of whoever had done the deed was still there, the doc went slowly upstairs. He pushed open the door of the old lady's room to find it wrecked and then went into Jason's room expecting to find Jason dead but his room was also wrecked.. He was just about to leave Jason's room when he noticed some torn up photos on the floor. He bent down and picked them up. It was like a jigsaw trying to fit the pieces together but it was worth the bother for the photos were taken in town. They were of the women who had been raped and one of them was Nickki. He pushed the pieces into his pocket and went back downstairs.

"I can't leave you like this," he said to the still form on the floor. He threw a blanket over her as he sat her back on the chair as best he could and wheeled it outside., He picked up a nearby shovel and went to dig a grave.

MEANTIME AT THE CITY AIRPORT

Susan had said goodbye to the commissioner and thanked him for taking her to the airport. She had breakfast at the airport and arrived at her friend Sally's florist shop.. She opened the door and as she did so a bell rang.

"With you in a second," called out Sally from behind the thin partition; she was busy making a wreath.

"I have reached the point of no return. If I let go now it will all fall apart., There done it," said Sally.

She wound up the piece of wire and cut it off. Then she came out into the shop. She looked up as she wiped her hands on her pinny.

"What can I do for you?" she asked politely.

Susan's back was turned; she was looking at some of the plants. She half turned.

"Susan," said Sally excitedly. "Susan is it really you? Well what a lovely surprise. What are you doing in the city? Deator told me you weren't coming."

Susan went over to Sally. She held out her hand and Sally grasped it.

"Hi," said Susan. "I hope you don't mind."

"No," said Sally. "Not at all. Did you come with your father?"

Sally looked at Susan and smiled. She dropped her hands.

"Want some tea?" she asked Susan. "I'm just about to have some myself."

"Yes please," said Susan, rather surprised at Sally's question.

"Has my father been here then?" Susan asked.

"Why yes. Didn't you know?" said Sally.

She put the kettle on in the compartment where she had been working.

"Come and sit down, and tell me what's been going on," said Sally.

"What do you mean?" asked Susan. She came in and sat on a tall stool.

" You tell me," said Sally.

She made some tea.

"I've been a grass widow for the last twenty four hours almost," said Sally.

She poured out the tea and handed Susan a cup.

"Deator worked all day yesterday and late last night. Your father phoned up and wanted him to collect something at one o'clock this morning. Oh, don't get me wrong. I'm used to him working all hours except on this occasion, this weekend was special. You see every four weeks we send the girls away. We've got relatives on the other side of the city, and the girls go there for a break," said Sally, laughing. "Well, it's us that gets the break really, but that's another story." Sally picked up her tea and took a sip.

"I see," said Susan. "But when did my father come? He didn't say anything to me. I never knew, when did he get here?"

"Oh, I'm not sure early this morning. I've tried to phone Deator to find out what time he's coming home. That's if he intends to come home at all." She winked at Susan. "Had a few heated words, I'm afraid, still never mind, it'll come out in the wash, so I'm told."

"Well, it's news to me," said Susan putting down her cup. "The last time I spoke to dad was about eight o'clock this morning after he sent me on this job."

"Oh, what's that then?" asked Sally. She put her cup down, the shop bell rang.

"Customer, back in a minute," said Sally.

"Can I help you?" asked Sally politely. She smiled at the man who was in his sixties.

"Yes, I'd like some flowers for my wife's birthday," he said.

Sally looked at the elderly man and recognised him immediately.

"Ah yes," she said. "Half a dozen red roses isn't it?" she asked and then went on to ask "how are you?"

"Oh I'm fine, thank you. Why you remember me?" he said and looked at Sally.

Sally got out half a dozen roses and wrapped them up in fancy paper and handed them to the man who paid her for them. Just before he left, he turned.

"You are most kind, thank you," he said.

"Nice old boy really," said Sally to Susan. "Now where were we? Oh yes, you said something about a job. More tea?" Sally asked as she noticed Susan's cup was empty.

"Yes please," said Susan. She pushed over her cup. "Thanks, dad gave me chance to spend an extra hour with Jamie. He's gone on a week's flight you know. We were to have a weekend together, so there we are… It just didn't work out the way I wanted, that's all."

"Has he? Oh dear," said Sally. Then she asked Susan. "When are you two going to settle down?"

"I don't know," said Susan.

She took the cup Sally offered. "That's what I'd like to know," Susan said. "Anyway I had to take …"

Susan went on to explain.

AT THE VILLAGE

There is a glimmer of light in Frank's eyes and he is aware of something next to him. He is vaguely aware that he is under cover but is not sure where, his senses seemed to tell him that much. Something damp is on his forehead and it's slippery. Suddenly he remembers the monster before he passed out, In a flash he pushes the cloth away and sits bolt upright only to feel excruciating pain in his shoulder and passes out again.

BACK AT THE FARM

Suchana is bringing in the washing that had been done earlier. Mark has now completed the bird cage and is fixing some bars in it for the mynah bird and starts to whistle.

James was now trying to teach Reaker to play hopscotch; he had drawn in the dust some squares to jump into. Ann was busy in the kitchen again getting their midday lunch ready. The time was about one forty five.

"Now Reaker, I'll show you once more," said James.

He stood in the first square and the chimp stood and watched.

"You throw a stone just a little way so it lands on the places I've marked., Then you stand on one leg and jump. You see it's quite easy if you try., Ok, you have a go. Here's a stone," said James to Reaker.

"What are you doing master James?" asked Suchana. She came over with the washing in her arms.

"Trying to teach him to play hopscotch, he's hopeless. All he does is fall down and mess up the lines I have made," said James

The chimp tried again but ended up falling over and doing just what James said. Suchana and James laughed at the chimp.

"Ha, ha, silly thing," they laughed.

"Well, what do you think of this then?" said Mark to Suchana and James.

Suchana and James went over to see Mark's completed birdcage leaving the chimp screeching and rolling in the dust and laughing at himself.

"Great, said James, "even though you are my brother."

He looked at Suchana.

"Don't you think so?" he said and grinned, that cheeky grin that brothers use when they are after something.

"It's true," said Mark. "Whenever he says anything of mine's good. I always know that he's scrounging. So there."

"What, you two at it again?" asked Ann as she came down the steps. "Why do you always have to argue? I don't know. James you can get off and play somewhere. Go on, go and play with Sophie or something."

Ann shielded her eyes as she saw a cloud of dust in the distance. She frowned.

"Don't go too far James, lunch will be ready," said Ann. "Mark, you go and get washed. I've changed my mind about playing. You can do that afterwards. Go on, get."

She tapped James on the backside as he went towards the bungalow. She turned to Suchana.

"Would you like a drink first?" Ann asked.

She looked at the cloud of dust getting nearer.

"Come on let's go in and get some lemonade," Ann said.

"Ma, Ma" yelled James from an upstairs window. "Someone's coming."

"Who is it? Is it your father back already?" called Ann from the porch steps.

"Can't say it looks like him." There was a pause and James came tearing down the stairs.

He rushed out past Ann and Suchana, and fell over when he reached the bottom of the steps. He got up brushed himself down and ran on.

"It's uncle Keith and he's got a baby elephant. Isn't he lovely?" said James.

Mark appeared at the window to see what all the commotion was about. Keith and JoJo got nearer and nearer.

"Oh my god, he's hurt," said Ann.

She and Suchana rushed down the steps towards the two men.

"Keith, JoJo what happened, are you all right? Where's Frank?" asked Ann.

"Hold on, hold on," said Keith "One question at a time, let me get down first I'm absolutely knackered. My leg is killing me, try riding that thing."

He got off the baby elephant with JoJo's help, and then he sat down and told them everything.

The children were sent to their rooms before Keith began his story. He told Ann about the bar and what happened there

"We have been raided by thousands of birds," said Ann as she bandaged Keith's ankle.

"We must find Frank and warn him," she said after she had heard Keith's story. "Did you see the birds?" she asked Keith.

"No we didn't," he said. "That's what I intend to do but first we must set up this radio link with Camagonga. But I believe your story. Very strange things are happening and I don't know why."

MEANWHILE UP IN THE AIRCRAFT

"Excuse me sir," said the blonde hostess. "Would you like something to eat?"

Steve was miles away, when he heard her voice. He was deep in his book.

"Sorry what did you say?" he asked the hostess.

"I said would you like something to eat?" she said smiling at him. She had some sandwiches on a tray.

"Er, yes please," said Steve. He looked up at her big blue eyes.

"What about those two?" she asked, looking at the prisoners. "Shall I give them something?"

"No," said Steve firmly. "Sorry, you'd better not, they are dangerous. I wouldn't put anything past them."

Bennett and Sied snarled at her.

"What have I done?" asked the hostess as she leaned forward.

Steve quickly took up the opportunity of talking and using his expertise to pull a bird.

"Take a seat," he said.

This request took the hostess by surprise.

"Well er, I, well er, ok, just for a few minutes," she said.

Steve began to tell her the story, laying it on a bit thick. Jenny at this time was looking out of the window while Barry was eyeing Jason up and down. He was listening to the radio through the earphones, but he was still carrying his bag.

"What business are you in?" asked the passenger who was sitting next to Harry, the coloured man.

"Why?" asked Harry. "I don't see that it's any of your business anyway."

Since Harry had been on board he had not spoken to anyone. He was thinking about his son's birthday, and how it was going on without him.

"Only trying to be sociable," said the other chap. "We've got eight hours of flight so I thought we could become friends. I'm not prejudiced, guess you could say you struck lucky sitting next to me."

"Don't bank on it," said Harry, giving the man a queer sort of look.

"Why?" asked the man. He took out his hanky and blew his nose.

"Because the mere fact that you said you are not prejudiced show that you are," said Harry.

"How extraordinary," said the man. "Do you know, I have never thought of it that way before." He put his hanky away. "You are right, here put it there." He held out his hand to Harry.

"What you crazy?" said Harry. "What's that for?"

"Your hand, you fool. I must admit it's not every day I meet an intelligent man, but you are one and I admire you for speaking your mind," said the man.

Harry hesitated, then he smiled and took the man's hand. He knew that this man had a great deal of pride and respect.

"Works every time," said the man. "Do you play chess?"

"What does?" asked Harry. "Yes, I do."

"Why don't you know? Get them all riled up, then apologise. All part of human nature and the best way to make friends," answered the man.

"Anyone ever tell you," said Harry, "you are sneaky."

"Many a time but I don't let it bother me. You see I'm a professor of human behaviour, and I could see you were not comfortable sitting next to me. I've also noticed that you carry a small black box, which means you are possibly a doctor. Seems to me you do not sound like a doctor therefore my conclusion is you are something to do with the mining business. Am I right? I'd even go as far to say that possibly you are carrying diamonds in there but I should imagine that's wrong," said the man.

"You clever bastard …" said Harry. "How the devil…"

"I thought so, but please don't tell me, having got this far there's only one other conclusion seeing you treat it so gently. I can guess the rest, does the captain know? And what if the other passengers find out? There's no need to worry about me, I'm not the panicky kind," said the man.

"Yes," said Harry. "And I'm not going to tell them. Only you know."

"My name is Brian," said the man, and then went on, "you must be expert at your job then?"

"Right again," said Harry. "Let's play chess, ok?"

They continued their conversation as they played.

"Excuse me," said Jenny as the hostess came by.

"Yes," said the hostess. "Can I help you?"

"Have you a blanket? My husband has gone to sleep at the back and I would like to cover him up," said Jenny, as she went to get up.

"Yes, that's all right, don't you bother, I'll do it," said the hostess.

"Thanks," said Jenny. "That's very kind of you. You see he has been working all night."

"Sure, I understand., It's no trouble," said the hostess. "I'll get one right away and cover him myself." She turned and went back the way she had come.

"Hey son," said the surgeon who was looking after the baby. "You've been sitting there staring at the baby for an hour., Aren't you tired?"

He was sitting opposite David and next to Mrs Heal.

"No," said David. looking across. In front of him was the incubator.

"Why are you so fascinated by her? Haven't you any brothers or sisters of your own?" asked the surgeon.

"No," said David"

He continued to stare at the baby. He rubbed his eye and rubbed his finger along the side of his nose.

"Any particular reason?" asked the surgeon. "Are you ok, you look awfully tired? Are you always so pale?"

"Yes I'm ok," said David. "She's nice, isn't she?" said the surgeon. "Perfect, but why is she here? Has she got a disease like me or something? She looks ok." He paused and went on, "Some days I'm ok, but others I'm sick all day long."

"Oh why's that?" asked the surgeon. "She'll be ok, it's just that she hasn't got a feeding tube. It's a bit complicated for you to understand."

"Is she going to die like me?" asked David suddenly. "I wouldn't like that."

"You are not going to die," said the surgeon. "Whatever makes you say that?"

It was a shock statement coming from one so young, but then he went on, "She's got to have some special treatment, that's all."

David looked at the surgeon who was fumbling for his hanky. "Mum says I've got something called leukaemia. I've seen many doctors, and been to loads of hospitals and all that stuff." David had taken out his hanky and he blew his nose and made a noise.

"Sorry," said David.

"That's ok," said the surgeon. He looked at David compassionately and asked. "Who told you, you were going to die?"

"No one at first," said David. "Then I heard one of the doctors telling my mother and she burst out crying so I guessed the news was not good. Later mum and I sat down and had a good talk. Now mum's scared of having any more children and won't get married again."

"Did she?" said the surgeon. "So what's going to happen now, I think it's a terrible shame".

"She told me the truth in the end, but it was hard you know. What I mean is mum did not want to hurt me, but I told her it was ok. I remember my dad had said to me once," said David.

"Oh, and what was that son?" asked the surgeon.

"He said to me before he died, when you are a boy, always be the man about things and when you are a man stay one. At first I didn't understand what he meant but now I do. It was like he was warning me."

"Excuse me," said the hostess. "May I get by? Your legs are in the way."

"Yes sure," said David, and he pulled his legs round.

The hostess went to get a blanket; while she was doing so, the other hostess got some more food ready.

"I see you had a word with that dishy policeman," said the dark haired hostess. "Lucky beast."

"Yes nice, I quite fancy him, but I don't think he really noticed me. He's a crack marksman," replied the blonde girl.

"Funny," said the hostess. "You could have fooled me."

"Why?" asked the blonde hostess, clutching the blanket.

"I could have sworn I saw Cupid's arrows sticking out of his forehead," she said laughing.

The blonde hostess laughed also as she went off with the blanket. She turned. "Oh, by the way, you had better check the old boy in one zero two. He's looking quite ill you know. Better check again with the captain," said the blonde hostess.

"Are you thinking what I'm thinking?" said Sied to Bennett.

He pulled at the cuffs and hurt Bennett's wrist.

"Lay off, you son of a bitch," said Bennett. "Don't yank on those cuffs, you fucking pig".

"Aw who's going to stop me? You then, huh?" "Aw, shut up you fool. We got to get out of these," said Sied.

David left his seat and walked down the gangway. Towards the back as he went he eyed the rest of the passengers and passed by the nurse and his mother.

"What are you doing David? You are not supposed to wander anywhere. Come and sit down," said his mother.

"In a minute mum," said David. "I want to go and look at those two men."

"Oh all right," said his mother. "But don't get into trouble."

As David walked back he eyed Jason but said nothing as he passed. He came upon the film couple and stopped and looked at the woman.

"I know who you are," said David.

The film couple were still in the middle of their conversation and had not finished.

"Don't be so cynical," the woman said to her husband. Then she saw David.

"Hello, sorry what did you say?" she asked.

She took out a silver cigarette case from her bag opened it and took out a cigarette and looked at David.

"Do you still make films?" asked David. He stood on one leg and scratched the other with his foot.

"I know who you are. I've seen you before in a film about birds. You are Cindy Ansty, aren't you?" asked David.

The hostess came past with the blanket for Dale and walked past the prisoners and up to where Dale was sleeping. She carefully laid the blanket over him. He still had his arm over his face. The hostess felt the cooler blowing on him so she leaned over and turned it off.

"Hey Miss," said Bennett to the hostess. She turned to Bennett.

"What can I do for you?" she asked coming over to him.

"What I want you to do, you can't do for me," he said winking at her. "Or can you?" he said sarcastically.

"Don't be so disgusting," said the hostess. "You make me sick." Bennett turned to Sied.

"I like this one," he said. "She's got a lot of life in her. That's just how I like them all spit and fury cow'r."????

"Well what do you want?" she asked and made a face, to show she was disgusted and Bennett turned back to her.

"We want something to eat and drink. If it ain't too fucking much to ask. We ain't had damn all since yesterday," said Bennett, staring at her.

Steve heard the conversation and leaned over the seat.

"Me and my companion want to go to the bog," said Sied. "Lessen you want us to shit ourselves." He was trying to take a chance or a way out.

"Now boys," said Steve. "That ain't no way to talk to a lady is it?" He rested his arm on the top of the seat. "Since she's doing all the fetching and carrying it might be a help if you spoke kindly to her." He put his head on one side.

David came nearer; he stopped just by the seat next to Steve.

"Are they murderers?" he asked looking at them.

"Sure we are," said Sied looking up at David. "Why do you ask?"

"What did you do then?" asked David. "Who did you kill, and did you mean to?"

"Hold it boy," said Bennett. "What's it to you anyway. Ain't you a bit young to ask such questions? I suggest you bug off and mind your own business."

"You lay off," said Steve. "Leave the kid alone, he ain't done you no harm."

Steve turned to the hostess and looked at her.

"Go on it's ok., Get them some food," he said.

"Well, who's being protective now?" said Sied. He held up his cuffs. "Shit, man. Get me out of these things I want to go to the bog."

He looked at David again.

"Boo. Get out of here," he shouted. "Boo."

David left and carried on further to the back of the plane as Steve uncuffed the first prisoner; David turned and looked back at them.

"You don't frighten me mister," said David.

"David" said his mother, as she came to get him. "I thought I told you not to go near them."

The hostess passed them in the gangway.

"It's all right," she said.

Bennett got up, and so did Sied and Steve removed his gun from its holster. Sied was annoyed at David's remark and his bravado and he shouted at David's mother.

"Get that kid out of here," he yelled.

He glared at David's mother and spat on the floor.

"Don't you speak to me like that," said David's mother.

She stood holding David to one side as they passed along the gangway.

"He's more man than you'll ever be," she said angrily.

"You are holding out on me Barry," said Jenny to Barry. "Do you know you've been sitting there for nearly an hour and you've hardly said a word? Not even to say you are looking forward to this holiday or anything. Have I done something wrong? Didn't you want to come?"

She turned and looked at him. Then she got out her bag that lay on the floor and took out a mirror and comb and began to tidy her hair. Then she put on some lipstick.

"Well, I'm waiting," she said. "What's the matter?" She wiped the lipstick off her finger with a tissue.

"Nothing," said Barry. He fiddled with a newspaper on his lap.

"Oh, come off it. Do you take me for some kind of fool? I know you are hiding something. We've lived quite some time together in the same house, so you can't kid me there's nothing wrong. So out with it. Don't be so bloody self centred," said Jenny.

"Why don't you get off my back?" asked Barry. "You are always fussing over me like a mother over her chick. Just because you've got no kids of your own you treat me like your own. I ain't a kid no more," he ended angrily.

"There's no need to be so rude," said Jenny. She was very hurt. "That remark is hardly fair, is it? Just like a man ready to throw rocks as soon as it suits you. You'd better watch your tongue young man; I can, and will throw out a few home truths of my own if you are not careful. But like most teenagers, you can see no further than the end of your nose when someone is trying to help."

"It's none of your business," said Barry. "It's got nothing to do with you."

"Then if you want my help it's about time you made it so," said Jenny.

"I don't," said Barry. "I can handle my own affairs ok?"

They lapsed into silence. Bennett and Sied passed and Bennett winked at Jenny.

"Go get him girl," said Sied. He looked at Bennett. "Now she's got a lot of spunk. You said you liked them sassy."

Sied made kissing signs to Jenny, Barry saw that and made to get up, but Steve pushed him back into his seat.

"I wouldn't if I were you," said Steve.

"Miss, Miss," called the old lady. "My husband's very sick. Someone get help."

The hostess heard her cry and came towards Bennett and Sied carefully squeezing past them both.

The surgeon heard the woman's cry and left his seat giving Mrs Heal a quick glance as he did so.

MEANWHILE BACK IN THE VILLAGE

Frank was aware of a damp cloth on his head when he came round for the second time; he had no idea how long he had been unconscious.

"Ah," said Frank as he opened his eyes.

He began to get things into focus. In the background he could hear strange noises but everything seemed to be a long way off.

"What's going on?" he asked.

A hand was placed over his mouth and he opened his eyes and looked up.

"Shh," said a voice. "Not so loud, keep your voice down."

"Why what's happening?" mumbled Frank.

He raised himself but the sharp pain in his arm stopped him going too far. So he used the other hand to pull off the cloth and then he tried to sit up.

"Ah Christ, that hurts," he said as he managed to get up on one elbow.

"You've broken your arm," said Fletcher.

Frank vaguely knew Fletcher by sight.

"You'll be ok, providing you take things easy" said Fletcher. "I've set your arm as best I can."

"What the hell's going on?" asked Frank.

He remembered what he had seen.

"What was that thing out there?" he asked. "Has it gone?"

"I don't know," said Fletcher. "All I know is that something got my mate Pete. Crazy fool. I told him not to touch anything. How are you feeling now?"

Fletcher had been kneeling down by Frank for most of the time.

"Much better thanks," said Frank. "What happened to that old man for Christ's sake? He came out to see me yesterday and told me some cock and bull story said people in this village used voodoo on him and his animals. He seemed ok, but Jesus what's going on? These cone things. What are they? They seem to have something to do with what's happening."

"God, I don't know," said Fletcher. "Maybe, I am not sure, Anyway, I'm not taking any chances. How much fuel have you got in your truck?"

"Why what are you going to do?" asked Frank.

"We are going to destroy as many of those things as we can find," said Fletcher. "And I need your help. Do you reckon we can do it?"

"Yes sure, but how?" asked Frank.

Fletcher stood up. They were in one of the huts.

"Here," said Fletcher. "I'll use one of these."

He pulled back the tarpaulin and underneath were two glass acid containers.

"We'll put them in these and fill them up with petrol and blow them up, ok?" said Fletcher.

"How the hell are we going to get out of here and away from that thing if we use ail the fuel?" asked Frank.

"We'll save some," said Fletcher dropping the cloth. "Come on we've got work to do I'll give you a hand. All right?"

MEANTIME BACK WITH THE NATIVES

The six natives whom JoJo had spoken to were nearing the village, but before they arrived to claim the boy's bride they were going to eat some of the snakes and get painted up. Because of the trouble, JoJo had forgotten to mention that Frank was at the village. The young boy sat half naked on the ground while the others made dye from roots and made marks on his back and on his face and arms. They had a pile of snakes tied up in a sack and were in a small gully near some scrub trees and bushes. They chatted in their own tongue while they made the boy up and smoked some sort of grass. They all laughed., It was now two fifteen or thereabouts. Suddenly all went silent and all the birds thereabouts flew into the air. From nowhere they were all deafened by the sound of buzzing. They held on to their ears and were then engulfed by the monster, a seething mass of red eyes and bodies, and within a few seconds they were gone. The monster was now much bigger, nearly twenty feet long and eight feet high.

"Ah, ah, ah," screamed the natives from inside the monster and it echoed around and around.

MEANWHILE AT THE FLORIST SHOP

Sally and Susan are still puzzled over why Deator was working so late when the phone rang; the time was now three o'clock.

Sally picked it up.

"Hello Florenteen's, the flower shop here," she said. "Can I help you?"

"Hello darling, it's me," said a voice.

Sally put her hand over the mouthpiece, as she turned to Susan who was trying to make a wreath.

"It's Deator," said Sally.

"Hi" said Sally. "Are you phoning me to tell me you are coming home? Thank god for that, because we have a visitor."

"Oh, have we?" said Deator. "Who's that then?"

"It's Susan," said Sally. She watched Susan who looked up at her.

"George didn't bring Susan, did he?" asked Deator. "He didn't tell me."

"Nor did Susan, come to that," said Sally. "Anyway, when are you coming home? I'm beginning to feel like a grass widow. That was until Susan came in. I felt completely lost. It's not much fun sitting and watching TV on your own."

"Give my love to Susan. Sorry darling, something really important has come up. I can't tell you on the phone so don't ask me, I'm truly sorry," said Deator.

"What's that then? Oh never mind, we'll come in later to see you if that's all right?" said Sally.

"No don't do that," said Deator abruptly.

"Why ever not?" said Sally. "What's wrong? You sound very worried,"

"I must go darling. I'll ring you later," said Deator. "Bye."

Sally pressed the button three or four times.

"Deator, Deator," she said. "Oh what's going on?"

The only reply was the buzzing of the disconnected phone.

"What's up?" asked Susan. "You look worried."

The wreath she had been working on fell to bits.

"I don't know," said Sally. "It's most unlike him."

MEANWHILE BACK AT FRANK'S BUNGALOW

Keith and JoJo had set up a temporary link with Camagonga, but the interference was very bad, and they still could not get a contact. Keith and Jojo then loaded the spare landrover with fuel and said goodbye to Ann, Suchana, and the boys. Keith told them what to do. They were to dig a large hole in the ground and cover it with planks of wood and make it so it couldn't be found. Keith thought the trouble may be a native uprising. He remembered the last few hours in the town the night before. The two men left Ann and the others to work out their hiding place; it shouldn't be too near the sheds or house in case of fire. They dug the hole and filled water cans with drinking water and put some cushions there as well. Keith left Ann, Suchana and the boys with the thought of what to do if anything strange happened.

BACK ON BOARD THE AIRCRAFT

Bennett and Sied had both been to the toilet and were on their way back to their seats. The blonde hostess had fetched the captain, as the old man had appeared to have passed out. On his arm was a nasty swelling. The surgeon was looking at it. The old lady had moved out of the seat to let the surgeon examine her husband.

"What's wrong with him?" asked the old lady. "I told him not to work so hard."

The young girl who had been sitting next to her fiancé had sat down beside the old lady. The young man was sat behind in an empty seat.

"Don't worry," said the girl. "I'm sure he will be all right."

She put her arm around the old lady.

"He never listens to me," said the old lady. She took out her hanky and wiped her eyes. "Why only yesterday he tidied the garden so that it would be nice when we got home and not look like a wilderness. I said it didn't matter, but he insisted. Now it's made him ill. We shall have to go home again. My son could not look after him like this."

"What's up?" asked the captain.

He pushed past the prisoners and bent down at the old man.

"He was all right when we got on board," said the lady. "A bit tired that's all."

"Heart attack?" said the captain as he looked at the surgeon.

"No, I don't think so," said the surgeon. "Here have a look at this." The captain picked up the old man's arm and had a closer look.

"What is it?" he asked.

Bennett and Sied walked by. Steve was behind them ready in case of trouble. Bennett stopped and looked down.,He recognised the man. It was the ex police chief, Warren.

"He's fucking had it," said Bennett, "if that's what I think it is."

"Oh," said the girl. "How can you be so cruel"?

The old lady began to cry.

"He's not dead," she sobbed into her hanky.

"No, he's not," she said looking up at Bennett.

"All right now come on," said the captain, looking into Bennett's eyes. "Why did you say that? Was it necessary to be so bloody cruel? Anyway how do you know what it is?" Steve asked Bennett.

"Anyone can see that it is a spider bite," said Bennett. He leaned over the surgeon and looked at the old man's arm and took a look at the colour of him. He then held up the old man's arm.

"See those two marks. I'd say it was a tarantula or black widow spider," said Bennett. He looked at Sied who nodded.

"What shall we do then if your diagnosis is right?" asked the surgeon.

"Excuse me, ma," said Bennett more politely this time. "Has your husband been digging the garden or something?"

"Why yes," said the old lady. "I've already told you that."

"Around the foundations of your house?" asked Bennett.

"Why yes? Why are you asking me all these questions? What's happening to Warr? Iis he going to be all right?" she asked.

Bennett turned to the captain and shrugged his shoulder., The captain knew of this spider's bite and saw he had no chance to get the man back in time. He put his hand on the surgeon's shoulder and looked at him.

"Do the best you can?" he said.

"I'll look after him," said the old lady. "He likes it when I fuss over him." She pulled the surgeon's arm and got back in her seat.

"Come on you, get out, and thank you, you've been so kind," she said.

"I'll get a blanket for him," said the hostess. There were tears in her eyes.

Bennett, Sied and Steve sat down again.

"Mam," said David. "Why are there so many empty seats?"

"Can you hear anything?" asked one of the passengers looking down to the back of the plane.

"My ears keep going funny," said the woman She shook her head to clear the noise.

"No," said her husband who was sitting next to her. "What do you mean?"

"A sort of high pitched buzzing. You know like ringing in your ears," she answered.

"Can't say I can," said her husband, looking at her. He was sat on the inside seat.

"Sometimes if you yawn it helps," he said. "Why don't you try that?"

"That's so more people can get on at the next airport," said David's nurse.

"How long has David got?" his mother asked the nurse.

"That's too difficult to tell Why?" asked the nurse; she looked at David's mother dauntingly.

"Oh, I just wondered that's all," said David's mother. She stared across at him.

"Really," said the nurse. "I've been watching you now for the last few months and so far I've been proud of the way you've held up, but ..."

"Yes," said David's mother looking at her. She was perplexed.

"Well, you can't fool me, that's all I can say for the time being," said the nurse.

"What do you mean?" asked David's mother. She eyed the nurse coolly.

"I'm not a fool you know," said the nurse. "I've seen the doctor's report on both you and David."

"So," said his mother.

"You can have more children. Oh yes, I know you've been told that before haven't you? But it's the truth," said the nurse. She put her hand on David's mother's and went on, "honest, try and believe it."

"Believe," said David's mother. "Believe, oh I've heard that so many times. Go to God. Believe in Him. How can I possibly believe in Him when in the past year he's taken my husband from me and now he will soon take David? You tell me what's there to believe in and is it worth it?" She began to cry.

"I know," said the nurse. "It's hard I've seen many things in my career, that don't seem fair. People dying and families hurt, but there is a reason for it all. Only we have the misfortune never to be able to see that. For what it's worth, it's wrong and you know it."

Dale was till fast asleep and wedged in the sea., Not much of him could be seen.

"Sandwiches and coffee?" asked the blonde hostess.

She put them down by Steve's seat.

"I'll leave you to give them to him if you don't mind," she said smiling at Steve. Steve shook his head and blinked his eye.

"You ok?" asked the hostess.

"Yes sure thanks, I think so," said Steve.

"What's the matter?" she asked.

"I've got a high pitched ringing in my ears," said Steve.

"Oh, I wouldn't worry about that. It's caused by the vibrations from the wings. Most people never notice it. Only those with very sensitive ears. That's what causes jet lag. It's time difference. It makes you very tired like thousands of small jumps in your brain. Can make some people sick, others suffer from a type of nausea," said the hostess.

She took hold of the back of Steve's seat.

"Would you believe some people even know that they suffer from it without them really being aware of the fact?. It's all in the mind," she said.

"You seem to know a lot about it," said Steve, "don't you? How?"

"I should do," she replied. "It was one of my pet subjects at college. My boy friend used to get frightened when I started to discuss it. It was going to be my career at one time."

"What are you doing in a job like this then?" asked Steve smiling at her. "Flying round the world.., Talk about contrasting jobs, there's absolutely no similarity".

"A girl's got to live, hasn't she?" said the blonde girl, laughing.

"Seems like we have something in common. We both travel a lot," said Steve.

"Have you finished yakking yet?" said Sied from behind. "We are bloody starving to death, while you make love with your little biddy eyes," he sneered.

The hostess blushed.

By now, the captain had returned to the cockpit and to his co-pilot who had been keeping an eye on things.

The co-pilot and the navigator had been chatting together.

"How's your wife and baby?" asked the navigator.

"Oh, they are coming along fine," said the co-pilot.

Back in the plane there was a long drawn-out sigh from the elderly man who had been covered with the blanket., He was dead, but the old lady did not realise it..

MEANWHILE OUTSIDE THE TOWN

Billy's two brothers stopped by a wide, free running river. They had set their fishing lines and had been there for sometime. Both had their rifles with them in case of any trouble. Nearby was a motorbike that they had used for their journey. It was a custom-built bike that one of the lads had painted himself. The petrol tank was painted with a picture of Elvis, one of the boy's favourite record covers.

"I hope we catch something this time," said Joe.

He was very like his dad with dark hair. He was seventeen and was wearing a navy t-shirt and old blue jeans

"You bet," said his brother Darren.

He too was dark, but shorter and more stockily built. He was fifteen.

"Have you brought that extra bait? I don't want to run out Darren, not like the last time," said Joe. "There's nothing worse than running out of fish food and being stuck next to a damn river and nothing to do."

He pulled in his line while his brother opened a small tin. There were lots of maggots inside. He picked one out and stuck it on his brother's hook.

"There, will that do?" asked Darren.

"What did you think of the party the other night?" asked Joe. He dropped his line.

Darren cast the line in and then out again. He paused and put another maggot on as it had come off.

"Bloody great," said Darren..

"How about that Pearl? Great isn't she? What knockers!" said Joe.

Joe picked up his fishing rod and cast it into the river again.

"Boy, she's a great little screw." Joe held up his arms and said, "What about it? I'd like that every night. I'd be in ecstasy. What about you? You have got a bird haven't you?" Joe asked Darren, cheekily.

He turned with a knowing look at his brother.

"I ain't a virgin anymore, that's a fact. Not after the other night, but for fuck's sake why did you have to palm me off with Hazel? She stinks. Boy, she stinks like a hyena. One night is enough. Phew!" said Darren.

Joe looked at him and laughed.

"Beggars can't be chooser., Besides, I was broken in by someone like her. Jesus, she was great, a great little raver," said Joe.

Suddenly his line went taught, and he yelled with delight.

"I got you, you son of a bitch. Hey up, he's a big bugger ain't he? Get a frigging net man, come on hurry," yelped Joe to Darren.

Darren put his line down and picked up the net that was in the river.

"Here let me help," said Darren. "Keep the friggin thing from moving."

He caught the fish in the net and Joe took the hook out.

"I never knew a woman who could talk so much, you know what I mean., There's me banging away, ten to the dozen, and she's chatting as if it's an every day thing. There's me nearly shitting myself," said Darren.

"Sorry, haven't had that much experience myself," said Joe laughing.

"You mean?" said Darren as he turned to his brother. He dropped his rod, so did Joe.

"You bastard, ,you did that on purpose, it was all planned," said Darren.

"Yer, why?" asked Joe and he laughed. Darren jumped on him.

"I'll get you for that you fucking idiot. You done that on purpose. How many of the others knew about it?" said Darren.

He landed on top of Joe. "Aw, come off it, it was only a bit of fun,"

"I don't care you fucking sod, you knew all the time," said Darren.

He hit Joe in the face. He hit him back still laughing. For a few minutes they fought taking in more water. All the wild birds flew up and away.

Suddenly they were aware of someone watching them. It was John, one of the cops from the town. He looked and felt very tired.

"Have you quite finished?" he asked standing by his car smoking.

"What's it to you what we are sodding doing?" asked Joe.

He climbed out of the water. He held out his hand and helped his brother to his feet.

"We ain't doing any harm are we? So what are you going to do about it?" Joe asked rudely.

"Nothing," John..

He took out a packet of cigarettes and offered them to the boys.

"Here want one?" John asked them.

"Thanks," said the boys as they walked over to John. They each took one.. John produced a lighter and lit all three cigarettes.

"What do you want?" asked Joe, eyeing him suspiciously, but not making it obvious.

"Not much," said John. "I've been looking for you that's all., Where's Billy, he been with you?"

"Why?" asked Darren. "We ain't done nothing wrong."

They all leant against the car.

"Shit, I'm soaked," said Joe as he spat out some water.

Then he put the cigarette in his mouth and puffed away on it.

" I heard you were at a party on the other side of town the other night," said John.

He took a deep drag on his cigarette and studied Darren's reactions. Joe looked at his brother and dared him to say anything.

"True," said Joe.

He left the side of the car and went and sat down on his bike and rested his foot on the stand.

"One of the girls at your party was badly beaten up that night. Do you know anything about it?" asked John.

"No," said Joe giving his brother a quick look. "Who was it?"

Darren got scared and he looked at Joe. For a second he thought John was talking about Hazel, and he got very annoyed with Joe and became agitated.

"If it's that bloody bitch Hazel Rodgers," said Darren, "then she's a bloody liar, she was a willing bitch, and if she says different …"

John looked at Darren and could see he was scared; this was because it had been his first time.

"No, we know all about her," said John.

He threw down his cigarette and stubbed it out.

"Where's Billy then?" he asked. "Around somewhere, I don't see him."

"No, he ain't here anyways. What's he gone and done now anyway? Up to his old tricks again?" asked Joe.

"Nothing much, anyway the chief dealt with it It's just that he found a gold chain and the chief wants to know where he found it and at what time. He seems to think that he might have picked it up near the scene of the crime. Could mean he may have seen the thing," said John.

He still had his lighter in his hand and he fiddled with it and then put it back into his pocket.

"Right thanks boys," said John.

He looked at the two boys.

"I suggest that you get back as it's getting late, and if you find Billy get him to come to the station. Oh, by the way you'd better go back the other way," said John as he got back into his car.

"Why's that?" asked Darren.

"There's a massive herd of wildebeest crossing just a few miles out of town. That thing is apt to make them stampede," said John, pointing to the bike.

Joe looked hard at the cop. Like most kids he hated his authority.

"Right," said Joe. "Thanks for the warning."

The cop raised his hand and drove away.

"Come on," said Joe. "Let's get out of here, I've suddenly gone off fishing. Ain't you?"

They packed up their things.

"Why didn't you tell him what happened about Barry?" asked Darren.

"Cause it ain't any of his business, that's why" said Joe. "You saw how drunk he was. How the hell would I know if it were him or not? All I know is that he is bloody wild, that's all. We ain't got no reason for pointing our bloody fingers, until we know the truth, ya hear me. Come on, let's get out of here," said Joe angrily.

The two boys got the bike packed with their fishing gear and rifles over their backs and left the river. They had only gone about two miles up the road when they saw something in the distance.

"Hey, stop, do you hear me?" said Darren and he tugged Joe's shoulder.

Joe skidded to a halt and dust flew all around them.

"Why did you do that you bloody fool? You nearly had both of us off," said Joe.

He looked around at Darren who was now staring at something in the distance.

"What the bloody hell's wrong with you?" Joe asked.

The dust had settled a bit by now.

"Would you say you know this area pretty well?" asked Darren.

"Of course you bloody idiot, why?" asked Joe.

"Then where did that mound come from, over there? Look!" said Darren pointing.

"Where?" asked Joe. "You going crazy or something, come on let's go home."

Joe revved up the engine and looked to where Darren had pointed and sure enough there was a mound.

"Maybe you are right. Ok, to please you we will go and see what it is," said Joe.

"Hold on to your hat," and he rode off in the direction of the mound.

They realised, as they got nearer that it was not natural, but they were fascinated by the size of it. Soon they came to a halt and before them lay a huge winged creature. They both became very scared but were afraid to run.

They knew they had no chance to run if it was still alive.

"Holy shit," said Joe. "What the heck's that?"

He got off his bike but left the engine running. Darren got slowly off the back.

They stood looking at the creature.

"What the hell is it?" asked Joe.

He ran his hand over his forehead, and removed his hat and held it in one hand.

"I ain't waiting to find out. The frigging thing may still be alive. Come on Joe, lets get the hell out of here" said Darren.

"No it ain't" said Joe, going nearer.

"What can you see?" asked Darren, as he held back.

"The vultures have had a go at it," said Joe; he beckoned Darren to come closer.

The creature was not unlike a giant bee; it lay with its faces on one side, three in all each with short claw-like teeth, able to rip an elephant in half with no trouble at all. Its eyes were made of thousands of honeycomb cells. At the back of its fish-type tail, and scaled body was a long sting edged with razor type blades. Its wings were almost transparent but as tough as any metal. Altogether it must have been about the size of a three or four storey building. It's colour blended in with the dry sandy desert where it had landed and was perfectly camouflaged from above.

"It's dead ain't it?" asked Darren. "Come on, let's go home."He pulled at Joe's shirt.

Suddenly a high pitched buzzing sound seemed to come from within the monster but it didn't move. Both men backed off.

"Let's get out of here," said Joe. "We must go and report this. Quick on the bike."

Joe dropped his hat and ran.

"Don't worry," said Darren shivering with fear. His eyes were wide with terror. "I ain't staying round to find out if it's dead or not."

They both made a dash for the bike and drove off towards the town leaving the creature and a cloud of dust behind them.

BACK AT THE VILLAGE

With both bottles now filled with cones and petrol, Fletcher and Frank set to work blowing them up. They were very careful not to go anywhere near the area that the old man had last been seen. Altogether they had collected about a hundred and sixty cones in each bottle.

"Right," said Fletcher. "Are you ready?" He waited for an ok from Frank.

He had a lighted waft of burning grass in his hand., Petrol led its way to the two large bottles that Frank had laid down as best he could.

"I'm going to light it now," said Fletcher. Holding it ready, he asked. "Did you throw that spare can of petrol in the landrover?".

Frank carefully did as he was told and stayed back under cover and soon the other man joined him.

"Right all clear, ready, here goes," said Fletcher.

Frank ducked down behind the landrover and with great anticipation watched as the flames shot along the petrol fuse.

"Keep your head down you bloody fool," screamed Fletcher.

Suddenly two bottles blew scattering burning cones onto the huts and setting them on fire.

"Save us the job," said Fletcher. He fell to the ground and stuck his face close to the sand. Then they both got back into the landrover.

 "What about the old man?" asked Frank. "We can't leave him here."

He got into the landrover as best he could. His arm was extremely painful.

"Somehow we must destroy him the same way we did the cones." He held onto his arm.

"Ow," he said as he knocked it.

"Ok," said Fletcher. "We'll drive round and try and get in on the other side of the village. I need some more fuel in my truck, so hold on it's going to be a bumpy ride, I'm afraid."

Fletcher crashed the gears into first and they drove off. Within minutes they had reached the other vehicle. Fletcher got out and grabbed the jerry cans of petrol and put them in the back of the landrover, where Keith waited.

"This ain't going to work," Frank stated. "How the hell are we going to get it over him? As soon as the buzzing starts we have had it. It's impossible."

"We'll have to work it out as best as we can," said Fletcher.

Keith was left with the other landrover and they headed back to the place where they had last seen the monster. The huts were now an inferno.

"He's gone," cried Frank, as he pulled up.

"How the hell…" said Fletcher. "Shit. The fire must have scared it away."

He banged his fist hard down and in Fletcher's anger his foot slipped off the accelerator and the engine stopped.

"Where the hell's it gone?" he asked.

"Come on get going," said Fletcher to the engine. As he tried to get it started again, the sound of buzzing had started to be heard again.

"Come on you bloody thing," said Fletcher as he fought to get the motor going.

"Hurry" screamed Frank. "It's coming back, come on, come on or we'll be …"

Suddenly the engine burst into life and the two men sped out of the place. The ground was very uneven and the sound grew louder and louder.

"Let's get out of here," cried Frank. "We've got to warn the others"

They sped off in the direction of Keith's landrover. They had only gone a few yards when something huge loomed up in front of them, causing Fletcher to swerve and he hit a mound. He was thrown out of the driving seat, leaving Frank helpless and going straight for the monster. Frank let out a scream as he was thrown out of the vehicle and sailed towards the creature., He was helpless to stop himself. Fletcher hit his head on a rock, but in his dazed condition he saw Frank being completely engulfed by a mass of maggots. Frank's cries faded and Fletcher passed out. Keith saw this and saved him and then left in the direction of Frank's farm. They both feared it was too late.

BACK IN THE TOWN, AT THE POLICE STATION

"Hi, where is everyone?" asked one of the officers as he came through the door. He walked over to the main desk. Rob who had taken over from John was busy writing out some reports.

"I don't know," he said, recognising his mate's voice.

He didn't bother to look up to see who was asking the question. "Ah ha, I can see you are your usual jocular self today," said the officer leaning on the counter. "Who put curry in your tea? And where's everyone gone, it's like a morgue in here today. Everyone's going mad."

"Mmm, to the jumble sale down at the hall I suppose," replied Rob.

"I can see by the conversation that there is not much left of your tongue, let's have a look, open your mouth. Hmm." He waited and Rob opened his mouth without thinking. "Hmm, as I thought," he went on. "Only one cure for that, we should go and have a beer." He knew his friend's sense of humour.

"May I enquire as to who is paying?" asked Rob. "Sounds like a good idea."

"Ah ha, you did hear what I said then?" said the officer. "Your ears are ok".

"Of course I did.. Do you think I am bloody idiot?" said Rob.

"Sorry, I can't answer that on the grounds that it might incriminate me," said his mate.

"That'll be easy to do, you fool.., You steal enough drinks from me, it's about time you treated me," said Rob looking up and putting down his pen.

The chief came out of his office and walked down the corridor. He swung open the doors and looked at the two men.

"Where's Frost? Have you seen him?" the chief called out, impatiently.

"No sir. Why?" asked Rob looking across.

"Damn stupid man, he's supposed to be looking after the bar and I can't see him from my window anymore," said the chief.

At this point the doc drove up very fast and jumped out of his car and came rushing through the door. He was very worried about something.

"George, I want a word with you. It's very urgent."

"Yeh, sure", said George. He turned towards his office.

"In my office," he said to doc.

"Sergeant," said the chief.

"Yes sir," said the sergeant.

"Get someone down to the bar to find Frost," said the chief.

He left the desk and followed doc to his office.

"Oh and get the fire brigade to clear up that mess," he said.

"Right away sir," said the sergeant.

Both men walked to the chief's office.

"Right, sit down," said the chief to doc. "What's all the fuss about?"

The chief rubbed the back of his neck again.

"Boy, I'm pooped. I can tell you doc if I took a day off the whole damn force would fall apart," he said as he sat down.

"Now take it easy George," said the doc. "You've been on the go now for some sixteen hours. I've warned you to slow up, but you never listen."

"Yes I know, it's time I retired but who the hell do I get to take over? Anyway what are you doing back in town so early?" asked the chief, pressing the intercom button.

"Yes sir?" asked a voice.

"Get us some coffee", said the chief.

"Yes sir," answered the voice.

"Here, said doc. He threw the torn photos on the chief's desk.

"They might be able to help you solve the riddle of the rapes," he said.

"What's that?, Where did you get those from?" asked the chief as he looked at the doc. He shifted the pieces from side to side.

"Had to call at Jason's gran's. You know I told you earlier on. I found the old lady dead, and the house upside down. At first I thought it had been done by natives until I saw these."

The chief looked at the torn photos and began to fit them together on his desk.

"You mean Jason?" asked the chief, as he leant over and looked at them.

"Yeh, I guess you could say we've caught him red handed. You wanted evidence now you've got it", said the doc.

The chief once again pressed the intercom button, and waited for it to be answered.

"Yes sir?" asked the officer.

"Someone pick up Jason Peters, I want him pulled in for questioning," ordered the chief.

He could hear a lot of noise at the main desk as he ordered this done.

"What the hell's going on out there?" asked the chief.

"We've got to see the chief right away," said the two boys.

"For Christ's sake, don't mess me around asking questions, send them in," said the chief.

Joe and Darren left the main hall and ran down the chief's office. They burst through the door; they nearly knocked over the person who was bringing in the coffee the chief had ordered.

"Oh, for heaven's sake watch where you are going?. You nearly had the damn lot over me. You damn fools."

"Sir," said the boys. "We'd better get everyone out of town, quick."

"Hold it, hold it. What the hell's going on? Why do we have to get everyone out?" asked the chief.

"There's this thing out there," said Joe. "It's huge and ... you wanna see it, it's horrible and it's still alive I think."

"What the hell are you talking about?" asked the chief.

Doc was sitting on the side of the desk. The two lads told him and the chief what they had seen. There was a knock on the door and the coffee arrived and the boys stopped talking.

"Come in," said the chief. "What is it?"

The lady came in with the coffee and was followed by Rob.

"Sir," said Rob, "no one has seen Frost. I've tried his home and there is no answer and no one around the town has seen him."

"Tried his girlfriend's house?" asked the chief. "Damn incompetence I call it, first the kid now Frost. What the bloody hell's going on round here?"

He stood up angrily and stomped around the room.

"Can you lads go with Rob?" asked the chief to the boys. He turned to Rob. "Rob, you write out their report," he said. "Right away, please, Thanks."

Rob handed the chief the reports, which had been asked for earlier and then left the office with the two boys.

After the door closed behind them the chief turned to the doc.

"Maybe it's all got something to do with what happened last night in the bar, I think it could be connected," said the chief. "Now these lads have found something."

He scratched the back of his neck again and rubbed his head.

"If it is, then we are going to need help. Right?" said the chief. He picked up the phone.

"Yes sir?" asked the voice. The phone crackled.

"Get me a free line to Camagonga," said the chief.

"Sorry sir, all the lines to the city are unobtainable," said the voice.

"Why's that? What's wrong?" asked the chief.

"Some form of electrical interference, sir, we've tried several times but get nothing," said the voice.

"Ok, damn it," he said and slammed down the phone.

"Deator was the only one who could help us," said the chief looking at doc. "I only hope Keith got to Frank's place and set up that radio link."

"What do you intend to do?" asked the doc.

"We'll have to get all the men ready, and everyone else for the worst," said the chief. He pressed the intercom button. Rob answered.

"Rob are those lads still there?" he asked.

"Yes sir," replied Rob.

"OK," said doc. "What do you want me to do?"

The chief put up his hand for him to wait a second.

"Get the lads to round up all their pals, and tell them to say nothing of what they saw and get them down here. I'll do all the talking. Do you understand me? I don't want anyone to run away, I want everyone accounted for," said the chief.

"Yes sir," said Rob.

"Get someone down to the sale. Tell them that I want everyone who is able bodied to report to the station, then get my chopper ready to call base and tell them

I want it ready in five minutes. Then get me another car," said the chief. He let go of the button.

"Doc, you get everyone when the boys get back to get every woman and child down to the hall." He snapped his fingers.. "You know where the sale is, I don't want anyone to leave until I get back."

"Yes," said doc. "Anything else?"

"Yes, take a portable radio with you from the desk and see if you can contact Frank Parker and Keith, and see if they can get a message through to Deator in Camagonga .Tell, them exactly what's happened and tell them to get help to us as soon as possible, in double quick time," said the chief.

"Yes sure," said doc.

"Right let's go," said the chief.

He made his way to the front desk where he caught sight of the boys just about to leave.

"Hey, hang on a sec," he called to Darren. "You come with me I want you to show me where that thing is."

"Yes sir," said Darren.

BACK IN THE CITY

Many tests have now been carried out on the cones, and Ken and Deator have worked hard and fast to find out what and how everything works. So has Ben, the assistant. They are all sitting back enjoying coffee in a small room just off the lab when they heard a cry from Ben. They are in the middle of a conversation and discussing the information they have found.

"I don't believe it," said Deator. "It's not possible."

"It is and what's more there is nothing we can do about it. We've let it grow to four times its size. It sets off these strange impulses, we can't hear them at the moment, it's far beyond our sound range. If we let it grow by the time it reaches the size of a man, who knows what harm it may do us. I'm not willing to take that chance, are you?" said Ken.

"But where does it come from?" asked Deator. "I just can't believe that it came from space like you have said. Surely it would have been reported if you say its intended size is what you say Why, hundreds would have seen it."

"Not necessarily so," said Ken. "Anyway how do we know if its so-called parent has landed and what it looks like? At the moment it's just a mass of honeycomb crustations living of human blood and cells, or anything come to that. Tell you what, I'll contact the air base, and find out if anything has been reported. We'd better get help to the town too," said Deator. And he picked up the phone. "Hello, hello, is that the air base?" he asked. The line was very bad, it crackled and he could hardly hear anything. "Put me though to air control," asked Deator. He put his hand over the mouthpiece. "Bloody awful line, I can hardly hear anything," he said to Ken.

"Yes can I help you?" asked a voice., It was male and completely distorted.

"Yes what's wrong with this line? Can you hear me?" Deator shouted. Ben came into the room.

"Sir," said Ben. He looked scared. "Something has happened to that cone."

"What?" asked Ken.

Deator slammed down the phone and they all rushed into the lab. They went over to where the cone was behind the glass and looked at it.

"I was bombarding it like you said sir, first with gamma rays and then with radio active material and nothing happened. Then I thought I'd try just ordinary ground heat, seeing that it was found in that village., I got to wondering. Why there? I looked up the area on the map," said Ben.

"So what did you find out?" asked Ken "and how did you cut your hand?"

"Oh, that's nothing sir. That area if you look on the map is like a crater, it's over a hundred miles wide in places. The ground heat is very high and it stays the same more or less all day long only to drop at night, but although it's cooler it's only a damp humid coldness like that of a cool summer night. I tried to keep to those temperatures and look what happened," said Ben.

"So you've got some brains after all then in your head?" said Deator.

They all looked at the cone. It had now opened up like a flower in bloom in the glass cabinet.

"Where did you cut your hand?" asked Deator.

"Cut it on the wire mesh on one of the samples I was doing," said Ben. "But it's ok. I was standing here and it shot across towards me."

"What are they?" asked Ken, getting out a magnifying glass and looking.

He pointed to two minute fish-like things stuck on the glass.

"Was the cabinet clean when you put those things in it?" he asked Ben.

"Yes," said Deator. "Ben, you had better go and get your hand fixed."

"Yes sir, thanks," replied Ben. As he passed the cabinet they moved again.

"Yes, it was sterilised completely, there was nothing in there except for the cones," said Deator.

"Get me a slide," said Deator. "And some gloves and a suit, I'll have to see what they are." Ken obliged..

Ben left the room. Ken returned with the suit and gloves. He carefully picked up the case and carried it to the sealed room after putting on a special suit.

"Lock me in," he said to Deator. "Don't let me out until I say it's ok. While I'm in there destroy the other monster so that it won't grow any bigger. I'm not taking any chances."

"Yes, all right," said Ben, and he went off to get his hand seen to.

"Deator, you make sure he does it right, and don't let anything happen. When I press the buzzer then you can open the door. As you know this room is electrically, intensified and if anything should happen to me you then know what to do. Now lock the door," said Ken.

"Ben, you make sure all the samples are safe," said Deator. "I'll see to the rest."

Deator locked the door behind Ken and went over and started work on what he had found. Ben got on with his job. He still had not removed the bottle with the remains of the barman in it.., Unknown to them all, one of the tiny fishlike creatures was in the bottle. A small drop of blood from Ben's hand had managed to get into the flask and this enabled the tiny creature to start laying thousands upon thousands of minute eggs.

Usually in a lab there are two sinks, one marked drinking water and the other, waste. This sink had underneath it a large container marked lab waste to be burned. Deator got to work on the job of destroying the monster. It had now grown to about seven inches long, with a mass of honeycomb cells and what looked like a maggot in the middle. It was in another room in a glass. In this case the heat was intensified also. Deator pressed a red button while Ben looked on.

"If it thinks it's going to have us for its next meal it's very much mistaken," said Deator.

He gently pushed the button and the room glowed with a fierce white light and the creature within the glass disappeared completely, letting out a shrill cry of pain as it did so.

"Thank god for intensified lasers," said Deator "and in fact if we can ..."

"Pretty scary," said Ben. He shivered as if someone had walked over his grave.

"Right," said Deator. "We had better get back and find out how Ken's getting on."

They left the room after Deator had switched off. Ben had left the samples safely behind the wire mesh basket and put the lid back on.

"How's it coming along?" asked Deator through the intercom.

"So far so good, I've looked at this thing under a slide and it's not good I'm afraid. I've tried saline and other things but its main source of food is blood (any blood)."

"Why?" asked Deator.

"Seems whatever it is it's laying thousands of eggs. There is a thin tail thing on its back. I've checked this and something comes out, a liquid. It's not unlike a bee sting only much more lethal. It contains a sedative; it puts its prey to sleep. I should imagine slowly at first and then when it's dead it gets to work," said Ken. "Mass production on a grand scale."

"Are you telling me that that minute thing is responsible for that creature we have just destroyed?" asked Deator.

"Yes, I'm afraid so," said Ken. "It's not unlike the corn we grow. I've tried other tests too since I've been in here. Look, I'll turn on the magnifying glass and you can see for yourself. It has small fins and a sucker at the back so it's able to fix itself inside the cone until the temperature is right, then somehow it shoots itself out and into the victim. If left in a bottle of blood or a solution I dread to think of what could happen. I'm scared, bloody scared, if this ever got in to the human blood stream there would be no chance to save any of us."

"Why?" asked Deator.

"Somehow it seems attracted to blood. I'm safe because I have a suit on. I put a small drop of blood on the slide and within seconds it had propelled itself onto it," said Ken. "Tell me are there many more of these in the village?"

"Get me the report Ben," said Deator, "it's on my desk.

Ben went off. He came back with it and handed it to Deator.

"Yes quite a few," said Deator as he read the report.

"Jesus Christ," said Ken. "Then that kid's story was true."

"We'd better get out there fast," said Deator. "If you say it goes for large quantities of blood, then the town is next on its list."

"Right," said Ken.

He left the slides underneath the microscope checking first to make sure the tiny fish-ike creatures were still there, and then checked the other one. They were both in place.

He then left the room and went through another area and took off his suit and put it in an incinerator, where it was burned to a cinder, along with other things he had on over his own clothes. He turned and left the room and returned to the lab. "Destroy those two immediately," he told Deator.

"We'd better get help to the town as quickly as possible," said Ken.

He turned to the window that Deator had been looking through and pressed the red button. The room lit up and the creatures were destroyed.

"But we can't contact them," said Deator. "I've just phoned the airport but there was some form of interference. I can't get through it's impossible."

Suddenly, his face paled.

"Are you thinking what I'm thinking?" asked Ken. "My god, heaven help them."

"Come on, we have not got much time," said Deator. He turned to Ben. "Right, Ben you clear up the lab and make sure everything is sterilised and put away. I'm depending on you.. You understand the consequences as you have seen it for yourself."

"Yes sir," said Ben. He glared at them both. He hated being told anything.

The two men left the lab shouting to each other as they went.

"Where's the nearest army base?" asked Ken.

"About five miles outside the city," said Deator running alongside Ken.

"Good," said Ken. "Just pray to god that they have one of those new laser beam guns because if not we are all dead."

MEANWHILE UP IN THE PLANE

Dale was still curled up fast asleep, it was nearly two hours and no one had disturbed him. The hostesses were busy serving the dinner; the old lady still didn't know her husband was dead. One of the hostesses came round with food. She, too, did not realise that the man was dead..

"Ah, there you are Mr and Mrs Bates," said the hostess smiling at Mr Bates.

"Shhh," said the old lady. "Warr's gone to sleep, don't wake him."

"Oh, sorry," said the hostess. She looked at him and she saw that he was dead. He was blue around the face.

"He's always in a terrible mood you know, when he wakes up.Hhe's been like that ever since we have been married," said the old lady.

The hostess looked at her compassionately. She didn't want to panic her.

"Childhood sweethearts that's what we were," said the old lady proudly as she patted his hand.

"My, my your hand's cold Warr. Why didn't you say so you silly boy?" She fretted, pulling the blanket round him, and tucking him in.

"I don't know," she said. "He doesn't like being fussed over. Have you got a sweetheart?"

"No," said the blonde hostess. "That is, not a permanent one."

"Oh haven't you my dear?" said the old lady. "Never mind, I suppose it's got something to do with this modern day and age. In our time it was so romantic. Warr and I can dance you know, the waltz and the quickstep. We used to belong to a dancing school. He's so handsome and me I'm just a plain Jane really. I fell for him right away …"

The old lady drifted away in a dream after closing her eyes.

"Mrs Bates, your dinner's getting cold," said the hostess.

"Oh sorry dear, now where was I? Oh yes, my dinner. Thank you," said Mrs Bates.

"I'll have the chicken please," said the film lady to the dark hostess.

"Beef for me," said her husband. "Thanks."

The hostess handed them each a tray. She had four-stacked one on top of the other.

"Is everything all right?" she asked them. "Anything else?"

"Thanks," said Cindy. "At least this will break up the boredom," she sighed. The hostess made no reply; she could see what was up.

"David, you had better have the chicken," said his mother "It will be better for your stomach."

"Right mum," said David. "What are you having Theresa?"

"Oh, I don't really mind," said Theresa. "Let's see, yes I'll have chicken the same as David."

She smiled at David and took a tray from the hostess.

"You know something Theresa," said David. "You've never talked about yourself or your family. You've been half way round the world with us, and we don't know you really, and if it hadn't been for the boys at school we would have never been able to come on this safari. Don't you think they are a swell bunch of friends? Mum got the money but the school gave me spending money."

"I do," said Theresa.

They both got on with their meals.

"If you promise not to get excited," said Theresa. "I'll tell you about myself."

"Oh yes please," said David. "I'd like that."

He looked at Theresa and gave her a wide grin.

"You know," he said to her. "I've got a feeling I've seen you somewhere before this trip."

"Well," said Theresa. "I'm one of a big family. I have eight brothers and two sisters," she sighed. "And yes, you have seen me before, but not like you see me now. I was a nun you spoke to." David didn't hear.

"Eleven," said David. "Eleven brothers and sisters. Boy, that must have been fun at Christmas. Where have I seen you before? That's where, I thought so."

"Hectic I'd say," said Theresa. "With all those mouths to feed, well what do you expect? We met at the hospital, remember?"

"Yes. How marvellous," said David's mother. She smiled. "Why didn't you say so before? You kept that a big secret didn't you?"

"Yes I think so," said Theresa proudly. "My mother married a second time when I was quite young and already had a family of six then. She married a divorced man, and he had children of his own, so that's why I became a nun ..."

"I tried to escape from the world and that was wrong, I know now."

David's mother looked very surprised., She knew then why she had said what she had. Anything for a bit of peace of mind, she thought.

"Hey cop," said Bennett. "I said hey you in front." Steve had changed seats.

"What do you want?" asked Steve, turning round and leaning over the seat.

"I want to be moved from here," said Bennett, staring at him.

"Why?" asked Steve. "Give me one good reason, why the likes of you should sit with the others up there?"

"My ears hurt," said Bennett. "I'm picking up some damn vibrations and they are making me feel bloody sick. I want to go to the bog."

"Ok, Ok," said Steve. He got up

He uncuffed Bennett and then cuffed Sied back to the seat.

"That I can allow you, but you'll have to come back here afterwards, ok?" said Steve.

"Sir," said the co pilot; he was keeping a check on things while the captain had a kip. Then he noticed something was wrong.

"Yes, what's up?" asked the captain opening one eye.

"Something's strange," said the co-pilot. He rechecked the dials. "Although we are on automatic pilot the controls don't correspond with the way we are flying."

"What the hell are you talking about?" asked the captain. "Of course they do. Automatic pilot is automatic pilot. It flys itself. Ok?"

"Then why are we turning round?" asked the co-pilot.

"What do you mean?" asked the captain. Unbelievingly, he opened his eyes. He turned to the navigator. "Have we turned round?" he asked.

"Nah, not to my knowledge," he replied. "It seems pretty straight forward to me, the compass seems to check," he said looking at it. "But we have …"

"Better check again," said the captain, "and find out what's going on."

"Funny," said Garry to the captain.

He had his meal tray with a metal trim on his lap, and it was vibrating.

"What?" asked his friend; he had his drink in his hand.

"The sun was over there a short while ago and now it's over the other way. Look," said Garry.

"Must be your imagination," said his friend. "The sun don't move."

A small red warning light flickered on the incubator and the surgeon noticed it and went in search of a hostess.

"Excuse me," he said to her. "Where do you keep the back up system on the plane? Something is possibly wrong with the incubator."

"Why?" asked the hostess. "I believe it's kept in there." She pointed to the cabin floor level.

"Something's wrong with the unit," the surgeon said. "The light keeps flickering on and off. I can't afford to take any chances."

"I'll ask the captain for the keys," said the hostess.

She went in the direction of the flight deck.

"Check all the dials," said the captain. "And double check them."

Bennett returned down the aisle with Steve behind him.

Dale was still asleep and Jenny looked back to check he was all right. Barry was watching Jason. He still had the feeling he had seen him before. Jason was still acting in a very strange manner. Barry still didn't recognise him.

"I think he's running away," said Barry.

He still could not remember where he had seen Jason before.

"Why?" asked Jenny. She sat down and clipped on her seat belt.

"He hasn't let of that bag all the time we've been flying .He's even taken it to the toilet with him. I'm sure I know him but from where?"

He looked at Jenny as she fastened her belt.

"Why are you doing that?" he asked her.

"I feel safer," she said "Why?"

"Can you hear anything?" asked a woman passenger.

She put her hands over her ears.

"Can't you hear it?" she cried out to her husband. "It's awful."

She shook her head trying to get rid of the sound., She was sat on the outside of her husband.

The dark hostess walked up the gangway and passed Sied. She put some trays back on the shelves and threw some rubbish away. Then she left to get some more trays. She peered at Dale as she passed. The woman at the front of the plane got out of her seat, and slowly began to walk to the back of the plane. David had already gone beyond Sied and was looking out of the window.

"Where are you going darling?" asked the woman's husband. "What are you doing?"

"It's him, I must go to him," she said. "He's calling me."

"Who's calling you? I can't hear anything," said her husband. "Come on darling, sit down and don't be silly."

Suddenly in the cockpit the dials went wild and the lights started to flash. The red lights indicated a malfunction and a loud buzzing rang out. All the metal objects in the cockpit flew to the side of the plane. The crew's rings were drawn off their fingers, as were their watches from their wrists. Then the plane began to shake violently. There was panic in the main area of the plane as everything from the cabin started to fly about including the passengers. Their watches, rings and bracelets left them and stuck to the side of the plane. The trays that had contained their meals also went to the side of the plane. Miraculously, Sied's cuffs became unfastened and he saw his chance to get away, to God knows where. But he was determined to try anyway.

The tray that was on Harry's lap flew into the air and hit him sharply on the forehead and knocked him out. The old lady screamed as her dead husband was thrown onto her lap. Bennett and Steve ducked as best they could as the things flew around and the captain fought to regain control of the aircraft.

"What the bloody hell's happening?" yelled the captain to the co-pilot. "Grab hold of the controls and maybe the two of us can do it."

Passengers who had kept their seat belts on found that they could not get them off no matter how much they clutched at them and tried to get out. Jenny and Barry found themselves well strapped in and Jason's bag flew open scattering the contents all over. The bits and pieces he had stolen from his victims were stuck to the side of the plane for all to see. Only Dale knew nothing of what was going on. He was still asleep. Nickki's earrings flew out with the rest of the stuff and Jason tried to grab them. Barry saw them and remembered where he had seen them before, on Nickki the night of the party.

The buzzing got so loud that everyone could hear it. Sied got up and grabbed hold of the hostess and pulled her to his chest and she screamed. He pushed her up the gangway threatening to kill her with his bare hands if any of the passengers didn't do as he said.

People screamed and the plane shook violently, terror was in the eyes of the dark hostess and Sied pressed his arm tightly around her neck. Steve and Bennett got up when they saw what had happened. They were helpless to do anything.

"What the bloody hell?" said Steve. He searched for his moment.

"Don't come any nearer or I'll break her neck," cried Sied.

He seemed to be unaffected by the noise. The woman who had first got up out of her seat was slowly walking to the back of the plane, leaving her husband securely and helplessly strapped in his seat.

"Get back I mean it, get back," said Sied.., He was starting to panic.

"Do as he says, please," screamed the hostess. "Please."

But the woman walked on. She seemed to be in some sort of trance and she kept moving forward. Sied, seeing that she wasn't going to stop, panicked even more and threw the hostess to the floor and grabbed hold of the woman instead. The woman struggled and screamed.

"He wants me. I must go to him, I must," she said.

"Keep quiet you brat," said Sied, "or your next cry will be your last."

Slowly, Sied worked his way forward pushing the woman in front of him. The woman whose eyes were bloodshot from crying and screaming was still looking to the back of the plane. Sied because of this was half turned.

"Hey Bennett, get his gun," yelled Sied. He nodded towards Steve and squeezed the woman's neck even harder. Steve turned to Bennett and gave him a flashing look as if to say 'no'.

"Over my dead body," said Bennett. "You go to hell."

Steve was very relieved to hear Bennett's answer but could not understand why.

"What?" said Sied. "You bloody fool, get it or she's dead."

"Why for fuck's sake, don't you understand?" the woman screamed.

"Shut up bitch," said Sied. He spat and looked at Bennett. Sweating profusely, he pulled even harder as the woman struggled.

"I thought you were with me," he said.

"I was," said Bennett. "But can't you see there is no hope in hell up in this damn thing and what's doing this anyway, for god's sake?"

"Now what the hell are you on about?" asked Sied. "Get that gun. Do you hear me, or I'll bust your head off?"

"You fool, we will all be sucked out of the side of the plane," said Steve. "Can't you see we are all going to die anyway?"

"Aw shut up," said Sied. "I ain't got time to listen to your blabber."

"What the hell's going on?" asked Jenny. "And why hasn't Dale woken up?"

"Shhh," whispered Barry. "If he hears you he'll waken him up and hold him hostage instead. Free, he has a chance to save us, or we are all dead."

"Oh my god, no," said Jenny. One thing she didn't want was to see Dale harmed.

While all the things had been flying round, David had ducked down and now Sied had worked his way up the gangway. David had been looking out of the window, unseen by Sied. He popped his head up and was seen by all the passengers as well as Steve. He was three or four seats behind him.

Jenny's mind flashed back to when they were all packing and she remembered that Dale had packed his revolver, a small handgun in her travel case. It was now in the rack above their heads. If only she could get it down. The other passengers were still panic stricken and the old lady was in a world of her own.

"Oh, War it's been many years since you slept with your head on my lap. Do you remember the picnics when you took me on the river? Now, where was that? Ah yes, in Cambridge, England. Oh, such lively days we had there. If you had retired earlier we could have gone back there," she said.

"Tony," said the young girl to the boy she thought she was married to.

"I'm scared. We are going to die and we have only just started to live," she said. She clung to him and was most distressed. "I…"

"Shhh honey," he said. "Don't cry." He cradled her in his arms and began to wish he had not played that cruel and terrible trick on her. Alas too late now.

"What's going on?" she asked. "And why is everything sticking to the sides of the plane like that? What's that noise, it's awful?"

A sudden thought of death had made the boy realise that he really loved the girl after all. He regretted everything he had done but couldn't see his way to tell her the truth.

"I'll always love you darling, always remember that," he said as he kissed her tenderly. "I'm so…"

"Where's my camera?" asked the film producer. "I've got to get this on film. It's fantastic no one will believe it, that this is really happening."

He waved his hands about and managed to get his bag unzipped but as he did so the camera flew out and crashed to the sides with the rest of the things. It ended up facing towards Sied at the back of the plane. It clicked on.

"Keep still you brat," said Sied to the woman. She still struggled.

David looked at Sied and stood perfectly still.

"Let me go, let me go," she cried out. "Please, you're hurting me."

Slowly, Sied backed down towards David..

MEANWHILE UP IN THE HELICOPTER

The chief, Joe and the pilot headed to the place where Darren had seen the creature.

"There it is," cried Darren. It was almost hidden from view.

"Holy mother of god," said the chief. "What the hell is it?"

"Exactly my sentiment," said Darren. "Scared the hell out of us two."

"How the hell do we fight a thing off that size? As big as that?" asked Joe.

"I see what you mean," said the chief. "We haven't a hope in hell."

"Maybe we can't fight it but at least some of us could be saved," said Joe.

"What do you mean by that?" asked the chief. He looked at him.

"I was thinking about the old underground shelter sir," said Joe. "Just on the outskirts of the town. If you think about it we …"

"Yes great, but there's not enough room for all of us out there, is there?" replied the chief, "but your right, it's our only hope."

"Better some of us perish than all of us sir," said Joe. "The women and children first. We can at least save a few."

"True," said the chief "You are right. Ok, better get back to the town and sort something out. Better start to evacuate straight away."

"Dad," said Darren, and then he changed his mind. "Perhaps Billy was with them."

"What son?" asked his father.

"Nothing," said Darren. "Forget it." He was putting two and two together.

"Joe," said the chief. "When we land I want you to go and assemble all the men available, men who will help you carry out my instructions and get food and water down into the shelter. I can trust you to do that job Joe?" asked the chief.

"Yes sir, don't you worry. I'll get on fine," said Joe.

"See if you can get through to the city again," said the chief. "Maybe it's a lot clearer up here."

Joe tried again but still there was no reply. The airways were completely useless.

IN THE CITY

Ken and Deator had reached the army base and had seen the top authorities. After some debate they had got what they asked for. Their latest secret weapon was, a laser gun. This was after the story had been told to the governor., He saw that they knew how to use it and had no option but to release it to them.

Three thousand men and machinery, tank guns and ammunition were speedily dispatched to the assistance of the town. Plus a high secret back up system.

None of them knew what to expect.
Under the circumstances, Deator thought it best not to tell Sally or Susan.

MEANWHILE AT THE TOWN

The chief and Joe landed at the base and the chief's instructions were well on the way. The chief headed back to his office. As he got through the door he threw some keys at one of the men.

"Get going," he said. "Don't ask questions, get some men and go to the armoury. Take all the guns and ammo there and get down to the underground shelter at the end of town. Move, move, move."

"You," he said turning to another officer. "Get all the women and children out of their houses. Doc will be helping. Get them to take as much food as they can but be quick about it.".

"Sir," said Marlene. "What can I do to help?"

She looked dreadfully worried. Dare she assume she had at last found love?

"You help doc and get all the medical supplies to the shelter. Some of you others can help too. Thanks," retorted the chief. He knew she was scared.

They were all scared as they didn't know what was going on but they each did as they were told without question.

"Go, go, go," yelled the chief. "Get food and water and whatever we might need, blankets and stuff like that. You see to the children," he asked Marlene.

Joe arrived back from the base and went straight to the chief's office.

"Joe," said the chief. "You get back to the hall. Tell doc what's happened and see that everything's ok with him. I haven't time to tell everyone what's happening so you see to that. If you have any problems then you see that they are sorted, right get going…"

"Yes sir," said Joe, and he left the office.

IN THE HALL

Everyone was being assembled into the hall and they were all afraid and worried.. One woman who couldn't find her son, cried out.

"Where's my Michael? Michael, Michael. Where are you?" she called.

"Mum," answered her son. He was at the other end of the hall.

"I'm here, I'm ok," he said.

Then another woman rushed through the door screaming. Doc slapped her face to calm her down. Then she started to cry. "I can't find my boyfriend," she said.

"Calm down everybody! For god's sake we mustn't panic or everything will go wrong," Doc said to them.

At the same time he comforted the woman. "What's his name, when did you last see him?"

Joe entered and told Doc what the chief had asked.

They all headed towards the shelter.

AT THE POLICE STATION

A woman came rushing through the door. Her face was pale and worried. Behind her was her son. His face was paler than the moon.

"My husband," said the woman "He went into the bar ruins, please, please help me," she pleaded to the chief. "I was the other boy's mother."

"Why what happened?" asked the chief.

He had a thousand and one things to do. The boy with her was Billy's friend. He looked at the chief.

"Dad never came out, he only went in to look for the ball," said the boy.

"I was down the road and I heard an awful cry, and that awful noise. It's all my fault I kicked the ball in there."

The boy began to cry.

"Billy went in there too," he said. "I'm sure he did. I've not seen him since."

"Do something," said the woman. "Get someone to search or something, please. What's happening?"

"Where was Frost?" asked the chief. "He was supposed to be keeping an eye on that place."

The chief had a vision of what might have happened, after the incident at the bar. It meant that Billy, the dogs, Frost and the woman's husband had all been killed by the creature underneath the burnt -out bar.

"Ok," said the chief; he tried to pacify the woman. "Quick, get everyone out of the town, there must be two of these things."

The few men left in the station grabbed hold of the woman and boy and they all rushed out and down the street to the shelter. The chief was now very uptight, as he had no idea how to fight whatever it was.

MEANWHILE UP IN THE PLANE

"Sir, what's happening?" asked the co-pilot.

"I don't know," replied the captain.

"I can't control the plane any longer; it's as if we've been taken over by some unforeseen force. I don't know what it is.," said the co-pilot.

The navigator who had been studying his charts looked up.

"Sir, I've just checked the charts and we are heading back the way we came," he said.

"What?" asked the captain. "Jesus what's going on?"

"Ok" he went on "Go and check the passengers, I expect there's absolute panic back there by now. See if you can calm them down, see what you can do. Ok, the force field is making all those …"

"Yes sir," said the co pilot.

"When everyone is a little calmer I want a full report on all the damage," said the captain.

The navigator got up from his seat.

"Yes sir," he said,

When he reached the passage he was confronted by a load of terrified people. The first one to speak was the surgeon.

"The incubator has cut off, I shall need another unit straight away or she'll die," he said.

"What the hell's going on out here?" asked the navigator as he looked down the gangway. He saw the back of Steve and Bennett.

"Sit down," he said to them. "There's no need for panic. Everything's under control." Well I hope to god it is, he thought to himself. He wasn't sure.

The blonde hostess was lying on the floor. She had been knocked off balance by a flying object.

"Here let me help you up," said the film lady.

"Thanks," said the hostess, "What happened?" She was terribly dazed.

"Will someone help this man?" asked Harry's companion.

Harry was losing a lot of blood from a wound on his head caused by the flying tray.

"For Christ's sake, do something," said the man.

The surgeon was more worried about Mrs Heal and the baby.

"I'll help," said Jenny. "If someone can cut me free from this strap."

"No," shouted Sied. "Everyone stay where they are. You!" he pointed at Steve. "Throw your gun over here."

Steve hesitated, then unclipped his gun and threw it at Sied who pulled the woman closer and bent down to pick it up.

Bennett caught David's eye and David knew what to do. The woman who could still hear buzzing in her ears, found the call getting stronger and louder.

"Ah, I've got to go to him," she shouted.

"Darling, keep still or he'll kill you," said her frightened husband. He looked daggers at Steve. He did not approve of what he was doing.

"Why did you have to give him your gun?" he demanded. "You bloody fool!"

Sied suddenly saw the black case on Harry's arm. He'd seen such before.

"You," he said to Jason who had been keeping very quiet all this time He pointed the gun at him, and Jason was sweating. "Get that," he beckoned pointing.

"I'm on your side man," said Jason. He felt in Harry's pocket for the key and removed the box carefully.

"Now I remember," said Barry to Jenny. "I saw him raping Nickki."

"Why didn't you report it, you bloody fool?" said Jenny.

"I don't know. When I woke up it was morning and time for us to leave. I just didn't think, it was like a bad dream," said Barry. "He's changed his appearance."

Jason picked up the case and handed it to Sied, sniggering at Barry.

While all this was going on David was edging out of his seat and back towards Dale who was still asleep. David's ears began to hurt as he got nearer to Dale and he shook his head to clear it. Then he reached out and grabbed the blanket ready to pull it off on the signal from Bennett.

"You lot," said Sied, to the passengers who were still free.

"Move up the front of the plane," he told them, and pointed the gun. They moved and Jason stayed in his seat and held the case then eased out slowly.

"You," he said pointing at Harry's companion "Get out of there Back up all of you." He headed back towards David's position.

"Help us," said the old lad, "Warr's very sick. He's not moving and he's very cold. Please you must do something. Why's everyone standing up?" She got up and walked down the gangway unaware of what was going to happen., Steve made a grab for her but she pushed him aside.

"Take your hands off me young man!" she said, pushing past everyone.

"Sir," said the co-pilot. "We are going down. We've dropped over a hundred feet and we are losing height rapidly."

"Whatever it is guiding us must be landing us. Its put down the landing gear," said the captain. "God knows how."

"What are you doing young man?" asked the old lady as she walked towards Sied. "How dare you point that thing at me. Why not see to Warr, he's sick?"

She turned to Steve.

"Why can't you control your men?" she asked. "Warr would never have allowed this to happen. I don't know what the world is coming to, and why isn't someone seeing to this poor man? He's bleeding all over the place."

"Get back you old buzzard," said Sied, "or you'll be dead."

"Don't be so impertinent young man," said the old lady. "Put that thing down. Don't you know, it's dangerous to point those things at people?"

OUTSIDE THE TOWN AND DOWN AT THE OTHER END IN THE SHELTER

Doc had managed to keep everyone under control, but was unaware of what was going on outside. He had herded as many people as he could into the shelter and suddenly from out of the silence the ground began to shake as the huge creature that had engulfed Ann and Suchana hit the town to look for its mate. Everyone screamed and clung together as the roof began to cave in, in some places.

Dust and dirt fell on them all. The smell of the creature as it passed was terrible, the noise even worse. It clung to their ears; others were compelled to leave unable to control themselves. It was useless trying to stop them. Others were ripped through the roof of the shelter as if sucked up by a vacuum cleaner. No escape was possible.

MEANWHILE OUT IN THE SCRUBLAND

Keith and JoJo found the broken landrover and the injured Fletcher and were on their way back to the farm. When they arrived they found Mark and James barely alive and scared out of their wits. Their hair had gone completely white with shock. They bundled the boys in the back of the landrover with Fletcher and made their way towards town. They did not realise the danger into which they were heading.

No signs of Suchana and Ann could be found along with the animals.

DOWN IN THE TOWN

Everyone was still trying to rush to the old dugout. They were all carrying food and such like.

The chief and some of his men rushed down the road towards the burnt-out bar. A bright red light hung over it, cloudy and misty. As soon as they got near it the men put their hands to their ears and, walking and screaming at the same time, they seemed to be dragged towards it, as were many other people. They seemed to be in a trance of some sort.

"Get back, get back!" cried the chief.

The men took no notice, neither did the people. He was suddenly deafened by a high-pitched buzzing and began to hold his ears, even though he could only hear with one ear. He with the others tried to grab hold of anything to stop themselves being dragged towards the creature's clutches. It loomed up in front of them. As they were pulled towards it some had their arms pulled out of their sockets as they tried to save themselves. The huge crustated monster was now bigger as it had been living off the people that it had engulfed. It sent out a sound that seemed to be calling all its other parts together for some unknown reason.

"Oh Jesus Christ, help us," screamed the chief as he was pulled towards the huge creature.

"Help us for Christ's sake," he cried, but it was to no avail.

But he and all the others hadn't a hope in hell; they were all going to one place and that was it.

MEANWHILE BACK IN THE CITY

Susan and Sally had been to the lab to find out what was going on and to have a word with Deator. When they got there they met two cleaning ladies at the lab door. They were just about to start cleaning the place, as they had not been allowed into the lab for the last two days.

"Excuse me," said Sally. "Have you seen my husband?" She'd seen one of them before.

"Well not lately Mrs," said the cleaning woman. "But I do know he's gone out. I saw him go."

"Ok, well where did he go?" asked Sally. She turned to Susan. "This is typical of him just what I was talking about earlier isn't it?"

"He went off, sometime ago Mrs," said the woman, "screaming something about a blaze I don't really know. But he nearly knocked me over. It's not like him at all, is it?" she asked her friend as she turned to her.

Her friend nodded in agreement.

"Thanks," said Sally.

"Oh, that's all right Mrs," said the woman. She turned to her friend. "Come on, I want to get these rooms done or we'll never get home."

The two women went into the lab and Susan and Sally went down the hall. One of the women had a large polishing machine to do the floors and the other some cloths in her pinny pocket. In her other hand she had a mop which she leant against the sink.

"Are you going to the party tonight?" asked the woman's friend, who was dark, short, curly hair and was in her early forties. She had a nice soft featured face. She turned on the machine and then it turned off.

"I don't know" the other replied, polishing the lab taps.

She was younger than her friend by about three years.

"What's it for?" she asked.

"Oh it's nothing much," the other replied.

She leant against the bench, and placed the mop beside her. As she went on speaking to her friend she saw the mop move out of the corner of her eye but took no notice and carried on with her conversation.

"It's one of those parties where you can choose and try on clothes. They bring a range of dresses from England, quite good really you know," said the dark woman. "It's the new idea, all the rage they say."

"Sounds ok," said the other. She had not started to use the polisher yet.

"Why not come?" said the dark woman. "I'll come and pick you up, you'll love it." She started the machine again, did a bit, and then turned it off.

"Ok, you've convinced me. I was only going to stay in anyway and wash my hair."

The mop moved slightly again but the woman still ignored it.

"What time will you pick me up?" the first woman asked her friend. She turned on the polisher and the mop moved again.

"Eight thirty, if that's ok with you?" the dark woman replied.

"All right that's ok, by me," said the first woman.

The machine swung into action and the vibration made the mop move and slide along the bench. The dark woman saw it go by, could not save it and it fell on the other side of the sink.

"Watch out, the mop!" she called to her friend.

It was too late and the mop fell down on the wire mesh basket that contained the samples the lab technician had forgotten to put away. The handle hit some papers which in turn hit the basket sending it crashing to the sink and it broke the top off the container and the contents spilled out into the sink.

"Christ," said the woman. "Sorry, it was too late to save it. Never mind."

It had fallen into the sink marked drinking water. Without thinking, she turned on the tap and washed away the samples that the men had been working on. Sam's remains had been put into the bottle and the tiny fish-like creature had been laying thousands of eggs. The sample had contained just enough blood and now the lot was washed down the sink.

"Oh no," cried the dark haired woman.

"God, what have I done? I didn't know, now I'll get the sack won't I?" said her friend.

"You stupid bitch," said the dark haired woman. "Now we are for it."

"If we don't tell anyone then they will never know. It probably wasn't important or they wouldn't have left it there," the other woman replied.

"I suppose you are right," said her friend "But for Christ's sake don't you do anything like that again. Here turn off that damn machine. If I hadn't turned it on we wouldn't be in this mess."

She bent down and picked up the pieces of broken bottle and looked round to find something that looked the same to replace in the mesh cage.

"There," she said. "No one will know the difference with distilled water."

The two women finished the room and went off. No one would be any the wiser.

IN THE PLANE

"We've dropped another two thousand feet," said the captain. "I've no control over what's happening."

"The landing gears are down sir," said the co pilot.

The navigator and the passengers were all falling over.

David's ears were hurting but he bravely tugged at the blanket. One of the men who was nearest to Steve, turned. It was the professor.

"I can see a way out of this," he said to Steve, "if you are willing to take a chance."

"What?" asked Steve "What are you talking about?"

"Barry, see if you can attract the attention of the film lady, but don't let him see you whatever you do. Ok?"

Barry tried to do as he was asked but failed. So Steve tried.

"What do you want me to do now?" he asked Steve.

"Haven't you noticed," said Jenny. "We are going down, we are going to crash in a few seconds."

Barry looked out of the nearest window.

"That's Zimba over there," he said. "The captain's trying to land, seems the captain's got everything under control after all".

Steve thought the same but did not say so.

"I can't get her attention," said Barry. "And the only other one left is him." He pointed to Bennett, who was still watching the old lady.

"He's on our side ain't he?" said Steve. "He wouldn't pass the gun to that man, so if not why is he here with us".

Barry tugged at Bennett's trouser leg. Bennett felt this and looked down at him.

Jenny had taken a piece of paper from her bag and had written on it. She passed it to Barry who hesitated and then handed it to Bennett. The note said, 'There is a small hand case above your head, the case is open. There is a gun inside. See if you can get it out and pass it to Steve.' It was taking a chance for none of them knew what Bennett would do. Would he do what they asked him?

Bennett nodded at Jenny after reading the note.

"I said stay back you old fool," shouted Sied at the old lady backing up.

He fired a shot and everyone screamed. In that split second Bennett's hand went into the case. He felt for the gun, found it and in a flash threw it to Steve.

The old lady opened her eyes wide as she felt the red-hot bullet hit her in the head and she slowly fell to the floor. Steve aimed.

David at this point pulled the blanket off Dale to wake him but to his horror he found a mass of honeycomb crustations, a moving mass of cells, living off Dale's blood cells. His eyes, nose and ears were sealed by the creatures. The thing zoomed at David and he let out a terrified scream.

Sied saw the monster and let off three shots at it and let go of the woman in sheer terror. She ran towards the mass of creature instead of away from it. The creature had now got hold of David. He was spreadeagled across him and consuming him at a terrific rate. The woman was sucked into it. Everyone was screaming at the terrible sight. Barry and Jenny tried to get out of their belts, and so did the other trapped passengers.

"What the hell's up?" cried the captain.

He could see the chaos in front of him. People were running up and down and screaming, while parts of the monster rained down on them in the streets below.

It had grown to the size of a three-storey building and people were being sucked in like flies to a lollipop.

Above the creature there hung a cloud of red dust and a strong smell of ammonia and from nowhere there seemed to be a wind as it drew the people to it. Houses from the town were being sucked up as the plane was only a short distance from the ground.

Steve caught the gun that Bennett had thrown to him. Someone yelled out.

"Aim for the black case, it has explosives in it."

Within a flash after firing the gun the plane hit the ground and the tail section of the plane blew off, taking with it Jason, Sied and the monster. The other passengers were thrown from the other parts still screaming. The tail section was drawn towards the monster and sucked in like everything else.

Then like the eye of a storm everything went quiet..

Bennett found himself miraculously still alive. His head was badly cut and his arm was broken.

David's mother lay unconscious, as were Steve and Jenny, but Barry had disappeared. He was nowhere to be found. The seat belt strap was still round Jenny but it had broken off Barry's seat. Flames were seen licking around them.

"Ah, what the hell?" asked Bennett and he looked round.

The remains of the plane had buried itself nose down in the soft ground. Some of the passengers were still alive and they were crying out for help but there was no one around. Their bodies were broken and bleeding. Some were alight.

"Barry," called Jenny "Where are you?" She was safe from the fire.

She had badly cut legs. She remembered the horror she had seen inside the plane. But she was still in shock. Her hair had gone completely white, so had Steve's. In the remains of the plane there lay the bodies of the crew and Brenda but the body of the baby could not be seen anywhere, just the broken incubator. Nearby were the bodies of the film couple and the two young lovers.

The old lady lay on top of her dead husband, as if to prove that they would not be separated even in death.

When the red dust finally settled the people began to come out and then they saw the monster that had caused the crash. In front of them was a great chrysalis and to their horror and dismay they saw the people who had been dragged in alive, ready to be consumed as soon as the cycle had taken place. They were food for the bug inside.

Jenny looked in horror as she could clearly see the chief and others banging on the sides to get out.

"Oh my god," she cried to Steve. He was nursing his head and arm.

"Look," she said.

Steve had now come to slightly, his leg was broken. The bone stuck out and he was in agony.

"Oh Jesus," he cried out. "My leg!"

By now the doc had collected a few men from the town and had returned to help. He saw the horror and got to work on those he could.

"Get them out for Christ's sake," screamed Bennett. "We've got to get them out."

The doc beckoned to some of the men and they came running over to help. Everywhere, people were still moaning and crying for help.

"See what you can do for these," he said to them..

"Take all those who can walk to the shelter," said the doc.

He looked at the giant bug and scratched the back of his head.

'Holy shit,' he said to himself as he saw the chief inside the case. He was banging like fury.

"Get us out," cried the chief.

Pieces of the monster had sucked up and were all round them. So with the other survivors he got them to pick up the sharp pieces of metal and bang on the side to try to crack the skin. It was useless. They were also nearly overcome by the terrible smell of ammonia. The buzzing sound the monster made could no longer be heard, only the thunderous sound of frightened heartbeats for miles around.

"Go and get some dynamite," yelled doc. As he bent to attend to David's mother she was just beginning to come round.

"David, David. Where's my David?" called his mother.

"Sorry," said doc. "Who's David?"

"My son," she said. She looked at the wrecked plane.

"What happened? Where am I?" she asked. She seemed to be unhurt and tried to get up but in doing so held onto her head. The nurse lay dead.

"Oh that hurts," she said. "Then, seeing Bennett she put her hand to her mouth.

"You'll be all right in a minute or two," said the doc "Too late for her."

He turned to the other men.

"Hurry up with that dynamite," he yelled,. "and the blankets."

"No," said Bennett. "You are not going to blow them all up are you?"

"It's them or us," said doc. "I'd say that I've got no choice wouldn't you?"

Suddenly there came the sound of buzzing and the doc looked up. He couldn't see anything

"Not another one," he yelled and panicked like the rest.

"Run for your lives," he screamed.

"No, no," cried out David's mother. "Look."

At first their fear was enough to give them all heart attacks, but now it turned to utter relief. From the distance they saw three helicopters arriving to assist them.

"Thank god," cried Jenny, "thank god." She rocked back and forth on the ground.

Doc stood up and waved frantically as did some of the others., The baby was still alive. She had been catapulted into Jason's empty bag. Joe's boy who had been at his side had disappeared.

The choppers landed and Doc soon found that Deator was with them. He had persuaded the authorities to let him have a laser gun that hopefully would kill off the monster. But now he was having second thoughts about it as he saw the size of the thing. He was glad he had brought a back up team and that more troops would soon be on their way. Three thousand men and equipment arrived at a safe distance and set up their camp.

Tanks and guns could be seen moving in from the direction of the base, and joining up with the rest of the force, soldiers came and helped load the injured into the choppers and they were flown away to safety.

Only David's mother, Jenny, the Doc, Steve had remained behind. They had asked to be left till last.

Ken and Deator were late too. They were trying to find a way to get the others out of the monster and it was now getting dark again.

The giant chrysalis glowed in the dark of the night sky and the men assembled the laser gun and set it in place, The only hope was to use the gun to cut a hole in the side of the thing to get them out. But they didn't know just how long they had before the creature hatched out.

"Right sir," said the sergeant as he came forward. "We've got it all ready now and are awaiting your orders. We understand sir that if this doesn't work what we have got to do".

"Thanks," said Deator. He turned to Doc and the others.

"You should have gone while you had the chance," he said to them. "If that thing starts to buzz again then heaven help us all. And if that's a baby then god help us if we can't destroy it, and it grows to full size."

Joe remembered what his two sons had told him and fortunately Joe's sons had come along on the flight.

"My sons saw something out in the bush," said Joe.

"What another one of these things?" said Deator. "Where? You had better show me, so that I can get an idea of what it is we are up against."

"We'll have to use one of your choppers sir," said Joe.

"Ok, come on let's go. Where is your son?" he asked Joe.

Joe looked around and saw his son helping to load some of the bodies on to the remaining chopper.

As all this was going on, Garry's accumulator was being won.

"There he is," said Joe, and he called him over.

Within a few minutes they took off in the chopper and Deator left Ken in charge in case something else should happen before he got back.

"Your father tells me you saw one of these things out in the bush?" said Deator.

All the races run, he and his dead friend had won. one hundred thousand dollars.

"Is that true?"

"Yes sir, and it was not like the one we have down there, it's much larger and…"

The noises of the chopper made it hard for Deator to hear what the boy was saying but he more or less had an idea of what he was going to say and the description of what he had seen. He told Deator that thousands of birds were in the vicinity and that they had left not much more than a skeleton of the thing. What was left were just a few birds and they appeared to be eating small maggots or something. Deator nodded his head.

"What does it look like?" asked Deator.

"It had three heads sir, huge about three times the size of that thing down there," replied Joe's son.

"From what I gather," said Deator, "we have had reports of birds migrating by the thousands and this freak storm and much interference on all radios and phones. Planes, have had to be diverted to other airports." He turned to Joe's son. "Are we nearly there?"

"Yes, down there," said the boy pointing.

"Yes, I can see it clearly now," said Deator.

There was the skeleton of the creature; Deator tapped the pilot on the shoulder.

"Let's get back," he said. "I only hope Ken has done what I asked him to do so that everything is ready when we get back. If that's the female down there then I'm glad it's dead, and thank god for the birds, for without them we would all be dead by now. By the time they have digested the maggots in their stomachs we shall only have the problem of getting rid of that baby down there in town.. Joe, I have something to tell you ,but not now," said Deator

Joe and his son looked puzzled at Deator's remark. They landed the chopper not far from where the laser gun had been set up and Ken was waiting for them. The generator had been connected.

"Sir," interrupted one of the officers. "It's all ready."

"Thanks," said Ken. His face was scared and worried. "I'll set the beam. It will cut through the toughest metal or simply burn everything to a cinder. Its range is formidable, so I have to judge it carefully."

"Right," said Deator. "I'm turning it on now."

"Doc," said Deator. "You be ready as soon as they get out. I want all of you loaded and away in the last chopper."

"I want to stay here," said David's mother.

"So do I," said Jenny.

Her hair had turned white as had Bennett's and Steve's.

"Me too," said Joe and his son. They all shrugged.

"I hope you are all aware of the consequences," asked Ken.., He looked at Deator.

"You are the youngest here," he said to Joe's son. "Are you sure you want to stay?"

"Yes sir," said Joe's boy and Joe looked at him proudly.

They all knew what was meant and so did the boy but he still wanted to stay with his dad. For he had not the heart to tell him about Billy's death.

"If the plane is on time, and he received a signal from me then that is it," said Deator.

An officer stepped forward.

"Ready when you are sir" he said, and saluted.

"God help us all," said Doc.

"Right here goes," said Ken and he pressed the button.

A thin beam of light sped its way towards the cocoon, which contained the beast that had killed nearly a hundred people. As it did so the chief began to get everyone who was inside ready so that as soon as a hole appeared they could escape. Soon the strong smell of ammonia became sickening and turned everyone's stomach. All guns were trained on the monster; the men would obey their orders or die in the attempt to save their country, or the world come to that. Sweat was pouring down Ken's face as he watched the hole get larger and larger, and finally it was big enough for the chief and the others to crawl through. All those who had been trapped ran for the helicopter as fast as they could as none knew what was in store for them. Not one of them realised just how close to death they had been. Deator raised his hand to give the signal. They all cried with relief and shock as they ran away. Expecting the worse to happen Ken nodded as Deator's hand was ready to fall.

Bennett looked at David's mother, Joe looked at his son, as if to say farewell then the hole that Ken had burned in the shell suddenly cracked all over, like a thousand pieces of glass all breaking at once. Then like a waterfall it fell to the ground. They were all spellbound, their mouths dropped open. Ken's hand paused as if in a sign of friendship. They all gazed at the beautiful sight in front of them. It was not a creature like the one that had caused such panic, horrid like the one that had wrecked the plane, but it was breathtakingly beautiful. It had large silver wings and three heads. All who saw it were spellbound. Panic had gone and they stood flabbergasted when suddenly the creature spread its wings and took flight a few feet into the air. Then it gave a few feeble buzzing sounds and fell slowly to the ground. It was dead. Not quite knowing what to do they stood without speaking. The relief hit then all at once. They were elated but sad for they didn't know why.

SOME HOURS LATER

Steve and Bennett and all the others had received hospital treatment. Steve had to stay in hospital but Bennett was allowed out as was Jenny and David's mother. Then it was time for the questions to be asked. The reporters all arrived and rallied round asking things, some of which had no answers. Joe had been told about Billy and was saddened by the news of his death. But he was consoled by his other two sons, both of whom had become men in the last few hours. The world's press snapped photos of them as they walked down the corridors. News of the accumulator and Garry's death meant the baby got all. She had to be operated on and was ok.

"Why this inquiry?" asked a reporter.

"None of your damn business," snapped the chief.

"How many were killed?" asked another, "and have their relatives been told?

"All in good time," said Doc. "Please don't crowd us."

Susan came running through the crowd calling out for her father, and Jamie.

"Dad, where's Jamie?" she asked. "Where's Jamie?"

The chief heard her cry and he looked at her sadly as if to say he was dead, and she broke down and cried. Sally tried to give her some comfort but found it impossible to console her as the tears rolled down her cheeks. "Someone get her a drink of water please," she asked.

The cleaning lady fetched her one.

"Seems we shouldn't have used our latest secret weapon," whispered Ken to Deator.

"I think we will have to tell them. It will make them see it can be used in times of peace and war," said Deator. "Don't you think so?"

"Doc," said Joe. "They were really going to …"

"Yes," said Doc. "In cases like this it would be far better for a few to die for the sake of the human race., After all who really knows what the thing could have done to our world? We could all have been destroyed so we have to be ready for the worst".

David's mother came through the door.. She was escorted by a polite and courteous Bennett. She looked at Doc. Her hair had turned white like the rest of the survivors. Looking at Bennett compassionately she said, "There was a moment in my life and that now seems a thousand years away now when I found out that David was going to die, the same way as his father. At that time the thought was, what have I done wrong to be treated this way? I lost my belief in God and wanted to die. I even thought of taking my own life. I know now that there was a reason for God to take David from me." Bennett comforted her. She went on, "And if he can hear me now I say with all our thanks and love, David died and without knowing it he saved all our lives. He lost his knowing that he would not live much longer, and in doing so saved all the human race. I only hope he knows what he did." Her eyes turned to heaven and she whispered "Thank you son."

Susan was still crying bitterly when she suddenly heard Jamie's voice calling out to her. Her shaking hands clutched her drink.

"Susan, Susan," he called as he came down the corridor.

"Oh, Jamie darling, Jamie," she said standing up. "Oh, Jamie, you're safe." She rushed into his arms and they kissed.

"Gee, what would have happened if that thing had wanted a drink of water?"

THE END

Printed in the United Kingdom
by Lightning Source UK Ltd.
126500UK00001B/189/P